Praise for Susanna Kearsley

Winner of the Catherine Cookson Fiction Prize

Named of the Dragon

"Evocative and entertaining. *Named of the Dragon* [has] warm, living, breathing, utterly believable characters and a background as beautifully illustrated as a watercolor painting. . . . I will read it again and again." —Christina Jones, award-winning author of *Going the Distance*

"A very interesting contemporary romance. . . . The story line is character-driven, which works because the prime players are different in temperament yet add much to the mix . . . a complex relationship drama." —Harriet Klausner

"A marvelous story . . . intriguing . . . impossible to put down." —*Rendezvous*

"Reading Kearsley is like reading Barbara Michaels, Mary Stewart, and Elizabeth Harris all rolled into one. She serves up an intriguing story, interesting and compelling characters, and a sense of the history and people of Wales. I was thoroughly engrossed by this suspenseful, well-written novel." —*Old Book Barn Gazette*

continued on next page . . .

THE SHADOWY HORSES

"Gripping [and] atmospheric." —*Ms.* (London)

"The plot may seem fanciful, but the liveliness with which Susanna Kearsley writes and her ability to convey atmosphere more than compensate." —*The London Times*

"*The Shadowy Horses* is like vintage Mary Stewart by way of Rosemary Sutcliffe; *The Eagle of the Ninth* updated with a sprinkling of the supernatural." —*Scotland on Sunday*

"The plot elements . . . are beautifully managed . . . the characters are original and colorful." —*The Denver Post*

"[Kearsley] is such a good writer that she breathes vigorous new life into a time-honored formula. . . . A splendid writer . . . The hallmarks of her fiction are smart heroines with dream jobs, fascinating settings, and storytelling which respects the reader's intelligence rather than insults it. All of these are excellent reasons to read *The Shadowy Horses,* and to look for the author's other books as well."

—*The Romance Reader*

"Filled with charming and eccentric characters that add a delightful depth to the plotline. Ms. Kearsley has woven archaeology, history, mystery, the paranormal, and love together, to create a wonderful story sure to please."

—*Rendezvous*

"A brilliant romantic thriller . . . The story line is exciting and filled with non-stop action. However, it is the fully developed, wonderful characters who make this into a winning tale." —Harriet Klausner

SEASON OF STORMS

SUSANNA KEARSLEY

McArthur & Company
Toronto

Published in Canada in 2001 by
McArthur & Company
322 King Street West, Suite 402
Toronto, ON M5V 1J2

This is a work of fiction. Names, characters, places, and incidents are either the product of the author's imagination or are used fictitiously, and any resemblance to actual persons, living or dead, business establishments, events, or locales is entirely coincidental.

National Library of Canada Cataloguing in Publication Data

Kearsley, Susanna
Season of storms

ISBN 1-55278-188-7

I. Title.

PS8571.E57S42 2001 C813'.6 C2001-930713-6
PR9199.4.K44S42 2001

Printed in Canada by *Transcontinental Printing Inc.*

The publisher would like to acknowledge the financial support of the Government of Canada through the Book Publishing Industry Development Program (BPIDP) and the Canada Council for our publishing activities. The publisher further wishes to acknowledge the financial support of the Ontario Arts Council for our publishing program.

10 9 8 7 6 5 4 3 2 1

For my mother,
my first and best reader,
with love.

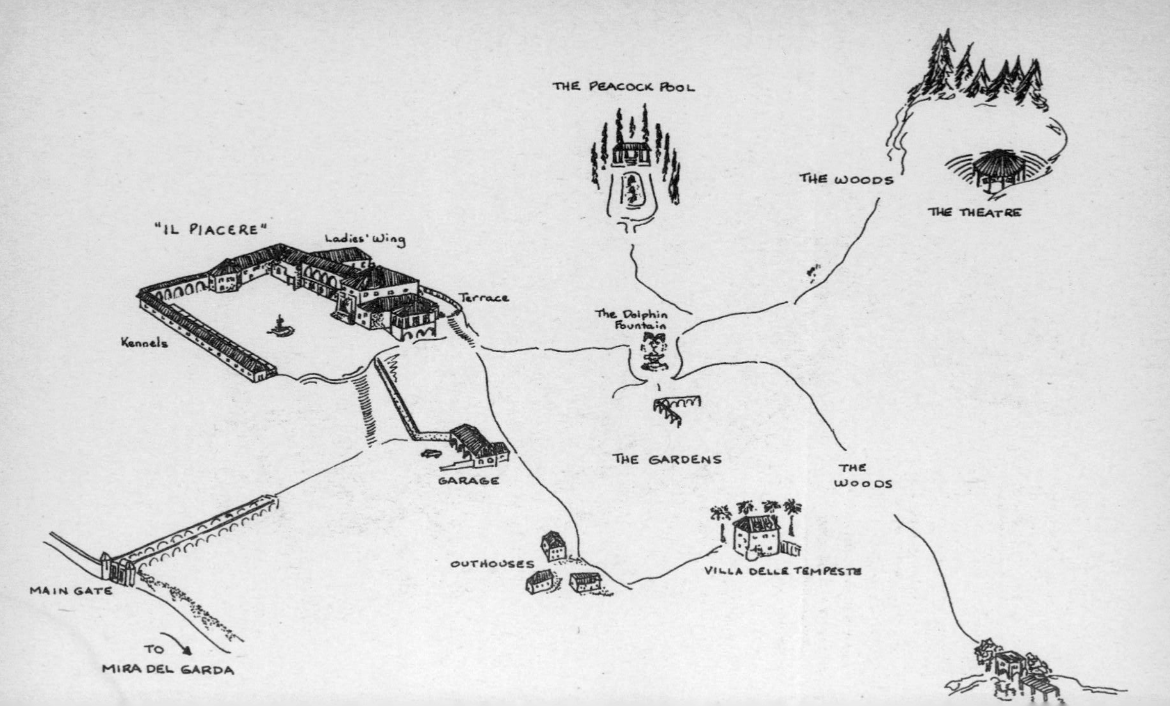
THE PEACOCK POOL
THE WOODS
THE THEATRE
"IL PIACERE"
Ladies' Wing
Terrace
Kennels
The Dolphin Fountain
THE GARDENS
THE WOODS
GARAGE
OUTHOUSES
VILLA DELLE TEMPESTE
MAIN GATE
TO MIRA DEL GARDA

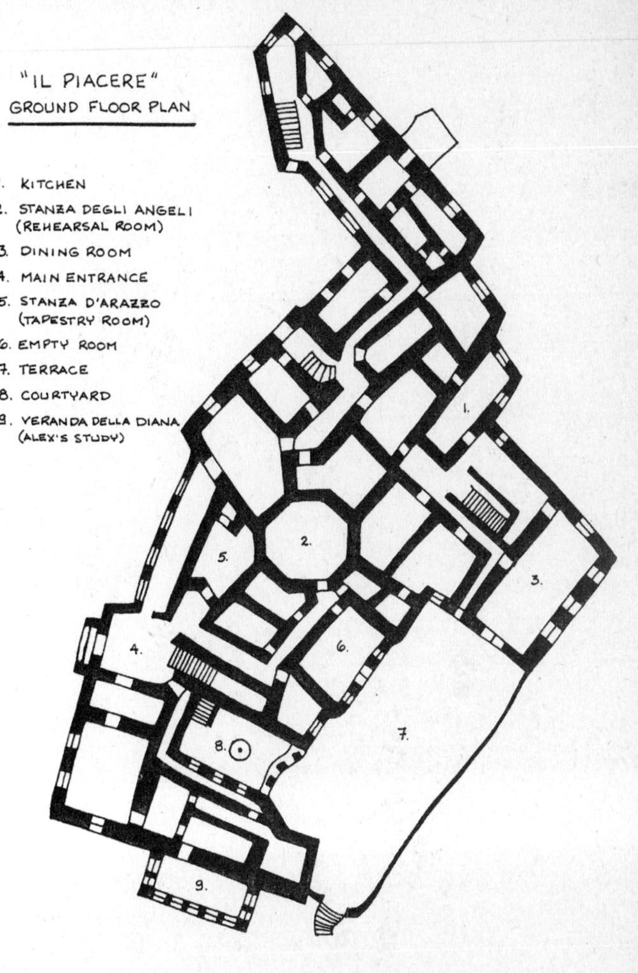
"IL PIACERE"
GROUND FLOOR PLAN
1. KITCHEN
2. STANZA DEGLI ANGELI (REHEARSAL ROOM)
3. DINING ROOM
4. MAIN ENTRANCE
5. STANZA D'ARAZZO (TAPESTRY ROOM)
6. EMPTY ROOM
7. TERRACE
8. COURTYARD
9. VERANDA DELLA DIANA (ALEX'S STUDY)
1.
2.
3.
4.
5.
6.
7.
8.
9.

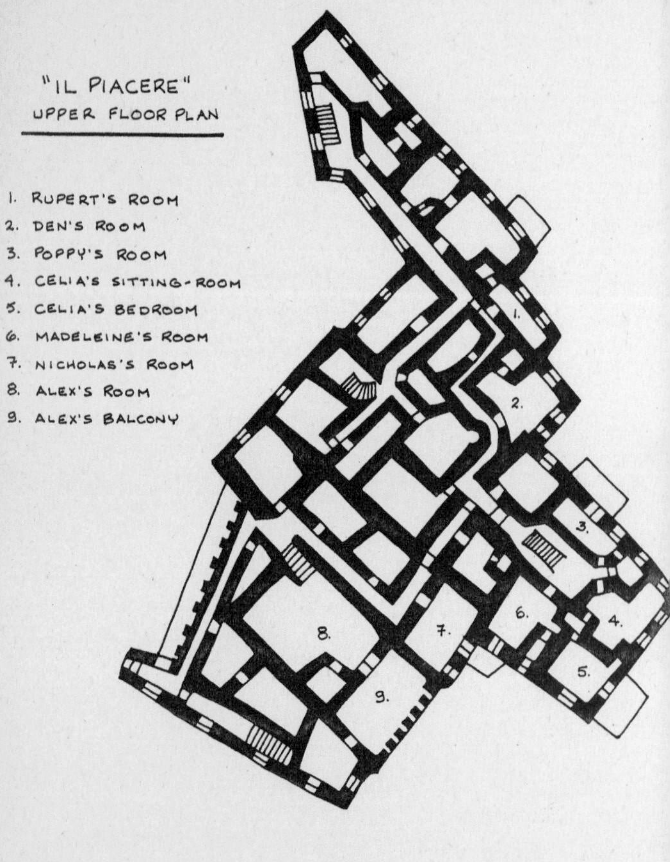
"IL PIACERE"
UPPER FLOOR PLAN
1. RUPERT'S ROOM
2. DEN'S ROOM
3. POPPY'S ROOM
4. CELIA'S SITTING-ROOM
5. CELIA'S BEDROOM
6. MADELEINE'S ROOM
7. NICHOLAS'S ROOM
8. ALEX'S ROOM
9. ALEX'S BALCONY
1.
2.
3.
4.
5.
6.
7.
8.
9.

PROLOGUE

And these she does apply for warnings and portents,
And evils imminent;

Shakespeare: *Julius Caesar,* Act II, Scene II

THE letter arrived by the afternoon post. I found it waiting for me on the front hall table when, having finished a particularly long luncheon shift at the restaurant, I'd dragged myself up to the small fourth-floor flat that I shared, for the moment, with Sally, my flatmate.

She showed me the envelope straight off. "It's from your agent. Maybe she's got you another audition."

I shook my head. "She'd ring me for that, not send a letter."

"Well, maybe it's a birthday card, then. Happy birthday, by the way—I didn't get a chance to tell you that this morning, you went out too early."

"Thanks." Mornings, for Sally, began around ten. She'd been busy today, from the looks of it. Another stack of boxes packed with clothes from her bedroom now blocked my way into the sitting-room. Stepping round, I slumped into the nearest cushioned chair and let my head fall back, caught fully in the power of the wearying midafternoon, when every tiny movement seems an effort and the dull light weights your eyelids. I felt like I'd just turned a hundred, instead of twenty-two.

Sally followed me and sat cross-legged on the floor by the bookcases, getting back to the business of sorting the books into piles of hers, mine, and those that she coveted. She sent me a knowing glance. "Long day?"

"Hellish. They didn't get round to the hoovering up last night so I had to do it this morning when I got in. Things just sort of went downhill from there."

"Oh, poor you. There's still tea in the pot."

"No, thanks." The idea of rising to pour another cup of tea, even if it was for myself and not for someone else, seemed far too much like work. I turned my head against the chair back—Sally's chair, I thought morosely, so presumably it, too, would be leaving the flat at the end of the week.

She glanced over again, homing in on my mood with that particular awareness of hers that had often led me to wonder if the Wiccan altar with its candles in her room might not be more than just an offbeat decoration. She'd have made a good witch, with her wild curling hair and diaphanous clothes that came straight from some Indian version of Oxfam. Everything about her floated, and one always had the impression she'd flare up like a torch if she came too near a lighted match.

We'd met last year, waitressing, but since then her handmade jewellery stall had done good enough business that she'd been able to leave the restaurant, and now she was leaving me, too, to set up house with her boyfriend—a drummer and nice enough bloke, I supposed, once you got past the piercings.

"Aren't you going to open it?" She nodded at the letter I was holding.

I felt a little apprehensive, actually. The envelope, with its printed address, seemed suspiciously official, and the way things had been going all week I was rather afraid this would be more bad news—another agent dumping me because I'd failed to make them any money. Reluctantly, I slipped a finger underneath one corner and started peeling up the flap. "I take it no one's phoned?" I asked. I took it for granted that my mother wouldn't have, she never remembered my birthday, but there was always—

"Oh, that friend of yours did," Sally told me. "You know who I mean . . . that older man, the director . . ."

"Rupert?"

"That's him. He seemed a bit surprised that you were working today."

"Yes, well, someone has to pay the rent." I spoke without thinking, then wished I could take the words back when her face sagged with guilt.

"Look, I can leave you a little extra, if it would help . . ."

"I'm fine." I wasn't, really. Fledgling actresses made next to nothing, even when they waitressed on the side. We'd been barely scraping by together as it was, eating lots of rice and things from tins, and wrapping ourselves in quilts instead of turning on the fires, to save on the electric bill. I'd hoped to have found someone to take Sally's place by the time she moved out, but so far no one had responded to my ad, and without a new flatmate I didn't know how long I'd be able to cope.

"Anyway," said Sally, "you're to meet what's-his-name—Rupert—this evening at St. Paul's."

My hand stopped in surprise, and I looked up. "St. Paul's? Why does he want me to go all the way over there?"

"Not the cathedral, silly. The church. It's a five-minute walk."

"Are you sure he meant the church?"

"I wrote it down. He made me write it down." She retrieved the piece of paper as evidence. "There you are, you see? St. Paul's Church, Covent Garden, sixish. Dinner at the club." She smiled at the expression on my face. "Yes, he said that that might cheer you up. Nice place, is it, Rupert's club?"

"Very nice." Returning my attention to the envelope, I finally got the flap up and discovered that it wasn't a letter at all—at least, not from my agent. Inside was a second, smaller envelope, addressed to me and postmarked Italy. Turning it over, I read the return address in open disbelief. "It's from Il Piacere," I told Sally, giving it the true pronunciation so it came out as 'Il Pia-*chair*-ray.'

"Who is he?"

"It's not a person, it's a house. A rather famous house. It belonged to Galeazzo D'Ascanio." Galeazzo D'Ascanio, self-proclaimed Prince of the Decadent Movement that had blossomed like a black rose in the Europe of the 1890s, languid with drugs and perversity, darkly erotic, committed to nothing but the taking of pleasure. That's what the name Il Piacere meant—the full name of the house where he'd lived in the twenties and thirties had been Il Piacere del Vecchio . . . 'The Pleasure of an Old Man.'

When Sally still looked blank I explained, "He was a writer. Poetry, mostly, though he also did novels and plays. See those books on the second shelf up? They're all his."

I wasn't especially fond of his writing. I found it too dark for my tastes, for the most part, but I'd always had an interest in the writer himself, for the simple reason that his last great love—the mistress he had called his 'muse,' the joy of his old age—had been, like myself, a young actress from London, with whom I had shared, across time, the same love of the stage, and a name: Celia Sands.

I had no claim to bear her name; we weren't related. I'd been named at the whim of my mother, an actress herself, not so much in homage to a legend of the British stage, but rather, I suspect, because my mother's narrow mind so rarely ventured from the theatre that she couldn't think of any other name to go with Sands, her surname at the time. If we had been Bernhardts I should have been Sarah, and suffered as greatly.

My mother never gave much thought to consequences. Certainly she'd never considered what problems I'd face if I followed her onto the stage, having to carry the name of a woman who had so electrified England and France in the months that had followed the Great War.

I'd sought refuge in a stage name, Celia Sullivan, which still allowed me to use the monogrammed luggage that Rupert had given me for my twelfth birthday but gave me some degree of confidence that I was being given parts because of my abilities, and not because of Mother's fame or some dead woman's name.

My agent knew, on pain of death, to not reveal my real name when she represented me . . . and yet here was this letter now, forwarded on by my agent from someone at Il Piacere, and clearly addressed: Celia Sands.

It was one page, typed neatly and signed with a masculine, no-nonsense hand at the bottom. I read it twice through, to be sure that I'd read it correctly.

Sally asked, "Well, for heaven's sake, what does it say?"

"I'm being offered a part in a play," I said, still unable to believe it.

"Just like that, with no audition?"

"Just like that."

"Is it a good part?"

"It's the lead. And it's a very famous play, the last one that Galeazzo D'Ascanio ever wrote. They're going to stage it in his private theatre, there on the estate."

"In Italy? How marvellous. Good work by your agent, I'd say."

"I don't imagine she had much to do with it," I said, and turned the letter round as evidence. "Rupert's going to be directing."

"Ah. Well, nepotism has its advantages. Good work by Rupert, then." Her smile faded slightly as she studied my expression. "Don't you want to take the part?"

"It isn't that. It's just . . . it says here that I'd have to use my real name."

She reached out a hand for the letter, to read it herself. "Why would they make a condition like that? What on earth does it matter what name you use?"

I imagined it would matter quite a bit, in this instance. Aloud, I explained, "Galeazzo D'Ascanio wrote his last play for his mistress, an actress—he gave her the starring role. Her name was Celia Sands, too. That's why I use a stage name. She was pretty famous, Galeazzo's mistress. People still know her name in the theatre, and I don't want to trade on it."

"Even if it means a paying job?" She was watching my face, and she saw the flash of indecision. "Wait, I'll get the cards."

Sally's tarot deck made an appearance at least once a week, whenever she wanted—or thought that *I* wanted—direction on some question or another. I endured it as a harmless entertainment, like reading one's horoscope in the tabloids, but to Sally it was dead serious.

Returning, she made herself comfortable on the floor in front of me. "Here, give those a shuffle and ask the cards if you should go to Italy. Oh, wait a second, I need to keep out your Significator." Searching for the Queen of Cups, which supposedly 'signified' me, representing as it did a woman with light brown hair and light eyes who had more sensibility than sense, Sally passed the rest of the deck over for me to shuffle, then took it back and split it neatly into three face-down stacks on the carpet, gathering them up again in one hand. My Significator, on its own, sat patiently face-up and waiting.

"Right then, here you are. This covers you," she said, laying a card down directly on the Queen of Cups. The covering card, I knew, was meant to show the atmosphere in which I'd asked my question. In my case, this apparently had something to do with a blindfolded woman holding two crossed swords above her head. "The Two of Swords," said Sally. "That means indecision."

"Fair enough."

"This crosses you." She set a card across the first two. "This will oppose you, for evil or good. Oh, the Moon—that's a Major Arcana card, a powerful force. It's the card of the psychic, you know. It can mean vivid dreams, the discovery of your own powers. Or it can mean bad things: people deceiving you, bad luck for someone you know." She turned the next card over, laid it directly below the three others. "And this is beneath you."

The supposed 'foundation' of my question was a Court card—the matching card, actually, to my own Significator.

"The King of Cups," Sally identified him. "That's a man with light brown hair, a businessman, responsible, but interested in the arts. He can look quite calm on the outside, this man, but inside he's emotional. Know anybody like that?"

"I wish."

"Well, he's at the bottom of all of this, anyway. And this," she said, setting another card down, "is what's passing away, what's behind you. The Queen of Wands, reversed." Her upwards glance was dry. "A blonde, blue-eyed woman who's jealous, unfaithful, and lies a lot. Gosh, who could that be?"

I couldn't help smiling. Sally had only met my mother once, but obviously the encounter had made an impression. There was no mistaking who she thought the Queen of Wands, reversed, might be.

She dealt the next card. "This is over you."

A card that was supposed to show me something that

might happen in my future. Again there were swords, this time nine of them, suspended rather ominously over the despairing figure of a woman burying her face in her hands.

Sally paused, and her eyes for a moment grew troubled. "This isn't a good card. It means suffering, tragedy. Loss of a loved one."

I couldn't say to her, as I wanted to say, that it was only a silly game, and could no more tell my fortune than could a mess of soggy tea-leaves, because Sally would likely have believed in the tea-leaves, too. But I did manage to cheer her a little by reminding her that the card only showed what *might* happen. "Keep going," I said. "Maybe things will get better."

But they didn't. "This is before you." Again she turned over a card from the Major Arcana, the High Priestess card, in reverse. "This isn't good, either. It means you'll meet up with a selfish, cruel woman. She'll cause you some trouble." She was frowning now, turning the cards over with obvious reluctance. "These are your fears . . ." The Fool, reversed, a ghoulish-looking character who leered at me from his upside-down position. "You're afraid that you'll make the wrong choice." And the next card, revealing the influence of family and friends, offered no more encouragement. There were swords again, three of them, piercing a heart, with dark storm clouds behind and hard rain pelting down in the background. "Oh, Celia. This means quarrels and things going wrong in your family."

The second-to-last card, my 'hopes,' was all right, which stood to reason, since one didn't often 'hope' for anything unpleasant. Mine came out the Ace of Wands, an optimistic card that meant a new creative venture, and a journey. But that didn't take the frown from Sally's face. She chose the last card for the reading and held it out, suspended, hesitating . . . then in one quick movement, as a child takes its medicine, she turned it over.

"Hell."

I didn't need her interpretation to tell me it wasn't an auspicious outcome. The image spoke for itself: a castle turret wrapped in flames, with human figures toppling from it, arms outstretched and screaming, and behind the flames a storm, with jagged lightning.

"That's not good," I said, "is it?"

Sally looked up at me, serious. "Celia, you mustn't take this job. There's something bad there, something evil . . ."

"Well,"—I put the letter to one side—"that settles that, then, doesn't it?" But still I couldn't help but look again towards the printed image of Il Piacere on the letterhead, and wonder . . .

Venice, 1921

His anger had not vanished by the afternoon; merely retreated to a place where he could manage it. He pulled another packing-crate across the library floor, uncaring of the scars it left, and went on emptying the shelves of books.

His valet watched him. "Sir, you're certain this is wise?"

He should never have hired an English valet, he thought. Anyone else would have understood, would have helped him, not stood there prudishly in judgement. "Of course it is wise! It is just! To say that I must leave this house," he said, in indignation, "after all that I have done here, this is criminal. To simply say, 'Get out,' like that"—he snapped his fingers—"to me . . . to me." He glared as if that insult in itself were cause enough.

"But sir . . ."

"They said I could not keep the house. They did not say a word about the contents." With a smile he pulled an ancient volume from the shelves, caressed its leather binding. "I will have my compensation." In sudden decision he turned to the valet. "We will go to the house on Lake Garda. The air there is good for my health." To emphasize the point he crossed to pull the window shut against the stale infernal dampness rising from the green canal below.

And then he heard the voice.

A woman's voice—an English voice—melodic, clear and lovely, floating upwards from a point below his balcony. "I don't suppose he'd be at home to visitors?"

A man replied, "You're mad, you know that?"

"Stop and let's find out."

"He'd never see you, Celia." A gondola creaked and a single oar splashed, resolute.

He stood transfixed and watched, his hand forgotten on the window-latch as the black boat slid out of his balcony's shadow and into the light. The man, to him, was but a shape; the gondolier invisible—he only saw the woman, half-reclining in the bow with one hand trailing in the water and a faintly pouting frown upon her face. She was exquisite, pale like porcelain, and the sunlight seemed to gather in her spun-gold hair and ivory dress and radiate around her like the aura of an angel. If she looked up now, he thought, their eyes would meet . . . but she did not look up. The gondola slipped on and round the corner, out of sight and hearing, but he didn't leave the window. He felt breathless, almost giddy. He felt young.

He looked where she had gone and spoke her name to try its taste upon his lips, and having tasted it he knew a sudden hunger for possession: "Celia."

ACT I

Enter Four or Five Players.

Sir, the scene is set, and everything is ready to begin if you please.—

Sheridan: *The Critic*

i

"IT isn't me he wants, it's just the name," I said to Rupert.

We'd stopped walking now to stand beneath the central southern window that was glowing with that softly golden light that seems to seek out empty churches in the quiet early evening. I had to tilt my head a long way back to read the lettering cut in the marble stone above. And though I'd read it countless times before, it still felt strange to see my own name spelled there: CELIA SANDS.

Rupert, at my shoulder, gave a cough that stirred my hair, and from the angle of the sound I knew that he was looking up as well. "Perhaps," he said, his quiet voice not echoing as mine had in the soaring space. His tone was noncommittal. Rupert rarely offered an opinion. I'd always found that maddening, especially when as a child I'd wanted his advice, but it was one of those small things that made him such a good director, his ability to let a thing develop, not to interfere.

That said, I didn't think it wholly accidental that he'd wanted me to meet him here, at St. Paul's, Covent Garden.

This was the 'actor's church,' a landmark of the theatre district, the names on its marble memorials reading like some sort of heavenly cast list: Sir Michael Redgrave, Dame Edith Evans, Sir Noël Coward . . . all properly humbling to someone like me, who had only just cracked the West End, and that in a role with ten minutes onstage and three lines, barely noticed by anyone. Still, here in St. Paul's I felt rather more than that, part of a larger community.

Even the building was one of us, having taken its role over from the original church, which fell victim to fire in the reign of Queen Anne. The original had been the creation of architect Inigo Jones, whose love of the Italian Renaissance had inspired him to try to reshape the whole of Covent Garden into one of the grand open squares, or piazzas, he'd so admired in Italy, and this second St. Paul's, built to copy the first, was ladylike and graceful. With its plain glass Palladian windows, etched here and there with a tracing of gold, its white and gilded ceiling and its candle chandeliers, it looked—as Inigo had intended it to look—like a small bit of Italy transplanted whole to the centre of London.

Rupert, I knew, would have thought of that, too. He'd always been a master at manipulating people's moods through setting. And although he'd never tell me outright whether I should take the job, I knew which way his mind lay from the fact that he had steered me to this place, where my subconscious would be bathed in thoughts Italian while I contemplated Celia.

'Celia the First,' Rupert always called her, as though we had both sprung from the same royal line. In truth I'd come to feel a kind of kinship with her, even though we had no bond of blood. I had so few true relations—just my mother, and an uncle who'd died childless in New Zealand—that adopting Celia the First as an honourary ancestor had given me that sense of continuity that comes from spotting one's own eyes in ageing photographs of youthful strangers, knowing that they're family.

She hadn't actually been buried here, at this church. No one knew for certain where her body lay, or if in fact she were actually dead, though her death was assumed from the fact that the memorial stone I was looking at now had been placed in St. Paul's by the one man who ought to have known what became of her—the actor, himself now forgotten and buried, for whom she'd allegedly left Galeazzo D'Ascanio. I say 'allegedly' because there were some who said that Galeazzo had killed her himself, and that the whole tale of her running away with that young English actor had been a fabrication, and an unconvincing one at that. What actress, after all, would run away the night before her play was set to open?

I, for one, almost preferred the murder angle. I didn't like to think of Celia the First growing old in obscurity.

I breathed a little sigh that swirled with scents of musty oiled wood and dust upon the marble and, still looking up, said to Rupert, "I can't believe you kept it a secret, your doing this play. You were hired when? Last autumn? And you didn't think to tell me?"

"I thought it would make a nice surprise for your birthday."

Only Rupert would have thought of that. But then, he'd always been able to hold on to information much longer than anyone else I knew. He was patient with a secret.

"Well," I said, "I take it that you've met this chap who's putting on the play?"

"D'Ascanio's grandson, yes. He stopped in on his way to New York last October, took me out to lunch."

"And what's he like?"

Rupert had always been a good judge of character. As a teenager, I'd made a point of bringing all my boyfriends round to meet him, so that later I could grill him on their weaknesses and strengths. He'd never tell me who to date, of course, but his keen observations had saved me a small lake of tears. I watched him now while he considered my question. "Rather quiet," he said at last, "and not overly social. A bit bloody-minded. But then he'd have to be, wouldn't he, to do what he's trying to do. It's not only the theatre he's restoring, it's the house as well. He's giving the whole estate over to the Forlani Trust to manage, so I'm told, and they'll be helping with the cost of restoration, but even so it must be costing him a fortune. The house, he said, was closed up in his father's day, and no one's lived there since."

An image flashed across my mind of cobwebbed corridors and shadowed rooms devoured by dust—a Gothic setting worthy of the poet who had written plays with names like *A Love Decayed* and *City of the Damned*.

I'd seen both plays performed, but I had never seen the one that Galeazzo's grandson hoped to stage, *Il Prezzo*. No one had. *Il Prezzo—The Price*—had been written as a gift of love for Celia the First. After fifteen years of silence, during which he'd only written a few forgettable verses, Galeazzo had on some sudden inspiration inked his pen again and in one fevered month of creation had produced, in English yet, the play that every critic called his best. That same inspiration had moved him to construct a theatre on the grounds of his estate where he could mount his own production of the play, and where his beloved Celia could once again weave her spell over an audience.

It would have been a triumph, if she hadn't up and vanished on the night of final dress rehearsal, never to be seen again.

Since then, the play had gathered something of a reputation. Several companies had tried to put it on, but each had faced its own disaster, from an actress falling through the stage trapdoor and breaking both her ankles, to a roof collapsing under a torrential rain that flooded out the set. If Shakespeare's *Macbeth* was considered 'the unlucky play' among actors, Galeazzo's *Il Prezzo* was the proverbial black cat passing under a ladder—the 'unstageable play.'

Which was probably, I thought, why the project so appealed to Rupert. He had always liked a challenge.

Mind you, if anyone could put the damned play on, it would be Rupert. He was a bit bloody-minded himself, and one of the best directors in the business. Galeazzo D'Ascanio's grandson had done well to snag him—Rupert's name alone assured a play success.

And I was tempted.

"I don't know, Roo." I exhaled a breath that fell short of a sigh and looked down again, turning away from the memorial stone. "I don't know that I'd feel quite comfortable taking a role like this."

"Why not?" His question made no judgement.

"Well, for one thing, I haven't auditioned. He's never even seen me act. He'd never have known I existed if you hadn't told him." There was an accusation in my tone, and he responded with a calm defense.

"You only came up in conversation because—"

"Because of my name. I know."

Silence for a minute, as both of us looked up again at the marble memorial stone. Rupert coughed. "He does have my word for your abilities."

"Yes, well." I glanced back, slanting him a smile. "You are a little biased, don't you think? And anyhow, that's just what I've been saying—I don't want to get a part because of who I know, or whose daughter I am, or whose name I happen to have. Besides," I said, "I'm building a career as Celia Sullivan, I can't just throw that all away, not now. And if I do this play as Celia Sands, I might as well forget about my stage name, because everyone else will—it's going to get attention, this play, because of what it is, and where it's being done. If I do it, I'll be Celia Sands for the rest of my life."

"You have to do what you think best, of course." Glancing down at his watch, he said, "Come on, time we were going. I told Bryan we'd meet him at the club at seven sharp, and it doesn't do to leave him sitting too long in the bar."

"You think I should take the part."

"I haven't said anything."

"But you think I should take it."

He smiled, not replying; turned and, hands in pockets, led me back along the peaceful dimness of the aisle towards the door, while from the shadows in the corners all the actors who still haunted St. Paul's Church appeared to watch and wait, as I did, for his answer.

ii

I'D always loved Rupert's club—one of those secretive places tucked well out of sight down a tight cobbled alley. After all these years I still wasn't sure just which turning to take, and had to trust to Rupert's memory. He found it unerringly, leading me down through the crowded brick buildings and dark unmarked doorways that looked as though they hadn't changed since the days of Dickens, as though they remembered the gaslight and coal dust and hansom cabs clopping unseen through the neighbouring streets.

At a nondescript green door he stopped, and rang the bell.

I heard the sound of footsteps coming down the stairs inside, and then a small square panel high up on the door swung halfway open on its hinges—my favourite part of the ritual. The porter's eyes held faint suspicion till they saw the man beside me.

"Evening, Mr. Neville, sir." The bolt slid back, and we were ushered in. "You're expected upstairs."

The staircase was my second-favourite feature of the club—it looked so deliciously ancient and rickety, rising a full storey up at an angle that only the fittest of members could manage unaided.

I had no idea how the porter did it, puffing up and down all afternoon and evening. He had to be, by my reckoning, rising seventy at least—he'd been porter here long before Rupert had become a member, and one had the impression that he'd been here as long as the building had, eternally condemned like poor old Sisyphus to climb and descend for eternity.

It was a killer of a staircase. Even I, at twenty-two and with aerobics classes twice a week, felt slightly winded at the top. There, in the narrow panelled room that served as entry hall and cloakroom, the porter took my coat in silence—to conserve his own breath, I suspected—and, turning, led us down along the corridor, with glimpses here and there through open doors of quiet drawing rooms and lounges lit with warmth. This had been a private house, once, though I couldn't really picture it as anybody's home, this rabbit's warren of tiny rooms with creaking floors and twelve-foot ceilings. Still, it was a matter of record that up to the 1750s a doctor had lived here, whose love of the theatre had led him to leave his entire estate to be used as a club for directors and actors and others who worked with the stage.

Rather a progressive establishment, for its time, it had allowed women as guests since before the first war, and as members since the early 1970s, and though children were not technically permitted Bryan and Rupert had brought me here for birthday lunches every year since I'd turned six. "And why not?" Bryan had once asked my mother. "She's much better behaved than most actresses one sees at dinner these days." Which was a straight shot at my mother, I think—though she probably wouldn't have noticed.

Bryan was waiting for us now beside the bar, with his back to the elegant windows whose curtains had not yet been drawn against the waning evening light. From the level of Scotch in his glass I could tell that he'd been here awhile, which meant that we were late, since Bryan was always dead on time.

The Scotch had strengthened his Aussie drawl. "We did say seven," he reminded Rupert, leaning round to kiss my cheek. "Happy birthday, Angel."

"Thanks." I kissed him back. "It's my fault, really—"

"We were over to St. Paul's Church," said Rupert. Greeting the barman, he ordered a Scotch for himself. "And what will you have, Celia? Sherry? Right. And a glass of the Amontillado, please."

"And what were you doing," asked Bryan, "at St. Paul's?" But he knew. I could tell from the smile at the edge of his eyes. Bryan had marvellous eyes—they could speak in a silence.

He was older than Rupert by several years, but seemed younger for some reason, maybe because he was more energetic, less languid, more given to moods. His face, too, was sharper in outline, expressive, with that prominent jaw and cleft chin that seemed somehow reserved for Australians. His skin, after twenty-odd years in our pallid weather, still bore the marks of a youth spent in subequatorial sunshine, creased deeply round his eyes and mouth to reveal the way he smiled. He'd looked the same for as long as I could remember—restless activity kept him from ageing. His golden hair had only just started to show at the temples the grey that had long ago sneaked into Rupert's.

Since childhood I had played a secret game of giving roles from Shakespeare's plays to the people around me. Bryan I had cast as *Romeo and Juliet*'s Mercutio, witty and clever and swaggering round with a sword in his hand, whereas Rupert was more of a Brutus from *Julius Caesar,* reflective and careful. They balanced each other, like all well-matched couples.

They'd met quite by chance in the year of my birth, on a lazy hot Sunday in St. James's Park. Bryan had still had his dog then—a lurcher named Oscar—who'd taken a liking to Rupert in passing and bounced him clean over. "And that," Bryan told me, "was that."

In the theatrical world, where people changed partners the way they changed socks, Bryan and Roo were a rarity. Bryan and Roo—I always thought of them like that, like bookends, each one incomplete without the other. Theirs was the only truly stable relationship I'd ever observed. It helped, I think, that Bryan was *not* theatrical. He worked in R and D for a pharmaceuticals firm, probably the furthest thing from Rupert's world and mine one could imagine. Having lived for years at a microscopic level, he saw things with precision.

"You've had your letter, then," he said, "from Italy."

"How did you know about that?"

He shrugged. "Roo told me it was coming. And you have that look you get when you're trying to make up your mind about something. You haven't decided?"

"Not yet, no."

Picking up his glass again he nodded understanding. "It'll be the name thing. If you want *my* opinion—"

Rupert interrupted. "We'll just let her make her own decision, shall we?" Passing me my sherry, he said, "Now then, do you want your presents now, or after dinner?"

"Now, please."

"Oh, big surprise," said Bryan, drily. But he was as much of a child as I was, and from the way he bent to fetch my birthday presents from his briefcase I could tell he hadn't wanted to wait, either. There were two gifts, one small and square like a jewellery box and one flat like a book. "The book's from Roo. Mine isn't as well-wrapped as his, and it's Christmas paper, all I could find in the house, but I reckoned you wouldn't mind."

I didn't. I opened his first, and stared at the blue box. "From Tiffany's?"

"Yeah, well, I took a walk down Bond Street last week, and—"

"Oh, Bryan." I drew out the delicate pendant and chain, let it trickle across my splayed fingers. "It's beautiful." A tiny golden angel with a diamond for her head, its facets trapping every colour of the rainbow in the soft light of the bar. It was Bryan's pet name for me, 'Angel'—he had called me that forever.

"It just looked like you," was his excuse for spending so much money, when I thanked him with a moist-eyed hug and kiss. "A little guardian angel to keep you safe; we could all use one of those."

He stepped in behind me to fasten it on while I picked up my second gift. Rupert sent me a dry look. "I can't top Tiffany's, I'm afraid."

He was no slouch when it came to gift-giving either, though. Rupert nearly always gave books, but they weren't just any books—he had a penchant for rare volumes, little treasures he'd mined from the shelves of some tucked-away secondhand bookshop. This year's gift was no exception.

The book itself was small and slim and physically lovely in the way that well-made books are, with a tooled red leather binding and pages whose edges gleamed gold. *The Season of*

Storms, read the cover, in fanciful gilt lettering, and under that, *The Celia Poems*. I looked at Rupert, disbelieving. "Where did you find this?"

My reaction had pleased him. "Little shop near the British Museum."

"I've been looking for *ages* . . ."

"I know."

Bryan, still fiddling with the clasp of the angel pendant, leaned in and had a look over my shoulder. "What is it?"

I held the book higher to show him. "The poems that Galeazzo D'Ascanio wrote for Celia Sands, or at least the ones he dedicated to her. Some of them he wrote afterwards."

"Afterwards?"

"After she went to . . . wherever she went to."

"Ah. I hope they've been translated."

"No need," I said. "They're in English, he wrote them in English." The frontispiece was a hand-coloured photograph of Celia the First posed like a classical statue against a stone parapet, presumably on the terrace of Il Piacere itself, with a tableau of mountains and blue lake behind her. I touched the picture gently, as though seeking a connection.

Bryan turned to Rupert with a grin and threw his own words back at him. "'We'll just let her make her own decision, shall we?' You old fake. You're trying to nobble the girl."

"I'm doing nothing of the kind. I saw the book and remembered she'd been wanting it, so I bought it, that's all."

But I had to admit he'd timed the gift conveniently, just like our meeting tonight at St. Paul's, and I couldn't help but wonder why Rupert, who usually took such pains not to influence me one way or another, was coming so perilously close to offering an opinion.

Bryan by contrast had never been reluctant to tell me what *he* thought I ought to do. Picking up his drink again, he settled back to take stock of my problem. "I am right, though, aren't I, Angel? It's the name thing that's stopping you?"

"Well, yes. I mean, not having to audition for a role is strange enough, but knowing I've been chosen for my name, and only that . . . I'm just not sure it's what I want."

Bryan, who'd watched me fight to earn a reputation based on my own merits, not my mother's, nodded understanding. "Then again," he said, "from what I've heard D'Ascanio isn't the type to go throwing his money about without doing his research, and considering he's already got Maddy Hedrick and Nicholas Rutherford he'll at least have made sure you can speak two lines together before offering the role. And even if he *does* just—"

I interrupted him, my voice coming rather more sharply than I'd intended. "Madeleine Hedrick is doing the play?"

"Didn't Roo tell you?"

"No." There was an accusation in the gaze I turned on Rupert. "No, he left that bit out."

Rupert raised his eyebrows. "Did I? I can't imagine why." And then, switching focus abruptly, he straightened and set down his Scotch and looked past me towards the main dining room. "I'll just go and see what's happening with our table."

Watching his departing back I drained my glass in one long swallow, suddenly wishing I'd ordered a much stronger drink.

He turned from the window.

"Thompson," he asked the valet, "you are English. Where do the English tourists like to go in Venice? Do you know?"

"I should think they would go to the usual places, sir."

"Yes, yes, of course they would." Forgetting the packing-crate half-full of books, he crossed the long floor with a purpose. "I expect I'll be out for the day."

"Very good, sir."

"And Thompson . . ."

"Yes, sir?"

"If you should see a young woman, a young Englishwoman with bright golden hair and the face of an angel . . . if you should see her in the street outside, or if she comes to call, you must not let her leave, you hear?"

The valet had been with him a long time. With no change of expression, he nodded. "Yes, sir."

"And tell the others, also. She is in Venice somewhere," he said, turning at the door, "and I will find her."

iii

I saw her step out of a taxi at Fortnum and Mason.

I didn't recognize the man at her side, but then Mother changed her men like top designers changed their fashions: something new for every season with a few choice bits thrown in for winter holidays. This man, with even blonder hair than hers and a strong Germanic jaw, might have been a remnant of the holiday collection—he looked the type she might have found while skiing over New Year's at Gstaad—but from the way she clutched his arm and looked at him and laughed I thought it far more likely he was new, her first selection from the spring-and-summer line.

Moving in close to the nearest shop window, I pretended an interest in silk lingerie while I kept my head half-turned to watch them. I wasn't the only one watching. All along the pavement at my back I caught the quickening of interest and the faint excited lift of expectation as the midday shoppers nudged and pointed, whispering her name.

She would have been difficult to miss, even if she'd wanted to be missed, and Mother seldom wanted that. She loved attention. And why not, I wondered? Why should people not go mad whenever she appeared? She had talent, she had presence, she was lovely . . .

She *was* lovely. I had always thought so, always wished my own eyes could have been as large, my features half as delicate. Instead I'd inherited only her small hands and her allergy to cats. The rest of my genes I presumably owed to my father, whoever he was. Mother, I suspected, didn't really know herself, although her husband at the time—the one whose surname I'd been given—had been working in Hong

Kong all that summer and so could be safely ruled out as a candidate.

I remembered asking Rupert once, when I was very little, if *he* was my father. Hunching deep into his armchair by the window, he'd told me no, he wasn't, and that I should count myself lucky.

Which had puzzled me a bit and hurt my feelings, until Bryan had hoisted me beside him on the sofa and explained that I should take no notice, that Rupert was just out of sorts because his mother wasn't well.

I'd snuggled close to Bryan, my cheek against the smoothness of his shirt, wrapped in the comfortable soap-and-Scotch smell of him. "Bryan?"

"Yes, Angel?"

"Are *you* my father?"

He'd pulled back to look at me, and then he'd asked why I was asking, and scrunching closer I'd explained that one of the girls at my school had told me everybody had to have a father, even if he lived somewhere else; that you couldn't be born if you didn't have a father; and I'd told her, well, *I* didn't, and she'd said that it wasn't normal, my not having one.

And Bryan had laughed and he'd told me that I was better off than the other girls at my school—that I had two fathers, him and Roo.

To which I'd said something like, "But you're not my *real* fathers though, are you?"

And Bryan had admitted no, they weren't. He'd shared a longish look with Rupert that hadn't meant anything to me at the time but which, in hindsight, I assumed had been a silent plea for help. And then on inspiration he had said that sometimes, every now and then, real fathers needed helpers.

"Oh," I'd said, as I'd absorbed this in a child's frame of reference. "Like the men who pretend to be Father Christmas, because he can't be everywhere at once."

And Bryan had gathered me close in his arms. I could still feel his kiss on the top of my head, and his cheek rubbing warm on my hair. "Exactly like that, Angel."

So though I'd never had a father of my own, I'd had his helpers, which had seemed to me to be the next-best thing.

As for Mother . . . well, Mother had always been absent. I'd thought that all mothers were like that, descending on you now and then, all smiles and scent and lavish frocks, to lead you by the hand past a bewildering array of staring faces, flashbulbs popping; fussing over you one minute and forgetting about you the next, and then depositing you back in your bed before you'd quite had time to sort out what was happening.

Rupert, in a rare burst of temper, had once accused her of using me as she might use a prop. It was, after all, common knowledge that she'd only permitted herself to get pregnant in the first place because one of her reviewers had remarked in print that a woman as beautiful as my mother would be bound to have beautiful children, an offhand comment that apparently had caught her shifting fancy. The problem was that having had me, she had no idea really what to *do* with me. It didn't help that I'd been born a very quiet baby. I'd almost never cried or fussed, which meant that Mother frequently forgot about me altogether, and if it hadn't been for the housekeeper I might have gone for days on end without so much as a nappy change.

Mother was just like that, though. Always had been, always would be. If you didn't make a noise she didn't see you.

I could have made a noise, now.

I could have called her name and waved and given her the chance to come the loving mother in full view of her adoring public. But I didn't. Instead, as her companion paid the taxi and she smiled in recognition of the crowd upon the pavement, I turned and briskly walked away down Picadilly.

iv

I found Bryan alone in the flat. Which wasn't unusual for a Saturday—Rupert liked to go off on his rounds of the antiquarian bookshops on a Saturday afternoon, and more often than not returned home with a bag full of volumes to pile on his already overstuffed shelves. Bryan often said it was a wonder that their front room didn't collapse from the weight of those shelves. "We'll go right through the floor someday," he'd warn, "end up in poor old Mrs. Potter's kitchen." But although he'd sigh and roll his eyes at the sight of yet another bag of books, he'd let it go at that, indulging Rupert's foibles just as Rupert indulged Bryan's love of American football.

He was watching a match now, in fact—one that he'd taped last weekend, I assumed, since he'd paused the action to answer the door, but when he would have stopped the tape altogether I told him not to, that I didn't mind if he watched it while I was there. Truth was, I'd been hoping that he'd have a match on. Seeing Mother always left me feeling woefully off balance, and I drew a certain comfort from the familiar trappings of a Saturday afternoon with Bryan: American football on the television and, close to hand, his bottled beer and cheese-and-onion–flavoured crisps and his remotes for video and television, lovingly arranged.

I took the chair beside him, Rupert's chair, and curled my legs up comfortably. No need to stand on ceremony here, or worry about my feet marking the upholstery. This was a man's house, and besides that, it was home.

"So," Bryan asked me, "did Sally get off all right?"

"Yes, she and her boyfriend took the last bits of furniture out last night." The flat had seemed strange without her.

Empty. Colder. That's what had driven me out in the first place today, a desire for companionship. And warmth. Rupert and Bryan's front room was deliciously cosy, compared to my own. Not that I ever complained about the way I lived—I didn't want Rupert or Bryan to know just how close I'd come to poverty, because they would have tried to give me money, help me out. I didn't want that. I wanted to stand on my own two feet, make my own way, just the same as I wanted to do in my acting.

But I think Bryan had his suspicions. The sandwiches he made for me at half-time were enormous, bulging with chicken salad and served with a big hunk of cheddar and three pickled onions.

As I took the plate from him, I said, quite as if it didn't matter, "I saw Mother this morning, at Fortnum and Mason."

"Oh, yes? What did she have to say?"

"Nothing. She didn't see me." I didn't need to explain things, with Bryan. He glanced over briefly, but didn't say anything. I said, "She has a new man."

"What, the blond? Yes, I've seen him. He's Danish, I think." Then he suddenly grinned as though struck by some private thought.

"What?" I asked him.

"I was just wondering what your mother would say if she knew you'd been offered a leading role opposite Madeleine Hedrick."

I didn't see the humour. "Yes, well, I can't imagine Madeleine Hedrick being too thrilled to learn I've been offered the role, either."

"And why is that?"

"Because of what my mother did."

"Angel," he said, "that was ages ago. Ancient history."

"I remember it clearly enough." I'd have been unlikely to forget. Not only because it had been splashed across the tabloids, but because I'd been responsible. I'd been twelve at the time, just back from a school trip to Stratford-upon-Avon and the Royal Shakespeare Theatre, where I'd sat in the dark watching Madeleine Hedrick play Lady Macbeth. I'd been spellbound. I could still close my eyes and recall her performance, and how, when I'd returned home, I'd told Mother I was going to be an actress.

To begin with, I think, she'd been flattered. But when she'd realized that it had been not her, but Madeleine Hedrick who'd inspired my decision, her reaction had been predictable. Mother might not have owned a magic mirror, nor would she necessarily have resorted to poisoned apples, but she did have a need to be fairest of all.

I'd forgotten by now what she'd actually said, but her unjust attack on the actress I'd just seen and loved had stung me to retort, in the know-it-all tone of a twelve-year-old, that Madeleine Hedrick was more beautiful and talented than anyone; than Mother, even. I'd actually said that: "She's better than you."

"Is she really?" my mother had asked with that small inward smile that spelled trouble. "We'll see."

Two weeks later the tabloids had printed the picture—*that* picture—of Mother lying topless in a man's arms on a beach in Monte Carlo, laughing without shame and pretending to be unaware of the cameras that she surely had known would be trained on them. The man had been famous as well—Jason Hedrick, the well-known film actor . . . and Madeleine's husband.

I could still feel it now, deep down in the pit of my stomach, the way that I'd felt when I'd first seen that picture, seen it staring back accusingly at me from every newsstand as I'd walked that day to school.

The guilt had eaten holes in me, great holes I'd filled with silence as I'd watched the bitterly painful collapse of the Hedricks' marriage play out in the press through the following weeks. I'd wished a thousand times that I'd have had the sense to keep my mouth shut, knowing that without my goading Mother she would never have gone after Jason Hedrick, and the whole sordid scandal would never have happened.

But words, once spoken, couldn't be taken back, and mine had done their damage.

I'd been too ashamed to tell anyone it was my fault. To this day I had never discussed it with Rupert or Bryan. Which was why all I said now to Bryan was that I remembered what

Mother had done. "And I'm sure Madeleine Hedrick remembers it, too."

Bryan, very dry, pointed out that if I meant to avoid working with anyone my mother had offended, that wouldn't leave too many places I *could* work. "Maybe one or two small theatres in the Hebrides," he thought, "but you'd have to forget the entire West End."

"Oh, Bryan . . ."

"I'm only saying." He took a swig of beer. "She's a nice lady, Maddy Hedrick. I've met her. She doesn't seem the kind to hold a grudge."

"Even so." I drew breath; set my jaw. "I'm not taking the part."

"Not just because of Maddy, surely? Or . . . is it something else?" He slanted me a penetrating look. "What's the matter, Angel—don't you think that you can do the job?"

He saw too much, too easily. "Of course I do. It's just that, well, D'Ascanio's grandson said he wants the play to run through August, and that's a long time to be gone, and I've just had this audition for a part in the new Gareth Gwyn Morgan play . . ."

"Oh, really? What's the part?"

I looked down again. "Sort of a servant girl."

"I see."

"It's a fabulous play. Everyone says so. And my audition went really well; I think that—"

"Roo wants you to go."

I stopped short. Raised my head. Bryan's eyes were still trained on the television, but his face had the self-reproaching look of someone who had just betrayed a confidence, who'd spoken out of turn. "He'll never tell you so, you know how he is, but he wants you to go with him."

So I hadn't been wrong then, to think that Rupert's giving me the Celia poems for my birthday, and his taking me to St. Paul's Church, had been part of an effort to sway my decision. It wasn't like Rupert to do that, any more than it was like Bryan to break rank and tell me what Rupert wanted. "Why?" I asked.

"He's retiring."

He had dropped the bombshell squarely, and it took me several seconds to absorb the impact. "What?"

"He's been thinking about it for some time, we both have. We're not getting any younger . . ."

"You're only in your fifties; that's not old."

"Well, bless you for that, but it feels old, sometimes, and there are things we'd like to do together, places where we'd like to go. We've got no worries financially, so we figured, why not? I've already handed in my notice, and Roo"—here he looked at me—"Roo wants to do this one last play, for young D'Ascanio. And then he's finished, too."

"I see." It was an awful lot for me to take in, all at once. Bryan's retiring wasn't so much of a shock—he'd worked for the same firm forever and he did have a fair bit of money set by, but I couldn't imagine Rupert giving up the theatre. Directing, to him, was much more than a job . . . it was a calling.

"Don't you dare say I told you," said Bryan. "He'd bloody kill me. He wasn't going to tell you till the play's run was over. I'm only telling you now because I know what it would mean to him to have you there, your first leading role, and this the last play he's directing."

"Bryan . . ."

"Look, you know that I'm not one to tell you what to do—"

"Since when?"

"I only think—"

"You *always* tell me what to do."

"I only think," he carried on, with patience, "that you should think it over."

It was blackmail and he knew it. I would never have been able to bear disappointing Rupert, not after learning he had his heart set on my going to Italy with him. Rupert and Bryan meant more to me than anything, and if it came down to a choice between keeping my stage name and making Rupert happy, well . . . I sighed, and looked at Bryan.

He said, "So you'll go?"

"I'll think about it."

"That's my girl." He smiled. "You never know, you might enjoy it."

"Oh right, I'm sure I'd have a marvellous time. Madeleine Hedrick would hate me for sure, and D'Ascanio's grandson just wants to have my name for his publicity."

He shrugged. "So take it as an opportunity to show the bastard—show them all—that you can bloody act." As he passed me the crisps he reminded me, "Chances like this one aren't thick on the ground, Angel. And playing a servant girl isn't the same thing as playing the lead."

v

I was not a good traveller. Planes made me nervous and driving in anything other than a car made me queasy and besides that I never knew what I should pack. An open suitcase always seemed to be inviting me to fill it, which I invariably did, to the point where it became impossible to lift and carry for more than a yard at a time.

This morning had challenged me on all three fronts—our flight had been rough, and when we'd landed at the Marco Polo airport we had transferred to an overcrowded, overheated bus that had carried us over the causeway to Venice, and when the bus had let us off I'd had to drag my heavy suitcases for what had seemed miles, up and over the little arched bridges that were, I imagined—at times when you *weren't* hauling suitcases—quite picturesque, but whose endless stone steps had at the time been sheer torture. I'd felt like the porter at Rupert's club, like poor Sisyphus endlessly rolling his boulder uphill, labouring up to the summit of each bridge only to find there was one more beyond that to climb . . . down and up, down and up . . . in the heat and the crowds it was hell.

Rupert would have helped me with my suitcase if he hadn't been weighted down with two himself—it had probably been Rupert, I'd realized, who'd taught me to pack in the first place, though he'd seemed a good deal more cheerful with his load. After the first half-mile or so I had, rather hopefully, suggested a taxi, only to be told there were no cars in Venice. Not a one. Visitors and residents were forced to leave their vehicles in car parks at the city's edge, and enter the Venetian maze on foot. There were water taxis, of course, Rupert had said, and a sort of bus system involving larger boats called *va-*

poretti which patrolled the Grand Canal. But our hotel, as luck would have it, wasn't on the Grand Canal. So we had walked.

But I hadn't complained.

Rupert had been like a child at a holiday camp since I'd said I was taking the part in *Il Prezzo*—I'd never seen him so openly happy, and it was clear from the way he had gone about planning things that he wanted this trip to be special, something that we'd both remember fondly in the years to come. As Bryan had pointed out, this would be my first 'big' play, and Rupert's last, so it was natural, I suppose, that Rupert would want to make everything perfect.

And starting in Venice had been a big part of his plan. Rupert loved Venice. He'd managed to take me to nearly all his other favourite travel spots, but what with school schedules and his work, one thing or another, we never had made it to Venice.

Not only had Rupert made special arrangements to give us a night's stopover here, on our way to D'Ascanio's villa, but he'd spent the past fortnight showering me with coloured brochures and maps, showing me the sights we'd see and telling me the history of this strangest of all European cities. Founded by people who'd literally gone to the edge of the land to find safety in those dark days that had followed the fall of the Roman Empire, when barbaric marauders had terrorized Italy, Venice was an engineering triumph, built on water—or, more correctly, on piles sunk into a marshy lagoon—its hundred islands held fast by a labyrinth of bridges and canals.

The very name Venice had seemed to me ancient and rich, filled with romance.

So far, though, reality hadn't lived up to the image.

The hotel was nice enough, but it was modern and might have been anywhere. I did appreciate the shower, though. I stepped clean from it now, wrapping myself in the thick hotel towel as I padded across to my suitcase in search of fresh clothes.

I had just finished dressing when Rupert knocked at my door.

"Well," he said, as I let him in, "we've had a fax from Il Piacere. Seems our SM is flying into Venice today, as well, and young D'Ascanio's given him the name of our hotel here, so we'll meet up for dinner and go on together tomorrow by train."

I knew he'd already told me the name of our stage manager—there weren't too many people in the business that Rupert didn't know—but I'd forgotten. "Who's our SM, again?"

"Bill Melansky. Nice chap, American, I've worked with him before. You'll like him." Looking down, he fiddled with his camera, checked the settings. "I do hope I've brought enough film."

"I thought you'd been here a dozen times."

"I have, but not with you."

Which prodded me to put my own ambivalence aside and try to let on I was having a good time, that I was loving Venice just as much as he was.

And I wanted to love it, I did. As we left the hotel and came into the main tourist thoroughfare I focussed my weary eyes harder, and tried, but the Venice I saw was a city of commerce, of shops selling Carnivale masks and hand-blown glass and leather goods and marbled paper, jewellers' windows dotted in between to make things glitter, and Italian ice-cream stands on every corner.

Not that this was anything new, I thought. Venice must always have been one great market, a Babel of languages. Even now, in late March with the Carnivale over, the hotels were full and the streets thick with tourists, and I heard English spoken more often, it seemed, than Italian.

Aware of Rupert's scrutiny, I summoned all my acting skills and smiled. "Where to first? The Rialto?" I remembered he'd said that he liked the Rialto especially, not only the lovely white high-arched bridge itself, but the district that surrounded it—a shopper's mecca, he had called it.

He watched my face a moment longer; looked away. "You know, the best way to see the Rialto would be from the water. Come on." Stepping clear of the current of tourists he towed me behind him, one hand on my arm, as though I were still a small child he might easily lose. "We'll take a gondola."

Visions of seasickness rose to my mind but I kept my face deliberately cheerful as he detoured me off to the nearest stone bridge on a narrow canal where two young men in identical outfits—black trousers and jackets, and shirts horizontally striped red-and-white, and flat-brimmed straw hats and white trainers—lounged together against the stone railing and called by turns "Gondola-Gondola!" over the heads of the swift passing crowd.

The taller one straightened, arms folded, as Rupert approached him, preparing to bargain a price. Rupert appeared to be losing the battle until, turning, he pointed at me and said something—my name, I think. Both the gondoliers looked, and the taller one smiled. Then he nodded, replying to Rupert, who motioned me forwards.

"He says he can take us."

I glanced down at the moored gondola bobbing by the stone steps that led down to the canal, below the bridge. "Take us where?"

But Rupert only smiled. "You'll see."

Near the sottoportego *a gondolier leaned on his oar, trading gossip with a woman who was hanging out her washing from the window-ledge, above. The pair of them stopped talking as he bore down on them, his mind alive with purpose like a hound that had just caught the scent of its quarry.*

"An Englishwoman," he demanded of the gondolier, "a blonde young Englishwoman, beautiful. She travels with a man. Have they been passengers of yours this morning?"

"No, signore, no. I have had no one." The gondolier shrugged off his luck. "But I have seen a couple like this, maybe half an hour ago?" He glanced upwards at the woman in her window to confirm the time, and at her nod repeated, "Yes, half an hour ago they came by, in the gondola of my friend Paolo."

"Do you know where he was taking them?"

"I think to the Rialto."

"Then quickly," he commanded, stepping down into the gondola as though it were his private launch. "Quickly, we must go to the Rialto."

If he could have urged the craft to travel faster, he'd have done it. As it was, he could barely restrain himself from reaching over in his seat to paddle with his hands, to speed their progress. But the gondola cut through the green canals as swiftly as it could, as if the gondolier had caught his fever.

A thrill raced through him as they turned into the turmoil of the Grand Canal and made towards the graceful white-arched bridge of the Rialto. He was close now, he thought. Very close . . .

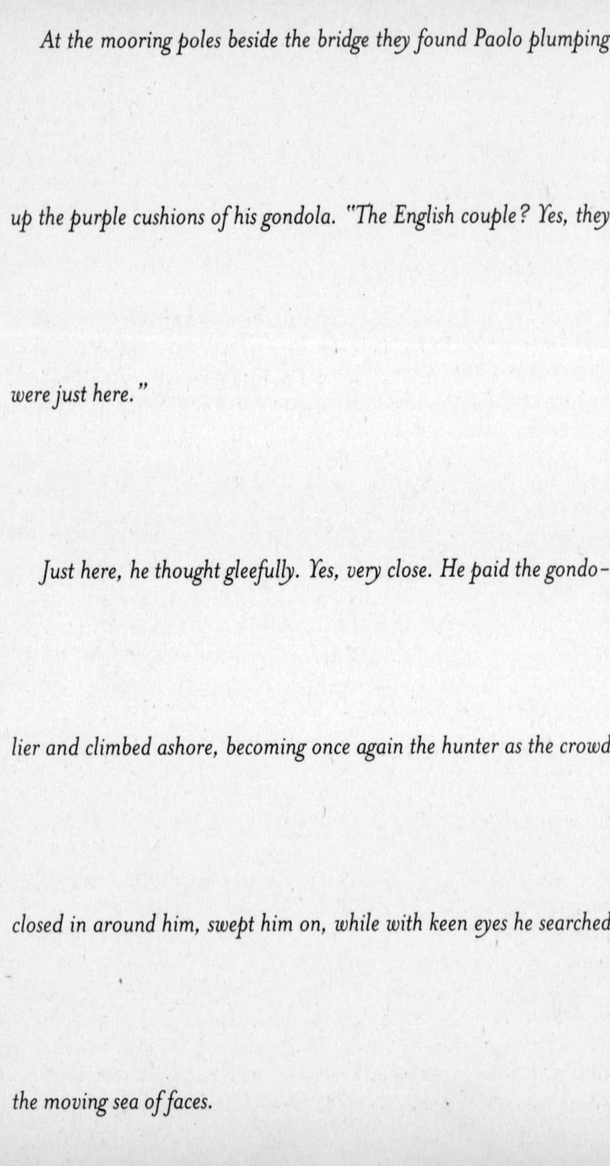

At the mooring poles beside the bridge they found Paolo plumping up the purple cushions of his gondola. "The English couple? Yes, they were just here."

Just here, he thought gleefully. Yes, very close. He paid the gondolier and climbed ashore, becoming once again the hunter as the crowd closed in around him, swept him on, while with keen eyes he searched the moving sea of faces.

vi

IT was an odd sensation, stepping from firm and predictable land onto something unstable, a surface that quivered like something alive. I sat hastily, seeking balance in the long and narrow boat that suddenly seemed far too narrow, too wobbly.

Casting round for reassurance I took heart in the gondola's obvious age. Its lacquered black sides had been lovingly polished for years, I decided, as had the arching brass dolphins who held the red cords on which soft padded bumpers were strung, to each side of the seat. The seat itself was leather, smooth and yielding underneath me, and in case of extra passengers a rather ornate chair had been positioned to my right, in front. The only less-than-reassuring feature was the gleaming silver ornament that topped the long, up-curling prow—a curious thing like the blade of an executioner's axe, pointed perpetually outwards as if to keep all other boats at a distance.

Rupert got in and the gondola rolled and I clutched at its sides; grasped them harder when the gondolier stepped on behind us, taking up his oar and pushing off with a cheerful farewell to his partner, left back at the bridge calling 'Gondola-Gondola!' all by himself.

Rupert settled himself on the cushion beside me, adjusting his camera. "Relax," he said, testing his lens with an experimental snap of me in profile. "It's perfectly safe. Just like punting on the Cam."

"Yes, well, we didn't all go to Cambridge," I reminded him, but I tried to relax all the same. I didn't want to spoil Rupert's pleasure at showing me the sights. To distract my rolling stomach I glanced over my shoulder and watched as our gondolier shifted his feet on the small Persian rug that protected the polished black boards in the stern, using his own weight as much as his oar as he steered us through the shadows underneath the little bridge.

Rupert, mistaking my fierce concentration for a lack of confidence, said, "It's a mostly inherited trade, gondolier. There can only ever be five hundred of them at any given time, that's the law, so it tends to get passed on from father to son. Our chap here is probably not the first man in his family to do this." The gondolier, when asked, confirmed in passable English that he was indeed fourth-generation. "You see?" Rupert told me. "So no need to worry, he knows what he's doing. Ah, look there," he said, distracting me by pointing to the left as we passed an intersecting canal. "See way up there, that bit of land in the lagoon, that's where they blow the glass. The island of Murano."

I caught only a glimpse as we glided by, and a bracing clean whiff of the sea—the first time I'd smelled anything at all on these canals, in spite of all the things I'd read and heard. Perhaps the recent rains, I thought, had cleansed the ancient waterways, or maybe it was simply that we'd come in spring and not a few months later, when the summer's heat and still more tourists took their toll on the city's hygiene. Whatever the reason, apart from a faint breath of sea air from time to time all I could smell was the rich scent of greenery, lacy pale branches of trees hanging high overhead and the ivy that clung to the crumbled brick walls of a small side canal.

My stomach settled. The noise of the crowds at our backs grew progressively fainter, disappearing entirely as we rounded the next corner, leaving only the lulling splash and pull of the gondolier's oar and the creak of the boards as he balanced himself. The hushed and huddled buildings pressed us closely, painted pink and green and ivory, windows shuttered, with a laundry line hung here and there between the rusting railings of their balconies. I heard the small repeating click of Rupert's camera shutter, and the slap of pigeons' wings as they rose flapping from their hidden perches, seeking higher places; heard the water gently lapping at the old walls with their softly greening stones. And as I exhaled on a sigh I knew that Rupert, who'd been watching me again, could now rest satisfied.

Here, at last, was the Venice I'd dreamed of, the Venice of Shakespeare, of Byron, of Browning; faded a little, perhaps, like a magnificent Renaissance painting that had lain too long in the sunlight, but still standing, silent and agelessly beautiful; still worthy of the name La Serenissima—the Most Serene.

We floated on peacefully, our gondolier calling out "Oi!" as a warning each time he manouevred us round another corner of the labyrinth. From time to time he pointed out an interesting sight that we were passing—the Church of St. Madelena, the house of the explorers Antonio and Nicola Zeno, the palazzos of a half a dozen dukes whose names I didn't know—buildings whose facades were set with marble carved in deep relief above columns and colonnades shaped with those strange pointed arches that looked as though they'd come straight out of the Arabian Nights . . . a legacy, I supposed, from the days when the trade winds had carried to Venice tall galleons laden with spices and silks from the East.

And then, as we entered a narrow canal where a peeling pink building with iron-barred windows rose out of its dappled reflection in water the colour of olives, our gondolier tapped Rupert once on the shoulder.

"Ecco," he told him. *"La Casetta Fiorita."*

And I knew then why Rupert had wanted to bring me this way, in the gondola.

Leaning forward in my seat, I took a closer look up at the crumbling 'Little House of Flowers' where Galeazzo D'Ascanio had spent his years in Venice. He had written of this house in *The Season of Storms,* the book of poems Rupert had given me for my birthday, and I wished I had the book in my hands now so I could read the lines again and get their full effect, but the book was still packed in my suitcase back at the hotel, and all I could remember was one fragment of a verse in which he'd called the Casetta Fiorita 'that birthplace of our passion.'

I had pictured it quite differently, a grander house than this one . . . but I wasn't disappointed. This was better, really. More romantic.

I couldn't see flowers, but twisting vines trailed down one side of the building and clung to the curving stone balcony two storeys up, from whose window, I thought, Galeazzo had first glimpsed his Celia as she passed by in a gondola, as I was passing now. I sighed, and looking up I fancied I saw something for an instant break the shadows at the window, like a ghostly face forgotten, gazing out.

"No one lives here anymore," said Rupert sadly. "A shame, but there it is. It isn't safe."

"Why not? Is it sinking?"

"I should think that would be a large part of it, yes. All of Venice is sinking. But part of it, too, is the age of the house. This one's ancient, you know. Thirteenth-century."

I shaded my eyes with one hand as I studied the structure, imagining what it must have looked like all those years ago; what sights it must have seen. "It's a pity he doesn't restore this house, too."

"Sorry?"

"Galeazzo's grandson."

"I'm sure that he would, if he owned it."

"Wasn't this part of his inheritance, then?"

Rupert, with a shake of his head, informed me that Galeazzo D'Ascanio had only rented the Casetta Fiorita. "It belonged, I believe, to an Austrian financier, and when the First World War got going it was sequestrated—"

"Sequestrated?"

"Confiscated," he said, simplifying, "by the government, who rented it to Galeazzo, furnished."

"Hardly fair on the Austrian," I remarked.

Rupert, with a patient shrug, reminded me that war was rarely fair. "Though he had his revenge. He trained as an aviator and got himself selected for the squadron that bombed Venice. Apparently he took delight in dropping bombs on his old neighbours. Even hit his own house a few times. See?" He pointed out the scars along the roofline as we glided underneath the jutting balcony, where a carved stone lion's head appeared in the tangle of vines, blindly snarling.

My initial sympathy for the displaced Austrian vanished. “What a bloody stupid thing to do.”

“I’m sure it didn’t help the house much,” Rupert said, squinting as he focussed his lens on the lion’s head. “And it would be lovely, as you say, if someone would restore it. But Venetian laws are strict about what can and can’t be done to these old buildings, and many owners simply can’t afford to do the work. Cheaper to clear out and leave the house empty.”

Not entirely empty, I thought. There were ghosts here. From behind the black window I felt the eyes watching me, silently following, as our gondolier called out an echoing “Oi!” and we slipped round another corner in the canal, leaving the decaying pink Casetta Fiorita alone and softly dreaming of the grandeur it had known.

It was noon when he reached the Piazza San Marco.

The midday sun had bleached the square and cast a haze across the piazzetta, so that even the statues of San Teodoro and San Marco's winged lion, they who had for these eight centuries stood vigilant, their eyes fixed ever eastward over the serene lagoon, appeared today to slumber on their columns while below them at the edge of the canal the water barely swelled beneath the waiting row of gondolas.

He turned his back upon the gleaming pinnacles and domes of the basilica and searched among the faces in the strolling crowd for hers. No easy task, that. All of Venice seemed to be here, standing idly sharing gossip in the shadow of the bell-tower, or lunching at café tables by the Moorish colonnades. Music rose and met from either side of the piazza where the orchestras competed for attention from beneath their café awnings, a cultivated duel of rival melodies and rhythm that yet managed to produce a pleasing harmony.

"Maître!" a delighted voice behind him cried and, turning, he recognized the oldest of the waiters from the café on his right, a sun-creased man from Corsica whose thick French accent clung to every word. "Maître, what a joy to see you here again. You must sit here, where all who pass can see you and pay tribute to your talent."

He hesitated . . . he had not meant to stop here, but rather, like one of his own hounds, to keep to the chase, to find the scent and pursue it, relentless . . . but the waiter's words, the blatant adoration, moved him suddenly. He sat. What did it matter, he thought, if he paused for a meal? Did not his own hounds hunt the better when they were refreshed?

He ate and drank deliberately, in honour of the watching eyes.

A scraping of chairs at the table behind him announced the arrival of a new party, young, gay with laughter. A man in English said: "Oh no, but it really was too bad of you, John, not to stop the boat and let her have a go. She might have done it."

"Nonsense. From what I've heard, nobody gets in to see him. That man of his guards him like a Gurkha."

And then a woman, in amusement, said: "I fancy Celia's a match for any man's man. Aren't you, darling?"

Still with his back to their table he froze, his glass half-lifted to his lips, as something wonderful and warm began to tingle all along his spine. Fighting the impulse to leap to his feet at that moment and face her, he felt in his pockets for pencil and paper. Their meeting, this first meeting, mustn't be ordinary. It must be creative, it must have appropriate drama. He wrote quickly, and signalled the waiter.

"Yes, maître?"

Keeping his voice hushed he urged the man closer, conspiring. "Behind me—the blonde at the table behind me . . ."

A glance flickered over his head and then back again. "Yes, maître?"

"There is only one blonde?"

"There is, maître."

"Excellent. When I am gone, you will give her this note," he said, folding the paper and pressing it into the waiter's hand. "You will give it to her privately, pretending it is something she has dropped, perhaps. Do this for me, and I will be forever in your debt."

The waiter bowed his head and left.

Once more the laughter of the English party rang out close behind him, and he raised his glass and drank the sweetness of the wine and smiled.

vii

I had seen the Piazza San Marco in films.

I had known that it would be the most enormous public square I'd ever seen, alive with flocks of beating pigeons swirling upwards, wheeling, settling, then rising once again to spread their wings above the multitude. When I stood at the centre of the square, in the shadow of the soaring red-brick campanile, or bell-tower, I felt that I was standing on the very spot where East met West, with the onion-domed Byzantine splendour of St. Mark's Basilica glittering gold and white beneath the sun before me and the other three sides of the square at my back ringed with porticoed buildings in an echo of the ancient Roman forum, pale stone arcades and shaded cloistered walkways.

To the right of the basilica, the pastel-patterned walls of the exquisite Doge's Palace, with its pointed Moorish arches, formed the north side of the smaller piazzetta that opened from the great piazza onto the fresh sea-salt–scented breezes and wide blue of the lagoon.

We'd arrived that way, disembarking from our gondola beneath the watchful eyes of St. Mark's lion and St. Teodoro standing on his crocodile, set high upon their matching red Egyptian granite pillars that for centuries had stood as both a welcome and a warning to those entering the city from the sea. Often, Rupert told me, foreign visitors in olden times were greeted by the sight of a body hung to swing between the pillars—an executed traitor, perhaps, or some unfortunate citizen who had fallen afoul of the Council of Ten, that secretive band of assassins and spies who'd scuttled through the shadows of the Doge's Palace like a plague of rats and kept their stealthy vigil with an ear at every door, earning themselves, by their methods of torture and terror, a fearsome reputation throughout Europe that had rivalled that of the Inquisition.

There hadn't, of course, been a dead body hanging between the twin pillars today, although Rupert had taken great pains in describing what one might have looked like, to give me the proper effect. Rupert had a director's compulsion for setting the scene.

Which was why, after we had spent an hour or so at the Rialto, breathing the breezes that washed the high bridge, and indulging in some rather wistful window-shopping, Rupert had insisted we hire a second gondola to take us further down the Grand Canal, so I could see the Doge's Palace as its architects had meant it to be seen—from the water.

"I'm giving you a memory," he had said, in explanation. "You only see anything once for the first time. The sight should be one you'll remember."

And to make sure that I did, he'd snapped a photo of the pointed palace arches rising out of the lagoon as we'd approached.

He took another photo of me now, as I half-turned from my admiration of the basilica. The camera clicked and whirred as the film began to rewind automatically, and Rupert swore. "I knew I should have brought a second film." Zipping his camera case closed he squinted down the length of the piazza. "There must be a shop around, surely . . ."

"There," I said, and pointed. "I'll wait here for you, if you don't mind. I want to feed the pigeons."

Rupert smiled. "Right then, I won't be long. And then we'll have a cup of tea at one of the cafés, whichever one you like."

I considered this briefly as he headed off to buy his film. There were several cafés sheltering in the long and shadowed galleries behind the arching porticoes that ringed the huge piazza, each one having extended its territory out onto the paving stones with a tidy array of tables and woven-backed chairs whose colour marked them—and the customers who sat in them—as the property of that particular establishment. One had yellow chairs; another cream ones, but the café closest to me had done theirs a lovely pea-green, a colour that seemed to have succeeded in attracting patrons. Nearly all the pea-green chairs were occupied by people slowly sipping wine or nursing single cups of coffee; people watching people, reading papers, reading guidebooks, simply lounging, half an ear tuned to the compact little orchestra that sat upon its awning-covered platform underneath one rounded archway, playing waltzes.

Any melody, apparently, would do—traditional or modern, from an opera or a Broadway show—so long as it was in three-quarter time.

The pea-green-chair café, I decided, was definitely the one we ought to choose. But for the moment, I was in no hurry to have a drink. There were pigeons to feed.

The maize-sellers dotted the piazza, perched on folding chairs and stools behind their wheeled white stands, cheerily scooping the hard yellow kernels into little plastic bags. They did a smashing business. I bought three bags all at once from a middle-aged man with friendly eyes whose cigarette appeared to be permanently attached to one side of his mouth—it bobbed when he smiled but stayed firmly in place, sending up a curling wreath of pure white smoke as he took my money in his work-creased fingers.

I loved feeding pigeons, no matter what anyone told me about their being dirty birds. I loved their plump grey bodies and their warm contented cooing and the bobbing of their iridescent heads. And I'd always had a feeling that they liked me, too.

Certainly the birds here in the Piazza San Marco seemed to find me irresistible. As I tossed my first handful of maize they rose around me in a flapping mass, cooing madly in encouragement, their small pricking feet settling on my sleeves, my back, my hair, while a flurry of wings fanned the air by my face. Some of the greedy ones didn't wait for me to throw the maize, or even to gather it into my hand, but thrust their searching beaks into the open bag and took what they were after. "Now then, that's bad manners," I told them, and nudged them aside as I tried to make sure that they all got their share. The bag began to empty, and my covering of pigeons subsided a bit, dropping to my shoulders and my forearms and then fluttering by twos and threes towards the ground.

It was then I first became aware that I was being watched.

He was sitting alone at a table some fifteen feet in front of me, drumming a folded newspaper with fingers that were restless with energy. A youthful-looking man, with one of those faces that might have been thirty or forty-five, handsome in that easy, open way that always looked to me American. His hair in the sunlight was a light brown, carelessly cut, and his clothes were the casual clothes of the tourist. He'd apparently been reading the paper, but had lowered it to look at me, as though he found me much more entertaining.

I registered this quickly and glanced down with careful nonchalance, opening another bag of maize to bring the pigeons back around me, swarming upwards like a living screen. But when the grey whirlwind of wings slowed and sank again, calming, the man was still there. This time he grinned, a flash of perfect white, and in a clear voice he called over: "Need some help?"

I'd been right about him being an American.

I shook my head. "No, thank you."

"You're sure?"

"Quite sure." However appealing I might find the smile and the accent, I thought, it wouldn't do for me to be chatting with a strange man when Rupert came back, not with all of the lectures he'd given me over the years on the dangers of doing just that. I moved off a step or two, hoping that would send a stronger signal to the American.

But a few minutes later, when I'd finished doling out the contents of my third and final bag of maize, I looked round to find him still sitting there watching me, drinking a beer now, his newspaper set to one side. "All done?" he asked. "Then come and have a drink."

He said it just like that, as though we knew each other well, as though there wasn't any reason why I wouldn't want to join him. I didn't for a moment consider doing it, but having never been faced with this particular pick-up technique, I wasn't entirely sure what to do. If he'd been more aggressive, or lewd and suggestive, like most of the men who came on to me were, then it would have been simple. I could have been rude. I could have made a haughty exit, parting with a comment that would cut him down to size. But rudeness in this case seemed rather excessive. Instead I shook my head again and answered him coolly, "No, thank you, I'm waiting for someone."

"You can wait as well sitting as standing. And anyway, Rupert won't mind." He stood himself, with hand outstretched. "I'm Den O'Malley."

I must have looked a blank, because he added, "Your stage manager."

"Oh."

The man who'd be in charge of every detail of rehearsal and performance, taking care of the practical, technical matters so Rupert could concentrate on the creative; the man who'd be responsible for scheduling my life and who would be by turns my advocate, my taskmaster, my sympathetic ear. This wasn't quite how I'd expected to meet him, and his name didn't ring any bells—I was sure Rupert had mentioned someone else—but here was this man standing now with his hand out, and I didn't want to be rude.

"Celia Sands." It felt odd giving someone my real name in a professional context. I'd got so used to being Celia Sullivan. But Galeazzo D'Ascanio's grandson had hired me on as Celia Sands, and that would be the name used in the programmes, so I might as well get used to it. Still, it tumbled strangely from my tongue, like someone else's name.

"Yeah, I know," he said, over the handshake. "I got the package from your agent, with your picture, though I have to say it doesn't do you justice. You're much prettier in person."

It was not the most original of lines, and it shouldn't have worked, but something about the way he delivered it charmed me in spite of myself. I sat down. "Thank you."

"That's a fortunate name, Celia Sands. And it's your real one, is that right? But you're not a relation? Damn, that's too bad—it would have made a great story for the newspapers. Oh, well. What can I get you to drink?"

"I don't really—"

"This beer's kind of weak, but there's wine, or tea, or . . . hang on, here's Rupert." As he raised his arm, calling to Rupert across the scattering of tables that divided us, I took the opportunity to study him more closely. I had never met a man who talked as quickly—or as much—as me, till now, and it felt odd to be the one who couldn't get a word in edgeways. He'd have made a good Henry the Fifth, I thought, playing my little Shakespearean casting game. He certainly appeared to have the restlessness, the energy, the natural bent for leadership. Watching him stand and call a second time to Rupert I could easily imagine him rallying the troops at Agincourt, though there was something playful round his eyes that made me think he might not have had the stick-to-it-iveness to take part in the actual battle.

Rupert had stopped at the edge of the pea-green-chair tables, and was staring.

"There, he's seen us now," said Den. He waved again and grinned and sat. "He probably doesn't recognize me without my beard—he's got that fatherly protective look on."

He was certainly wearing some kind of a look, though I couldn't have said what it was, and it had vanished by the time he reached our table.

"Dennis, this is a surprise." He greeted Den O'Malley with a smile and a handshake but his eyes . . . well, there was something in his eyes that wasn't right. "You're here with Bill?"

That was the name that Rupert had told me earlier, I remembered now—the man who was supposed to be our SM. Bill Melansky.

"I'm here instead of Bill. He's had some trouble with his heart—his doctor said he shouldn't make the trip. Didn't D'Ascanio fax you? He said he was going to."

"He did, yes, he just didn't say . . . well, it doesn't matter, really. Bill's all right, though, is he?"

"Cranky as ever. Here, have a seat, it's good to see you. It must be . . . what, three years?"

"About that, I should think."

Den shook his head in disbelief. "Where does the time go? You're looking well. And Bryan? How is he? The two of you are still . . . ? Yeah? Well, that's great." He raised his glass in a salute. "You're an example to us all, you and Bryan. I don't know how you do it. My wife's become an ex-wife since I saw you, did you hear?"

"I did, yes," Rupert said. "I'm sorry."

"Nothing to be sorry for, she knew what she was doing. I'm no good at being married. And besides, she's less expensive this way—no more bills from Bloomingdale's." His blue eyes laughed, without regret. "This being single isn't bad, you know. It has its . . ."—and he looked at me—"its compensations."

Rupert smiled and warned him, "Careful, Dennis. That's my little girl you're leering at."

"Was I leering? Sorry, force of habit. Let's order a drink, then, OK?" He hailed the waiter.

Rupert surprised me by ordering Scotch. Unlike Bryan, Rupert rarely drank anything stronger than tea in the daytime. He leaned back in his chair, taking up the dropped reins of the conversation. "So, Dennis, where are you staying?"

He named the hotel. "Little place down an alley near the train station. I always stay there. D'Ascanio offered to put me up at the same hotel where he's got you, but I have kind of a loyalty thing going with the place I'm in, and anyway I've gotten so I like my hotels cheap and cheerful. Makes the trip more interesting. Besides, I won't have to drag my luggage too far in the morning. What time does our train leave, do you know?"

Rupert said, "Not offhand. I left the schedule back at the hotel. I know it's early, though. Supposedly the tickets will be waiting for us at the station, young D'Ascanio has it all arranged."

"Then I'm sure the tickets will be there. He's done a pretty good job of arranging things so far. Have you met him? What's he like?"

"He seems a decent chap, and very keen."

"Yeah, that was my impression on the phone. We'll see." Lifting his beer, Den leaned back in his chair and directed another quick smile at me. "But here it is your first visit to

Venice—it is your first visit? And we're spoiling it by talking shop."

I didn't mind, and told him so, but he refused to be convinced.

"No, we'll have to stop. Have you been inside the basilica? The Doge's Palace? Seen the Bridge of Sighs?" When I shook my head to all of them he turned a half-accusing eye on Rupert. "What the heck have you done with her all day, then?"

"We took a gondola to the Rialto."

"Gondolas." Den gave a shudder.

"You don't like them?" I asked.

"Let's just say I think Oscar Wilde hit the nail on the head when he said seeing Venice from a gondola was like being ferried through the sewers in a coffin."

I'd always liked Oscar Wilde's wit. "But it wasn't like that, really. It was lovely. Very peaceful."

"And since when is a holiday meant to be peaceful?" Den grinned.

I would have smiled back, but something in the way Rupert was watching me over the rim of his glass made me reconsider, and I couldn't help feeling that somehow the peace of our trip had already been broken.

viii

I'D been right to think Den was the Henry the Fifth type. When we'd finished our drinks he took charge with military zeal, touring us round all the buildings that ringed the Piazza San Marco. At first Rupert appeared to be happy enough to relinquish the lead and fall back in the ranks—he directed much better from that angle, anyway, where he could see the whole picture—but it soon became apparent that he hadn't entirely surrendered his command.

A sort of competition had developed as we went along, with Den and Rupert trying to outdo each other in the tour guide department, coming up with interesting facts and curiosities, or pointing out some little-known detail about what we were seeing. A duel of knowledge, really, with me caught in between and doing my best to give them both my attention. It was wearying work. By the time we'd gone up the bell-tower and all through the Doge's Palace and across the Bridge of Sighs, my head was fairly spinning with facts that I'd never remember.

They were still at it now, as we came out again into the piazza.

". . . but then the doge, or duke, was really an elected dictator," Rupert was saying, "who ruled until death, like the Pope, and was almost as powerful."

"I always thought," said Den, "the doges hit their peak with Dandalo. Now *there* was a doge—the way he tricked all those Crusaders into doing his dirty work for him." He looked at me. "You know about the Fourth Crusade?"

"Well . . ."

"The one in 1204," said Rupert. "It began as a Crusade

against the Holy Land, but the Crusaders made the mistake of stopping in Venice, you see, to get ships and supplies, and Doge Dandalo—a very old and blind and very crafty man—kept the Crusaders lingering on here with one excuse or another, long enough for them to spend all the money they'd come with, till they were all well in debt. Then he promised them he'd *overlook* the debt, and give them the ships that they'd wanted besides, if they'd do him a couple of favours . . . First he wanted them to help him take back the city of Zara, in what's now Yugoslavia—a city that Venice had ruled and lost. And then he wanted them to help him take Constantinople."

"I don't think he put it that bluntly, though," Den said. "I'm sure his intention, of course, was to sack Constantinople, because it was such a rich city . . ."

"And the only real rival to Venice for the Mediterranean trade."

"Yeah, but the way he actually got the Crusaders to go there was by using that king's son, the kid who'd come to Dandalo for help in getting back his father's throne. Then, once they *got* there, he got them all worked up—not too tough to do with a bunch of guys with swords who'd been waiting around for a chance to kill somebody. They tore the place apart."

"Laid waste to everything," Rupert went on. "Stripped the gold and silver right from the altars of the churches, and what they didn't vandalize they destroyed by fire. The Pope was livid, when he heard. He'd given the Crusaders his blessing to kill Muslims, not Christians, you see, so he called the whole thing off and sent them packing with their tails between their legs."

"But not before they'd divvied up their loot," Den interjected. "A lot of guys got rich off that Crusade."

Rupert pointed out that Doge Dandalo, who'd masterminded the escapade, had not been among those to profit. "He died there, at Constantinople. He was over eighty, anyway. They buried him, I believe, in one of the churches that his own men had only just desecrated—he was probably smiling in his coffin when they did it. Most of the wealth that they plundered came back here, to Venice."

"You'll see a good part of it," Den promised, "in the basilica. Ninety percent of the things in their treasury came from the Fourth Crusade."

Feeling like I'd just had a history lesson with not one but two teachers, I tried to absorb what I'd heard as we passed with the crowd through the massive stone entry of St. Mark's basilica. Someone jostled me and Den briefly shielded me with an arm round my shoulders, but it was Rupert who guided me forwards, his hand at my elbow, to give me my first full view of the basilica's interior.

Had I been a child, I would have thought I'd walked straight into heaven—a vaulted paradise of gleaming gold mosaic touched with jewel-like reds and blues and greens, soaring round domes over rich marble columns that seemed to go on to infinity.

Rupert tipped his head back to take in the mosaics. "You see how they've built it to draw your eyes upwards, by keeping the sunlight up there in the domes? And the rest of the space is quite dim, so that when you walk in you feel instantly that you're in the presence of the divine."

Small and insignificant and humbled, I should have said. I stood at his side gazing upwards for a long moment.

"Aladdin's cave," said Den, his breath skimming over the top of my head. And he explained how, when the basilica was being built, every merchant who set out from Venice had orders to bring something back to enhance the decor—a bit of gold or marble or some rare and stolen jewel. "The things from the Fourth Crusade are over there"—he pointed to the far southern wall—"in the treasury. Want to go see them?"

We had to pay an extra fee and pass a pair of guards to gain admittance to the treasury and its adjoining reliquary chamber, where a multitude of tiny caskets wrought in glass and precious metals held the preserved bones and body parts of various saints—a skeletal ring-finger here, and a scrap of skull there; a solitary molar, roots and all, displayed upon a tiny crimson pillow. I found it all very macabre.

Peering at a black and shrivelled something, Rupert remarked there was much to be said for a life full of sin. "At least when I die no one will put *my* bits and pieces under glass for all the world to see."

I smiled. "You hope."

"You do and I'll disinherit you."

"You can't disinherit someone once you're dead." Keeping my head bent, I sent a glance sideways to check that Den was still behind us, out of earshot. "Roo," I asked, tentatively, "is there anything I ought to know about Den O'Malley?"

He paused, then turned to look at me, his eyebrows raised. "Like what?"

"I don't know. I'm just getting the impression you don't like him."

"I like Dennis." His gaze drifted calmly away from mine, back to the display case. "He's a nice chap, and a good SM."

Unconvinced, I tried another tack. "How long have you two known each other?"

"Years."

"Then why haven't I met him till now?"

"Well, darling, he lives in New York."

"Yes, I know, but he must have been in London at least once in his life." He would have to have been, I thought, to have met Bryan—Bryan hadn't been to America.

"I don't know why you haven't met him, then. Is it important?"

I admitted it wasn't. "I just thought it odd, you know, because I've met nearly everyone else that you've worked with . . ."

"And now you've met Dennis," he said, summing up. Clasping his hands behind his back, he moved on to the next display.

For all the morbid fascination of the reliquary, I was ready to get clear of all the vials and the caskets with their gruesome little contents. The main room of the treasury seemed larger, less oppressive, and I spent a long time looking at the rare and lovely items the Crusaders had carried out of Constantinople—ancient glass goblets with dainty gold rims; bowls and vases and chalices; censers and swords—all gleaming in the strong lights in their floor-to-ceiling glass displays.

"Of course the great tragedy," Rupert said, "is what they destroyed in the process of getting all this. So much went in the fires. The museums, the libraries—think of the manuscripts that must have been lost. Medical teachings and histories; plays . . . did you know," he asked me, "that Constantinople till then had a copy of every play by Euripides, Sophocles . . . just think of it. Over a hundred plays by Sophocles alone. For fourteen centuries they'd managed to survive, and then—" His hands swept up and out to imitate a massive conflagration. "What do we have left, now? Seven of them? Eight? It's a crime."

Den, who'd rejoined us, pondered this a moment, then said, "Though you can't really blame the Venetians for stealing the horses. I might have been tempted to take those myself."

He meant, I knew, the four sculpted horses that I'd seen featured so often in the Venice travel brochures. Rupert had already pointed them out to me from the piazza, in their place of prominence high up along the gallery of the basilica, from where they could look down and over the square.

But when I mentioned to Den that I'd seen them, he shook his head. "No, those are replicas up there. The real ones are kept indoors now, in a special room—the weather was doing a number on them." As we came out of the treasury into the cavernous dimness of the basilica, with the golden mosaic domes glittering high overhead, he went on, "They've been around the block, those horses. They originally came from a place in Greece—Chios—but one of the Byzantine emperors stole them and took them to Constantinople to put them on top of his box at the Hippodrome, to look down on the chariot-races. Then the Crusaders in 1204 stole them again, brought them here."

Rupert wasn't sure he'd call it stealing. "They were stolen to begin with, don't forget. The emperor had no legitimate claim to them, no more than Venice does now. They merely got passed from one thief to another." And then, as we started up a well-travelled stairway to the level above, he trumped Den by pointing out that the horses had taken a few side trips as well, through the years. "Napoleon took them to Paris, part of his plunder after he'd forced the last of the doges to submit to him. They weren't returned till after Waterloo. And during the First World War they spent some time in Rome, for safety."

"Like I said," said Den, "they've been around. Typical horses; they like to be moving."

I couldn't get over the size of the beasts, when I saw them. Cast in some sort of metal that might have been bronze, they were set in a row, as if recently freed from their chariot's harness, one forefoot raised, prancing, necks arched, heads held proudly. A rubbing of verdigris green added depth to their gleaming gold coats and traced lines where their bridles had been, and their hooves, set on stone plinths, were nearly as large as my head. I tipped my head back, studying their faces and marvelling at the ancient sculptor's skill in giving each horse an expression all its own. The first one, farthest to my left, looked vaguely worried; the second looked kind; the third looked perplexed; but the fourth—and my favourite—was laughing.

"What do you think?" Rupert asked me.

"They're gorgeous."

Den remarked that they didn't look bad for their age. "Considering they've been kicking around since the time of Alexander the Great. Want to see the imposters?"

To get to the gallery outside we had to double back along a catwalk and a balcony set high above the shadowed aisle, high up amid the bright mosaics, close enough now to see and appreciate much of the detail. The walls curved over and around me, rich as an illuminated manuscript, with biblical figures and scenes large as life.

But my eyes, in the midst of this splendid confusion, came to rest instead on human figures, standing by the doorway to the treasury, below me. I noticed the woman, I think, because she wore yellow—a bright golden yellow designed to draw the eye, to make an artful contrast with her long dark hair. I couldn't see her features clearly from this height and angle, but I guessed that she'd be beautiful, a woman who wanted to be noticed. She had that look about her, indefinable. The man with her looked much more ordinary. They were arguing, which struck me, in these surroundings, as being almost a sacrilege.

"Come on." Den, reaching back, took my hand in a friendly grasp. "Come see the best view in Venice."

Rupert kept close; he always kept close when he thought that I needed protecting, and this long crowded open-air gallery so high above the piazza, with nothing but a chest-high open railing between me and a dangerous drop to the pavement beneath, would be in Rupert's eyes an accident waiting to happen.

As Den tugged me over to look at the replica horses, Rupert touched my sleeve and told me, "Do be careful."

And I had the odd impression that he wasn't speaking only of the height.

She came, as he had known she would. She came at the appointed hour that night; she came alone. It took all of his will not to leap from his chair when he heard the first knock at the door, not to bolt across the marble hall and wrest the great doors open himself, so urgent was his own desire to see her. But he clenched his hands and kept his place, determined that the scene should be played in the way he had staged it . . . she must find him here, sitting so, where the light from the candles fell just the right way to steal years from his face, and the tapestried wall at his back gave the proper effect.

She knocked a second time; he heard the measured tread of Thompson answering the summons; heard the scrape and creak of key and bolt and hinges; heard her voice within his hall.

With beating heart he listened to the footsteps coming nearer, arranging himself with great care in the armchair in the instant before Thompson opened the door to the study and announced, expressionless: "Signorina Celia Sands, signore."

"Thank you, Thompson."

And then the door swung closed again and there was only her.

ix

VENICE grew more beautiful at night.

Freed for a few stolen hours from the sunlight that showed every flaw in her fading complexion, she emerged in all her finery, transformed by the darkness that gave back her youth and her mystery. The brilliant stars above became her personal adornments, as did the moon, almost full, that threw its bright reflection into the thousand murmuring ripples of the canals.

Gone was the city of commerce and trade; in its place was a city of lights, of strolling couples and soft conversations half-caught in the shadows; the paddle and splash of a gondola's oar and the sound of a footfall in darkness, retreating.

I sighed, a small unconscious sigh, and scooted back my chair across the paving stones beneath the wide green awning of the family-run trattoria where we were eating dinner.

I'd chosen the place myself, more of necessity than anything else—Rupert and Den had been so locked into their rivalry, searching for the perfect restaurant, that we might never have eaten at all if I hadn't stepped in. Not that it was really a rivalry, in the proper sense of the word. After watching them all afternoon I'd come to the conclusion that Den was only being Den, he wasn't doing anything on purpose. He was simply one of those people who knew everything and had tried everything and no matter what story you told they could do you one better, though he did it in a non-annoying way. It was Rupert, I'd decided, who kept trying to compete.

At any rate, they'd paraded me for miles, it had seemed, through tight twisting streets and close alleys, along back canals and over bridges. I'd finally had enough. When we'd passed the trattoria, set along one of the smaller canals, I had dug in my heels and pointed. "There," I'd said. "That's where I want to eat."

I'd taken them both by surprise, I think, but they'd stopped, and now, my menu spread in front of me, I was finally enjoying a bit of peace. The night air felt soft and cool and relaxing, faintly scented by the sea but only now and then, when the breeze blew the right way along the canals. I lifted my face to it, looking across to where the high water with dapples of light lapped the mossy green steps of a derelict building. It made a nice picture, quite soothing.

To make sure that Rupert and Den didn't get going again and spoil it, I steered the conversation clear of anything to do with history or sightseeing, opting instead for the more neutral topic of food. "I wonder if they'd let me get away with just having one course, instead of all three. Any one of these pasta dishes would do me for a meal." I didn't think I'd be able to keep with Italian tradition and follow my pasta with a plate of meat and vegetables.

Rupert assured me he'd eat what I didn't. "Anyway, you could do with a good solid meal for once."

Den glanced up. "Don't you eat well at home?"

"She does not," Rupert said. "She eats things out of tins, with a spoon."

"Not always, I don't. I take some of my meals at the restaurant, when I'm working. I waitress part-time," I explained, for Den's benefit.

"So this must be kind of a treat, having someone serve *you* for a change."

He was very perceptive. I smiled. "Yes, it is. I've decided if I ever win the lottery I'm going to hire somebody to serve all my meals, and bring me breakfast in bed."

"Perhaps I'll apply for the job," Den said, with a wink and a smile. He was, I thought, an irrepressible flirt. It seemed as much a part of his nature as his fidgeting—even sitting here it seemed some part of him was always moving, poised for action. His restless hands twisted the thin paper wrapper from a breadstick into a little baton that he tapped on the table.

"So, Dennis," said Rupert, "I expect you've got the whole play memorized by now, have you?"

Den grinned. "Almost. I've been over it backwards and forwards and broken it down into sections of scenes that might do for rehearsals—you'll have to look those over later, tell me what you think. It wasn't easy, I can tell you. Three acts to the play, and every act essentially one scene . . . except for the first act, I guess you could see that as two separate scenes, couldn't you? Still," he said, shaking his head, "it's a bastard to break down."

I'd assumed that the play, having only three actors, a handful of props, and one standing set, would be something of a stage manager's dream, but recalling it now I could understand why it might pose a bit of a problem for Den. The SM eventually had to run all the play's performances from his prompt book—a ring binder holding the master copy of the script, on which he'd written all the technical cues and directions that came out of rehearsal—and to make up his prompt book he needed to break the play down into scenes.

The problem was that, except for the intervals between acts, D'Ascanio's *Il Prezzo* didn't really break anywhere, it simply went on in continuous motion.

So would I, come to that—my character appeared on the stage before anyone else and remained there until final curtain. The first and last speeches were mine.

I'd been trying not to think about that, trying not to dwell on the responsibility, but Den, as though reading my mind, asked me now, "Are you nervous at all, taking on the lead role?"

"I'll have Rupert to direct me." Not that that answered his question, but it certainly pleased Rupert, who smiled the first real smile I'd seen all afternoon, and said to Den, "She'll do just fine. She's very talented, you know."

"I'm sure." Den's voice was a little too carefully pitched to be convincing.

Determined not to let that shake my already wobbly confidence, I managed a fair imitation of my mother's casual sophistication. "And it really is such a wonderful part. The whole play is so beautifully written."

He agreed. "A little *too* beautifully written, for some people."

Leaning back so the waiter could set down my starter, I asked, "What do you mean?"

"Well, there's some question as to whether Galeazzo D'Ascanio actually wrote it, it's so unlike his other work."

I considered the plot of *Il Prezzo*: A World War I soldier purposely sacrifices himself going over the top in the trenches because he's been told by a spiritual medium that the first side to lose a man will win the battle, and his young widow then persuades the same medium to hold a séance and reunite her with her husband for one final evening, after which, unable to bear a second parting from the man she loves, the widow kills herself so she can follow him back to the spirit world. It was, I thought, high melodrama, just like all of Galeazzo's plays. But when I said as much aloud I found even Rupert was willing to argue the point.

"It's not the subject matter, darling, so much as the execution. There's more finesse in the plotting, the dialogue, of *Il Prezzo* than in his earlier plays."

"Well, that's because it's a more mature work," I defended the playwright. "He was only in his twenties or thirties when he wrote the other plays, wasn't he? And then there was that long period where he didn't write anything, really, so it would make sense that by the time he got round to *Il Prezzo* his style would have changed."

Den started in on his own antipasto. "Yeah, well, it's that 'long period where he didn't write anything' that makes me suspicious. Kind of convenient for the old guy to come out of his slump with a play like *Il Prezzo*—a bit *too* convenient."

"The question is," said Rupert, and I realized with a sinking heart that they were back at it again, the two of them, showing off their knowledge like a couple of kids playing Trivial Pursuit—"the question is, whose work did he plagiarize? I mean, the story itself is a straightforward knockoff of the Protesilaus myth, but I doubt that he took it directly from that. There was probably a work in between—someone else's adaptation of the myth."

I knew I'd be sorry for asking, but, "Who was Protesilaus?"

"Greek mythology," said Rupert, with a smile that gently chastised me for not remembering my classics. "The Trojan War. Protesilaus was a soldier, a Greek warrior, who let himself be killed on the landing at Troy in order to fulfill the prophecy of an oracle who'd told the Greeks that victory would belong to the army that lost the first man."

"Oh," I said, with a dawning understanding.

Den nodded. "And his wife was Laodamia. She loved the guy so much that when she heard what had happened she begged the gods to let her see him one more time."

Exactly like our play, I thought. "And did they?"

"Oh, yeah. Hermes brought him up from the land of the dead for a visit—three hours, I think they had. And when that was up, Laodamia committed suicide, so she could go to the underworld, too. Sound familiar?"

"But that's not evidence of plagiarism, surely lots of people have stolen their plots from mythology, from Shakespeare on."

"Before that, even," Rupert said. "The ancient Greeks did it all the time."

"Well, then." It must have shown in my face that I wouldn't be easily convinced, because Rupert gave in with a smile of indulgence.

"All right," he said, "but consider this: He wrote his Celia poems, the ones in *The Season of Storms,* at around the same time. You read those, and then tell me the same person authored *Il Prezzo.*"

He had me there. I'd read half the poems since he'd given me the book, and I had found them very wordy, overwrought. I might have blamed it on the translation if he hadn't written both the poems and the play in English. Still, on behalf of Celia the First, who had loved the man, I felt I owed him loyalty. "I just don't think he would have risked his reputation, stealing someone else's work. What would have been his motive?"

Den raised an eyebrow. "Vanity."

I shrugged and let it go; let the lapping of the calm canal against its quiet buildings soothe me as I detached myself from the continuing conversation and freed my gaze to wander round the other tables, other patrons, interested as always in the niceties of other people's lives. The family to my left, I guessed, were also on holiday—two teenaged children on the brink of boredom and a fed-up-looking father and a mother on the brink of a nervous collapse, from the look of it. Even so, I envied them. Although I'd travelled a good deal with Rupert when I was a child, and enjoyed it, I'd never had the luxury of a real family holiday, with a mother and a father. Whatever the aggravation, I would have given anything to try it.

A few tables away from the family, an elderly man with a rumpled, academic look that made me think he might have been a teacher or a lecturer, was dining on his own. And next to him, a loving couple . . . here my gaze stopped wandering, with interest.

That had to be the same woman I'd seen in the basilica, I thought. There couldn't be two dresses in Venice that same colour, that same brilliant sunrise yellow—nor two women who could wear it quite that way. Her long dark hair was fastened back now with a clip, but it was definitely her. I had been right in my assumption she'd be beautiful, although it was the sort of hard-edged, self-aware beauty that tended to put me off a person, rather than draw me to them. Personal experience had taught me that a woman who looked like that wouldn't be someone I'd like.

And the way she was smiling now, all perfect teeth and dark eyes, at the man she was with only reinforced that opinion. It wasn't a genuine smile—it was cat-like, designed to manipulate.

I couldn't see the man's reaction. His back was to me, and to be honest all I really noticed was the bald spot that had begun to take hold on the back of his head, a perfect heart-shaped bald spot. I wondered how much larger it would need to grow before the woman seated opposite him ditched him for a more attractive model.

Mother, I thought, would have dropped him at the first sign of a fallen hair. She liked her young men flawless.

Once again Den seemed to read my mind. He asked, "So Celia, how's your mother?"

Jolted from my people-watching, I looked round. It would have been too much to hope, I supposed, that he wouldn't have made the connection between me and my mother. But then, I *was* using my real name, and he was in the business, and had known Rupert for years, so presumably he would have known about me. "She's fine, I guess. I really don't see much of her these days."

"I worked with her once, did you know? A long time ago. I was only a lowly assistant back then—ASM in charge of props. Never met your dad, though."

He could join the club, I thought. Across the table Rupert raised his head and looked from Den to me, his eyes vaguely worried, as though he were wondering whether he ought to divert the discussion to something that wouldn't upset me, but I smiled at him to show it was all right. Reaching for my wineglass, I asked Den, "And so what did you think of my mother?"

"Oh, I was dazzled," he admitted, with a reminiscent smile. "But then, I was meant to be, wasn't I?"

I was frankly surprised that it hadn't gone further than that, and told him so. "You're very much her type."

"Am I, now?" His smile became a grin. "And what's your type?"

Aware of Rupert's watching eyes I answered, "Dark and brooding. Like our waiter."

Den pretended to be crushed. "You know that men with light brown hair are lots more fun."

A man with light brown hair . . . The words repeated through my mind, but not in Den's voice—in my former flatmate Sally's. For a moment I was back again and sitting in the flat while Sally turned her tarot cards . . . *This is beneath you. The King of Cups . . . a man with light brown hair.* Only she'd also, as I recalled, described him as a businessman, responsible, and calm on the exterior, and Den was none of those.

And anyway, the tarot cards were just a game, they couldn't

tell the future. Which was just as well, I told myself, and smiled. Because if half of what the cards had said awaited me at Il Piacere were true, I'd have been heading for very big trouble.

And now, he thought, now he could die in contentment, for he had ascended the heavens and seen what must surely be God. Perhaps he had already died; his body had a weightlessness it had not known before. But no, he felt the blood returning to his veins now with the force of youth, and smiling turned his head upon the pillow.

She was sleeping. Like an angel, he decided, with her lovely golden head against his shoulder, hair spread fragrant on the linen, breathing sweetly, soft and deep. "Celia." The name flowed like springwater over his tongue. She stirred but did not wake.

He looked away again and sighed in satisfaction, his eyes moving over the tapestried walls of the room, taking in every detail: the shadows that clung to the corners, the dark textured hangings embroidered with faces and vines and a glitter of golden threads catching the light of the low-burning candles.

He would take this room, too, when he left—take the tapestries, the candles, and the sofa they were lying on. And from the old house on Lake Garda he would build for her a palace, and this room would be the centre of it.

Yes, he thought, this was but the beginning . . .

X

THE morning was clear and my view from the train stretched for miles. After we passed through Vicenza, some thirty minutes inland from Venice, the hills to either side grew more pronounced, ridged with dark green points of cypress trees above flat farmland rich with red-brown soil. In the distance now and then a turret or a steeple would appear against the cypresses—medieval-looking structures, tile roofs and ochre walls, and if I squinted as I looked at them the modern buildings in between us vanished and I saw the landscape as it might have looked to those who travelled in the time before the Renaissance, the days of holy pilgrims, roving merchants and Crusaders.

I'd been a little sorry to leave Venice, in the end, and my arms were still aching from hauling my suitcases from the hotel to the station, but it did feel exciting to be on the move again, following the route that Celia the First would have taken when she had left the stage to go with Galeazzo to his villa on Lake Garda.

I had to admit that geography wasn't my strong point, and I hadn't known exactly where Lake Garda was, in Italy. Before leaving London I'd made a point of consulting the antiquated atlas that held up one leg of a table in Roo and Bryan's front room. Bryan had long threatened to bin both atlas and table—the latter because it was falling apart and the former because it was so out of date half the names of the countries no longer applied—whereupon Rupert had flipped to a page that showed all of the 'new' Balkan states set out in more or less the proper places: Croatia, Bosnia and Herzegovina . . .

"A few more wars and revolutions," he'd predicted, "and this whole book will be right again."

I wasn't so sure. According to the atlas, half the world was still stained British red, and the Austrian Empire straddled the Alps with one foot firmly planted in Italy. Along this northern border, nestled snugly in the foothills of the Alps, lay the Italian lakes, a series of brilliant blue squiggles and dots on the map. Lake Garda, the largest of all and the one farthest east, had a shape like a pipe—long and narrow in the neck and bulbous at the bottom—and a marvellous location just below the snow-capped Dolomites, halfway along the rail line between Venice and Milan.

The rail line we were travelling this morning.

I'd intended to get lots of work done, of course, on the journey. I did have a heap of lines to learn. My copy of the script, in fact, lay open on my lap now, to the séance scene in which the medium summons the dead soldier's ghost to appear to his widow.

That the medium would be able to do this at all—let alone bring the soldier back intact in body and smoking a cigarette—ought to have strained one's credulity, but it didn't, a credit to the playwright's skill in crafting his characters.

I, of course, was the widow. And my husband, the unfortunate soldier, was to be played by Nicholas Rutherford, who'd made a big splash in the West End last summer by taking the lead in a daring new play that had revisited the legend of Masada. The critics had given mixed reviews of his performance, but the general consensus among my acting friends had been that, with a face like his, performance hardly mattered. "Besides," one of them had said, "he's not stupid. He's latched on to Madeleine Hedrick, you know. He'll be huge."

I'd agreed. Since divorcing her unfaithful husband, Madeleine Hedrick had taken a series of young handsome actors in tow, and every one of them it seemed had gone on to success on stage or screen. Not that she approached my mother's head count when it came to lovers, and Madeleine Hedrick's relationships lasted a little bit longer—for years, in some cases. Certainly Nicholas Rutherford must have been with her for over a year, now.

Which left me as the odd one out, the one who had to prove herself. With renewed purpose I bent once again to my script, but the passing landscape proved too distracting. We flashed by a marbleyard, hard blocks of unpolished stone, stacked three deep, that gave way to a small grove of silver-tipped blossoming fruit trees, and vineyards carpeted with tiny yellow wildflowers. At Verona I pressed my face close to the window, hoping for a glimpse of the ancient, gracious city that had inspired Shakespeare to write the tales of his two gentlemen and Romeo and Juliet. I saw a lovely river and a bridge and rooftops peeking through the trees, but no sign of the Capulets' balcony.

"Anyway," Rupert was saying, beside me, "if everyone agrees I think we'll start right in on Monday with the read-through. That is, if Nicholas and Madeleine arrive today as planned."

Den checked his watch. "They should be there before us. D'Ascanio said they were flying to Milan and then renting a car. I gathered Nick was keen to take a crack at mountain driving."

"He's a better man than I am." Rupert gave a feeling shudder with a look towards the jagged hills that smudged the long horizon to the north.

"And me," said Den. "I'd rather drive blind on one of your English hedged lanes. But Nick likes to take risks."

"Does he?" Rupert turned from the window. "I wouldn't know, I've only met him once, and he was on his best behaviour."

"Oh, well, brace yourself then," Den advised him, grinning. "He's wild."

I'd heard rumours, myself, but I hadn't paid too much attention. At the time, I'd thought the chances of my ever working with someone like Nicholas Rutherford were practically nil, so it hardly mattered what he got up to backstage. Now, though, I hoped that he wouldn't be too hard to work with . . . it helped to have *some* sort of chemistry when you were playing a husband and wife.

Rupert said, "Not to worry. I've no doubt that Madeleine

keeps him in line," and directed my attention out the window. "There's the lake."

I didn't look quickly enough. All I caught was the end of a long streak of blue like the mouth of a river before the land rose up again to hide it as the train tracks angled inland. Still, just to know we were running along the south shore of Lake Garda was excitement enough.

"Nearly there," Den said. "Two more stops."

My excitement held and grew when we stepped off the train at Desenzano Station, bumping our luggage down the steps from the platform and into the tight, narrow, glass-fronted space overlooking the circular drive and the bus shelters.

"Who's meeting us?" I asked, peering eagerly out through the window.

Neither Rupert nor Den knew the answer to that. And as the minutes ticked on, it began to appear as though no one was meeting us.

I looked round, but apart from the ticket window and a tiny shop behind us there was nowhere anyone could have been standing where we might have missed them. "He did know which train we'd be on?" I asked Rupert.

"I should think so. He paid for the tickets." But just to be sure he found a telephone and rang Il Piacere. "Couldn't get through," he told us, on returning. "The operator said the lines were down, or something. Still, whoever D'Ascanio sent to collect us is probably on his way here, not to worry."

We had lunch, or at least as much of a lunch as one could assemble from what could be bought in the shop at the station—a sandwich and crisps and a bottle of juice. Then we waited what seemed like another full hour before I finally said, "I think we've been forgotten." Through the window I could see a large bus pulling into the shelter out front, and I pointed to the sign on its front. "Look, it's going to Mira del Garda. That's where we're headed, isn't it?"

Rupert and Den seemed reluctant to just up and leave the station, but I managed to persuade them we wouldn't be doing anything out of line, that no one could reasonably expect us to still be waiting here two hours after we'd arrived. And I, for one, was tired of waiting, eager to get on with it, to finally see the house that I had read about for all these years.

The bus was, I decided, every bit as comfortable as a car would have been—a modern, spacious vehicle with clean-smelling seats and a freshly cleaned windscreen that gave me a glass-bubble view from my seat in the front. And at long last, as we headed out of Desenzano, I got my first look at the lake.

It looked like a scene on a postcard from Switzerland—blue water held captive by mountains that rose to the north. Here at the bottom, where it was widest, the lake rippled out and across to a darker green shore flecked with pale specks of buildings that clustered in towns at the water's edge, some of them rising behind in a scatter of rooftops to terrace the forested hills. Farther north, where the lake narrowed and the mountains began, the hills purpled and rose steeper still, wreathed in cloud. And far up on the opposite shore I could see one peak higher than all of them, capped with pure snow.

"Monte Baldo," the bus driver gestured towards it with obvious pride. "It is in the winter a very good place to go skiing." He spoke English well, and thanked me when I told him so. "I work many years in America," he said. "New York."

Which of course started Den off. He might have gone on talking forever, I thought, if Rupert hadn't eventually leaned forward. "Our stop is the next one, I think."

Den looked round. "We're in Mira already? That was a quick trip."

It had actually taken an hour, a fact confirmed by the stiffness of my legs as I scrambled down the steps onto the pavement, filled with anticipation.

The bus stop at Mira del Garda was a rather unassuming little lay-by at the side of a narrow hill road. Presumably we were still on the fringes of the town itself. Across from us a steep grassy bank angled up to support a three-storey block of modern flats, while to our backs a flight of steps led down another level to a strip of pavement lined by older buildings, closely shuttered and unwelcoming, their rooftops rising high enough to block my view beyond them to the lake. But the sky was blue, the sun was shining, and at the edge of the bus stop a rectangle marked out in yellow paint enclosed a familiar word: TAXI. We shunted our luggage towards it . . . and waited.

At length, after a few cars had whizzed past us, Rupert shaded his eyes from the sun with one hand and remarked, "I would have thought there'd be a taxi to meet every bus, just in case."

Den suggested we might call for one.

"With what?" Rupert wanted to know. "There's no telephone here." Still shading his eyes, he tilted his head up to scan the balconies of the block of flats opposite. Spotting a middle-aged woman hanging her towels out over one rail, he waved an arm to attract her attention and shouted a question across in Italian.

"Ah," he said, when she'd called back her answer.

"Hell," said Den.

I frowned. "What is it?"

"Well," said Rupert, "it appears there are no taxis."

"None at all?"

"Not anymore, no. We'll have to walk."

I looked at my luggage and sagged. "Walk?"

Den, taking pity on me, slung the long strap of one of his own bags over his shoulder, freeing a hand so he could carry one of my suitcases. "Did I say D'Ascanio had things well-arranged?" he asked. "I take it back."

I frowned. "And you're positive, are you, that we were expected today?"

"Darling, of course we're expected," said Rupert. "Don't worry. I'm sure when we get there we'll find there's a good explanation for why we weren't met."

Den said drily, "I can't wait to hear it." And then, as a bright yellow sports car came rocketing past, he leaped back. "Let's cross over—it's too dangerous here."

On the other side of the road, a narrow pavement angled up the terraced hill, then flattened out six feet or so above street level, running along on the top of a pretty stone wall draped with vines that would soon be in flower. Walking here felt definitely safer.

If only, I thought as I struggled to manage the uneven stones, if only I'd had enough sense not to bring so much luggage. The single case I was carrying felt even heavier now than it had when we'd left our hotel that morning, and with every step the strap seemed to cut deeper into my shoulder and raise new raw welts in the palm of my hand. Rupert was similarly burdened, and Den, who appeared to have packed more economically than either of us, had my other suitcase now weighing him down.

He'd been gallant enough to take my larger case, the one with wheels, only it was so overstuffed and ungainly that it kept tipping over whenever the wheels caught the edge of a paving stone. It became a sort of pattern as we made our way along, the suitcase tipping and Den swearing while he righted it again with a decided thump, and then the rolling rumble of the wheels until he reached the next uneven spot. We must have made an entertaining sight to passing motorists.

There were surprisingly few cars that passed, but then I supposed it was still quite early in the season. This part of Lake Garda, south of the snow-covered mountains, probably wasn't suitable for skiers—the weather was too mild—so the tourists likely wouldn't start arriving here until late spring or summer, when they could enjoy the lake itself, the bathing beaches and the boats.

My own view of the water was still blocked by buildings and the pointed stands of cypress trees that rose between them, regally, like soldiers on parade. Now and then I caught a tantalizing flash of blue behind the darkness of the cypresses and the smooth plastered walls of the houses whose rich painted colours were lovely as flowers, in shades of deep gardenia pink and primrose yellow, marigold and soft leaf green.

I would have appreciated the beauty of my surroundings more if I hadn't had to concentrate on where I put my feet, and if my muscles weren't so trembly from the weight of what I carried, and if my shirt wasn't sticking wetly to my back between my shoulderblades—if, in short, I hadn't felt so beastly warm and sore and out of sorts.

I couldn't help but have the sinking feeling that Sally's tarot cards had been right—that I should have stayed at home.

"I need to rest a minute," I announced. When I stopped walking Den and Rupert stopped too, without argument, dropping their suitcases.

Den, leaning against a metal signpost marking where a smaller road had tumbled down the hill to meet our own, massaged his shoulder. "I'd suggest we hijack a car, but I don't have the energy."

I sat on my own case, disturbing a tiny brown lizard that shot from the ledge in the stone wall where it had been soaking up sun and vanished with a rustle in the vines. Rupert, right beside it, didn't notice. He was looking up.

"We're almost there," he said.

Den arched an eyebrow. "Yeah? And how do you know that?"

In answer Rupert nodded at the signpost and the sign above Den's head, a stylized arrow pointing up the hill with IL PIACERE spelled out in neat black letters, very plainly.

The sight of a hill didn't thrill me, but the name on the sign did—the knowledge that we were so close to our goal. Hefting my suitcase again, I took over the lead as we made the turn and started up. There was no pavement here, and we had to walk Indian file on the road itself, close to the verge and the hedge that enclosed it. My back was to the lake now and if I'd had the presence of mind to turn round and look I would probably have had a smashing view of it, with the mountains behind, but the mountain I was climbing now took all my concentration.

It was all I could do to stay upright, and keep placing one foot in front of the other, especially when each shuffling step raised a small cloud of dust from the road, to swirl and settle grittily into my eyes, my nose, my thirsty mouth.

More tiny lizards scattered every which way out of my path, seeking shelter in the tangle of wildflowers bordering the hedge. And then the hedge became a high stone wall, and in the wall I saw an iron gate.

"Thank God." Den's words were heartfelt.

Rupert reached around me; rang the bell. The intercom crackled. A woman's voice asked something brief, in Italian, and Rupert replied with our names.

For a minute we waited. And then something clicked and the tall iron gate started opening inwards.

And, like Celia the First, I passed through.

ACT II

The Palace.

The actors are come hither, my lord.

Shakespeare: *Hamlet,* Act II, Scene II

She moved through the gate like a child discovering paradise, hesitant, eyes wide with wonder, her hands half-raised and reaching out before her as though she wanted to touch everything.

With one great sweeping gesture she embraced the gardens and the cypress grove, the rows of white stone columns lining both sides of the long and graceful rose-red gravel drive on which they stood, the proud triumphal arches curving overhead, the little statues of Apollo, Venus and Diana posing silent in their niches. From somewhere close by came the sound of a fountain, the sound of water running, spilling laughingly from overflowing pools, and in the branches of the copper beech above them now a tiny sparrow trilled its joyful song, as though its breast could not contain its happiness.

He took her hand. "You have not seen the house, yet." With her fingers curled in his he led her up the shaded lane of arches, round the gentle bend that brought them face to face with a fierce-looking pair of gilded lions, guarding what he thought was the most properly imposing approach to a villa that he'd ever seen—a wide palatial staircase built of whitest stone and edged with roses, climbing to the terrace up the curving lawn.

She stopped to marvel at the sight.

He swelled with satisfaction. And when they'd reached the top and stood within the sheltered courtyard set before the house, with a second fountain scattering bright beads of water to the morning air and below them the tumble of gardens and trees spilling down to the placid blue

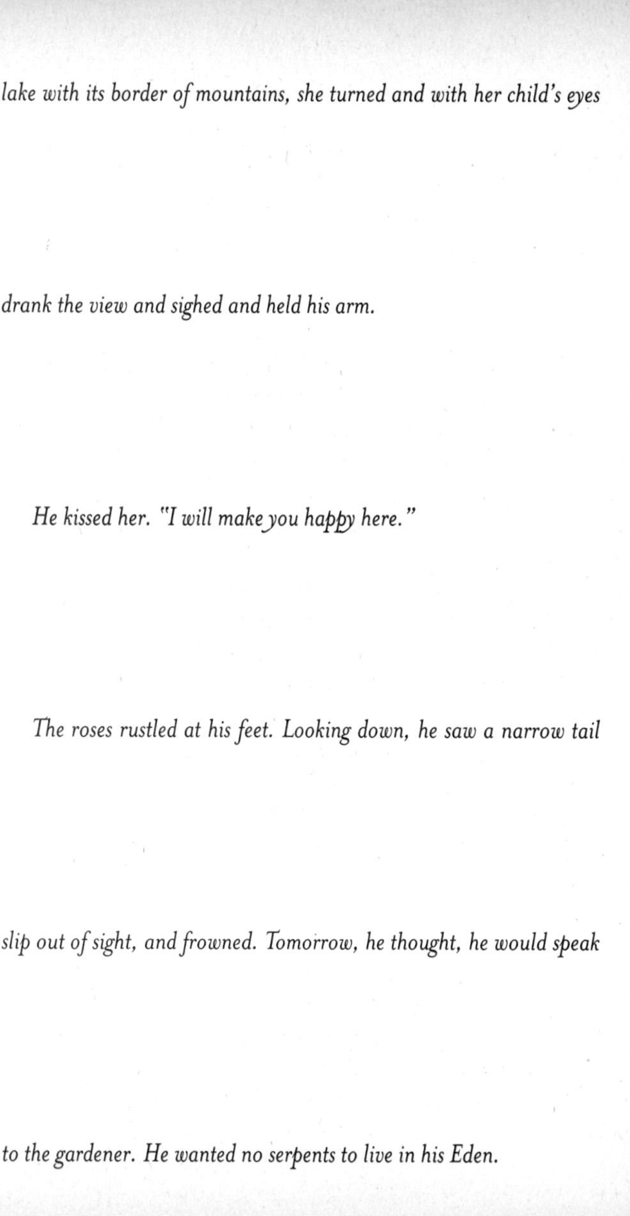

lake with its border of mountains, she turned and with her child's eyes drank the view and sighed and held his arm.

He kissed her. "I will make you happy here."

The roses rustled at his feet. Looking down, he saw a narrow tail slip out of sight, and frowned. Tomorrow, he thought, he would speak to the gardener. He wanted no serpents to live in his Eden.

i

"WHY do the rich always build their houses miles from the road?" Den wanted to know. "All they need is a little front yard and a driveway, but no . . . they have to put in all these columns and fountains and—"

"Dennis," Rupert cut in, puffing nearly as much as I was, "if you didn't waste all your breath complaining, you'd find it easier to walk."

"Oh, I've got plenty of breath," Den assured him. "That isn't a problem."

I couldn't help smiling, even in the midst of my exertions. I couldn't think of any situation in which Den would cease to talk. Perhaps in sleep, but even then he most likely muttered and tossed in his bed, restless. He was not a quiet man.

I, on the other hand, couldn't have spoken a word if I'd wanted to. My body needed every bit of oxygen to keep my muscles moving, propelling me up the long drive like an automaton . . . left foot, right foot, left foot, right foot, each step crunching on the gravel. I kept my head purposely down, focussing not on the way ahead but on the patch of gravel just in front of my feet—a much more attainable goal.

Even with the shoulder strap taking the brunt of the weight, my suitcase handle had raised blisters on my palms that stung whenever I shifted my grip, which I had to do rather often because my hands perspired and slipped. And my eyes stung as well from the sweat that had plastered my hair to my temples and neck.

I knew, from my limited, low-angled view of the flowering shrubs and ornate column bases I was passing, that we were walking through a place of beauty. Now and then I saw the feet of a statue resting in the trailing greenery and was tempted to look higher, but I didn't dare for fear I'd lose my footing. I'd be living here for several months, I told myself. Plenty of time to admire the scenery later. For now, all I wanted was to get up to the house and climb into a bath.

Behind me, Den stopped walking. "Jesus Christ!"

I lifted my head then to look, and wished that I hadn't. I sagged at the sight of the steps—a seemingly endless flight of them, ten feet wide and gleaming white, that angled steeply upwards, barring our way to the house like some cruel architectural joke. Even the lions that stood at its entrance appeared to be laughing.

It might have been the heat, or simple tiredness, but I nearly broke down at that point. And I might have disgraced myself entirely by dissolving in tears at the foot of the steps if I hadn't just then heard the sure, certain sound of someone coming down to meet us. Looking up through blurring eyes I saw the outline of a man, a young man, lean and dark and moving swiftly, with an athlete's grace. Halfway down he waved and called out, "Thought you might need help with those. It's a bloody long way up." An English voice, precise and very RADA.

I blinked away my unshed tears and watched with curiosity as Nicholas Rutherford came closer. I'd seen photographs, of course, but never the man in person. He was not as tall as I'd expected, but I didn't imagine most women would notice his height—it was his face that so entranced them, with its cleanly cut features and laugh lines and soul-searching eyes. And whereas we looked hot and straggly and were on the point of collapse, he looked cool and crisply pressed and managed the final few steps without apparent effort, smoking a cigarette.

"God, what happened to you lot?" He looked us up and down, amused. "Did Giancarlo make you get out and push, or something?"

"We walked," said Den.

"Walked? From where?"

"From town. Giancarlo, if that's who was supposed to

meet our train at Desenzano, never showed. We had to take a bus."

Rupert pointed out that we had rung the house. "But apparently your phones aren't working."

"It wouldn't surprise me," said Nicholas, smoothing his hair with one hand in what I would learn was an habitual gesture of his. "It's a bit of a madhouse around here today. One of the maids didn't turn up for work, and that seems to have thrown everything off. Maddy and I even had to go down into town for our lunch—we've only just got back, ourselves. Here, let me take that." He held out a hand for my suitcase.

It occurred to me, as I gladly passed the bag over, that no one had bothered to make any kind of introductions, though I supposed that in the circumstances introductions were superfluous. From the way Den had been talking last night I'd assumed he already knew Nicholas, and even though Rupert had only, to his recollection, met Nicholas once, it was a fair bet that Nicholas recognized Rupert—actors, especially young and ambitious ones, made a point of remembering people of influence. Which left only me, and since I was a woman my identity would have been relatively easy to deduce—there were only two women involved in the play after all, and Nicholas Rutherford was already intimately acquainted with one of them.

And if he didn't need to ask our names, he didn't think to offer his. Clearly he took it for granted we'd know him on sight. Putting the cigarette in his mouth he turned with my suitcase. "Come on, then, you've only a little bit farther to go and we'll get you set up with a drink. The boss is away, I'm afraid," he said, taunting us further by talking as he climbed, making me feel as inadequate and hopeless as I did when my aerobics instructor chatted on easily during a difficult class. "But Teresa is here"—in his educated voice the name came out in its proper Italian form, sounding like 'Ter-*ay*-za' with a skillfully rolled *r*—"and I'm sure she knows what rooms to put you in."

"Something on the main floor, I hope." Den thumped the cases he carried another step up, nearly hitting my ankles. "This climb must keep the visitors down."

Rupert said he expected that was the general idea. "Galeazzo D'Ascanio valued his privacy."

That much was evident from the landscaping. Everywhere I looked there were high walls and hedges to block prying eyes. Whoever had first built the house here, I thought, must have craved isolation.

I was high enough to see the huge expanse of tiled roof, now, and the dark foothills rising behind it, their peaks weighted down with a pale, smoke-like mist that was wrapped round the textured deep green of the trees. If Den hadn't been behind me on the steps I would have turned to look down at the lake, but from the closeness of his breathing behind me I knew that by stopping I would have risked being ploughed over.

"Privacy," he said, "is all well and good, but if this is the only way up to the house then our play's going to have a short run—half the audience will never make it."

Nicholas smiled. "Not to worry. From what I understand they're constructing a new car park for the coaches on the far side of the gardens, just above the theatre, so the tourists won't have far to walk."

It was a credit to the younger D'Ascanio's business acumen, I thought, that not only had he managed to interest the prestigious Forlani Trust in restoring the house and its grounds, but he'd also struck deals with a number of European tour operators, who had added our play, and the gardens of Il Piacere, to their itineraries. Starting six weeks from now there'd be people on escorted coach tours coming in to fill the theatre, four nights a week through the whole of the summer. Which explained how Galeazzo's grandson could afford to give the play so long a run.

Not that money would be a great worry for him, I decided, as we crested the top of the stairs and came into a broad cobbled courtyard, surrounded on three sides by the splendour that was Il Piacere.

The photographs I'd seen in books hadn't been able to capture it all, nor give a proper sense of scale. The house was huge. Presumably in its original form it had been a conventional villa, its back to the hillside, its front façade facing the lake, but Galeazzo D'Ascanio had changed all that, bringing in an architect who'd altered the house according to the poet's whims and fancies.

He had set a giant fountain at the centre of the courtyard, and surrounded it with flowers. To my left, a loggia with arches reminiscent of an aqueduct of ancient Rome enclosed a row of what I knew to be dog kennels—Galeazzo had been fond of his racing greyhounds. To the centre, directly in front of me, the oldest section of the house stood unrecognizable beneath the huge stone lintels and ornamental plaster plaques that Galeazzo's architect had added, brilliant white against the butter-yellow plaster of the walls. And to my right was Galeazzo's great addition, an enormous wing whose design had been added to and changed so often during its construction that it looked now like some crazy thing a child might build with blocks, its edges softened by the tumblings of wisteria that draped its upper storeys like long robes of royal purple, trailing down the nearest corner till the petals brushed the ground.

To be standing here, actually standing right here in the courtyard of Il Piacere, struck me speechless. I stood for a moment and tried to imagine how Celia the First must have felt when she'd seen it—she who, like me, had come from damp and dreary London at the end of a long winter. Of course, it wouldn't have looked *exactly* like this . . . most of it would still have been under construction, but the fountain would have been here, and the tree-green mountain rising up behind the pantiled roof, and everywhere the smell of the yet-unseen gardens—the thick ripe scents of mingled earth and plants that blended with a host of softer floral perfumes.

The sound of a door closing jolted me back to the present, and I looked around, curious. I couldn't tell which of the doors was intended to be the main entrance—there were several, all impressive with their steps and iron railings.

A woman was crossing the courtyard towards us. For an instant my heart did a coward's flip, stealing my breath, but I relaxed when I saw that it wasn't Madeleine Hedrick. This woman was younger, only in her midthirties or so, and rather more rounded, with black hair scraped back and a bustling walk.

"Oh, good, here's Teresa," said Nicholas. "She'll get things sorted."

She looked the kind of woman who could do that very capably. Dressed neatly in black skirt and blouse, her low-heeled shoes clicking on the cobblestones, she radiated competence. And though her face was plain and unremarkable, the sort of face one easily forgot, her eyes were busily aware.

They looked us up and down efficiently as she drew near, and I saw her expression crease into a frown as she noted our somewhat dishevelled appearance, our glistening faces, the way we were breathing. And then she looked at Nicholas, carrying my suitcase, and the frown for a moment showed worry.

"Giancarlo is not with you?" Her English was thick, but understandable; her voice low for a woman's but pleasantly pitched.

Nicholas shook his head. "No, your husband apparently never turned up at the station."

"We took the bus," said Den. But he had also seen the worry in the woman's eyes, and ever the charmer, he tried to reassure her with a smile. "We probably just missed him."

Teresa's dark gaze took Den's measure carefully, and seemed to find him worthy of approval. "Yes," she said, "Giancarlo is not always good with time." Turning to the rest of us, she said, "You will be tired. Please come, I will show you the rooms."

My thigh muscles burned a protest as I followed her back across the cobblestones and climbed the marble steps to a heavy dark wooden door framed with Corinthian columns and carvings of cherubs and gargoyles, weirdly combined.

Inside, for a second, I felt I'd gone blind. The sunlight couldn't penetrate more than a few feet into the entry hall, so intense was the darkness. I had to stop and wait until my eyes adjusted to the sudden change, before I finally saw the panelled walls that pressed in close on either side, years of varnish blackening the wood. The ceiling, too, was low and panelled, inset with what looked like squares of damask silk in some dark colour—green, perhaps, or brown. On the wooden floor a length of oriental carpet, black with a design of rose and gold, stretched away from us, travelling out of sight up a curved staircase that seemed to be the only way out of this windowless cell.

Den groaned at the sight of the stairs, but Teresa turned, her expression encouraging. "Is the best way to the bedrooms, very fast."

Nicholas nodded. "She's right, it's a much longer walk from the main entrance—too many corridors. The house," he complained, "is a damned rabbit warren. I'm still getting lost."

"Still?" Rupert raised an eyebrow. "I thought you'd only just arrived, yourselves."

"We came yesterday, actually. Maddy was keen to get settled. She doesn't like travel."

"Ah," said Rupert. "And where is she now?"

"She was resting. I'm sure she'll come down for a drink, though," he said, "now that you're here."

The idea seemed rather surreal to me still: 'drinks with Madeleine Hedrick.' As fanciful, almost, as 'tea with the Queen.' I'd been practising what I would say when I met her—a short speech, neither too formal nor too familiar, something that projected quiet confidence, maturity . . .

"Celia, dear, watch where you're going," said Rupert, reaching a parental hand to press my head down and safely under the low ceiling beam that spanned the top of the staircase.

"Sorry." I straightened, looking round me at the narrow corridors that ran in three directions, their walls, like the ones downstairs, panelled in dark varnished wood veneer. I wasn't good with wood—I couldn't tell what kind it was by looking, but when I trailed my hand along a wall it *felt* expensive.

"This way," said Teresa, leading us off to the left.

I could see why Nicholas got lost. I felt like a rat in a maze, turning this way and that, passing door after door, darkened alcoves, more corridors, lit by amber-tinged Art Deco wall sconces.

"This room is for Signor Neville," said Teresa, as she

stopped outside a door and waited. I didn't understand the pause at first, until I realized that of course she wouldn't know which man was which. "Is a small room," she hastened to add as Rupert sidled past her through the door, "but there are many books, and Signor D'Ascanio said you would like."

"I do." Rupert paused inside the doorway, looking round. I couldn't see much past him, only a section of yellow-striped wallpaper and half a shuttered window. "It's a lovely room, I like it very much," he said, smiling first at Teresa, then turning to share the smile with all of us. "I'll just clean up a little, then, and change before that drink. Where shall I meet you?"

"The terrace, probably." Nicholas gave directions. "If you lose your way just tap out an S.O.S. on the wall and we'll come find you."

"Jolly good."

Which left only Den and myself to be dealt with. Teresa stopped two doors down. "Signor O'Malley." This room I saw in more detail than Rupert's—a tall window draped in blue velvet, a long polished desk with a mirror above it, the post of a bed. Den seemed pleased. Dropping his cases, he passed the heavy one of mine that he'd been carrying to Nicholas. "Here you go, Nick, this goes with Celia. I think it's her rock collection." Turning to me, he asked, "And where will you be?"

"Signorina Sands," Teresa announced, with a hint of disapproval, "is in the ladies' wing."

"Oh right, the ladies' wing. I should have guessed." Den grinned. "That's where old Galeazzo kept his mistress, I believe."

"And other female guests," said Nicholas. He winked. "The lucky sod."

"Yes, well, we can't all have his stamina." Den shifted his suitcases further into the room with his foot, to let his door close. "See you shortly."

Teresa set off again down the dim corridor, but this time with a rather grim set to her face. I wondered if she didn't think me good enough to occupy the ladies' wing.

We had to hunch over to duck through the passage dividing the wing from the rest of the house, but on the other side the ceiling soared upwards, cathedral-like, over a broad, U-shaped landing surrounding a second small staircase that gracefully wound its way up from the lower floor, lit high above by a skylight of stained glass that dappled the dark Persian carpets with colour.

I counted four doors on the landing—one on its own to my right, and the other three set at angles in the far left-hand corner. It was to the last of these three that Teresa now led me, while Nicholas nodded across at the door on the right.

"That's Maddy's room," he told me. "There are only the two of you sharing this wing. And the stairs there go down to the dining-room passage. That's the best way to get to the terrace, for drinks—just go down and turn left, then turn right and go straight."

I only half-listened to what he was saying, because by that point Teresa had opened the door and I'd seen what lay inside.

ii

I was almost reluctant to step through the doorway, for fear I might spoil it.

"Is your sitting-room," Teresa said, moving ahead of me into the high-ceilinged gold-and-white space with its tall arching windows. She opened the shutters and expertly twitched back the filmy white curtains to let in the light.

Nicholas set down my cases on the kitten-soft carpet, looking round appreciatively. "God, and I thought Maddy's room was luxury. It must be nice to be producer's pet."

"I'm not," I said, and then because I didn't want to step on any toes I added, "Look, I'll gladly trade with Mrs. Hedrick, if she'd rather have this room. I really don't—"

"Relax," he calmed me. "Maddy doesn't have that kind of ego." Smoothing his hair back he glanced round again. "Lucky you."

And with that he made a practised exit, leaving me alone with Teresa. The look she sent after him seemed to imply that she didn't think much of the famous Nicholas Rutherford, but she kept her thoughts silent. "Here is your bathroom," she said, pointing out the door at the end of the room, "and also after that the bedroom."

"Thank you." I paused then and, wanting to get in her good books, I thanked her again in Italian, trying to remember Rupert's coaching on pronunciation, rolling my *r* and giving each vowel a separate sound: *"Grazie."*

Teresa nodded. *"Prego."* And then, with a final disapproving look around, she turned and left me.

As the door clicked shut behind her I fell into the embrace of the overstuffed sofa and revelled in the feel of it, the obvious expensiveness of everything around me. But I couldn't stay seated for long. There was too much to see, to explore. Rising, I crossed to the windows.

The view was more stunning than any I could have imagined. I hadn't realized quite how high we'd climbed until this moment, when I saw the pointed cypress tops beneath me falling sharply to the long blue lake below, a darkly fragrant forest into which the villa's gardens had intruded in an unexpected paradise of terraced lawns and shaded groves with flowers showing everywhere and footpaths winding through the mingled greens, beneath the clustered trees too numerous to count and much too varied to identify. I recognized the flaming glory of a copper beech directly underneath my window, and knew by sight the silvery leaves and gnarled trunks that marked the olive trees, but all the rest looked unfamiliar to me, wonderful and strange.

The air was scented, heavenly, and filled with warbling birdsong that went on and on incessantly, a sound so purely joyful that just hearing it restored my spirits, and suddenly it didn't seem to matter that we'd had to walk from town, or that Teresa didn't seem to think me worthy of occupying Celia the First's private suite, or that in half an hour's time I'd be sipping a drink beside Madeleine Hedrick, who'd most likely hate me because of what Mother had done. Nothing mattered. Only that I was here, in this beautiful room, with the lake shining blue in the sunlight below and the snow-covered mountain that rose from the further shore framed like a painting by neighbouring lavender peaks, and the hill rising high like a shield at my back.

Eager to unpack my things and make myself at home, I grabbed the handle of one of my suitcases, dragging it through the small adjoining bathroom—an oasis of polished green marble and brass—into the bedroom.

I should, by rights, have noticed the bed first. It was fabulous—antique-looking and painted in delicate tones, plump and soft with pillows stacked against the headboard and a coverlet of heavy damask, opulently ivory. And I ought to have noticed the thickly draped windows, the one on the end wall that faced me and the two on my left, close together, that travelled from ceiling to floor and so clearly led out to a balcony. At the very least, I should have admired the marble-topped dressing table in the corner by the wardrobe. I had always wanted a marble-topped dressing table. But the only thing that caught my eye at first was Celia's portrait.

It was *meant* to catch the eye—a life-sized canvas, hanging square above the bed, so real the eyes appeared to hold my own, the figure seemed to breathe.

But it surprised me, still, to hear the voice. A woman's voice. It spoke to me from thin air. "I do hope that you'll forgive me."

My heart gave a foolish leap upwards and lodged in my throat, but even as I felt the rush of unreasoning panic I knew that it wasn't a voice from the grave. And I would have recognized the speaker even if I hadn't wheeled in time to see the curtains billow at the long French windows opposite the bed.

"It's dreadfully rude of me, I know," said Madeleine Hedrick as she stepped in from the balcony, "but I thought that our first meeting ought to be private."

I'd never seen Madeleine Hedrick close up. In my schoolgirl remembrance her Lady Macbeth had been regal, commanding, and on television chat shows she looked willowy and tall, so it came as something of a surprise to find myself facing a woman not quite my own height, with such delicate bones, such a slender physique, that I felt like a great clumping ox by comparison.

Her voice, though, low and pleasant, held the strength and skilled control that I'd expected. "Did I frighten you? I'm sorry. I don't make a habit of trespassing, really, but I couldn't think of any other way." Like Nicholas, she didn't introduce herself. There wasn't any need. And she didn't immediately offer her hand. Instead she paused for a moment inside the French windows, head tipped as though she were onstage and awaiting a prompt from the wings.

I could have done with one, myself. The perfect speech that I'd so carefully constructed and rehearsed had somehow vanished from my memory. Wordless, I stood and looked back at her.

Finally, she spoke. "Did you have a good journey?"

A question I could answer. “Lovely, thank you.”

“I always did prefer the train to flying. So much more civilized, really, and of course one has the scenery . . . from an airplane one only sees clouds, for the most part. And even from a car,” she said, “when Nicky is driving, one can only see a blur.” She smiled. Moving from the window, she sat on the end of the elegant bed, and for the first time I saw the whole person—the simple clean lines of the cream-coloured dress she was wearing, the curling dark hair in its trademark short style, the rounded soft face with its engaging dimples and the large dark eyes that could by turns be sharp or gentle, widely innocent or tragic, as she chose. At the moment they hadn’t committed to any emotion, but watched my face and waited, rather as a border guard might watch someone approach a checkpoint—reasonably certain that the password would be given, but prepared at any moment to defend.

I tried one more time to remember my speech, then gave up and said simply, “You can’t know how much of a thrill it is for me to finally meet you.”

“You are sweet.”

“No, honestly, it was you who made me want to be an actress. Roo—I mean, Rupert,” I caught myself using the childish nickname and winced. “Rupert Neville, he did all he could to put me off the idea.” He had, in fact, told me that practically any profession was better than theatre; that being a lollipop lady was better, more sane. “But then our school took us to Stratford, you see, and I saw you do Lady Macbeth, and it . . . well, I can’t really describe *what* it did to me, not properly, but acting was all that I wanted to do after that.” Which came out sounding foolish, and I kicked myself for saying it at all. And why, oh why, had I made that remark about school? It was hopelessly impolitic, and surely impolite, to remind an older actress of the difference in our ages.

But one glance at Madeleine Hedrick revealed that I had, by some miracle, chosen the right thing to say; I had uttered the password. She sat back a little, relaxing, fingers laced around her knees. “How nice. I don’t know that I’ve ever been anyone’s inspiration before.” She smiled. “Was that Dennis O’Malley I saw coming in with you?”

I hadn't been aware that she'd been watching us arrive, but I said yes, it was, and explained how he'd stepped in at the last minute to replace the other man who was supposed to have been our SM.

"I haven't seen Dennis in years," she said. "Is he still incorrigible?"

That was, I thought, as good a word for Den as any. "Definitely."

"Good. I was afraid age might have sobered him. It changes us all, you know, age does." It hadn't treated her too badly, really. She would be about my mother's age, just entering her fifties, but unlike my mother her youthful complexion appeared to owe nothing to surgery. Still smiling, she stood. "But of course you'll be longing to tidy up after your travels. I ought to have thought. It's my worst fault," she told me, "not thinking. Nicky always makes comments. I expect," she went on, inviting me with a gesture to walk with her through to the sitting-room, "that he'll have arranged for us all to meet up for a drink on the terrace?"

"I think that's the plan, yes."

"I knew that he would. It's the actor in him, you know. Drinks on the terrace. So predictably theatrical. Mind you," she said, "as settings go, the terrace here *is* fabulous. You know the way?"

I dutifully repeated the instructions Nicholas had given me. "Down the stairs here, then turn left, turn right, and go straight on."

She nodded. We had reached the door. She turned and showed me once again that beatific smile that had as much impact up close as it did when one viewed it from the upper circle. "I'll see you down there, then."

And it felt to me as though, with that one sentence, she had given me some kind of blessing, as though she had set me a test and was pleased that I'd passed. Though I couldn't imagine what sort of a test she could have set—we'd barely said anything to each other, really, and nothing that I would have classed as important.

Unpacking my suitcase, I played the conversation over in my mind, editing my own words after the fact, as I often did, to make them say the things I should have said. Naturally, in this revised version, I came off sounding less of an idiot, but I still didn't think we'd accomplished anything short of breaking the ice, and I still couldn't tell, when she told me 'Of course you'll be longing to tidy up' whether she was being considerate or catty.

The last thing I took from the suitcase was my copy of *The Season of Storms.* I'd brought it along, not so much for bedtime reading—although Galeazzo's Celia poems, from what I'd read so far, promised to be very good at putting me to sleep—but because they *were* the Celia poems, and having the book sitting there at my bedside seemed almost an invocation of her spirit . . . a connection with the woman who'd once slept in this bedroom, this bed, and who probably wouldn't have been nervous at all at the prospect of drinks on the terrace with Madeleine Hedrick.

But then Celia the First had been famous herself, whereas I was a nobody. Hopelessly out of my league.

My flatmate Sally said that rooms absorbed the energies of people who had lived in them. I would have liked that to be true. I would have liked to think that some of Celia the First's poise, and her talent, might rub off on me while I stayed in her rooms, but I knew the odds on that were pretty long.

I looked up at her portrait and studied her face, and her all-knowing eyes seemed to smile at me. "What was I thinking?" I asked her. When no answer came I sighed, gathered up my travel-wrinkled clothes and, turning, went to run my bath.

iii

"LEFT," I reminded myself, "and then right." The narrow flight of stairs had brought me down into an equally narrow passage that swallowed the light from the stained glass so high overhead. There were several doors here, but in keeping with Nicholas's directions I turned left and followed the corridor round till it came to an end in front of yet another door, through which I glimpsed a length of polished table ringed round with tapestried chairs. Here the corridor swung to the right. I saw daylight, and felt on my face the late-afternoon breeze that was blowing unchallenged through leaded French windows that stood fully open, inviting me out to the terrace.

I had seen it before. The most famous—or at least the most widely reproduced—photograph of Galeazzo D'Ascanio in old age showed him here on this terrace, at rest with his back to the parapet, forsaking the view of the mountains and lake while he bent his head close to the muzzle of one of his well-beloved greyhounds. It was a smashing portrait—one could read in that creased face, that smile, the curve of the shoulders, the strange combination of arrogance and vulnerability that had marked the great poet. When I'd seen it for the first time I had thought I understood what had made Celia the First chuck the stage and her family and friends and run off with a man nearly three times her age. But standing on the terrace now my only thought was: How could he have turned his back on *that*?

Because the view was quite beyond belief—the sort that hit me squarely in that little hollow place behind my breastbone, made me catch my breath and wish I had a camera, even though I knew full well the camera's lens could never capture what my own two eyes were seeing.

So high were we above the lake, so steep the cypressed hills that plunged to meet the tiny town below, that for a moment I imagined I was standing at the summit of the world with nothing over me but eagles and the blue, blue arc of sky.

It was Den who brought me down to earth. "At last," he said, and raised his glass. "I thought we'd have to launch a search and rescue mission."

I didn't think I'd taken that long, really, getting ready, but the others had managed to get here ahead of me. They were fairly spread out—Nicholas wandering round at the far end while Madeleine lounged in a striped chair and chatted with Rupert, who stood a short distance from Den, near the parapet. Four people—five, counting me—would have filled most spaces, but the terrace was so huge it swallowed all of us, and the walk across the paving stones to where the others were seemed endless.

Madeleine stopped talking and turned in her chair to watch me. She'd changed clothes as well, and in place of the cream dress now wore a more casual trouser suit, her dark hair wrapped in a bright turquoise scarf. I thought it odd that she had bothered changing, she had looked so smart before. It was almost as if she'd deliberately chosen to dress to the nines for our first private meeting, as though she had needed, or felt that she'd needed, the armour that fashion provided; and that having once met me she now felt reassured of her advantage and could dress whatever way she liked.

The less paranoid explanation, of course, was that she'd worn the dress to lunch with Nicholas—he'd told us, after all, that they'd gone out, and it was perfectly conceivable they'd eaten someplace swish. She might have only changed for comfort. But it still made me curious.

She shaded her eyes with one hand as she watched me approach. "Hello again."

That caught Rupert, who'd been preparing to introduce us, off guard. "Oh, you've met?"

Madeleine said, "Yes, we ran into one another upstairs.

Come have a drink. We're just helping ourselves, they're short-staffed here today."

"Yeah, there's a little bit of a mystery in that, I guess," Den said, with the look of someone who had secret knowledge. "I heard Teresa talking on the phone when I came down. Apparently this maid who's missing left her house this morning, same as usual, all dressed for work. Her family's worried sick."

"I do hope nothing bad has happened to her," Madeleine said, with a look of concern. "She served us at dinner last night; she's a sweet little thing."

"Oh, she'll probably turn up," said Den.

"Who will?" Nicholas wanted to know, as he sauntered over to join us with a cigarette in hand.

Madeleine turned to look up at him. "The little maid who didn't come to work today." And she told him what Den had overheard Teresa saying on the telephone.

Nicholas's first reaction had nothing to do with the maid. He looked at Den in mild surprise. "You speak Italian?"

"Half the kids on my block growing up spoke Italian. It rubbed off."

"Ah." I didn't know how well Nicholas could speak Italian himself, but I gathered he spoke it well enough to have thought it should accord him special status in our group. He'd be even less pleased, I decided, when he found out that Rupert knew Italian, too. People like Nicholas liked to be frontstage and centre—they didn't like sharing the spotlight. "Anyhow," he said, to Madeleine, "I wouldn't worry about this maid of yours. I can't imagine anything would happen to her in a place like this." With a wicked smile he added, "Maybe she's run off with Giancarlo. It's rather suggestive, the two of them missing. And after all, Teresa's not the most attractive woman."

"Nicky, stop. You have a nasty mind," Madeleine accused him. But her tone was light. "Do make yourself useful. Fetch Celia a drink."

I saw his eyes in the instant before he smiled at her, and in my Shakespeare game I knew I would have cast him as Macbeth—he had the vanity, the shallowness, and all the self-centred ambition, and like Macbeth, I thought, he'd probably do anything to get what he'd decided he deserved. And because of that one glimpse into his nature, the smile he turned on me, although it would have weakened many women's knees, had no effect. "What will you have? We've got sherry or vodka martinis, your choice."

I chose a martini. Then, seeking the comfort of familiar company, I joined Rupert at the parapet, loving the feel of the breeze on my face as I gazed at the lake. "It's beautiful, isn't it?"

Rupert nodded. "Very. It's been a resort since the days of the Romans, you know. They built holiday villas here, and came to take the waters. There are mineral springs about, I'm told."

"At Sirmione, aren't they?" Den said, trying to recall.

I felt the small airborne ripples of Rupert's sigh as he was once again upstaged, but Den, who hadn't done it intentionally and at any rate hadn't noticed the sigh, went on, "I'm sure the Romans built a spa at Sirmione, down that way." He waved a hand to indicate the south shore, past the jagged headland jutting out to partly screen our view in that direction. "There are still some ruins there, I think, if you like that kind of thing."

I looked at him. "I gather you don't?"

He shrugged, refusing to commit himself, and Madeleine said, "Well, I love them."

Nicholas, who'd been getting himself a fresh drink, rejoined the conversation. "Love what?"

"Ruins."

"You'll be loving this house, then," he said. "Half the plaster on that wall over there only wants a good rain to dissolve it." He tapped his ash over the parapet, yawning. "Our boy hasn't half got his work cut out for him, restoring this place."

I took a look round at the high, yellow walls. "But he's got the Forlani Trust helping him, hasn't he?" I knew the Trust by reputation. I'd seen a television programme last year on a project they were doing near Florence, and they had looked to be a first-rate organization. Their intent seemed to be to acquire and restore as many of the great old Italian estates as they possibly could, in keeping with the wishes of their founder, the art-loving tycoon Leonardo Forlani. His widow still sat on the board of directors, and while she hadn't actually appeared on the programme I'd watched, she apparently still took a hand in all the restoration projects, though since her husband had been well into his nineties when he died, she likely did most of her own work from a walking-frame.

Nicholas agreed that the Trust must be a help to D'Ascanio's grandson. "But last night at dinner he was saying there were rooms that they hadn't so much as looked inside yet—wasn't he, Maddy?"

She nodded. "It must be a difficult job."

Den folded his arms as he lowered his glass. "So what's your opinion of D'Ascanio?"

Madeleine said, "He was very nice, I thought."

"Quiet," said Nicholas, blowing out smoke. "Didn't say any more than he had to at dinner. I don't think he knew what to do with us, really."

Rupert nodded agreement. "No, he's not very comfortable in social settings, I did notice that, the time we met in London."

Madeleine thought that it must be because of his upbringing. "Poor little rich boy, and all that."

"And where does he get all his money from?" Den asked. "Is it all inherited, or what?"

Nobody knew. Nicholas admitted that he didn't even know what D'Ascanio's father had done for a living.

Den grinned. "Well, you know Italians." Adopting the hoarse, reedy voice of a Hollywood mob boss, he told us, "They probably run a respectable olive oil business."

"I somehow don't think so," said Nicholas drily. "And you won't either, once you've seen him. Anyway, those Mafia types all have hard names like Guido and Vito and Tony, not Alessandro." He drew the name out with an exaggerated roll. "No, an *Alessandro* could never be a hit man. He'd have to be more like an opera singer, or a magician." Spreading his arms he announced with a music-hall flourish: "The great Alessandro D'Ascanio . . . Christ, that's a mouthful, that, isn't it?"

All of us laughed except Rupert, whose mild gaze had

moved past my shoulder. He coughed, a discreet little cough. I knew Rupert's looks; I knew what this expression meant, and I could feel my face flushing before I could turn.

Alessandro D'Ascanio was younger than I'd thought he'd be, certainly no older than thirty-five, with hair the same colour as Bryan's, the kind that could be either dark golden blond or sandy brown, depending on the light and time of year. Unlike Bryan's hair, though, his curled loosely. His eyes were in shadow. He stood very tall at the end of the terrace, between two long-legged greyhound dogs who held their brindled heads stone-steady, level with his knees, and waited, poised like matching statues.

Maybe, I thought, he was too far away to have heard us poke fun at his name. Ashamed, I bit my lip and watched him, hopeful, till his hand at last went out and touched the nearer dog and stroked its ears. His voice, when he spoke, carried clearly with only a trace of an accent.

"My mother called me Alex. She was English," he said calmly, "if you find that any easier."

I felt like a child who'd been caught calling somebody names in the playground. I know my face went crimson.

Madeleine Hedrick, by contrast, managed to strike the right balance of composure and apology. "You mustn't take notice. We actors are horribly lacking in manners."

"Especially me." Nicholas, far from being chastised, looked amused. He pitched his spent cigarette over the parapet. "Sorry, just a bit of fun, and no offence intended."

"Yes, of course." D'Ascanio's quiet voice neither forgave nor condemned, but he didn't smile back. As he stepped now from the shadows I could see he was a most attractive man, not flashily handsome like Nicholas, nor a dyed-in-the-wool charmer like Den, but attractive in the strong-and-silent way that caught my interest. Crossing the terrace towards us he turned his attention to Rupert, holding out his hand in greeting. "I'm so glad to see you made it. I apologize for your not being met at the station. I'm told you had quite an ordeal."

Rupert shrugged off the experience. "Oh, it wasn't so bad. We survived it. Well, some of us did," he amended, as he caught Den's wry sideways look. "Alex, you haven't met Dennis yet, have you?"

"No." He had hazel eyes, as quiet as the rest of him, that travelled Den's length as the two men shook hands. And then it was my turn.

Rupert, still in charge of introductions, started off, "And this is—"

"Celia." There was something quite decided in the way he said my name. His gaze raked me once as it had done with Den, but his expression didn't change. "I'm pleased to meet you."

I liked that he didn't take my hand as some men did, with that limp partial grasp of the fingers that so often passed for a feminine handshake. His touch was firm, and warm, and very sure. I only wished he would have smiled. It would have made me feel less nervous.

Clearing my throat, I said the only thing that came to mind. "You have a lovely home."

"Thank you."

"Yes," said Rupert, stepping in to save the conversation, "we've all been admiring the view from your terrace."

Alex D'Ascanio nodded, turning from me to glance round. "This was one of my grandfather's favourite places, I'm told. And mine."

Rupert smiled. "I see you share another of your grandfather's preferences." He nodded down at the dogs, who stayed obediently close to Alex's side but continually shifted position with a restlessness that hinted they'd much rather be out hunting.

One of them turned a long head and fixed me with a level gaze, assessing whether I was worth the effort to make friends, as Alex told Rupert, "Yes, these are descendants of one of his champions."

"Really?" Madeleine offered her hand to them. "What are their names?"

"This is Nero." He touched one sleek head. "And the other is Max."

Max, I decided, was the flirtatious one, the one who had been eyeing me. As though he knew I had him pegged, he looked away now, feigning indifference, and sniffed politely at Madeleine's fingers.

"I used to keep dogs," she said. "Corgis."

Nicholas grinned. "Like the Queen."

"Well, not exactly. Mine were rather fat. But that was when we had the house in Hampstead. We couldn't keep dogs now, not in the flat. They'd be miserable. Not that my daughter will ever stop trying to convince me otherwise."

I'd forgotten that she had a daughter—during the scandal with Mother the papers had made a great deal of the fact that Madeleine and her husband had only just had a baby together, but one never heard a mention of the child now. Madeleine, I thought, must keep the girl well under wraps. Not like my mother, who'd delighted in posing with me for the cameras, at least when I was very small. The practice had lost its appeal as I'd grown, mainly because Rupert had pointed out—rather cleverly, I'd always thought—that anyone looking at me with my mother was bound to start doing the maths. Mother hated revealing her age.

I assumed Madeleine, being an actress, would have the same hang-up, which was why it surprised me, when Den asked how old her daughter was, that she answered without hesitation. "Twelve," she said. "Going on twenty."

"A right little terror," said Nicholas.

"Yes, well, most little girls are at that age," her mother explained with a smile. "I was horrid, myself. I'm amazed that my parents didn't lock me in the cupboard till my eighteenth birthday, really."

"I'm sure the thought never occurred to them," Rupert said, but from the faint curve of his mouth I knew he was recalling scenes from my adolescence.

"Well, *I've* thought about it," said Nicholas, shaking out a cigarette and patting down his pockets for a light. "With Poppy, that is, not with Maddy."

"Oh, Nicky . . ."

"Not to worry," he said. "She's the school's problem now, till the end of the term."

"She's at boarding-school?" Den asked.

"Ordinarily, she doesn't board," said Madeleine. "She's a

day girl, and if I'm away then she stays with her father. Only this time—"

"Only this time," Nicholas finished for her, "the sodding selfish bastard told us no, he couldn't take her, so we had to make arrangements with the school. Where the devil is my lighter?"

"I've got it." Madeleine quietly handed it over. I watched her and wondered why a woman so beautiful and full of class would make the choices she had made with men.

"Thanks." Lighting his cigarette, Nicholas glanced over at Den. "What's wrong with you, O'Malley? What, are you afraid of dogs or something?"

Den, who had backed away a step as one of the dogs nosed his leg, gave a shrug. "Let's just say I have respect for anything with teeth."

Alex D'Ascanio had stayed silent through our conversation, so silent in fact that it would have been easy to forget he was there, if I hadn't been so physically aware of him. I caught the small movement of his mouth—not a smile, exactly, but the closest he had come to it. "These dogs don't bite," he said. "They wouldn't even if I told them to. They're very independent, they don't bother much with people."

Like their master, I suspected. He was not at all the sort of man I'd pictured. I had thought the poet Galeazzo's grandson would be older, more flamboyant, not so damned reserved and serious. Mind you, he had told us his mother was English, and this was what came, I supposed, of blending warm Italian blood with our more chilly Anglo Saxon.

Bending his head he examined his watch. "You will excuse me, there's something I must do before dinner. Teresa starts serving at seven exactly—you remember your way to the dining room?" This question, expectant, he directed at Madeleine. "Yes? Then you can show the others? Thank you. I shall see you later, then." And with that he nodded politely and left us, the dogs keeping close to his heels as he entered the house.

Nicholas lowered his voice this time, drawing on his cigarette. "You see? What did I tell you? Not the world's most social bastard, is he?"

"Oh, I don't know," said Madeleine, "I rather like him."

"Yes, well, you would. Women always mistake silence for substance."

"The problem with you is you never give people a chance," she replied. "And anyway, Nicky, the poor man did well to be civil at all after your making fun of him."

"Oh, the hell with that." He brushed it off. "If a chap can't laugh at himself . . ."

Rupert, always keen to get out of the way of a conflict, moved me along with a hand at my back. "Would you like another drink?"

"Yes, please."

Our martinis freshened, we walked off a short distance to stand by the parapet, looking down into the gardens, a fantasy landscape of manicured hedges and footpaths and fountains and thickets of trees, tumbling down the steep hill till it vanished from view in the dark of the soldier-like cypresses ringing the lake.

"And what did *you* think of our host?" Rupert asked.

I wondered uncomfortably whether his sharp eyes had noticed my interest in Alex D'Ascanio. "I don't—"

"Come on, let's play your game. What role from Shakespeare would you give him?"

I smiled. "Oh, Roo."

"I'm curious."

Leaning on the parapet, I thought about it. "Hamlet."

"And why Hamlet?"

"I really don't know. It just came to me, that's who he is."

He accepted this. "And Madeleine?"

I glanced over my shoulder. She and Nicholas were still talking, but more amicably now, and Den had joined them. "Cleopatra," I said without thinking. Always loving the wrong man, I thought. First Caesar, and then Antony, and both had been unfaithful to her.

Rupert saw it, too. He smiled. "'O, never was there queen so mightily betrayed!'" he quoted softly. "Is that the idea?"

Actually, watching Madeleine watch Nicholas, another line from Shakespeare's play had risen to my mind, more plaintive. *Why should I think you can be mine and true?*

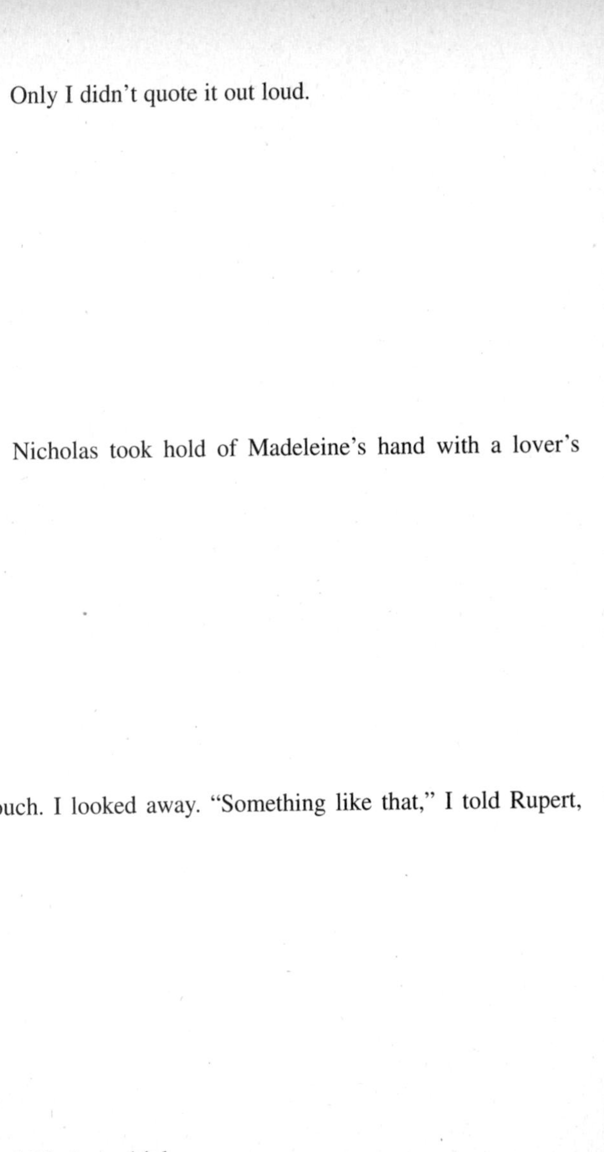

Only I didn't quote it out loud.

Nicholas took hold of Madeleine's hand with a lover's touch. I looked away. "Something like that," I told Rupert, and lifted my drink.

The knock on his door was expected.

"Your wife, sir," said Thompson, and ushered her in.

"Ah, Francesca," he greeted her, rising. "You do surprise me. I would have expected you long before this."

She sat. "I have been busy."

"Yes, I hear you have. A doctor, is he not?" His smile reminded her that he, too, had his sources of intelligence. "I'm glad you have not been too lonely, while I was away."

"No more than you have," she replied, crossing swords with the skill of long practice. "I have seen her."

"And?"

"She's very beautiful. Young for you, wouldn't you say?"

"Very."

"She's an actress?"

"She has a rare talent. Like you had."

She noted the past tense, as he had intended, but smiled all the same. "Then you will have to write a play for her, caro, *as you did for me."*

An underhanded thrust that hit its mark, but he refused to let her keep the advantage. He parried back, "Perhaps I will."

A play for Celia . . . his imagination grasped the thought, and turned it like a sculptor turning clay. Of course. And he would build a theatre also, where he'd always longed to build one, in the little hollow with the pines . . .

"You'll come and see your son?" Francesca asked him, rising.

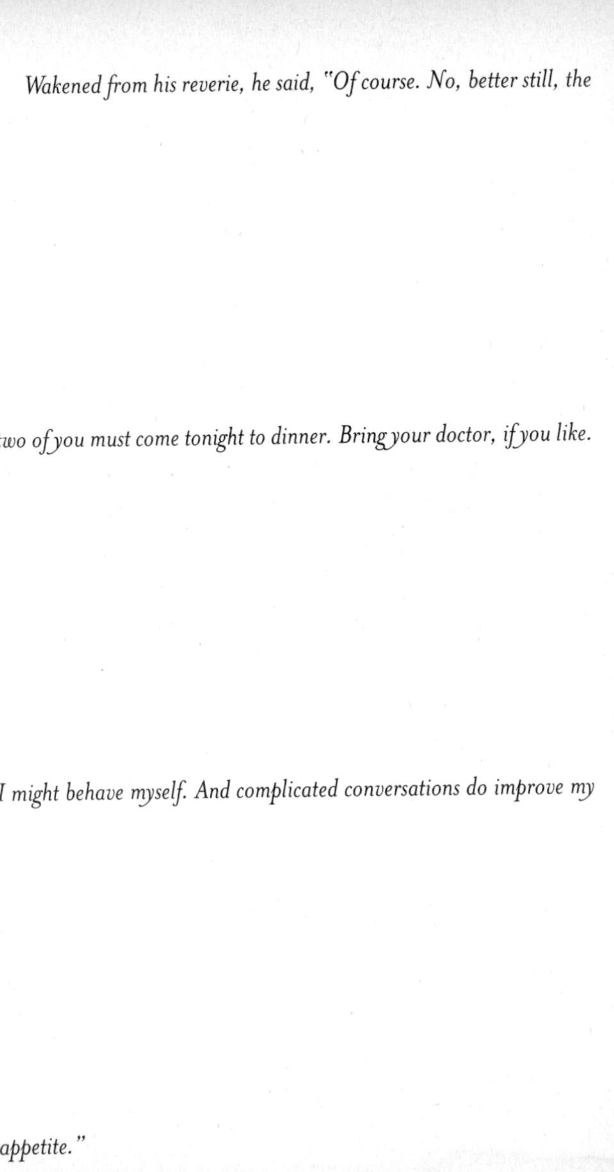

Wakened from his reverie, he said, "Of course. No, better still, the two of you must come tonight to dinner. Bring your doctor, if you like. I might behave myself. And complicated conversations do improve my appetite."

iv

WE didn't dress for dinner in the traditional sense, but the grandeur of the dining room—the room I'd glimpsed earlier on my way down—seemed to demand something smarter than the everyday. Even Rupert wore a jacket, which he rarely did outside his club, and only then because it was required.

But then, this was the sort of room that in the thirties had been meant for elegant women in long bias-cut satin gowns, and gentlemen in dinner jackets. It was not a room to lounge in, not a comfortable room, but in its day it must have been the height of fashion. The walls were black lacquerwork, polished like mirrors, and heavily gilded with gleaming bright gold. And the ceiling that arched overhead in a pattern of shells was gold, too. The effect was like being inside an exquisitely designed Chinese box.

All along the outside wall were opaque leaded windows cut in stylized geometric shapes, reflecting back the soft light from the room. I'd thought at first that they were made of painted glass, but Alex had informed me they were actually alabaster, and the masterpiece of one of the many skilled artists his grandfather had brought here to work on the estate. "I've been offered money for these windows, many times," he'd told us. "And they've recently been featured in a book of great twentieth-century art." So I wasn't surprised that there weren't any draperies to cover them.

The trestle table could have seated twenty people easily, though only six chairs had been set around it—rounded tub-like chairs with black-and-red tapestried seats that in spite of their stylized appearance weren't too bad for sitting, so long as you kept your back straight. I'd been placed at one end of the table, closest to the doorway to the corridor, with Den and Rupert to my left and Nicholas and Madeleine to my right. Alex D'Ascanio sat at the other end, facing me. Behind him, two gilded shell-shaped niches in the lacquered walls held the marble heads of a man and a woman, strongly illuminated, while at his shoulder a second door connected to the kitchen passage. Through this door from time to time Teresa came and went, bringing new dishes and clearing the old ones.

She didn't look overly pleased, and I wondered about this until Nicholas, catching me looking, leaned over and said, "I don't think it's her job to serve at table. The maid served us last night."

So the missing maid hadn't shown up yet. And I was guessing, from the black look on Teresa's face, that her husband, Giancarlo, had not come home, either. As we'd sat down to dinner Alex had apologized again for our not being met at Desenzano, and it was clear he'd been embarrassed by Giancarlo's unreliability, but something in the resignation of his tone had led me to believe that this wasn't the first time such a thing had happened. Which made me feel deep sympathy for poor Teresa—she was probably wavering, I thought, between wanting to wring her husband's neck and being worried to death.

I showed her a smile and said "*Grazie*" when she came to take my pasta plate, replacing it with a dish of roasted chicken and potatoes, but this time she didn't respond, merely nodded and moved on to Nicholas.

Ignoring her with the casual ease of someone accustomed to servants, he looked across at Rupert. "So now that we've assembled, what's the plan? When do we start?"

Rupert looked at Den for confirmation before answering. "We thought day after tomorrow, on Monday, if that's all right. We'll begin with a read-through, go over the schedule, see where we stand. That suit everyone? Lovely, then that's what we'll do."

Madeleine set down her fork. "And where are we rehearsing? In the theatre?"

"No." That was Alex. He shook his head. "No, there's still work to be done on the stage. I was thinking perhaps in the ballroom. I'll show you," he offered to Rupert and Den, "after dinner. It's a nice room, very large and bright, and I can have some chairs brought in, whatever you need."

I still hadn't reasoned out why my mind associated him with Shakespeare's Hamlet, so as the meal went on I tried to study him more closely without being obvious, keeping my head down so no one would notice and lifting it only to pretend an interest in the marble heads set in the niches just behind him. I wasn't having any luck until I saw him following in silence something Den was telling Rupert, and it hit me. I could see the intellect at work, and something else, a private kind of loneliness, and I suddenly felt very sure that I'd found the connection, that what had made me think of Hamlet was my sense that this man, too, was driven on by some internal force, and yet stayed always on the outside, looking in.

I was forming that thought when his head turned a fraction without any warning. His quiet gaze levelled on mine.

The contact was brief. But I couldn't help feeling, as he looked away unsmiling, that I'd once again been caught doing something I shouldn't have.

Den, having finished going over things with Rupert, leaned close to me and murmured, "You don't need to look so damned guilty."

I looked at him, surprised, because I didn't think he'd been aware . . .

"You'd need a superhuman appetite to finish that," he said. And with the smile of a conspirator he nudged his plate discreetly towards mine. "Here, let me give you a hand with those last few potatoes."

We were making the transfer when something, a tingling warmth on the side of my face, warned me someone was watching. Against my better judgement I glanced up, and for the second time my eyes locked with Alex D'Ascanio's. Only this time I thought that his mouth moved a little in what might have been the shadow of a smile. And this time it was I who was the first to look away.

v

I woke suddenly in darkness in the puzzled and disoriented state that came from sleeping in a strange bed in an unfamiliar room. I lay there a moment or two in confusion, unable to see much of anything, but gradually the outlines of the furniture and window-frames emerged from the shadows like a slowly developing film, and I relaxed as I remembered where I was.

The room was cold. I hadn't locked the French windows and one of them had come unlatched and drifted partway open, letting in a breeze that stirred the curtain. Shivering, I rose and went over to close it, and it was as I stood there at the open window that I first noticed the sound.

That might have been what had disturbed my sleep to begin with: the thrumming of an engine faintly underscored by the rolling crunch of tyres on gravel, coming on as careful as a thief. And then the sound abruptly died and for a minute, maybe longer, all was silent. I was putting out a hand to shut the window when the slumbering walls of the villa caught the echo of a car door's slam, and shortly after that I heard the scuffing steps of someone climbing, not the way we had come up at the front of the house from the gates at the entrance, but here at the back, climbing up to the terrace from somewhere below in the gardens.

Whoever it was wasn't taking great pains to be quiet. I rather expected the dogs to start barking, and when they didn't I wondered why. Maybe, I thought, they were very sound sleepers, and after all I didn't know where their master's room was, it might be round the other side of the house where the dogs couldn't hear . . .

On cue a feral growl rose low from underneath my balcony, and then was hushed by someone saying, *"Zitto."* A man's voice. Alex D'Ascanio's voice.

I couldn't close the window now, I thought—he'd surely hear me, and I didn't especially want him to know that I was awake and aware of his being there.

The climbing footsteps had reached the terrace, now—I could tell by their flattening tone and the change in their rhythm.

The voice beneath my balcony said calmly, "*Buon giorno,* Giancarlo."

The footsteps stopped dead. Giancarlo's reply was a short burst of words in Italian that, although I didn't understand it, was nonetheless easy to interpret. Bryan said much the same thing when I came up behind him and spoke without thinking . . . and then he'd accuse me of trying to give him a heart attack.

Alex D'Ascanio didn't seem very remorseful. He took his sweet time stepping forwards, and even the clicking of the dogs' toenails at his heels was leisurely. I didn't think he'd moved too far off, but the next time he spoke his voice was indistinct.

I didn't have any desire to witness him tearing a strip off an employee, and anyway it wasn't any of my business, so I started very quietly to pull the window shut. I didn't want to be obvious, didn't want anybody to see me and think I was one of those women who nosed about, spying through windows. But one of the dogs growled. The sound brought my head up and made me stop, motionless, as both men turned their heads to look.

It took me a minute to work out which man was which—they were much the same height and build, and in the end I only managed it because of the dogs, whose circular pacing kept bringing them round to the man on the left. At his knee, the dark shadowy figure of one of the greyhounds paused, poised with its nose pointed straight at my window, like a setter who had scented game. I didn't dare move.

Alex angled his head up to look at my balcony, too, but he mustn't have seen me because he once again said something to the dog before returning his attention to Giancarlo. The dog, though, sure of what he'd seen, kept watching me, and so for safety's sake I stayed exactly where I was, trying to keep still. Another few minutes, I thought wryly, and that wouldn't be a problem—I'd be frozen here, the night air was that chilly.

Come on, I urged the men silently, *finish talking and move off, so I can close this window and get back to bed.*

Giancarlo seemed to be doing most of the talking, gesturing a good deal with his hands, as though he were explaining himself, while Alex stood with hands in pockets, head tipped as he listened. Whatever excuses he was getting from Giancarlo, I could tell he wasn't pleased. He interrupted halfway through, impatient, and shrugging his shoulders he made a remark that was sharp and abrupt.

Giancarlo hovered in silence a moment, shifting his weight from one leg to the other, then opting for a dignified retreat he turned and came across the terrace, plainly heading for the doorway to the dining room, beneath my window. I shrank back without thinking, and the tiny movement brought another growl from the greyhound.

Alex didn't seem to notice. Instead he appeared to be looking at something. I followed his gaze and saw nothing at first, but as the night breeze stirred the shadowed mass of trees a small light showed, a tiny dab of yellow in the blackness at the bottom of the garden. Curious, my eyes came back to Alex.

He stood for a long time and looked at that light, then he gave a command to the dogs and walked off with his back to my window. The dogs, left behind, settled down on the terrace with protesting whines. Alex didn't go into the house. I heard footsteps on stone, but retreating this time, as he went down the steps that Giancarlo had climbed minutes earlier. And then that sound, too, faded and finally stilled and the silence wrapped around the house more closely than before.

vi

MORNING brought the sunlight and a symphony of birdsong. I'd never heard so many birds, all calling gaily back and forth to one another from the trees beyond my windows to the hedges and the rooftops and the hills behind the house. Bryan had once tried to teach me to recognize bird calls—he'd always been brilliant with things like that, knowing which species would nest in which hedgerows and such—but for all my gift of mimicry I'd been a very disappointing pupil.

Even now, after all his instruction, I still couldn't tell if that twittering song belonged to a sparrow or a finch. I was lying there trying my best to decide when a knock at the door interrupted my efforts. A single knock, too formal to be Rupert's. I combed my hair straight with my fingers and rolled out of bed, reaching for my dressing-gown. The mirrors in the bathroom reassured me as I passed. I didn't look too terrible for someone who had slept in fits and starts. Belting my dressing-gown tightly I went through into my private sitting-room and unlatched the door to the landing, to find Teresa on the other side, unsmiling, with a breakfast tray. *"Buon giorno."*

"Good morning." Surprised, I stepped back to let her by. "What's all this?"

"Is not for everyday," she warned. "Is only for this morning. Signor O'Malley asked me would I do this specially." Den must have worked his charm—her tone implied that if Signor O'Malley were to ask her if she'd mind moving the villa a foot to the east, she'd consider it.

I couldn't help smiling as she set the tray on the tea table near the sofa. Not technically 'in bed,' perhaps, but close enough. That had to be what all this was about, I thought—

my telling Den in Venice that, if I were rich, I'd have someone serve me my breakfasts in bed. Teresa, of all people, I thought, would probably have understood the sense of luxury I felt in being served instead of serving, but her face was so dour that I didn't try to explain. I only said, "Signor O'Malley is a very thoughtful man," and thanked her.

"*Prego.*" She moved to the window to open the blinds, her features still set in a look of supreme disapproval.

It occurred to me that, even if she didn't think me a fitting occupant for Celia the First's suite, I could perhaps pacify her a little by showing how much I appreciated being here. "These rooms are so lovely," I said, with a tentative smile. "And the bed—"

"Is no place to put guests." She surprised me with the force of her interruption. "These rooms are not good rooms. Things happen here."

Uncertain what to say to that, I asked, "What sort of things?"

Teresa looked at me, her eyes intense. "Things happen." And then shutting off that line of talk, she turned. "I must go and take care of the others."

I made one last attempt at friendliness. "At least you have help today."

"*Come?*" she asked me, which sounded like 'co-may' and clearly meant 'pardon.' She'd stopped by the door and was frowning.

"Your husband, I mean. He got back last night, didn't he?"

"No, signorina." Her frown had frozen over with professional reserve. "My husband has not yet come home." And then she sharply turned and left the room before I could respond.

Defeated and confused, I sat and poured my tea. "*Buon giorno,* Giancarlo." That's how Alex D'Ascanio had greeted the man on the terrace in the small hours of the morning, I was sure of it, and yet . . . I shrugged. I might have been mistaken. After all, I had just woken up, I might have still been half-asleep. I was pondering this when another short knock sounded at my door.

This one sounded like Rupert's. I called out, "Come in."

Den put his head round. "Morning. Are you decent?"

"Well, mostly." I wasn't in the habit of entertaining male visitors in my dressing-gown, but he'd already shut the door behind him and I had very little option but to pretend that I was more sophisticated than I actually was. Tightening the belt of my dressing-gown, I thanked him for my breakfast. "It was sweet of you to remember."

"I've been called many things in my lifetime," he confessed, "but never sweet." For all his smile was suggestive I felt quite sure that, with Den, the flirtation was only a habit, and harmless. I didn't feel threatened at all when he crossed to examine my breakfast tray. "Not bad. Teresa did a good job."

"You can have a roll or something, if you like. It's far too much for me."

"No thanks, I've had mine already, downstairs." But he did help himself to a seat in the armchair that faced me. Stretching his legs out, he looked round the room. "Very nice. I can see you're not suffering."

"No." It was my turn to smile.

"This was her suite, I take it? The first Celia Sands? Well then, likely you've got the best rooms in the house, except maybe for D'Ascanio's own. I'd imagine they're pretty impressive as well, if his grandfather did the decorating." Even sitting, he couldn't keep still. Reaching out a hand he felt a corner of the heavy fabric draping the table beside him, then turned to the trinkets arranged on its top: a porcelain box, a bowl of coloured glass, a tiny herd of silver elephants. Den picked each item up and flipped it over, felt its weight.

Trying to make conversation, I asked, "Do you visit all your actors at this hour?"

"What? Oh, I don't, no. Consider yourself privileged. Actually," he said, realigning the elephants, "I came to ask a favour. I've lost Rupert, you see, and—"

"He's probably gone for a walk. He usually does, after breakfast."

"The point is," said Den, "he's not here, and I wanted to measure the theatre this morning so I could do the marking out in our rehearsal room, and I need someone else to help me hold the tape. I'd have asked our host, but he's conveniently absent as well, and as Maddy and Nicholas haven't put in an appearance this morning I didn't think I should go knocking on either of *their* doors, if you know what I mean." His blue eyes danced mischief. "So that just leaves you."

"I'd be happy to help." I'd been hoping that someone would offer to show me the way to the theatre. After all of the pictures I'd seen I was dying to see the real thing. I'd even thought of trying to find it myself, although I had only the roughest idea of where it might be in the grounds, and the world's least reliable sense of direction. I'd be much better off with Den leading me.

Or at least, that's what I thought.

vii

WHEN we set out after breakfast it became apparent that Den, who'd led Rupert and me so unerringly through the confusion of back streets and alleys in Venice, found the garden paths here a bit difficult.

The layout of the gardens wasn't quite as bad, I don't think, as that of the house, but it had the same feel of the labyrinth—built on many levels, with enclosed and private spaces, some with shrubberies and fountains, others so completely wooded that I felt like I was walking through a forest in a fairy tale. Not minding being lost, I breathed the fresh and unfamiliar scents surrounding me, the dampened stones that lined the pathway, and the flowers and the trees whose names I didn't know. If Bryan were here he'd have named them all for me—the tall spindly ones with the elephant bark and the ones with the thick shiny leaves and the sprays of star-like flowers, white and yellow, hanging heavy with perfume. Bryan was clever with trees, as with birds, and some of these looked like they might have come straight from his part of the world, spiky and strange and decidedly tropical.

Den, who'd travelled more than I had, might have known what they were, but I didn't like to bother him when he was navigating. Not that he was having much success. As we stepped into the sunlight once again, into a level and orderly grove of small fruit trees contained by a classical border of columns and arches, Den reached for his hand-drawn map, frowning.

"Well, *this* should be the orchard. Which means right through there is the rose garden . . . yeah," he said, looking ahead to the next level down, where a tidy green pattern of hedges trimmed low to the ground ringed the beds where the rosebushes waited to bloom. "And that means," he went on, "that we've taken another wrong turning."

I smiled at his impatience. "That's all right, I'm quite enjoying this." I'd never been high on a hillside like this with the morning breeze cool on my face and the clear unspoilt blue of the lake far below me, its broad surface ruffled with streaks of pale silver that stretched to the opposite shore. I liked to look down to the lake and see the soaring points of cypress trees descending like the spears of giants, nearly black against the mingled greens of other trees. My gaze drifted sideways to take in the larger view. "What is that place, then?" I pointed to a narrow house whose rose-washed walls and tiled roof were only just now visible above the copper beeches at the bottom of the orchard.

Den consulted his map once again. "The Villa delle Tempeste, it says here. That means the 'House of Storms.'"

Appropriately named, I thought. The Villa delle Tempeste had been where Galeazzo kept his wife. She'd been an actress, too—Francesca Tutti, whom he'd married in his younger days, before his work had brought him fame. She'd acted in his early plays, although she'd never quite achieved the level of success or immortality that Celia the First had. Francesca Tutti had been very much an actress of her time, and when the fashions had changed she had faded from view like all those silent film stars talking pictures had displaced. Why she'd stayed with Galeazzo through his infidelities I didn't know. Certainly there didn't seem to have been much love lost on his side; in his later poems he'd written about Francesca rather savagely. They'd had one child that I knew about, a son—Alex's father, I presumed, still finding it strange to be able to put human faces to the people that I'd read about—and perhaps that alone had been the reason why Francesca Tutti hadn't left Il Piacere, why she'd stayed on in the Villa delle Tempeste.

I raised my hand to shade my eyes and took a closer look. The shutters stood open at one of the upper floor windows, a small sign of life.

Den, beside me, bent close to the map. "OK, I see what

we've done. We have to double back, then take the *second* turning at that little fountain with the dolphins."

I turned from the villa, and followed him. This time we found the right path.

We were back in the woods again, climbing through a tangle of slender-trunked trees stained with olive-green moss. Here the path was paved with grey stone cobbles, rounded carefully to shed the rain, and the gurgle of swift-running water, unseen but quite near, chased us up the short flights of steps meant to make the climb easier.

"No one told me," said Den, "that I'd have to go into training for this job. What's with D'Ascanio and stairs?" But I could tell that he, too, was impatient to get to the top; that he shared my excitement.

And then finally the trees thinned, the path levelled out and we stood at the edge of D'Ascanio's theatre.

viii

THERE are moments that lodge in the mind, as though somewhere a shutter has snapped and the whole thing's been captured; not only what you're looking at but everything: the things you smell, the way you feel, the angle of the sun, and at that moment you feel certain, you just know, that for as long as you are living you'll remember every detail. I'd had such a moment the first time I'd gone out onstage for a curtain call and seen people applauding in place of the darkness. I could never look at empty seats beneath a theatre's house lights without feeling that again, just as I knew that I would never smell a pine tree without thinking of this place.

It was a theatre-in-the-round, set in a hollow ringed by cypresses and pines. The hollow's grassy banks sloped downwards in a circle much too perfect to be natural, divided into quarters by four flights of steps descending from the pathway round the hollow's rim to where the stage lay nestled at the bottom.

Galeazzo, with his love of all things ancient and romantic, had built a wooden stage, with rising banks of seats beneath the tent-like shelter of a pointed roof on pillars, which left the stage and seats exposed to open air while keeping the rain off the heads of the actors and at least part of the audience. Those who opted for the less expensive seating on the grass had to take their chances with the weather, though the sloping lawn still offered them an unobstructed view.

Here at the top I could see the larger sweep of scenery, across the placid narrows of Lake Garda to the perfect snow-topped mountain peak that marked the farther shore, but as I started down the nearest of the four long aisles, venturing deeper into the hollow, that view gradually narrowed until, looking up from the bottom, I saw only treetops and the great blue bowl of sky.

I turned to continue on down to the stage, while behind me Den said to be careful. "The renovations aren't done yet, don't forget, and this would *not* be a good time for you to break a leg."

But the stage certainly looked sturdy enough, and there weren't any barricades or warnings to keep off it, and I couldn't resist the temptation. It was not a very large stage—maybe forty feet or so in diameter—and instead of being raised above the audience it sat in a depression at the centre of the rings of seats, so that those in the first row were actually looking down a bit at the actors; a rather unusual arrangement, but a practical one given the layout of the theatre since it guaranteed that everyone—those sitting under cover of the roof and those who'd spread their blankets on the grass—would see the play.

It felt odd, though, to have to climb *down* to a stage. The proper way to reach it, of course, would have been to begin my approach from the dressing-rooms and backstage areas, coming out through the tunnel-like gangway that opened out under the section of seats to my right. But since I hadn't started in the dressing-rooms, I had to go the slightly harder route of swinging myself over the edge of the first row of seats and dropping the short distance onto the circle of boards.

I'd never played a theatre-in-the-round before. Simply standing in one gave me quite an incredible feeling, exposed on all sides, with no elaborate scenery to hide behind. Rupert had once said that theatre-in-the-round was theatre stripped down to its essence, its primitive form, and standing here now I could see what he'd meant. When Thespis of Icaria, five centuries before the birth of Christ, had first stepped away from the chorus to say a few lines on his own, scandalizing the audience and changing forever not only the role of the actor but the whole nature of drama in theatre, he might have been standing on a stage much like this one.

Although, I amended, he wouldn't have had all those lights

pointed down from the rafters. He likely wouldn't have even had the rafters, come to think of it.

"Let's hear a soliloquy," Den said. He'd taken a seat in the front row to watch me, arms folded, expectant.

I took the dare. "Which would you like?"

"Oh, anything. Surprise me."

I surprised myself. The first great speech that came to mind was not from Shakespeare, but from Sophocles—Electra's opening lament. I hadn't spoken it since I'd left school, and yet the words were somehow there and flowed with ease, seeming fitting and right for this open-air stage with the hills sloping up on all sides to the trees, and the breeze blowing airily under the high pointed roof. I made it midway through:

"'. . . while I behold the sky, Glancing with myriad fires, or this fair day. But, like some brood-bereavèd nightingale, With far-heard wail . . .'" I faltered, then. "'With far-heard wail . . .' No, sorry, it's gone. I don't remember what comes next."

A pause, and then the answer came rather impressively out of the depths of the gangway behind me: "'Here at my father's door my voice shall sound.'"

And Rupert strolled out of the shadows to stand at the edge of the stage. He was smiling an odd little smile. "Very good, Celia. Very good indeed."

Recovering from my initial shock at hearing his voice coming out of the darkness like that without warning, I calmed my racing heartbeat with a hand on my breastbone. "Don't do that! I nearly went straight through the roof."

"Sorry," he said, but he looked more amused than contrite. "Fancy your remembering Electra after all these years. What made you think of that?"

I pushed back my hair, no longer the woman in mourning, no longer performing. "I don't know, it was probably all that talking you two did about the Fourth Crusade in Venice. You know, about the sacking of Constantinople and the library burning and all those Greek plays being lost in the fire. I've got Sophocles in the subconscious."

"And very appropriate, too." Hands on hips, Rupert surveyed the setting. "What do you think of it, Dennis?"

"Sorry, I'm still recovering," said Den, looking down from his seat. "That was terrific, Celia, it really was. Rupert, why didn't you tell me?"

The reply came back faintly indignant. "I said she could act."

"Yes, but I thought—" Den abandoned the sentence and leaned forwards, shaking his head. "Wow."

He sounded so sincere I couldn't help but feel a tiny flush of pride. Taking a sudden and intense interest in my feet, I mumbled my thanks, but I hadn't the chance to do more than that, really, because just then an angry shout shattered the peace of the morning.

I raised my head as Den and Rupert turned to face the hillside, where a giant of a man was thumping down the steps of one long aisle towards us, calling out words that could only be curses and waving his arms like he meant to do murder.

I sidled a step towards Rupert. "Roo?"

"Don't worry, darling. He probably thinks that we're trespassing. We'll get it sorted." But even he didn't look altogether certain of that.

Neither did Den. The big man was closing the distance between us with frightening speed, still shouting out phrases I didn't understand, his hands clenching now into fists. Den stood and called back something in Italian, but he might as well have thrown a pebble at a charging rhino.

And I could do little but watch as the man came on, now at the edge of the outer circle of covered seats, now halfway down the aisle, now nearly at the front row.

Rupert, very quietly beside me, told me, "Faint."

"But Roo—"

"For once, my love, just take direction, will you? Faint."

I dropped. I could have done it more dramatically, and maybe landed a little more softly, but given the circumstances and lack of preparation it wasn't too bad. As though a soundproof door had slammed, the tirade stopped.

A moment passed in silence before Den, catching on, started in on the stranger in his turn, accusingly. I didn't understand a word of what was being said, and from my prone position, eyes closed, I couldn't see anything, either, but Rupert, crouching down beside me, told me everything was going fine. "Good girl," he said. "Well done. Now just stay down there for a moment, and—"

Another man's voice, still far off, joined in. "Pietro!" That was Alex D'Ascanio, surely, I thought. I half-opened my eyes to be certain. At the sight of the figure in jeans and black jacket striding down the grassy slope, I struggled to sit. "Roo, I'm getting up."

"All right, but slowly, now. Don't spoil the effect."

He needn't have worried. The big man had his back to us, and wouldn't have noticed if I'd turned a cartwheel. And anyway, I didn't care. I wasn't going to have Alex D'Ascanio thinking of me as a weak, helpless woman. Standing, I rubbed the fresh bruise on my shoulder and watched Alex coming down between the seating sections, looking like an usher who'd been sent to deal with some disruptive member of the audience.

The man named Pietro launched an opening barrage of what I assumed were excuses, gesturing towards us with contempt, but Alex didn't appear to be much in the mood for explanations. His voice, his eyes, were very cold. With one sharp word he made the man fall silent.

It was not an easy silence, though. And when the glowering Pietro finally pulled his stare from Alex's, I sensed that he had merely shouldered arms and not submitted. As if to underline that point, he didn't leave the way he'd come but dropped to the stage and stalked straight to the gangway, past Rupert and me.

I hadn't got a good look at his face till now. A nasty face, with sullen eyes and bulldog jaw and heavy eyebrows drawn together darkly. Not a face I would have liked to have met in an alley; or anywhere else, for that matter.

"I am sorry," Alex told us, as the big man's footsteps faded in the darkness leading backstage. "I should have warned you, the theatre was meant to be off-limits today, so Pietro's men could do their work."

Den looked round, as though seeking evidence of the invisible workmen, and finding none returned to brushing off his leg. "Yeah, I can see they're hard at it."

Alex was looking at me. "Are you all right now?"

I'd hoped he hadn't seen me in my 'faint,' but it was clear from the tone of his voice, the concern in his eyes, that he had. *Blast,* I thought.

Rupert came to my aid. "She fainted on my orders, I'm afraid. Celia's really not so easy to intimidate, but I thought we could use a distraction, so . . ." He shrugged a good-natured apology. "Used to do it myself, years ago, playing football at school—not faint, exactly, but I'd grab my knee and drop and roll around. It always did the trick."

"Yes, well," I told him, still massaging my shoulder, "next time I'll remember that, and let you do the falling down, shall I?"

Den assured me I'd fallen down beautifully. "You're just showing off all your talents for me this morning, aren't you?" He was referring to my speech from Electra, I knew, but his choice of words and the smile that went with them seemed to suggest something rather more intimate.

Alex's eyes moved in silence from Den to myself and then, clasping his hands behind his back, he tipped his head up to study the lights in the rafters. "It's been the biggest project, this. We practically rebuilt it from the ruins."

"You did a good job," Den said, looking around. "It's a shame, though, that your dad let it fall apart in the first place."

The shutters came down then, as though Alex didn't like talking of anything personal. But he did say, "My father preferred to put his money into the family business."

Not content to leave it there, Den seized the opportunity to ask, "And what business is that?"

Alex smiled. "We build ships."

"Oh, I see." Den waited a few moments longer, presumably to see if any further details might be offered. When none were, he gave a small cough before asking, "Is there much work left to do here?"

"Enough," said Alex. "The stage needs refinishing. That's what the men will be doing today. They spent all of Friday sanding the stage and preparing the wood—it's all maple, imported, a very hard wood. We couldn't save all the old boards," he explained, as I looked down to study the pale amber floor at my feet. "When the roof went, the weather got in and ruined many of them, but we saved what we could, and the new parts blend in rather well."

I couldn't tell the new boards from the old, to be honest. Pietro's men had done an expert job.

"Then, when the stage is done," Alex went on, "there is the sound system to be installed. The acoustics here are very good, like in the old Greek theatres—the hills cast back the sound like the sides of a bowl, you understand, but with the microphones we can be certain everyone will hear. And then there are the dressing-rooms to finish. Nothing structural there, but they badly need paint and a bit of updating."

Rupert said he couldn't wait to see them. "I did try to have a look, but all the doors back there are locked."

"Pietro is protective of his tools," said Alex, and the sudden whine of some electric tool from down the gangway served as emphasis, reminding us that Pietro himself was still very much in evidence, backstage.

Den glanced towards the noise. "Yeah, well, he needs to learn some manners."

"I'm sorry he gave you a scare." It was the second time that Alex had been forced to make apologies for somebody who worked for him, I thought. It must have been an irritation, but he handled it with class. "It won't happen again."

Rupert said it was lucky that Alex had happened along when he did.

"Yes, I was looking out the window when the two of you went by"—this he addressed to Den and me—"and I could see that you were coming here, and that's when I remembered I'd forgotten to say anything last night about the theatre being off-limits. And then Pietro went by, after you, and so . . ." His shrug was full of meaning.

Rupert remarked that the theatre seemed to be a popular place this morning. "I only came to have a poke about, myself. I don't know what these two are doing, but—"

"We came to measure the stage," I explained. "So Den could do his marking out in the rehearsal room."

Rupert looked at Den. "Oh, yes?"

"That's right." Rummaging round in his jacket pocket,

Den produced a tape measure and held it up for Rupert with a smile before passing one end to me. "Celia, would you take this and go stand at the edge of the stage, please?"

Alex watched while we measured. "I thought that I sent you the designer's ground plan."

"Did you? I must have misplaced it," said Den. "Anyhow, there's no harm in checking things twice." Taking note of a number, he ordered me round to another position while I tried to keep my face straight. What a brat, I was thinking—he'd had the theatre measurements all along, he hadn't needed me at all. This whole escapade had been Den's way of getting me down here, with him, on my own.

Away from Rupert, I was guessing. Only Rupert wasn't stupid, he'd spent too many years being my chaperon to miss a trick. Stepping forward casually he said, "Here, let me help you with that, Dennis. I'm sure Celia has other things to do."

I surrendered my end of the measuring tape without argument, privately amused by his unwarranted concern, but when I would have pointed out that I had nowhere else to be just now, Alex said, "I'm heading back myself, if you'd like to walk with me."

That rather changed things. "Yes, I would," I told him. "Thanks." And reaching up I took the hand that he was offering to help me up and off the stage.

ix

I don't recall that anything momentous happened on that walk back to the house. Alex said something about the weather being cold for this time of year, and I said something nice about the gardens, and I asked him where the dogs were, and he told me that he'd kennelled them because they couldn't go where he had gone. And that was that.

But by the time we reached the terrace I was hopelessly infatuated. His quiet hazel eyes, the way he walked, the way he held his head to one side when he listened, made me feel all tangled-up inside and foolish. Foolish enough to be thinking again of Sally's tarot reading, and her 'man with light brown hair.' *The King of Cups . . . a businessman,* she'd said, *but with an interest in the arts.* Well, that was Alex, wasn't it? Serious on the outside, emotional inside. *He's at the bottom of all of this,* Sally had said—my foundation.

I tried not to go all adolescent over him, but the smile I gave when I thanked him for walking me back was a little too bright. He surprised me by smiling himself.

"You're very welcome. I enjoyed the company."

The terrace wasn't empty. Nicholas was there already, leaning on the parapet. "Teresa's been looking for you," he told Alex. "It's got something to do with a Mrs. Forlani's car."

I looked at Alex, curious. "Mrs. Forlani? Of the Trust, you mean? She's here?"

"Yes, she likes to come by every month or so, to check the progress of the workmen. You'll meet her at lunch."

She must be a very old lady, I thought, considering the age that her husband had been when he died. She'd be doing well to make it up the terrace steps.

Alex said, "You will excuse me?" and moved past me and into the house, presumably to look for Teresa to sort out the problem. Because I didn't want to appear to be following him, I stayed behind with Nicholas. He wasn't looking terribly sociable, but I didn't let that put me off. If I was going to work with him and Madeleine, I thought, then I would have to start behaving as their equal.

I strolled over to the parapet to join him, nonchalant. "We've been down to the theatre."

"Oh, yes? I wondered where everyone had got to. Den and Rupert, too?"

I nodded. "They're still down there, measuring."

"I haven't seen the theatre yet. We meant to go have a look yesterday, Maddy and I, but what with the maid crisis here and you lot showing up, we just never got round to it. Maybe we'll have another go at it this afternoon."

"Oh no, you can't. That is," I said, "the workmen will be finishing the stage today, so the theatre's off-limits—we weren't even supposed to be down there this morning, but nobody told us."

Nicholas had raised his eyebrows, as though marvelling at the audacity of an upstart like myself telling him what he could and couldn't do. "It's an open-air theatre, isn't it? Well then, they can hardly prevent us from taking a look. Or are there guards with guns?"

Unscathed by the sarcasm, I said, "Very nearly." And I told him how we'd almost been assaulted by that giant of a man, Pietro.

"Ah yes, Pietro." Nicholas pulled a face and paused to light a cigarette. "We ran into him, too, Maddy and I, the first night we were here—we came round a bend in the garden path and wham! There he was. It didn't half give me a turn, I can tell you."

I thought running into Pietro would give anyone a turn, and said so.

Nicholas agreed. "Ugly bastard, isn't he? He'd make a perfect Caliban."

The reference caught me off my guard. It was exactly how I'd have cast Pietro myself, in my Shakespeare game—as

Caliban, the brutish vengeful monster from *The Tempest*—but I hadn't expected that Nicholas would share my quirk of assigning people roles. I looked at him with a new interest.

Perhaps, I thought, he wasn't so shallow, after all. Perhaps he was someone worth getting to know. I might have misinterpreted his character, and been too quick to judge.

I was watching him, thinking this, when he lifted his head and looked past me. "Ah, there you are, darling. I wondered what was keeping you."

I turned and saw Madeleine's glance flick between us, unreadable, as she came across the terrace. Like a child accused unfairly of a wrongdoing, I wanted to explain, to let her know I didn't fancy Nicholas, that we'd only been talking—to shout to the world that I wasn't my mother.

But I sensed that my words, even if I'd had the courage to say them out loud, would have fallen on deaf ears. Madeleine appeared to be preoccupied. And as she drew nearer I could see that it was even more than that—her troubled frown was anything but absent. "I'm sorry." Her apology came automatically, the force of manners overriding her more personal concerns. "I've had a call from Poppy's school."

Nicholas reverted to his former shallow self. "Oh yes? And what has she done now?"

"She's got glandular fever."

"Poor thing," I said, in sympathy. I'd been spared that particular disease as a child, but one of my classmates had suffered through it. She'd missed a whole term.

"Rotten luck." That was Nicholas, blowing a smoke ring. "But it's hardly a fatal complaint, and the school does have a nurse."

Madeleine was only half-listening. Brushing a curl of dark hair from her forehead with a worried hand, she went on, "They said that she's been asking for me, wanting me. I don't know what to do."

"Darling, there's nothing you *can* do."

"I could bring her here."

He looked at her as if she'd gone quite mad. "We're rehearsing a play."

"Yes, I know, but I won't be rehearsing all day, every

day—I'll have time to look after her. She'll likely be in bed sleeping most of the time."

"And if we all come down with glandular fever? What then?"

I cut in. "It's a child's disease, really. Adults don't usually catch it."

Nicholas didn't thank me for the intrusion. Still looking at Madeleine, he said, "I just don't see why you have to—"

"Because she's my daughter."

I tried to imagine my own mother standing there, facing down a boyfriend with the simple explanation: 'Because she's my daughter.' I couldn't, of course.

And then Madeleine turned her head slightly and our eyes met, and I felt the strangest feeling of connection, as though she knew that I was on her side. "I'll ask Alex if he minds," she said.

Alex's voice asked, "If I mind what?"

He'd come out onto the terrace so quietly I hadn't even heard him, and he stood now a few yards away, looking from one to the other of us expectantly. He wasn't alone.

A woman had come with him, a young woman in a red dress with sunglasses hiding her eyes as she raised her hand to elegantly flick her long dark hair behind her shoulder.

I found myself staring, not only because she was with Alex, although I wasn't altogether pleased by the fact, but because I was certain I'd seen her before. And then I remembered: I'd seen her in Venice. The woman in yellow who'd been in the basilica, and later, at the restaurant.

A little stunned by the coincidence, I took the opportunity, in the brief interval while Madeleine explained the problem of her daughter's illness, to study the woman. I don't think she noticed, although of course with the sunglasses I couldn't see her eyes. Still, I didn't imagine that this was the sort of woman who would notice other people anyway. She had a bored expression that reminded me of Mother, of someone with a narrow, self-reflected view of life who'd grown accustomed to admiring stares and, when looking at crowds, saw not faces but one single entity.

She didn't shake our hands, but merely stood apart and

nodded when Alex, having assured Madeleine that of course her daughter must come to Il Piacere, introduced us round. He finished, "Everyone, may I present Daniela Forlani."

Again I could feel myself staring. Daniela Forlani! That couldn't be right, I thought. Leonardo Forlani had been in his nineties; his widow couldn't possibly be this woman, who looked thirty and probably wasn't much older. She had to be his daughter, surely. She couldn't be—

"Daniela's late husband was the founder of the Trust that is restoring this estate," said Alex. "She likes to visit now and then, to keep us all in line."

"Oh, *caro,* no, you know that is not true," she told him, in a languid voice whose command of English fell somewhere between Teresa's and Alex's—more educated than the housekeeper's, and with a better sense of structure, but still heavily accented. "No. I come because you spoil me so."

Nicholas frowned very faintly. "You will excuse me, but you did say your name was Forlani? I thought that here in Italy a woman didn't take her husband's name."

An eyebrow arched at the question. "This was my name as well, before I married. The families are, I believe, distantly related." Her tone implied it hardly mattered, and was certainly none of his business.

But Nicholas seemed to have taken an interest. Money, I thought, was more heady than any perfume. He shifted his long body against the parapet. "So you'll be in the ladies' wing, too, then?"

Her dark head turned a fraction till her sunglasses reflected his image. "No," she said, as though the very thought were quite absurd, "I stay in the villa."

The Villa delle Tempeste, I presumed. A good place for her. I had the feeling she'd be quite adept at brewing storms. I was wondering what had become of the man she had been with in Venice, the man with the heart-shaped bald spot, when Madeleine smiled and asked politely, "Have you only just arrived?"

I waited to hear what Daniela Forlani would answer—whether she'd mention where she'd come from, that she'd been in Venice. But she chose not to answer at all, as though

Madeleine hadn't said anything that needed a response. Clicking open her handbag she drew out a packet of long filtered cigarettes, shook one loose and lit it with a snap of her silver lighter. Inhaling elegantly, she moved to the parapet, the red of her dress vivid against the pointed dark spears of the cypresses that steeply dropped towards the lake. "There will be rain this afternoon," she said, and indeed it appeared that the weather was turning. A haze of cloud masked the summits of the mountains in the distance, and the colour of the lake had changed from blue to duller grey.

The air, too, felt colder, but I couldn't be sure whether that was the weather or simply Daniela Forlani.

X

"WELL, I'll tell you," said Den, "if she wasn't already taken, I'd be going after her myself." He gave a whistle of appreciation as he knelt again and went on with the marking out, using chalk to trace the stage's outline on the bare wood floor of our rehearsal room. Rupert and I were assisting, Rupert reading out the measurements while I, as before, held one end of the measuring tape.

Ordinarily the marking-out was done with coloured tape, but the floor of this room was such a marvel of polished parquetry that Den had been afraid of doing damage, so he'd opted for the chalk. He'd have to keep doing it over, as it wore off, but it seemed a small price to pay to safeguard the beauty of this room.

Like many of the rooms at Il Piacere, this one had a name: The Stanza degli Angeli, the Room of Angels. Unconsciously I found myself fingering my necklace, the little angel pendant Bryan had given me for my birthday, as I looked around at all the other angels that surrounded me. They hovered high above in the hand-painted ceiling, and smiled from the plaster rosettes set like pearls at the centre of each ceiling panel, and fluttered their wings round the huge gilded frames of the mirrors that lined every wall. My little gold-and-diamond guardian angel was, I thought, in quite elegant company.

Rupert was saying now, drily, to Den, that anyone who'd been at lunch with us an hour ago would have thought that he *was* going after Daniela Forlani. "You're not exactly subtle."

Den glanced up and grinned. "I was only being polite." Resuming his work he added, "But at least I've got one of my questions answered, now. I've been wondering what would make a guy like D'Ascanio hand over his family estate to the Forlani Trust . . . I mean, it's such a crazy thing to do, unless you're short of money, and that doesn't seem to be the case with him. Only now that I've seen what the Trust uses for bait, I can understand why he bit. Celia, honey, can you give me just a few more inches? There, that's great. Thanks." Glancing up again he said, to me, "You're awfully quiet."

"Am I? It's that lunch, I expect. Makes me drowsy."

I *was* feeling draggy and slow, though I expected my silence had more to do with Daniela Forlani than anything else; with the way that she had smiled and talked with Alex over lunch, and with my learning that she'd actually arrived at the Villa delle Tempeste last night, and that hers had doubtless been the light I'd noticed from my window, the light that had drawn Alex down from the terrace and into the gardens. And if I'd needed proof of that, the fact he'd left the dogs behind rather clinched things—Daniela had made it quite clear over lunch that she didn't much care for the greyhounds. Which meant Alex had probably been with her this morning as well, I thought, recalling how he'd told me he had kennelled Max and Nero because he couldn't take them where he'd gone. In fact, for all I knew he'd spent the night there, at the villa, with Daniela. It could very well have been *her* window he'd been looking out when he'd seen Den and me pass by on our way to the theatre.

I hadn't said anything, at lunch, about having seen her in Venice, or about her male companion with the heart-shaped bald spot. It wasn't my business, any of it. And besides, if she was with Alex, then however disappointed I might be, I wasn't going to interfere. I didn't make plays for other women's men. I wasn't Mother.

Rupert told me, "You should go and have a lie-down. We can manage."

"No, I'm fine." To prove it, I looked round and said, "I'm guessing that this was a ballroom?"

The answer came, not from Den or from Rupert, but from the doorway behind me. "My grandfather practised his fencing here," Alex said. "I'm told he was not fond of dancing."

I wheeled, and found him watching me.

He asked, "Does that disappoint you?"

"Not actually, no." I had an easier time imagining Galeazzo D'Ascanio fighting his reflection here than waltzing. From what I'd read of him in his biographies, he hadn't been particularly social, and for all he'd loved throwing wild and decadent parties, I thought it far more likely he'd have stood against the wall and watched, as his grandson was doing right now.

The dogs were at his side again, their long tails wagging. Max, the bolder one, took a step closer, accepting the invitation of my outstretched hand. As I petted the smooth brindled head Alex said, "He's not usually so friendly."

A few hours earlier I would have responded in kind to the tone of his voice, the rare smile, but now that I knew he was attached, I was careful to do nothing that could be considered flirting. "Yes, well, dogs can always tell the people who like them, can't they?"

And then I bit my tongue because that could have been taken as being a shot at Daniela Forlani—too close to Mother's cattiness for comfort.

Alex studied me a moment; turned to Rupert. "I have time now, if you'd like to come and choose the furniture, the tables and the chairs, that you would like to have in here for your rehearsals. I can have someone bring the things down later on."

I wondered who he would get to do that. He must surely be running out of servants, with the maid and his driver still missing. I didn't say anything out loud, of course, but Den had no such reservations.

"I can carry one end of a table, if you're running short of bodies," he offered cheerfully. "Still no sign of Giancarlo, I take it? Teresa was saying that sometimes he goes off for weeks at a time, is that right?"

"It has been known to happen." Alex tipped his head to one side. "When were you talking to Teresa?"

"Oh, just before lunch, for a minute. I was dying for a cup of coffee, and she made me one."

"You must have impressed her," said Alex, with the faintest of smiles. "Like Max, she usually isn't so friendly with strangers."

"She's friendly with me." Den scratched his head and flashed a boyish smile. "Guess I'm just lucky. Hey, speaking of coffee, Rupert, do you think you could grab me a cup on your way back from picking the furniture?"

Rupert hadn't looked too eager to go and do anything, but his professionalism won out over any reluctance he might have had to leave me in the room alone with Den. "Certainly. Celia? Would you like a coffee, too?"

"No, thanks, I'm fine."

"Right, I shouldn't be long."

"Take as long as you like," Den invited, with a wink. He really couldn't help himself, I supposed, as I watched him complete his chalk circle. When Rupert and Alex had gone he stood, brushing the dust from his hands. "There, that's it for the stage. Now I just have to figure out where the gangway goes."

I handed him the measurements to study. "So you've been chatting up Teresa, have you?"

"Just getting the gossip. She told me something interesting about the maid who's done a bunk—it seems the girl was hot and heavy with Pietro. Yeah," he said, as he saw my expression, "that's what I thought, too. I can't imagine any woman wanting to be with the guy, but there you go. There's someone for everyone, that's what they say. Anyhow, Teresa said the girl had been upset for a couple of days, so she thinks they'd had some kind of lovers' quarrel, and that's why the girl disappeared."

Having seen Pietro, I was inclined to think the maid had done the wisest thing. I had a sudden thought. "Next time you're talking to Teresa, see if you can find out why she doesn't like me."

Den took his end of the measuring tape and began backing up, with his eyes on the numbers. "It's not you," he said, shaking his head. "It's the ghost."

"Sorry?"

"She's got this idea that Celia Sands—the first one—is still hanging around her old rooms. You know, haunting the place."

"Ah." I remembered the emphatic way Teresa had told me

that my rooms were no place for guests. How had she put it, exactly? *Things happen.* "And what makes her think that?"

"She told me that she'd had a few . . . experiences. She didn't go into the details. Why, would you like me to ask her about it?"

"No, it doesn't matter, really." I didn't believe in ghosts.

"She's quite a character, Teresa is. What role did you give her?"

Again I looked lost and said, "Sorry?"

"In that game you play, the Shakespeare game."

"How did you know about that?"

"Rupert told us. Last night," he said, "after dinner—you'd gone up to your room, I think, and we all got talking about Shakespeare, I can't remember why, but Rupert told us how you're always giving roles to people."

"Ah." There was really no cause to be angry with Rupert, I thought. There was nothing particularly private about my game—all my friends knew I did it, and Rupert would never have purposely done anything to embarrass me. But I did feel embarrassed. I was so much younger than everyone here, and so much less accomplished, and I hadn't especially wanted them to know all my childish habits. Something stirred my memory. "Was Nicholas there, too, last night?"

"Yeah, why?"

"Oh, no reason." But that explained why, on the terrace this morning, he'd made that comment about Pietro being a perfect Caliban, and why he'd smiled when he'd said it. He'd been playing a game of his own, I thought. Which meant my first impression had been right: he was a rat. Like Bryan always told me, first impressions were the ones to trust. I smiled at Den. "In answer to your question, I haven't given any role to Teresa, not yet."

"She's a tough one," he admitted. "Not like you."

"Oh, yes? And how would you cast me?" I waited for him to pick one of the obvious ones—Juliet, or Ophelia, or—

"Cordelia," he said, without missing a beat.

Youngest daughter of King Lear. The loyal one, the one who had the kindest heart. I was flattered. "Wait a minute, though . . . didn't she get poisoned at the end?"

"I don't think you're in any immediate danger." He marked out his lines on the floor for the gangway. "There, we just need the furniture, now." As he knelt to replace the page of stage measurements in the ring binder he'd brought with him, he said, "Oh, hey, I almost forgot. Here you go, you'll need this for tomorrow."

I took the single page he handed me, a labyrinth of lines. "What's this?"

"A map of the hallways, from your room to this one."

He was nothing, I thought, if not meticulous. "You think I'll get lost, do you?"

"Not if you follow that map, you won't."

With a smile at the drawing I folded it over and tucked it away in my pocket.

xi

I got lost on my way to rehearsal next morning.

To be fair, in a house like Il Piacere my only hope of finding my way round would have been to leave a trail of biscuit crumbs or unwind a ball of thread behind me, like Theseus in the maze of the Minotaur. Of course, I could have used Den's map, but at the moment it was doing service as a bookmark in the little red volume of Galeazzo's Celia poems sitting on my bedside table. I'd been falling asleep last night reading the poems, and the map, neatly folded, had been right there beside me, and I'd put it in to hold my place, not thinking. And this morning I'd forgotten where it was, and what I'd done with it. I'd only just remembered now.

The problem was, I thought as I came round another bend in the dim corridor, that now I was lost, and about to be late.

I quickened my pace, spurred by the same irrational impulse that made me drive faster whenever I took a wrong turn, as though my mind had already dismissed everything around me as unfamiliar and was eager to look round the next corner. I knew I'd gone wrong because I wasn't in a corridor any longer, I was passing through a chain of formal rooms, eerily quiet and empty and smelling of polish and dusty old draperies. Confused, I stopped and nearly turned to double back . . . but then I heard a small and reassuring sound, as welcome as the beacon of a lighthouse to a sailor, certain evidence another human being was nearby: the industrious clacking of a computer's keyboard.

I tracked it to a closed door on my right. The clacking stopped, but I heard movement, someone walking on a creaking floor and a snuffling sound that *wasn't* human. Alex, I thought, and the dogs. I hesitated, not altogether sure that I wanted to let Alex know I was lost, but the pressures of time overrode my reluctance. I was raising my hand to knock when the door opened suddenly, making me jump.

He was startled as well, but he recovered more quickly than I did. "Good morning."

"Good morning. I—"

"Shouldn't you be at rehearsal?" He checked his watch. "I thought it was supposed to start at ten."

"It was. It is. I mean, that's the problem, I can't find the room . . ."

"Ah." His nod held comprehension. "You came down the main staircase, did you? You should have turned right at the bottom, not left, that's all." He raised a hand as though to direct me back again, then appeared to think better of it. Stepping fully through the door he pulled it closed behind him. "I think it might be simpler if I showed you."

Following, I tried to keep track of the route we were taking, back into one of the rooms I'd just come through then out by a different door into a short passage that in turn brought us into a cloister-like corridor looking down over an idyllic courtyard . . . but these things only registered in part. I was much more aware of the time and the man at my side, of his breathing and the way he walked and how often the dogs at his knee sought his hands. Bryan always said a dog could tell you more about a man than people could. "You can fool another person," he'd once told me, "but you'll never fool a dog. They know the stuff you're really made of."

I found myself wondering whether, in Daniela Forlani's case, it was a matter of her not liking the greyhounds, or of them not liking *her.*

I said, "It's kind of you to do this, really. I didn't mean to interrupt your work."

"I was finished. And anyway, I was only on the computer reading my mail."

"Oh, you have e-mail?" I said that too quickly, and with rather too much interest.

Alex noticed. "Is there someone you would like to send a message to?"

"No, no, it's not—"

"You are most welcome," he invited me. "It wouldn't be a problem."

"Well . . ." I thought for a moment, then finally caved in. "If you're sure . . . I mean, thank you, I'd love to send something to Bryan. I'm sure he's dying to know how we're getting on. We rang him from Venice, of course, and I know Roo was planning to phone at the weekend, but it's so expensive talking on the telephone and he does have his computer at the flat . . ." My voice trailed off as it occurred to me that Alex might not know who Bryan was; that he might not, in fact, know anything of Rupert's private life. Even in these more enlightened times in our society, not everyone approved.

But Alex's expression hadn't changed. "No problem," he said. We'd arrived at the foot of the stairs I'd come down from the first floor. "So now you go this way," he told me, "and turn, and the passage will bring you right into the Stanza degli Angeli." He angled his wrist and looked down at his watch. "You still have two minutes. You'll get there on time."

"Thanks."

"You do get a break before lunch?" he asked, as I was turning.

I paused. "Yes, I think so. A short one."

"Come then if you like and I'll help you to e-mail your friend. You'll remember the way?"

"Heavens, no. I've a horrible sense of direction. But not to worry," I said. "I'll just come to this stairway and then try to find my way back to the rehearsal room."

I think his smile surprised him, too. He looked at that instant unguarded, approachable. Only I knew that I couldn't approach him in the way I would have liked to. The moment passed.

Still, watching him walk off, the two dogs trotting at his side, I felt the stirring of a feeling that I recognized—a faint but certain tightness in my chest that almost tingled. Damn, I thought. I didn't *want* to be attracted to the man. No good

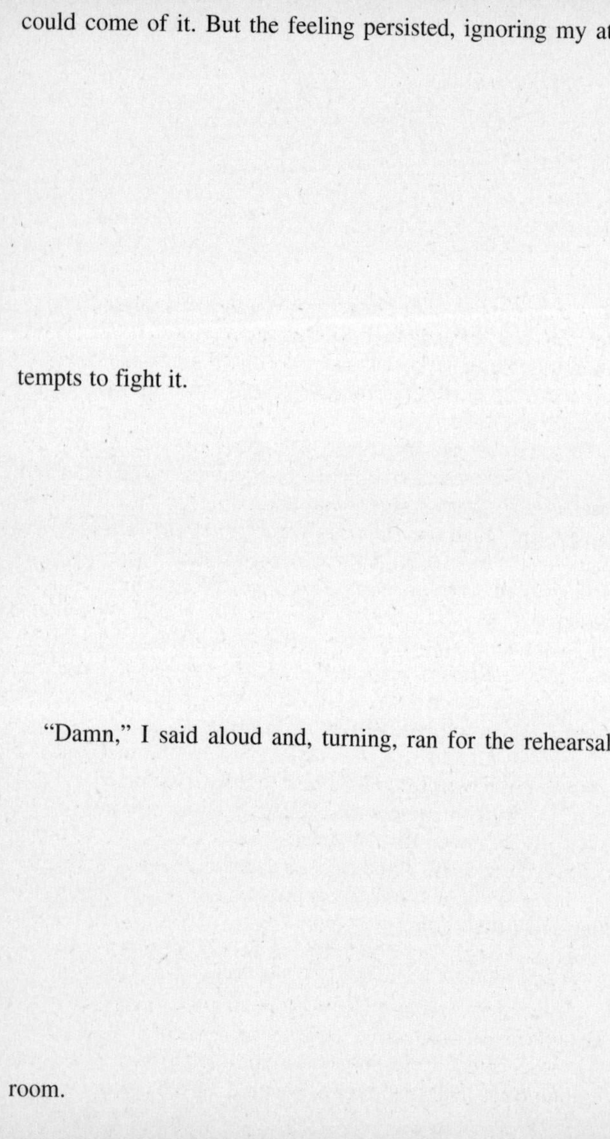

could come of it. But the feeling persisted, ignoring my attempts to fight it.

"Damn," I said aloud and, turning, ran for the rehearsal room.

xii

FIRST rehearsals always made me nervous. It didn't matter that I had already met the other actors, or that Rupert was directing, or that all we had to do this first time out was sit around a table reading through the play out loud. I still felt beastly nervous.

For one thing, there were strangers present. Everybody came to first rehearsal—the people who would be in charge of make-up and our costumes and the set design, they all turned up this first time out, although we mightn't see many of them until the final days before performance. They were all friendly, all fairly young, all Italian, though none of them came from the town and the one who lived furthest away had had to come from Verona this morning, which must have been a fair drive for him. Rupert introduced us round, but though I shook their hands and smiled I didn't retain any faces or names. My mind just wouldn't concentrate.

The room didn't help. In this echoing space with the mirrors all round me I couldn't help feeling small and insignificant, a child in grown-up clothing, fooling no one. And it didn't help, either, that Madeleine was sitting directly across from me, graceful, composed, every inch the professional.

For assistance I looked heavenward, my eyes seeking the angels in the ceiling paintings—more cherubs than angels, with soft wings and sweet childish faces that offered encouragement.

Rupert was talking. Having already shown us the overall design for the production, he'd moved on to the finer points. "... And that, I think, covers the rules and procedures. Is everyone clear on those? Good. If you do have a problem, just let Dennis know. Are there any objections to Nicholas smoking?" he asked without breaking stride, as Nicholas, rocking back in his chair at the opposite end of the table, touched the flame of his lighter to a cigarette.

The pause that followed held surprise. From the look on Nicholas's face I could tell it had never occurred to him to ask permission; he was used to doing as he pleased.

"Right," said Rupert, when no one objected. "Then I think we'll get on with the read-through. I'm going to let you just feel your way through this first time, let you make the first contact with your character, and we'll see how that goes, all right? Dennis, would you call the cues, please?"

Rupert settled back as Den picked up his stopwatch and started us off with a brilliant imitation of a chiming clock, the sound that first opened the play. Some stage managers, when calling cues, would simply read 'A clock chimes four' and be done with it, but Den's way was better. It helped set the mood.

I set my script flat on the table to hide the fact my hands were shaking, took a deep breath and read out the first line. My voice came out flat, rather tense, not at all what I'd wanted; the harder I tried to correct it, the worse it became. And it went on like that, with me stumbling over the words and Madeleine coming back smoothly while everyone else simply followed along. I could feel them all watching me, wondering why in God's name I'd been given the part—or at least, that's what I would have wondered, in their place. I couldn't even bear to raise my eyes to look at Rupert; didn't want to face his pity or, worse still, his disappointment.

Head down and desperate I soldiered on, reading too quickly in my effort to get to the end of the first act, to the séance scene in which Nicholas's character would at last come in, beginning as a disembodied offstage voice, then making a dramatic appearance in the flesh at the next-to-last line, relieving the long unbroken dialogue between myself and Madeleine.

Only when he finally spoke it didn't come as a relief. If anything, it threw me more off balance.

Nicholas read without any expression—his voice was a monotone, lifeless and dull. I had friends who knew actors who did this, kept their first readings free of emotion so as not to commit themselves to any particular interpretation of their character; but I'd never had somebody do it with *me*. It was highly unnerving.

"Well," said Rupert, as I miserably spoke the last line of Act One, "I think that's as good a place as any for a break, don't you?"

Den agreed. "I'll go see if Teresa can make us some tea."

Thank heavens I had an excuse to escape, I reminded myself, gratefully remembering Alex's invitation to come e-mail Bryan when we had our break. I stood, self-conscious. "I think I'll go and stretch my legs a bit."

Rupert nodded his consent. Nicholas, in the act of lighting a cigarette, didn't react at all. The others merely smiled. But Madeleine pushed back her chair. "I'll come with you."

I hadn't planned on that. I must have looked a bit confused, because she said, "That is, if you don't mind?"

And what, I wondered, could I say to that? Except, "Of course I don't." The problem was, I thought as we left the mirrored ballroom and went out into the corridor—the problem was that now I couldn't do what I had meant to do. I couldn't take Madeleine with me to Alex's study, not after I'd said I just wanted to go stretch my legs. But if not to Alex's study, then where . . . ?

"Let's go out to the terrace," said Madeleine. "I could do with a breath of fresh air."

xiii

SHE had clearly been learning her way round the house. Whereas I would have got all turned around trying to decide which way was which, Madeleine simply opened a door from the corridor and led me through an empty room whose long French windows opened out directly to the terrace.

The stones were still wet with the rain that had fallen at breakfast, and the heavy mist clung to the darkly treed hillside behind us and shrouded the opposite shore of the lake. The high golden walls of the house at my back showed the only real colour, and even that had flattened in the absence of the sun. But for the present, anyway, the rain had stopped, and the breeze blew clean and cool and had a brisk, reviving scent.

Madeleine breathed it in deeply and tipped her face up like a child. "That's better. I can't stay too long in a room without windows." She stretched and moved forwards to stand by the parapet.

Even just standing at rest she commanded attention, I thought bleakly. I could never look like that. Oh, why had I taken this part? Madeleine and Nicholas were in another league, I'd never match them in performance. Kicking myself, I looked up and across at the mist-covered mountains, only half-aware that Madeleine was speaking.

". . . And Rupert reminds me so much of the man who directed my first West End play—he was quiet, like Rupert, but brilliant, and here I was barely nineteen with my first leading role and they had me playing opposite Sebastian Boyd, of all people, and I was absolutely terrified. I wanted so badly to please everyone that I went all to pieces." Her voice was quite light, and her gaze was still turned to the lake, and she might have been simply relating an anecdote. Only I knew better. Focussing my full attention on her, I stayed silent as she went on, "By the end of the first week I was certain they were going to recast my part, I was that awful. And then one day Sebastian came up to me after rehearsal—I'll never forget, he'd grown a beard for the play and he had those fierce eyebrows, you know, and he looked just like Moses come down from the mountain to give me an earful. I felt sure he was going to tell me I'd chosen the wrong line of work. But he didn't. He asked me," she said, with a smile of remembrance, "if I'd ever heard the fable of the old man and the donkey. You know the one, about the old man and his grandson and the donkey, and they're going along and someone they meet says that one of them ought to be riding the donkey, so the old man puts the boy on the donkey and the next person they pass says how horrible, look at that young able boy on the donkey and the old man struggling along. So the boy gets down and the old man rides the donkey, and of course that doesn't do either, because the next person thinks that the little boy shouldn't be made to walk; so they *both* get on the donkey, and then everyone says oh, how cruel, to make the donkey carry so much weight. And in the end I think they wind up carrying the donkey, and they have a fall, or something, and then none of them can ride. At any rate," she said, "Sebastian asked me did I know the fable, and I told him yes, I did. And he said, 'Well then'"—she did a fair imitation of the venerable Shakespearean actor, catching his booming voice and trademark glare—"'Well then, stop worrying so much what the rest of us think; just get on the damned donkey and ride it.'" She turned her head then, and her smile was deliberately kind. "I always thought that good advice," she said.

I thought it good advice as well, and took it.

Back in the rehearsal room I shut my mind to everyone else and, ignoring Nicholas's deadpan delivery, gave myself over to reading the part. The second and third acts went off like a dream. When I'd finished I looked up and saw Rupert's eyes and I knew I'd done well.

"Very good," he said, pleased. "Very good, everyone. After lunch, we'll go back then and take it by scenes, all right?"

A chair scraped beside me as Den rose and stretched with a grin. "That was one hell of a comeback," he murmured. "What did Madeleine *do* to you at break?"

"Nothing," I said. "We just talked."

"I thought maybe she was out there feeding you triple martinis, or something, to make you relax." His grin grew broader as he reached an arm across to hug my shoulders. "Good work, anyway. You'll do just fine."

The tempting smells of roasting meat came wafting through the passage as we left the rehearsal room, beckoning us to our lunch, but there was something I needed to do first. "I'll catch you up—won't be a minute," I said to the others, and parting from them went the other way along the corridor.

xiv

I had no guarantee, of course, that Alex would even still be there. He'd said to come at morning break, and not at noon, but even so I thought it worth a try.

For once I had no trouble finding my way—the rooms, as before, led neatly one into the other, the thickly laid carpets hushing my steps as I moved through the dust-scented shadows. Only this time, as I was approaching the closed door of the room that I assumed was Alex's office or study, I saw someone else coming, too, from the other direction. A man, middle-aged, wearing working clothes.

He didn't see me. I was still a good room-length away, and at any rate he wasn't looking up. His head was bent as though in thought, his walk purposeful. Reaching Alex's door he knocked and then, not waiting for an answer, opened the door and looked in. In profile his face had a fierce, hawk-like quality, helped by the hooked nose and hard, thin-lipped mouth.

He said something urgent and sharp, Alex answered, and then with a slight frown the hawk-faced man went in and shut the door behind him.

Probably one of the workmen, I thought, with a problem. Not wanting to interrupt their business for something as frivolous as my e-mail to Bryan, I turned again, retreating quietly through the semidarkened rooms, and let my stomach lead me through the twisting corridors to where the others had already gathered in the dining room for lunch.

XV

THE afternoon flew.

Six o'clock came quickly, and before I knew it everyone was packing up their scripts and getting to their feet with yawns and stretches, and the Italians were shaking our hands again and saying their goodbyes, and that was that. The first day over.

I debated whether I should try one more time to reach Alex in his study, but in the end I reasoned that he probably wouldn't be there anymore, so I went upstairs instead to bathe and change, telling myself I could talk to him later, at dinner.

But he wasn't at dinner. His chair at the head of the table stayed empty while our starters were served, and when Rupert asked Teresa if we shouldn't wait she shook her head and answered something back to the effect that Signor D'Ascanio had been called out on business and wouldn't be joining us.

Teresa seemed more sociable today. She had a young woman helping her with the serving tonight—a quietly nervous young woman whose tentative movements reminded me of the time I'd been in training myself as a waitress. The new maid, I assumed, and her presence explained why Teresa looked less strained.

Looking at the two empty chairs near the head of the table, I found myself wondering what sort of business had called Alex away this evening, and whether he was alone, but my wondering stopped when Daniela Forlani arrived, coming late to the table with the nonchalance of someone who was used to having others adapt to her schedule.

Again, as before, her appearance distracted the men. All except Rupert, of course, and even he seemed to find her of interest, eyeing her the way he might admire a classic sculpture. And that didn't make me like her any better.

She sat—I thought deliberately—between Nicholas and Madeleine, and shaking out her napkin asked for wine. "This rain makes me cold, and I have spent much time outdoors today with my men, to see how they progress with their work."

Rupert, always first to get a conversation started, asked her if her men lived in the town.

"No, here," she corrected him. "Here in the grounds. If you take the path down towards my villa, you will pass the outhouses where they stay."

Den glanced up from his plate, eyebrow lifting. "Your men stay in outhouses?"

Rupert was smiling. "Not American outhouses, Dennis. They're not outdoor lavs, they're just outbuildings on the estate."

"Well, why didn't you say so?" Den grinned.

Daniela, unconcerned with the differences between British and American English, took a look around. "Where is Alessandro?"

Rupert said, "Teresa told us he'd been called away."

"Oh, yes? I hope he is not late," she said. "He promised to come down and light my fires tonight." I thought that a remarkably racy statement for her to make in the company of strangers, until I looked at her face and realized she wasn't aware of the English double meaning of the phrase. To our raised eyebrows, she explained, "The fires in my house are so old, I cannot make them light. And it is still so cold for spring."

Den leaned forwards, all charm. "I could come and take a look at them, if you like. I'm not too bad at lighting fires." The double meaning came across more plainly in his words, but once again Daniela missed it, acknowledging his offer with a wave of one manicured hand.

"Oh, no, it is all right. It will be easier for Alessandro, he has done it many times."

Den lifted his wineglass and murmured, "I'm sure he has,

the lucky bastard." Then more clearly, he asked, "Do you always stay down in the villa? Why not in the main house?"

She shrugged. "I am used to much space. To have only one room to myself, that I would not like."

She must, I thought, be used to quite a lot of space, to judge the rooms of Il Piacere as being too small, too confining. My own suite was larger by half than my flat. I said aloud, "Your work must keep you busy."

"Yes, I am always travelling. This past week alone I have been to Sardinia, Rome." Still no mention of Venice, I thought. She went on, "The Trust has many properties. But that is good. It was the wish of my late husband that the most beautiful homes of our country be kept for all Italians to enjoy. He would be very happy that we have Il Piacere. He was a great admirer of Alessandro's grandfather."

They'd both had a lech for young women, I thought. Although in Daniela's late husband's case, it had probably been the other way around. I might be willing to believe that Celia the First had stayed with Galeazzo out of love, but from my short acquaintance with Daniela I somehow doubted love had been the motive for her marriage to an old and wealthy man. I doubted, too, that love had any role to play in her relationship with Alex. He was wealthy, too.

Madeleine was asking, "Where will Alex live, when the Trust takes possession of Il Piacere? Do you know?"

"He has other homes, of course," Daniela said, her tone implying that everyone had a few homes scattered round. "And he will have the use of this one for his lifetime." Switching subjects out of boredom, she asked Madeleine in turn, "I am told your daughter comes this weekend, this is true?"

Madeleine confirmed it with a smile. "Alex has been very kind in making the arrangements."

"And this will not interfere with your work, having a child to look after?"

"Oh, I shouldn't think so. I expect she'll be sleeping for most of the time. She's got glandular fever."

Den looked over. "What's glandular fever?"

Rupert, again translating British to American, said, "Mononucleosis."

"Oh. Yeah, mono knocks you flat on your back, poor kid."

"If she actually has it," said Nicholas. "I wouldn't put it past Poppy to fake being ill just to get what she wants."

Madeleine sighed. "Nicky . . ."

"I'm only saying."

"Poppy?" Daniela arched her eyebrows. "This is your daughter's name? It is peculiar."

Madeleine only smiled politely and went on with her dinner, but I couldn't help cutting in, "I think it's a lovely name, actually."

"Celia," said Rupert, "could you pass the carrots, please?"

"I'd have loved to have had a name like Poppy, something distinctive, instead of having to share the name Celia with three other girls in my class."

"But then," Daniela said, "you would not have been given a role in this play, yes?"

"Celia love, the carrots." Rupert tried again, and this time, biting my tongue with an effort, I gave in and passed him the serving dish as Daniela, oblivious, turned her attention to Nicholas.

"So, you have started rehearsals today, I hear?"

"Yes, that's right."

"I must come one day and watch you. I have wanted many times to see the way a play develops in the days before it is performed."

Madeleine's gaze lifted briefly, so subtle a movement that I would have missed it if I hadn't been looking right at her. But Rupert saw. Sending her a silent glance of reassurance, he said to Daniela, "I'm afraid we don't have visitors at this stage of rehearsal. It's a little too distracting."

"I see." In spite of her light tone I sensed that she, like Nicholas, was not at all accustomed to being told what she could and couldn't do. And if she truly wanted something, I suspected that she wouldn't be put off.

xvi

I had just settled in with *The Season of Storms* on my sitting-room sofa when somebody knocked at my door.

It was Teresa.

"Signorina Sands, Signor D'Ascanio says would you like to come now. He waits in the Veranda della Diana."

"I'm sorry . . . where?"

"The Veranda della Diana. Is the room where he works. I will take you."

I would have liked some time to tidy up, to brush my hair at least, but already she was moving off and I didn't trust myself to find the room without her help. It was much easier, admittedly, to follow someone else through the corridors, though Teresa's straight back and formal efficiency made me feel rather as though I'd been summoned to an audience with royalty. Descending the main sweep of stairs to the ground floor entrance hall, I felt the watching eyes of disembodied statuary heads set into niches in the wall, and fancied they were living courtiers looking on as I was being ushered to the presence of the king.

I could have found my way from there—I'd done it twice today already. But Teresa insisted on taking me all the way through to the door of the study, even knocking to announce me and then melting back into the shadowy rooms we had passed through before I could thank her.

A single sharp 'woof' replied to the knock, and one of the greyhounds padded to the door and sniffed as Alex's voice called out, "Come in."

I pushed the door open with caution, because of the dog, but Max had already stepped back, long tail wagging a gentlemanly welcome. Stretching his head to examine the hand I held out, he permitted me to briefly stroke one ear before he wheeled and trotted back to take his place beside his master.

He had a fair distance to cover; the room was quite long. It was, though, the cosiest room I'd seen yet in the villa, a sort of blend of study and conservatory that jutted out from the house, a true enclosed veranda, with long windows running round the three outer walls and bookshelves with leaded glass fronts lining the fourth. The ubiquitous oriental carpets added warmth here, worn though they were, and the faded striped draperies had been drawn against the night, holding in the glow of floor and desk lamps at the far end of the room. There were several chairs set round haphazardly—a couple in woven cane with cushions in the same striped drapery fabric, and another leather armchair that was clearly meant for reading—but the room had been designed, I thought, for work.

The wide wooden desk at the far end was littered with papers and books that competed for room with a bulky computer. Behind that sat Alex, and behind *him* a bronze statue posed on a pillar, a female figure holding bow and arrow with a hound curled round her feet. The goddess Diana, I thought. Hence the name of the room.

Alex glanced up from his desk. In the light of his computer screen his face looked deathly tired. "Good," he said, "I'm glad she found you. I felt very bad for missing you this morning."

"No, that's my fault," I rushed to explain. "I couldn't get away at break, you see, and when I came at lunch you were busy with someone . . ."

He looked up a second time, rather more quickly, and finding his eyes too intense, too distracting, I finished off lamely, ". . . and I didn't want to bother you, so I thought I'd just leave it till later."

Again his gaze dropped as he pushed his own chair back and pulled another forwards, making room for me at the computer. "It is later now," he said. "Come send your e-mail."

The dogs made room as well, retreating to the corner behind Alex where they lay like coiled springs, their eyes alert. Nero, I thought, was more wary than Max, more aloof, and less likely to want to make friends. But Max kindly perked up his ears when I looked at him, and as Alex guided me through the Italian instructions onscreen Max crept forwards on the carpet till his nose was near my ankle.

"Then the address," Alex told me, "and you type your message here."

He turned away politely while I wrote, occupying himself with the contents of a file folder spread open on his desk. He seemed to be checking a column of figures, and that action combined with the companionable silence took me instantly back to the days of my childhood, with me sitting at one end of the old front-room table, the one with its leg held level by the out-of-date atlas, scribbling at my homework while Bryan, beside me, bent over the household accounts.

I felt a twist of something that was mostly missing Bryan, but partly, too, a flash of feelings harder to identify, a sense of familiarity and rightness. Stealing a quick glance at Alex, I had a peculiar sensation of continuity, as though this were a moment that would be repeated many times in years to come. Which was, of course, ridiculous. Smiling at my fancies, I turned my concentration to the letter I was writing.

I didn't tell Bryan everything—it would have taken pages. But I did ask him, out of curiosity, what he knew about Den. I didn't like to come right out and say that Rupert had been acting strangely since we'd met Den in Venice, but I thought there was a chance that Bryan might know some small detail of their history that would help me understand what was between them. I asked the question casually, and followed it by telling him about the theatre, and my rooms, and our first day rehearsing. *And Madeleine Hedrick is lovely,* I wrote. *You were right. (Aren't you always?) With much love, your Angel.*

"There," I said. "I'm finished. Shall I send it now?"

Alex nodded, showed me how. "And I will, of course, let you know when he replies."

"Oh, I hadn't thought of that. I mean, I didn't tell him *not* to reply, so of course . . . but I don't want to put you to any more trouble."

He shrugged it off. "We Italians are great romantics, you know. We understand the matters of the heart."

I was slow on the uptake. "Matters of the . . . ? Oh no, it isn't that at all," I set him straight, and smiled. "No, Bryan's not my boyfriend, he's my . . . well, he's like my father. One of them, anyway." And then, to his questioning eyes, I explained, "He and Rupert practically raised me."

"Ah," he said. "He's Rupert's partner."

He said that evenly, but still I thought I caught a change of tone. Not everyone, I reminded myself, had grown up in the theatre, where such things were common. "I'm sorry, does that shock you?"

His sideways glance was dry. "I went to public school."

I would have let the matter drop, but Alex, with his eyes still on my face, appeared to feel the need to add, "It's not a way of life I understand. But that doesn't mean I disapprove. As it happens, I like Rupert very much, and how he lives is not my business." He turned his chair a fraction more, as though he found me rather interesting. "You say that he raised you?"

"My school was very near their flat. My mother wasn't home much. So most nights I stayed with Roo and Bryan."

"Ah." He accepted this with a nod and looked away, and it was my turn now to study him. He must have felt my scrutiny, because his gaze came back, and held a silent query.

I said, "Sorry," looking back to the computer screen. "It's only that most people make comments, you know, about homosexuals bringing up children."

"Most people are not fit themselves to raise a child." A hint of a personal bitterness touched his calm voice, and Max, at my feet, raised his head as if to gauge his master's mood, ears cocked, eyes questioning. Alex dropped an automatic hand to stroke the side of Max's face. Satisfied, the greyhound subsided again with a soft whuff of breath as Alex flashed the tight brief smile that gave little away. "If it matters, I think you were lucky," he said, "to be loved."

Then he looked at his watch. Which was my cue, I thought, to make my exit. "Look, I'd better be going." I pushed back my chair. "Thanks for letting me do this"—I nodded towards the computer—"it really was . . ."

"I'll walk you back." He stood with me. The dogs, like small bodyguards, sprang to their feet, long tails wagging, preparing for action. Nero, being brave, nudged my knee with his nose and I offered my hand to him cautiously.

"He won't bite," said Alex.

But Nero had already moved off. Like his master, I noticed, he didn't like anyone getting too near. As Alex and I made our way through the corridors, the dogs went ahead, circling back now and then to be sure we were following.

Glad as I was of the escort, I found the long silence unnerving. I tried to think of something we could talk about that wasn't controversial. "We missed you at dinner," I said. "Teresa told us you'd been called away on business?"

"Yes, I was."

And that was that. I tried again. "You know Mrs. Forlani's been trying to find you. She wanted help lighting her fires."

There, I'd caught his attention. His mouth quirked. "She did, did she?"

"That's what she told us."

"Then I must see what I can do."

We'd reached the ladies' wing, the softly lighted landing with the stairway leading down, and overhead the stained glass ceiling set against the dark night sky. I could hear quiet music and voices from Madeleine's room, and I lowered my own voice accordingly. "Thank you again, I—"

"My pleasure." He turned with the dogs and was walking away when he stopped. Paused. Looked back. "Do you have a day off from rehearsals?"

"Yes, Sundays. Why?"

"There are quite a lot of sights to see, around Mira. Perhaps one Sunday you would like to take a drive."

Was he actually asking me out on a date, I wondered?

Caught completely unprepared, I dodged the question with a nonanswer. "It's very kind of you to offer."

"Not at all." Again he turned and walked off with the greyhounds at his heels.

I watched them out of sight, then closed my door and went through to the bedroom. Collapsing full-length on the bed with my feet on the pillows, I sent an imploring look up at the portrait of Celia the First.

"Well, what would *you* do?" I asked, begging for guidance. But she, with her soft, knowing eyes, only smiled.

ACT III

Enter a Ghost.

All her particular worth grows to this sum:
She stains the time past: lights the time to come.

Webster: *The Duchess of Malfi,* Act I, Scene II

i

NEXT morning I woke early and went looking for Madeleine. I found her on the terrace, where she'd set herself up comfortably with sweet rolls and a pot of tea and a chair pulled up close to the parapet, from which she could admire the morning view. Watching me approach, she raised a hand to shade her eyes and smiled. "You're all dressed up this morning," was her greeting.

"Oh. Rehearsal clothes," I explained away the belted long skirt and the blouse. "I thought it might help me to get a feel for my character, you know, to dress for the period."

"Ah." Her nod held the understanding of a veteran. "You believe in the outside-in method, then, do you? Like Larry Olivier. He always said you put shoes on your character first, get the externals right, and the rest will follow. Whereas dear old Ralph Richardson worked from the inside out, focussing mainly on feelings."

"Well, I sort of do both," I admitted. "I'm more concerned, I guess, with how my character feels than what she's wearing, but the clothes you wear affect the way you move, and that affects the way you feel, so . . ."

". . . you're not bound to one technique." She smiled. "I understand completely. Do sit down. There ought to be another chair around here somewhere."

"This is fine." I moved forwards, taking a seat on the parapet, facing her.

"Have some tea, there's plenty in the pot. That new girl brought it out for me, poor thing. She's a bundle of nerves, working under Teresa."

I poured myself a cup of tea and sugared it. "Teresa's husband's still not back?"

"I don't believe so, no. Unless," she reasoned with a smile, "she's done him in for all the worry that he's caused her."

"She'd be justified at that," I said. "I'd hate to have a man do that to me, take off for days on end."

Again, under Madeleine's warm, patient eyes, I felt the difference in our ages and experience. "Every man has imperfections. And every woman," she went on, her head turning a fraction at the sound of someone bounding up the stone steps from the garden, "has her own level of tolerance."

Nicholas, showing impeccable timing as always, appeared at the top of the stairs, dark hair ruffled by the breeze. He smoothed it with a hand and smiled. "There you are, darling. I thought I might find you out here." Strolling forwards, he bent down to kiss her.

"You've been for a walk," she observed.

"Mm. Down to the theatre and back. Did you miss me?"

"Celia's been keeping me company."

"Ah." Straightening, he looked me over. "Formal dress for breakfast, is it? Someone might have told me."

"Mind what you mock, darling," Madeleine warned. "I've been known to dress the part for my rehearsals too, from time to time."

"I'm not mocking it." Stepping back a pace he lit a cigarette and lounged against the parapet, beside me. "Whatever works, I say. So long as I can show up in my jeans, that's all I ask."

Madeleine tilted her head. "I don't know. I'd rather like to see you every day in military uniform."

"You will in performance," he promised. "But rehearsing in uniform won't make me feel like a soldier. That comes from in here." He tapped the centre of his chest. "To act like a soldier I have to feel a soldier's pride, a fear of being seen to be afraid, a sense of duty . . ." As he spoke the words his body straightened to attention, shoulders back, chin out. "And there you are, you see? That's Johnny in a nutshell," he told us, naming his character.

"Oh, but surely Johnny's more than that," said Madeleine.

"Not much. He's duty-driven, Johnny is. Why else would he throw himself into the front lines because somebody's told him if he does, his side will win?"

"I wondered," she said, "if perhaps he wasn't plagued by guilt."

"For what?"

She lowered her eyes, lifting one shoulder in a noncommittal gesture. "Was he faithful to his wife? It's left rather open to question, I think, in the play."

Nicholas relaxed again against the parapet, lifting his cigarette and blowing out a thoughtful stream of smoke, watching her face. And then his quick, easy smile returned. "What do you think?"

"I'm really not sure."

"Well, I am. He was faithful." Turning to tap his ash over the edge of the terrace, he said, "The whistle must have blown. There go the workmen."

I saw only the sleeve of someone's shirt disappearing into the trees. "I hope they're doing indoor work." I cast a doubtful look towards the deep blue bank of cloud that lay along the farther shore, flattening the colour of the lake to choppy grey. "It doesn't look as though this sun will last."

I don't think Madeleine was listening; her eyes were still on Nicholas. I thought for a moment she might question him further about where he'd been, but she didn't, and after a moment he glanced at her breakfast tray. "Any tea left in that pot?"

"If there is, it'll be stone cold."

"Give it here, then. I'll get us a fresh pot. Be back in a minute."

I found myself looking at Madeleine's face as she watched him walk off. She held her head motionless, calm, eyes quite clear of emotion. And then she glanced towards me and she smiled, a bit self-consciously. "He'll leave me, of course," she said lightly. "They all do. But he is a diversion."

She said that, I thought, almost as a kind of apology, which made me feel all the more guilty. If it hadn't been for me and that one stupid, stupid argument with Mother, Madeleine's life would have gone on quite peacefully—no scandal, no di-

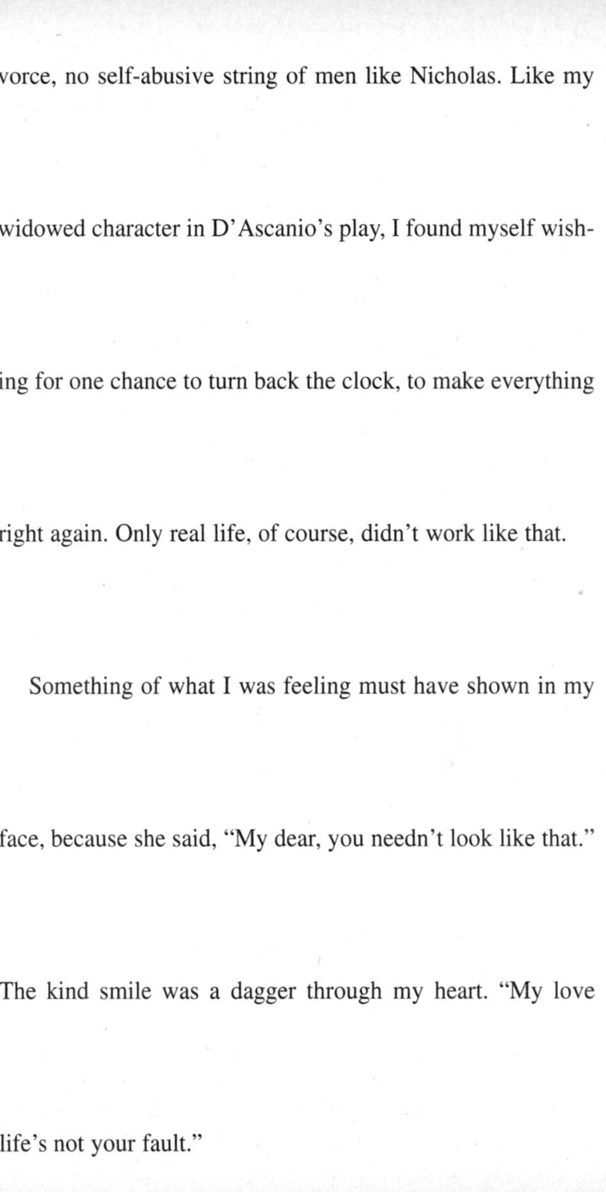

vorce, no self-abusive string of men like Nicholas. Like my widowed character in D'Ascanio's play, I found myself wishing for one chance to turn back the clock, to make everything right again. Only real life, of course, didn't work like that.

Something of what I was feeling must have shown in my face, because she said, "My dear, you needn't look like that." The kind smile was a dagger through my heart. "My love life's not your fault."

ii

UPSTAIRS, a piece of paper had been slipped beneath my door—Bryan's e-mailed reply to my note from last night.

As always, Bryan's presence in any form made me feel a bit better, and having read the warmly chatty message through I felt my mood improving. He didn't bother hiding his surprise at my news that Den O'Malley had replaced the SM we were meant to have, but apart from a few minor details about Den—that he'd once lived in London and that he and Rupert had worked with each other a couple of times—Bryan didn't tell me anything that might have helped me understand why Rupert was behaving as he was.

I put it down, myself, to his being overprotective and fatherly, not wanting his little girl to be corrupted by an obvious, if likeable, cad. That, or the fact that, having set this up to be a special time for just the two of us, the first and last play we would ever do together, Rupert now found himself having to share my attention. I couldn't do much about the latter problem, short of making an effort to spend time together with Rupert, but I tackled the first concern head-on before our rehearsal.

". . . So you see," I said to Rupert, as I finished with my speech, "you needn't worry. I mean, Den is nearly as old as you are . . ."

"Ancient," Rupert agreed with a solemn nod, holding back his smile.

"You know what I mean."

"Mm." He was only half-listening, yawning and cradling a coffee. "The thing about Dennis is—"

"Morning, gorgeous," Den said as he entered the rehearsal room, charged up with morning energy. "I missed you at breakfast."

"I came down at eight," I explained. "And I didn't stay long. I had to go back to my room and do my warm-ups." As unself-conscious as I might be onstage, I'd never felt entirely comfortable doing body and voice exercises with everyone watching—and anyway, I much preferred the flattering acoustics of my bathroom.

"On your own? How boring. See, I could have kept you company." He wasn't being serious; it wasn't even flirting. It was more the sort of teasing that one did with friends. I smiled.

"No, thanks. I don't need the distraction."

"Well, at least that's something, now," he told me, pleased. "I'm a distraction."

Rupert, at the table, said without looking up, "Dennis, you are many things. And if you don't stop talking and have a seat so we can start working, I'm liable to tell you what a few of them are."

His tone was light and I was fairly certain he was joking, but you couldn't really tell with Rupert, sometimes.

iii

WE did table work the next few days, and by week's end were getting to our feet with books in hand to make our first tentative efforts at blocking the first act. The long table was pushed against the side wall, out of the way, and new furniture brought in to form a makeshift set within the marked chalk circle of our rehearsal 'stage'—a smaller round table and two uncomfortably stuffed armchairs that were, along with an imaginary chandelier suspended from the ceiling, the only real set elements we had to work around.

Rupert, as was his custom, let us find the movements that seemed most natural to our characters. Saying little, he circled us constantly, watching, assessing, and stopping us only when something looked wrong. I had to think more about position than I'd ever had to on a normal stage. Theatre-in-the-round demanded motion, subtle sometimes but carefully planned, so that all the audience could have a chance to see more than our backs, to feel involved.

By Saturday evening I was so exhausted that I stumbled from my after-dinner bath straight into bed, looking forward to a lie-in and a restful day off.

I should have known better.

The birds woke me early with a chattering of song that seemed determined to announce a break in the rain that had fallen more or less steadily these past few days. Although the mist still clung to the darkly treed hills like the smoke from a forest fire, blending seamlessly into the grey, cloud-filled sky, I could see at least into the gardens and down to the lake, and the constant dull patter of rain on my windows had ceased. In its place, behind the birdsong, was the random drip of leaves and flowers shaking themselves dry. And something else . . . a voice below the terrace, speaking freely at full volume with no fear of waking anyone. A woman's voice, an English voice, but one I didn't recognize.

A car door slammed, and footsteps, small and dragging, started up the stairs, followed in a moment by a second set, more firm and sure, that climbed with steady purpose. I looked through my window in time to see a slight figure, half-drowned in a bright silver raincoat and hat, appear at the end of the terrace. Madeleine's daughter, I thought, had arrived.

The woman behind her was tallish and lean with a mass of white hair, and wore only a thick Irish sweater and trousers in defiance of the wet. She carried a plain leather suitcase in either hand. Why they'd come up the back way and not used the front entrance I didn't know, but then remembering that the man Alex had met that first night we were here had also come up by the terrace, I wondered if maybe this wasn't the quickest way up to the house from the garage, or wherever it was that people parked their cars upon arriving.

At any rate, as the woman and girl crossed the slick grey terrace I heard the door beneath me, near the dining room, swing open and Teresa hurried out to take their bags, still wearing her apron, as though she'd been caught unprepared for the pair's arrival.

Madeleine must have been watching as well. I heard movement in the next room, then the click of her door and a creak from the landing as she headed downstairs. It took me slightly longer to get dressed and ready myself, partly because I thought it only polite to give mother and daughter a moment to themselves before the entire household descended upon them. In fact, I'd half-expected Poppy Hedrick would be up and settled in her room by the time I went down for my breakfast, but she wasn't. She was sitting in the dining room with Madeleine and the older woman, sipping tea and trying with all the earnestness of a twelve-year-old to look grown up.

She was, I thought, quite an attractive child, with a slight edge of sullenness that kept her from being pretty. But that, too, went with being twelve, as I remembered. Freed from the folds of the raincoat, she looked rather fragile, long-limbed and fine-boned, with dark hair like her mother's that fell in loose waves past her narrow shoulders, framing a pale, large-eyed face; more pale now, I expected, from illness.

Her eyes moved to me as I entered, but she waited for a proper introduction.

Madeleine gave it. "Poppy, this is Celia Sands, another actress in the play. Celia, come and meet my daughter."

Poppy's handshake was very precise, very careful. "How do you do."

"And this," went on Madeleine, turning, "is Mrs. Farrow, who's done escort duty all the way from England."

"Mrs. Farrow." I held out my hand, and was greeted with an iron grasp that brooked no hesitation.

"Edwina," she corrected me, in a cultured voice clearly above mine in class. "I feel ancient when young women call me Mrs. Farrow, like I'm in a home, or hospital, or something. So"—she looked me up and down—"you're the girl with the famous name, are you?"

"That's right." Rising to the challenge, I met her gaze squarely and smiled. "I'm afraid I don't look much like the original."

She brushed that off as immaterial. "She was more of an image, you know, than a flesh-and-blood person. All attitude."

Something in the way she said that, coupled with the fact that I couldn't determine her age, made me ask, "Did you know her, then?"

"Me? Heavens, no. I was only a girl. But I did see her once at the Old Vic, one of the last performances she ever gave, I believe. I don't remember the play. I barely remember her, as I said, though I thought at the time she was lovely." She looked at me in realization. "But of course, you're in her rooms, aren't you? You'll have seen the portrait."

"Yes."

Madeleine said, "Such a shame she died young."

Edwina Farrow arched her eyebrows. "Inevitable, I should have said. She had an unfortunate aura."

I might have asked her what she meant by that, if her gaze at that moment hadn't gone up and over my shoulder. "Ah, there you are, Alex. Teresa said she thought you might be up.

She didn't wake you, did she? Good. I told her not to. Nero, Max, my darling boys," she greeted the enthusiastic greyhounds, who had bounded forwards joyfully to meet her, their whole bodies wagging, each seeming determined to be the first onto her lap. She pushed them off laughing and made a great fuss of them, rumpling their ears. "Now that's the sort of welcome that I like," she said, and then, to Alex, "I don't expect the same exuberance from you, my dear, but 'good morning' would do, for a start."

Alex, standing in the doorway, looked closer to my own age this morning in his polo-neck and jeans, his waving hair damp at the ends as though he'd just showered. But there was still a certain stiffness to his shoulders, a formality of habit, and it showed now in his face as he stepped forwards, as the dogs had, and bent to kiss Edwina Farrow's cheek.

"Good morning, Grandmother," he said.

I'd known all along, of course, that Alex was half-English, a fact that was apparent when I saw him with Daniela or Teresa—his reserve, his quiet movements, seemed distinctly un-Italian. So it was odd that now, beside Edwina, he should suddenly strike me as being so very *un*-English, so foreign. It was, I supposed, a simple matter of perception, like a frock that looked blue when you viewed it in one light, and green in another.

I was pondering this when he straightened and said to Edwina, "How did you get here? I thought I was supposed to meet your train at Desenzano after lunch."

"Yes, well, we had a change of plan. There were so many delays coming down through the Alps that our train didn't get into Milan until the wee hours of this morning, and there seemed no point to me then in stopping at an hotel like I'd planned, and no point either in waiting around for hours for our connection, not with Poppy feeling ill. So I thought, bother it, I'll hire a car."

"You drove?" His eyebrows lifted, though I didn't think he looked particularly shocked by her actions. "You drove from Milan?"

"And why not? I have my licence. And the car can be returned at Brescia—I asked. Giancarlo can do it tomorrow."

"I'll do it myself," he said.

Edwina Farrow had sharp eyes. "Gone off again, has he? I thought that might be it, when Teresa came out on her own to collect Poppy's bags. On one of his binges, is he?"

"I really wouldn't know," said Alex, tolerant. "He hasn't been in touch."

"Yes, well, that's typical. How long has he been away this time?"

Alex shrugged. "Just a week. He'll be back soon, I'm sure."

"Just a week." She shook her head. "Your father would never have stood for it—Giancarlo would have been out on his ear, and Teresa's cooking wouldn't have saved him. Still," she softened the statement with a smile, "Teresa is a damned good cook. I wonder if you could convince her, Alex, to make her wonderful gnocchi for me while I'm here."

"I'm sure she'd be delighted." A pause, then he asked her, a little too casually, "Will you be staying long?"

"Only a few days. I've booked myself on a tour of the Greek isles that leaves from Brindisi on Saturday next, and I'll want to spend a bit of time in Rome before that, I should think. We'll see." Glancing down at the greyhounds she scratched Max's head. "For now all I want is a meal and a hot bath and maybe a rest. Would you be a dear, Alex, and see that my cases get down to the villa? I tried to explain to your man at the garage, but he didn't seem terribly swift."

Avoiding her eyes, he said, "Ah. Well, I'm afraid that there might be a slight complication. Daniela Forlani—you remember Daniela?"

"Vividly," his grandmother replied in a tone of voice that made me warm to her.

"Daniela is here for a visit as well, and she's settled in already at the villa, so . . ."

"The Villa delle Tempeste," she said, "is fully capable of housing twenty people, let alone two women. And besides, I always stay there. Your Daniela will simply have to suffer through my company, these next few days. I'm sure that she'll survive."

I found I liked Edwina Farrow more and more. So much so

that, when Madeleine and Poppy had excused themselves and gone upstairs, and Alex and the dogs had gone to see about the luggage, I hung back and poured a second cup of coffee from the silver pot the new maid had just brought out to the sideboard. As I stirred in the sugar I tried to think of ways to get to know this woman better, things to say.

I turned to find her taking stock of me. "Did you think he didn't have one?" she asked, catching me off guard.

"I'm sorry?"

"Did you think that Alex didn't have a grandmother?"

"Oh. Well, I—"

"It's only," she said, "that you looked so surprised when you learned who I was."

"It did surprise me, rather," I confessed. "But only because Galeazzo D'Ascanio's been dead for fifty years, and if I've done the maths right then his son—Alex's dad—must be well into his eighties, if he's still alive . . ."

"He's not."

". . . so I didn't imagine that Alex would have any grandparents left."

"Only me." She smiled. "My daughter was quite a bit younger than Alex's father, as you might have guessed." I didn't ask for further information, but she supplied it anyway, matter-of-factly as though the details were public knowledge. "She was just out of school when they married, and he was already a pensioner. Not very bright of her, really. I expect she was hoping to be a rich widow, but she was the one who died first. Cancer," she told me. "And *he* went on fifteen years longer, as fit as a horse, more's the pity for Alex." That, too, she said as though I ought to understand exactly what she meant by it, although I didn't.

I assumed she was telling me Alex's childhood had been less than happy, a point I'd already inferred from a few of the comments he'd made.

"Did he never remarry, then, Alex's father?"

"Oh, no. Heavens, no." The idea amused her. "He was hardly a sociable man. No one but my daughter would have ever put up with him. Fancy shutting up this place"—she spread her hands feelingly, invoking the forces of reason—"and letting it all run to ruin. Sheer madness."

"He didn't sell the house, though."

"No, at least he showed some sense, there. And I'm glad that Alex decided to put the work into it, open it up again, however misguided his reasons might be."

A voice from the door interrupted. "Good morning." Den came in yawning so widely I don't think he noticed Edwina straight off, but when he did he shook himself awake enough to smile his charming smile. "What is it with this house?" he asked. "Every time I turn my back another beautiful woman springs out of the woodwork. I'm Dennis O'Malley, my friends call me Den. And you are . . . ?"

"Far too old to fall for lines like that, my boy," she told him, but she shook the hand he offered all the same. "Edwina Farrow."

It had probably, I thought, been quite a while since anybody had called Den 'my boy.' For a moment it threw him clear out of his stride. Then he grinned. "You're English, too. That's great. I have a thing for Englishwomen."

Edwina's intelligent eyes moved from Den's face to mine and then back again, and I saw the slight settling back and the change of expression that signalled a shift in her interest. *Oh no, not her, too,* I groaned inwardly. It was bad enough Rupert read more into my interactions with Den than he ought to, but now total strangers were doing the same.

Aloud, I told Den, "Mrs. Farrow brought Madeleine's daughter down with her. They've only just got here."

"Travel with a twelve-year-old." He shuddered at the thought. "I couldn't do it myself. Not sober, anyway. So, you must be from Poppy's school then, are you? Or did Alex hire you privately?"

"Wrong on both counts."

I tried to cut in. "Den . . ."

But he wasn't listening. "Oh? Then how did you—?"

"I'm Alex D'Ascanio's grandmother, Mr. O'Malley. And you needn't bother telling me I look too young and all that rubbish—women of my age have highly developed malarkey detectors. And speaking of age," she said, standing, "I've had quite a late night and I'm starting to feel the effects, so if you'll both excuse me I think I'll go down and get settled and have a bit of a rest."

Den stood with her, a gentleman, and when she'd departed he took his seat smiling. "Now *that,*" he informed me, "is one tough old granny."

"You don't know the half of it. Guess where she's staying."

"Where?"

"The Villa delle Tempeste."

"But isn't Daniela . . . ?"

"She is, yes. She'll have to make space for a housemate. Can I have a roll, please?"

Den passed me the basket with open amusement. "Daniela won't like that."

"No." I honeyed my roll with private satisfaction. "No, I don't imagine that she will."

iv

I joined Rupert for his after-breakfast walk in the gardens. He walked at a good pace—it took all my breath to keep up, but I had wanted to be sure that we did some things on our own together, just as he'd planned. And besides, after eating Teresa's wonderful cooking all week, I felt in need of exercise.

I hadn't been outside for so long, on account of the rain, that I'd nearly forgotten how sweet the gardens smelled, the thick rich scents of water-laden blossoms drifting upwards like a tropical perfume, and behind that the sharper, more pungent aroma of wet grass and earth.

We went round by the theatre and down through the wood, past the orchard and into the rose garden. Here the path ended, and Rupert, to my relief, paused for an admiring look round.

I hadn't seen any gardeners at work yet on the estate, but someone had been turning over a new bed in one corner of the rose garden—the soil was dark, its fresh smell carrying across to where we stood. Rupert breathed it in deeply. "It looks very English, this garden, doesn't it?"

I told him, "Yes, well, it would. Galeazzo designed it especially for Celia the First. I suppose he didn't want her feeling homesick."

He smiled. "When they open this place to the public, you ought to apply for a job as a tour guide. I had no idea you were such an expert on Il Piacere."

I caught the faint regretful tone and gave myself a mental kick, knowing how Rupert enjoyed playing tour guide himself. It made him feel useful. Aloud I assured him I wasn't an expert. "I only know about the rose garden because Galeazzo wrote a poem about it in *The Season of Storms.* I've finished the book, finally, did I tell you? I'm on my second reading, now."

"And do you still think that the same man who wrote those poems wrote *Il Prezzo*?"

The poems *were* very different from the style of the play, and I admitted that. "But you'd still have to prove to me that Galeazzo was a plagiarist."

"I may yet do that. If the proof exists at all, it would most likely be here. I'll have to hunt around a bit. I've already had a look through the books in my own room—there are some quite nice volumes there, but no plays, and I think it would have to have been a play . . ."

"Well, I'll believe it when I see it," I lifted my chin stubbornly. From here I couldn't see the lake at all—the copper beeches blocked my view—and the mountains showed as little more than shadows through their covering of cloud; only the church bells below in the town gave any sign there might be a world that existed beyond the high walls of the gardens of Il Piacere.

At the sound of the church bells Rupert glanced at his watch. "Good Lord, is that the time already? I wanted to try phoning Bryan before lunch, before his American football comes on."

I would have liked to talk to Bryan, too, but I'd already told him all the news I had to tell last Monday, in my e-mail, and he and Rupert after all deserved a little privacy.

I said, "You go ahead. I think I'll stay out here and walk a while longer."

He looked round from habit, assessing the safety of where he was leaving me. "You know your way back to the house?"

"Yes."

"All right, then. Just be careful." He gave me a fatherly kiss on the cheek. "Don't get lost."

What was it about me, I wondered, that made everybody so sure I'd get lost? "I won't," I said, and looking my most competent, went off to have a stroll around the rosebushes.

v

IT was the fountain with the dolphins that defeated me.

Three times I set my back to it and took the path—a different one each time—that I felt sure would lead me to the house, and three times I came back again to stand before the dolphins, water pouring from the bronze mouths open wide with silent laughter.

"Well, this is just ridiculous," I told the nearest dolphin. "There has to be a way out."

I could *see* the terrace parapet from where I stood; the red-tiled roofs . . . so close, and yet I couldn't seem to get to them.

"Ridiculous," I said again, and cast a quick look skywards at the thickening clouds. I could practically smell the rain coming, it wouldn't be long. All right, I thought, if I couldn't get anywhere heading *towards* the house, maybe I'd do better heading away from it—sort of an Alice in Wonderland logic. Choosing the path that I thought was *least* likely to lead to the house, I squared my shoulders and started off.

I passed through a thicket of trees and then out again, down a short flight of brick steps between shrubberies heavy with flowers, pale yellow and white, that gave off a sweet scent in the dampness. A little further on I passed beneath a curving arbour dripping with wisteria that showered me with violet-coloured petals scattered by the rising breeze. And then, as the first raindrop splatted heavily on the top of my head, I came into the open and found myself facing the graceful, rose-walled Villa delle Tempeste.

It stood in a clearing with cypresses behind it and a meadow-like lawn with a sprinkling of what looked like buttercups stretching out from the façade, with its balconied windows and grand outside staircase. Most impressive of all were the palm trees in front—an uneven row of them, slender trunks soaring to vanish in tufts of broad leaves, lending the villa a Mediterranean elegance.

Small wonder both Daniela and Edwina Farrow wanted to stay here. It really was beautiful. Though, as Edwina had said, perhaps rather too large for one person.

I hoped it was large enough to shelter me, as well—the raindrops were falling more steadily now, and the clouds had rolled over dark grey. Tucking my head down, I made a dash for it across the lawn.

I'd nearly reached the palm trees when a hand of stone descended on my shoulder.

I jumped as my heart lurched and lodged in the back of my throat. Wheeling, I saw only a stained denim shirt-front. The wind whipped a blast of rain into my eyes, making me squint as my gaze travelled up to the face of the man who was holding me pinned now by both arms—an ill-tempered face with the jaw of a bulldog. The workman Pietro.

I'd only felt fear, real fear, a few times in my life: once when strange footsteps had followed me home on the street late one night; once when I'd found myself stuck on the tube all alone with a gang of drunken yobs; and now, this instant, with Pietro glaring down at me and no one else in sight.

He asked me a question, short, sharp, and unpleasant.

I pushed back the fear, tried to smile. "I'm sorry, I don't understand. I—"

Grabbing me harder, he gave me a shake and repeated whatever he'd asked, his voice rising.

"Look, I'm sorry, but—"

"What *are* you doing?" Edwina's voice sliced over mine, firm and clear and demanding, from somewhere above both our heads. I looked up to see her leaning from one of the villa's upstairs windows, her own face nearly as cross as Pietro's. "Stop it!" she ordered him. "Stop it this instant!"

I doubted whether Pietro actually understood English, but he clearly got the message. And incredibly, he stopped. Letting go my arms, he took a slow step back, uncertainly.

"Now go away," Edwina said. "Go on," she told him, "shoo!"

He glowered at the peremptory wave of her hand from the window, and muttered a bit to himself, but he left all the same, turning hard on his heel as Edwina leaned out further, calling down, "Are you all right, my dear?"

I rubbed my bruising arms. "I'm fine, yes. Thank you."

"Well, come in, child, don't stand there. Come in." And with that, like the Queen, she withdrew through the balconied window, and pulled the shutters tight against the weather.

vi

"NASTY day," Edwina said, and promptly shut the door upon it, handing me a towelling robe—bright pink, with flowers—and steering me into a small bathroom off the entry hall. "Here, take off those wet clothes and put this on, before you catch your death." As I emerged, she said, "The stupid man. What was he thinking, harassing a guest like that? He didn't frighten you too much, my dear, I hope? No? Good. Now, give those to me." She collected my wet clothes. "I'll just go ring Alex, to tell him you'll be stopping here with me for lunch."

Belting the pink robe, I glanced up in protest. "Oh, no, I couldn't possibly impose . . ."

"It's not a question of imposing. It's already a quarter to twelve, and the clothes-dryer won't work that quickly." She smiled. "And I don't think you'd want to sit at table in that outfit, would you?"

Pushing up the sleeves, I shook my head and tucked a strand of dripping hair behind my ear. The small movement caught her attention.

"And I'll fetch you a towel," she said, "for your hair. Have a seat." She was waving one arm at the spacious front room opening off the entry—a bright room, and airy, surprisingly so, considering the darkly claustrophobic decor that Galeazzo D'Ascanio had favoured nearly everywhere else.

"Ah, yes, but this was his wife's house," Edwina explained, when she returned. "And my daughter moved in here with Alex's father, after he'd closed up the main house. She had a hand in the decorating, my daughter did, as I'm sure you'll be able to tell."

Indeed the look was almost English Country: flowered chintz and needlepoint and bowls of tulips on the windowsills. Over the mantel a large gilt-framed mirror reflected the room and enlarged it, while in the grate below a modest fire burned to take the chill edge off the air.

I looked round with interest. "So this is the house where Alex grew up, then?"

"And his father before him. Though Alex didn't spend much time here, really. He was off at school." She took a step closer to the fire and rubbed her arms. "I've never known it to be so cold in April. The weather is very unsettled this year." Seeing that I'd finished towelling dry my hair and was holding the towel uncertainly, she said, "Just put it over the back of that chair, dear. Daniela isn't here to make a fuss."

I did as instructed, feeling relief. "She's gone out, then?"

"Took off in a temper. I expect that she's gone to give Alex an earful. Serves him right, mind," she said. "What he sees in that woman . . ."

"She is very lovely."

"Mm." It was an unconvincing syllable. "Now then, what will you have with your sandwiches? Tea? Right, I'll go put the kettle on. Shan't be a tick."

Left alone for the moment, I wandered the room, admiring the artwork that hung on the walls and exploring the bookshelves and the narrow glass curio cabinet. I was bending for a better look at one of the objects in the cabinet when Edwina returned.

"This goblet," I asked her, and pointed it out, "do you know I saw one very like it in Venice, in St. Mark's Basilica?"

"The chalice, do you mean? Yes, well, the two of them probably came from the same place," she said. "Stolen from Constantinople as part of the spoils of the Fourth Crusade. Do you know about the Fourth Crusade?"

Still mindful of Den and Rupert's lecturing in Venice, I smiled. "Well, actually . . ."

But Edwina, assuming that I wouldn't know, had already launched into the history of it, and from politeness I let her tell me the story all over again, of how the Venetians had tricked the Crusaders into attacking the Christian city of Constantinople, and how they had stolen away with its treasures.

While she was speaking, I studied the medieval lines of the chalice, the pale clouded bowl that looked like alabaster set within a tracery of gold that had been studded with square gemstones and inscribed with strange words in block letters that might have been Greek. "But how did this come to be here, in this house?"

"That was theft again, theft of a more modern sort," said Edwina. "During the first war, Galeazzo D'Ascanio took a place in Venice . . ."

"The Casetta Fiorita."

"Yes, exactly. It properly belonged to some poor Austrian, but war being what it is . . ." She shrugged. "Anyhow, the story goes that the original builder of the Casetta Fiorita was a Crusader, or the son of a Crusader—I never can remember which—who'd kept a few choice souvenirs from the plunder of Constantinople. And through the years these were passed down through the family, the last of whom—a daughter—married the Austrian chap."

"The one who lost the house in World War I?" I asked, to check I'd got things straight.

"That's right. He was out of the country, I believe, when the Casetta Fiorita was sequestrated by the government, so all his belongings, the furniture, everything was still in the house when Galeazzo moved in. And naturally, seeing the treasures of Constantinople . . ." She smiled. "He was a great lover of relics, of beautiful things. So when he was told, after the war, that the Austrian was getting the Casetta Fiorita back, he took what he wanted before he moved on. Stripped the library bare, and a room full of tapestries, and helped himself to small things like that chalice."

"Didn't the Austrian complain?"

"Very likely. But I doubt anyone would have listened. After all, he'd spent the last years of the war dropping bombs on the Casetta Fiorita himself, out of spite, and Galeazzo made a rather clever defence of that, claiming the bombings had destroyed many things in the house. Besides, the authorities did tend to look the other way, I'm told, when Galeazzo was involved. He had that kind of charm."

A whistle sounded in the kitchen as the kettle came to the boil, and excusing herself she went to make the tea, leaving me alone again. This time, as I moved round to settle myself in an armchair pulled close to the fire, I spotted another small object of obvious value: an expensively slimline gold cigarette lighter that lay on the little round table beside me. Daniela's, I assumed, though I'd thought hers was silver.

Edwina, returning with our sandwiches and tea, shunted lighter and ashtray aside to make room for the tray she was carrying. "We won't be needing those," she said. "You're not a smoker, are you? Good girl. I was, once. It's a beastly hard habit to break."

"I was always too afraid it would ruin my voice," I confessed.

"Yes, I should think you would have to take care, as an actress." Taking the armchair opposite, she offered me the plate of sandwiches, curious constructions of meat and tomato between rounds of flattened bread. "I can't guarantee how they'll taste—I didn't make them, only bought them at the station in Milan this morning, just in case the girl got hungry on the drive. But she didn't. She hasn't got much of an appetite, that one, and I don't believe that's the fault of her illness. She's far too thin, I think. In *my* day, girls were not encouraged to be skeletons, not like they are today. It isn't healthy."

Beneath the accusation of her eyes, I took two sandwiches and sat back. "What is Poppy like?"

"I couldn't tell you, really. Quiet girl, she barely said two words the whole way down. Well mannered. But not—and this is only my impression, mind—not a very happy child. That might just be her age. I wasn't filled with joy myself, at twelve. But still, in Poppy's case, I feel it might be something more," she said. "Her parents are divorced, I take it?"

Feeling once again that stab of guilt, I answered, "Yes."

"Well, that might be it. Some children are able to cope, and some aren't."

"I believe she was only a baby," I said, "when her parents split up."

"But a child still feels the absence of a father." Luckily, she wasn't looking at my face when she said that. She'd bent her head to pour the tea. "Milk and sugar?"

"Please." I looked for something else to talk about, and saw in the adjoining room a small stack of packing crates half-covered by a canvas sheet. "Are they doing restorations down here, as well?"

She followed my gaze. "Oh, no, those are some of the more fragile items brought down from the house, you know, for safety, while the work is going on. This is the one place the workmen won't be touching."

"Is this villa not part of the gift to the Trust, then?"

"Oh yes," she said. "Everything goes. The house, this villa, the gardens, the theatre; everything. Alex will have private use of a few select rooms for his lifetime, but after this summer the whole thing will really belong to the public."

She sounded disapproving. I studied her over my teacup, remembering what she'd said that morning about being pleased with what Alex had done to the house, though she didn't think much of his motives.

Exploring this, I said, "It's very generous, what he's doing."

"Yes." The single word came on a sigh, unexpectedly. "Well, he was always a giving little boy, you know. But I'm afraid giving Il Piacere to the public won't make the Italians accept him as one of their own." Her voice, though sympathetic, held the resignation of one who has lived long and seen much and knows how things truly are. "It hasn't been easy for Alex, you understand, growing up half an Italian, half English—never fully belonging to either culture, always being viewed as foreigner. It hasn't been easy at all. But this Trust business isn't the answer." Decisively, she took another sandwich. "Still, when Alex sets his mind to something, there's no turning him from it. It was one of his friends, I believe, put him on to the Trust—some chap who'd given them his own villa, to save on the taxes. And once Alex had the idea in his head, well"—she shrugged—"that was that. I did tell him about the warnings I'd been getting, but he wasn't having any of it."

"Warnings?"

"Daniela Forlani's late husband has come to converse with my circle a number of times."

She said that so naturally, without pause, that at first I wasn't sure I'd heard her properly. I did a mental double-take. "With your . . . ?"

"Circle," she repeated. "I'm a Spiritualist, my dear."

"Oh, I see." A number of images rose in my mind—of my former flatmate Sally, with her crystals and her tarot cards; of old detective stories in which scatty old ladies in dimly lit drawing rooms huddled round Ouija boards, receiving clues from those who had "passed over"; of mediums speaking in trances at séances . . .

"Have I alarmed you?"

"No, not at all. I was just thinking of our play," I told her, trying to explain the change in my expression that had been caused, not by alarm, but by inspiration. "Do you know it at all?"

"Very vaguely."

"Well, part of the first act and almost all of the second is a séance, you see, and Madeleine—she plays the medium—she and I have been having some trouble with our movements, and I wondered . . . that is, since you *are* a Spiritualist, I wondered if I might ask your opinion?"

Edwina Farrow looked at me a moment, her eyes unsettlingly intense. And then she smiled. Topping up her teacup she leaned back in invitation. "Ask me anything you like."

vii

"I can't wait to meet her," said Nicholas, drily. "She sounds a rare treat."

"So anyway," I went on, ignoring him, "Edwina said she'd gladly come and give a demonstration at rehearsal, if we wanted, of what a séance should be like."

Madeleine, clearly interested, curled her legs beneath her on the crackled leather sofa. We were gathered in the Stanza d'Arazzo—the tapestry room—for drinks before our dinner, it being too cold and too wet on the terrace. This room, though dark and draped with the familiar rich fabrics that D'Ascanio had favoured, nonetheless managed to feel rather cosy. It might have been the warming pools of light cast by the floor lamps with their fringed silk shades, or the presence, in the corner, of a baby grand piano that had obviously been much played, its finish worn and mellowed.

Den had gravitated to the instrument the moment he'd come in, and now was sitting at it trying to assess whether it was in tune by playing arpeggios, with Poppy Hedrick sitting at his side on the piano bench, her thin legs swinging. She still looked deathly pale and, having only just woken from a long afternoon nap, had the groggy, half-sedated look of someone who was ill, but being around Den seemed to make her more cheerful. He'd actually got her to smile, just a moment ago.

I didn't think she'd been listening at all to what I'd been saying, but she turned now and asked, "What's a Spiritualist?"

Madeleine answered in the same way she appeared to answer all of Poppy's questions, with patience and intelligence. "Well, Spiritualism, darling, is an actual organized movement, a kind of religion, whose members believe that people's bodies die but their spirits don't, and that these spirits can communicate through mediums—people who are especially sensitive, and who can act as go-betweens at séances. Like the woman I play in *Il Prezzo*."

Poppy absorbed this. "And is Mrs. Farrow a medium?"

I was about to reply that she claimed to be, when Nicholas intercepted the question.

In a tone that knew better, he said, "Of course she isn't." He rolled his eyes at me. "I hope you didn't encourage her."

Madeleine smiled at him. "But darling, think of the fun. A séance! I'd love to see a real medium in action; it would help me with my part."

"There's no such thing as a real medium. And there certainly aren't any spirits."

Poppy turned to argue. "Yes there are. Mummy saw a ghost once, didn't you, Mummy?"

Madeleine smiled. "Well, I *thought* I did, darling. I was very young."

"There are too ghosts," said Poppy in a stubborn tone, to Nicholas. She clearly didn't like him much. I couldn't say I blamed her, though it must have made things difficult for Madeleine.

Rupert, who'd been following the conversation from the corner where he'd quietly been studying the contents of the room's only bookcase, said, "It's very kind of Alex's grandmother to offer. Shall we have her come tomorrow?"

"You're not serious?" asked Nicholas.

"I don't see any harm in it," said Rupert. "I'm sure if we were playing this in London, Dennis and I would have thought about bringing in a medium to demonstrate séance technique for you. Wouldn't we, Dennis?"

"Mm? Oh, yeah, sure," came the absent reply from the piano corner.

Nicholas exhaled sharply in impatience. "She's not a medium, she's only a dotty old woman."

"Not so dotty," Den warned him, his smile showing briefly in profile. "Old she may be, but she's sharp enough to kill a man at fifty paces, take my word."

"Madness," said Nicholas under his breath as he shook a

cigarette loose from its packet and struck a match to light it. I frowned as I watched him, not because of what he'd said but because of the match—he'd never used matches before, at least not around me. He usually used his lighter . . .

And then all of a sudden my memory kicked in and I knew where he'd left his gold lighter. I'd seen it today, as a matter of fact—on a table by an armchair at the Villa delle Tempeste.

Edwina hadn't mentioned him, which meant he must have been to see Daniela. *The rat,* I thought. I looked away, disgusted, and discovered I was being watched. Across the room young Poppy Hedrick glanced from me to Nicholas and back again, and sensing that she'd found a kindred spirit, shyly smiled.

viii

WE worked through the second act just after lunch the next day, and Edwina, at Rupert's request, came to give us a lesson on how to converse with the dead.

Poppy was there as well, all of us having given our consent to let her sit in on rehearsals, for Madeleine's sake, although in Nicholas's case that consent hadn't come without grumbling. "She'll throw me off," he'd warned.

"You won't even know that she's there," had been Madeleine's promise.

And in actual fact, the girl was quiet as a mouse. She was sitting now at the table next to Den, who appeared to have made her his unofficial assistant, giving her paper and pen and introducing her to the basics of running a rehearsal.

Not that he was really running anything, this afternoon. Edwina, from the moment she arrived, assumed control.

"Young man," she told Nicholas, "kindly do *not* blow that smoke in my face when I'm trying to speak. Thank you." Taking a chair between Madeleine and me at the small round table that formed the centrepiece of our set, she said, "Now then, Celia, what was it you told me was giving you difficulties? The placement of hands, wasn't it?"

I nodded. "We've tried holding hands, like this." I reached out for Madeleine's hands, to demonstrate. "But it's awkward with the table, and there only being two of us."

"I see, yes. Your play is set when?"

"Sometime during World War I."

"Certainly hand-holding would have been popular then—table-rapping was still a common form of communicating with the spirit world, and holding hands kept people honest;

let you know the person sitting next to you wasn't doing the rapping himself, as a trick. But I sat for a time in the home circle of a man who would have been around in those days, and he always made us lay our hands this way, palms down, on top of the table. Is that easier?"

"Heaps," I said.

Rupert agreed it looked better from where he was sitting. "Would you like the room darker?"

"Yes, please, if you can," said Edwina. "They would certainly have dimmed the lights—gaslights, it would have been then, I'd imagine. But again, you'd want to see the members of your circle, to make certain they weren't cheating, so you wouldn't have the room in total darkness."

Rupert looked at Den, who obligingly threw the switches for two of the three chandeliers. As the room's walls and corners were swallowed by shadows I felt a childish tingle of anticipation, as though we were preparing to do this for real and not making believe.

"So," said Madeleine, "how do we begin?"

"You're playing the medium, yes? Ordinarily you'd start by inviting any spirits who are present to come forward. Although in this case, if you're after one particular spirit, you might simply ask for him by name."

Nicholas, standing behind us, gave a snort of derision that Madeleine tried to cover by saying, "Well, good, that's just what my character does in the play. And then what?"

"Then we wait."

Drily, and to no one in particular, Nicholas remarked, "*That* ought to be especially thrilling for the audience."

Half-turning with the air of someone bothered by an insect, Edwina sent him the same sort of look that in my years with Rupert and Bryan had meant I was one step away from being sent to my room. "Of course when you're playing the scene you may take a certain amount of dramatic licence, but there still should be a pause," she went on, turning back to Madeleine. "The spirits rarely manage an immediate response."

There was an obliging pause. Poppy looked around the

room a little nervously, I thought, and asked, "How can you tell when the spirits are here? Do you see them?"

"Some people do, but not me," said Edwina. "I'm not a clairvoyant, my dear, I'm clairaudient. I only hear their voices." Getting back to the business at hand, she instructed Madeleine, "Now, let's assume that you've asked this young man to come forward, this soldier. He may not be the first one who appears, there may be others more determined to be heard."

"Oh, heaven help us," muttered Nicholas, moving a few paces off in search of an ashtray.

"For instance," Edwina went on, "Mr. Rutherford's mother might want to cut in to remind him of manners. Or somebody else's relations or friends who've passed over may want to send greetings, you never can tell. But eventually, if you're in luck, the person whom you wish to speak to finally does turn up. And then you start to ask him questions."

"So at this point, I'd be in a trance?" asked Madeleine.

"Oh, no. You can't ask questions if you're truly in a trance. When you're in a trance the spirit speaks *through* you, you understand, uses your body. Your consciousness goes somewhere else entirely. It's up to the others in your circle to ask questions of the spirit, then, because you're essentially not there, and when the séance ends and you come out of your trance you haven't a clue what's gone on."

"Ah." Madeleine frowned. "Because the script, as it's written, demands that I be in a trance, and I can't seem to make that feel comfortable. It feels too . . . well, melodramatic."

Edwina assured her it needn't be. "Generally people in trances just look like they're sleeping."

"It's the voice I have problems with," Madeleine said.

Rupert, patient in the shadows, interjected. "Perhaps, Celia love, if you'd read a few lines from the scene, from the part where you're trying to make certain that it really is your husband talking, then Edwina could show Madeleine the proper way to answer in a trance. Would that suit everyone?"

Madeleine thought it a wonderful idea. Passing her book to Edwina, she pointed out the page on which to start, and the lines she should read.

"All right," said Edwina, positioning the open book between her hands, still flat upon the table, as she straightened her shoulders and bent her head forwards. "I'm ready."

Finding the page, I began with the series of questions my character asked of the spirit, to prove that he actually was her dead lover. "Won't you tell me your name?"

"Don't you know it?" Edwina's voice came very calmly, relaxed, almost drifting, as though she were speaking from out of a dream.

"Why must you play games? I do want to believe, but—"

"Then ask me . . ." She paused, and her head angled slightly as though she'd heard something just off to the side. Then she slowly went on, ". . . ask me something more personal, something that matters. My name will prove nothing."

"All right then, your mother's name. What was that?"

"Rose."

"And your father's?"

Again the pause. "Edward."

"And where did you live as a child?"

"By the sea, in a house with a beautiful . . . beautiful . . ."

She's lost her place, I thought, and tried to help her with a prompt. "Beautiful garden."

"The garden—oh, yes, I can still smell the roses. They seemed to be always in bloom." She was improvising now, creating lines that weren't in the script, but I didn't react. After all, Edwina wasn't young, and the script's type was small—she likely found it difficult to make out the words.

"Where was this house?"

"Sussex."

It was definitely her eyesight, I decided. The proper word was *Surrey* but again I let it pass. "Tell me, how did you die?"

"I was murdered."

That one I had to correct, I thought, smiling, or else the rest of the reading would be nonsensical. "No, Edwina, that's wrong, you're supposed to—"

"*She* did it; she wanted me dead."

She said it so matter-of-factly I stopped, and leaned closer to look at her face. Her eyes were closed, her features relaxed and quite free of emotion. She carried on speaking: "She said she would tell him that I'd run away, but I didn't. I'm here. I'm still here . . ."

I tried prompting her again. "Edwina?"

Poppy's voice, out of the darkness, said anxiously, "Mummy . . ."

"It's all right, dear," Madeleine said. "Don't be frightened. It's only a play."

But it wasn't the play anymore. Edwina slowly turned her head towards me, and I had the uncomfortable feeling she could see me through her still-closed eyelids. Whispering, she told me, "Do be careful. There is evil in this house."

I felt a slow chill on my spine. "Edwina . . ."

"Celia," she replied, and in my slightly rattled state I half-believed she wasn't calling me by name so much as telling me her own.

Only Madeleine was close enough to hear. For a moment the hush held, and we exchanged glances.

And then Edwina stirred between us, opening her eyes. "Oh, I *am* sorry," she said, seeing us staring. "Did I fall asleep? The curse of age, you know—this room's so very warm. Well, shall we try that bit again?" she asked us, picking up her book. "From the beginning?"

ix

I couldn't sleep. Above my bed the portrait of Celia the First gazed down with newly haunted eyes, and every creaking timber of the old house had a voice. *Evil,* breathed the walls around me . . . *evil in this house.* And then a whisper, even fainter: *I was murdered . . .*

In childhood I'd have only had to call out for Rupert or Bryan and one of them would have been there at my side in an instant, turning the light on, dispelling my fears, even sitting as sentinel close by my bedside to hold all the monsters at bay till I'd fallen asleep. But I wasn't a child anymore.

Which left me uncomfortably tossing and trying to be brave. To this end I reminded myself that Edwina's performance, her séance, was all of a piece with Sally's much-consulted tarot cards—a simple entertainment, rather eerily close to the mark at times, maybe, but not to be taken too seriously.

Not that I thought for a minute that Edwina had deliberately tried to lead us down the garden path; but people who believed in things could sometimes fool themselves, could shape reality to suit their expectations. Just as the faithful might swear they saw tears in the eyes of a marble church statue, I thought, Edwina heard the voices of spirits. And being convinced of their realness, repeated their words without ever once doubting that she was relaying not thoughts that had sprung from her subconscious mind, but the words of the dead.

But she didn't intend to deceive. And she had been surprised to learn what she had said while she was 'napping' at rehearsal. "Extraordinary," she'd pronounced it, eyebrows raised. "I haven't gone into a trance for some years."

Madeleine, eager, had asked, "Could you do it again?"

But Edwina had turned her attention to Poppy, who sat very straight and waiting, eyes intense. As though she'd realized she was frightening the child, Edwina had said, "I'm afraid not. The spirit is no longer with us. She's gone."

Round my bed now the walls changed their whisper. *I'm here . . . I'm still here . . .*

Rolling over, I deliberately drowned out the voices with Alex's calm one, recalling what he'd said to me that evening before dinner. He'd come looking for me, purposely, with Max and Nero padding at his side as soft as shadows. They'd found me alone in the long empty room overlooking the terrace, across from our rehearsal room—the room through which Madeleine had ushered me the morning of that first appalling read-through, when she'd taken me outside to have a chat.

We couldn't have stood on the terrace this evening. The rain had returned with a vengeance, transforming the wide stretch of stone to a mournfully grey and abandoned place, lost in a landscape of mist.

I'd been watching the scatter of raindrops on puddles when Alex had suddenly spoken behind me. "You haven't had very good weather," he'd said, in a tone of apology.

Wheeling, I had willed my startled heartbeat to return to normal, gathering my thoughts. "I didn't hear you," I'd explained, as an excuse for my reaction.

"No? I'm sorry." Stepping forwards, he'd drawn something from a pocket, held it out. "You've had another e-mail."

"Oh." I took it from him. "Thank you." Unfolding the single page I scanned it and smiled. Just a small bit of nonsense from Bryan—a joke he had heard at the office, that's all—but it helped to restore my lost balance and grounded me after the day's goings-on as surely as if Bryan himself had been standing there telling it to me.

"I thought you might want to reply," Alex said.

"Now?" I glanced at my watch. "But it's nearly dinner . . ."

"There is time."

"All right," I said, deciding that as master of the house he wasn't likely to be punished if he turned up late for dinner, and by being in his company I could expect a similar immunity. Truth be told, I liked being in his company. He wasn't one of 'us'; didn't belong to the world of the theatre, a highly charged world in which places like Il Piacere seemed wholly at home. No, Alex, like Bryan, was solid and real, and in his presence things seemed very plain and reassuring. Mountains were mountains and molehills were molehills. It was too bad, I thought, he was already taken.

I walked with him through the long corridors, letting my eyes roam a few of the portraits and paintings that lined the walls as thickly and as randomly as posters pasted on a hoarding. In the quiet space beside me Alex coughed as if to clear his throat. "I heard about what happened in rehearsal." I felt his gaze slant briefly down at me, and away again. "I feel responsible. I'm sorry. I should perhaps have warned you of my grandmother's . . . eccentricities."

"Nothing to be sorry for," I told him. "And besides, I'm the one who sort of egged her on to do it in the first place—hold the séance for us, I mean. There's a séance in the play, you see . . ."

"I know, I've read it," he said, reminding me that this entire project was his brainchild, after all; that he was not simply the descendant of the playwright and our host, but our producer, and as such was probably at least as familiar with the material as any of us.

"Yes, well," I covered my embarrassment, "we've been having a problem with blocking that scene, and it sometimes helps to have an expert show you."

"Expert." The word came out softly, between speech and laughter. "She would like to hear you call her that, I'm sure."

"Well, what I mean is, she's a Spiritualist, and she knows what a séance should look like."

"You might have asked me," he replied, and the trace of amusement still left in his voice was surprising to me, unexpected. "I sat in on enough of the damned things when I was a boy, I could have told you exactly what they looked like."

We turned a corner in the corridor. Encouraged by his open

mood, I asked, "And what were you doing sitting in on séances?"

"Part of my penance. I went to school in England—part of my mother's dying wish, I'm told, that I should know her homeland. And it suited Father well enough. He didn't have the time to take care of me, so most half-terms and holidays I was sent to my grandmother's. She has a very draughty house," he said, "in Norfolk. With a forest out the back. And ducks," he added, as though it stood to reason that a woman like Edwina would keep ducks. "She had a group of friends who met on Saturdays—they probably still do—and she insisted I sit in," he said, "to broaden my horizons."

"And did it?"

"Most times it put me to sleep."

"Oh."

"I'm only saying," he went on, "that you shouldn't take it seriously, all the things my grandmother believes."

"I don't." And to prove it I told him about Sally and her white-witchcraft. "It's the same sort of thing, though Edwina's not so flaky." I didn't tell him Sally, too, had talked about an evil in this house—I was trying my best to ignore that part, actually.

"My grandmother," he said in full agreement, "is a woman of intelligence."

"Was your mother very like her?" I asked, tentatively treading on this new uncertain ground.

"I wouldn't know. I don't remember my mother. She died when I was very young. I'm told she was an affectionate woman," he said. And then, after a pause, "My grandmother's not overly affectionate, but she notices. She noticed me." He smiled a tight, self-conscious smile. "She bought me models, model ships, because I liked to build things." And then, as if he'd felt he had revealed too much, he'd almost visibly withdrawn inside himself, his shoulders straightening, his tone of voice more formal. "That's why I asked her to bring Madeleine's daughter down here, on the train. I knew she'd look after the girl."

I personally hadn't thought Poppy Hedrick needed much

looking after, and had said so. "She seems quite a clever young lady, and very mature for her age."

At least, that's what I'd thought then, in that hour before dinner, when I'd walked and talked with Alex.

Only now, as I lay huddled in my bed, my racing thoughts were interrupted by a sudden wild commotion on the landing—a pounding and sounds of a childish sobbing that showed me my opinion had been wrong. Poppy wasn't as poised and mature as she tried to appear. She was twelve, and in need of her mother.

"Mummy!" More pounding. Her voice rose in panic. "Mummy, please!"

When the sobbing went on, without any apparent response from Madeleine, I rose and shrugged into the sleeves of my dressing-gown, belting it tightly around me as I went through to the sitting-room and opened the door to the landing a crack—only enough to see by, not enough to intrude.

Poppy, her pale face streaked with tears, had plastered herself to the door of her mother's room, as if by sheer will she could force her body through the solid wood. Arms outstretched, small fists pounding, she seemed to be nearing a state of hysteria. "Mummy!"

I pushed my door all the way open. "Poppy?" I said, hesitantly. "Poppy, what's the matter?"

I was completely unprepared for her response. No longer the self-controlled almost-adult, she rushed headlong towards me and clung like a child being chased by a legion of bogeymen. Taken by surprise and oddly touched, I wrapped my arms around her narrow shoulders, holding her more closely as she cried. I asked, more gently, "What's the matter?"

The answer came out muffled in my shoulder. All I heard was: ". . . my bed."

"What about your bed?"

"*She* was standing beside it."

"Who was?"

"The woman in the photographs. It was her ghost Mrs. Farrow talked to, Mummy said." A shuddering sob. "She tried to t-touch me."

"Oh, darling." My hand moved of its own accord to stroke

her hair, to calm her, as long ago Rupert and Bryan had sought to calm me in the wake of a nightmare. "It was only a dream, you know—that's all it was."

She sniffed, and moved her head a fraction. "Where's my mother?" she asked, sounding even younger than she looked.

I hadn't a clue, though given the noise that Poppy had been making I felt reasonably certain that Madeleine wasn't asleep in her room. I couldn't imagine where else . . . *Oh,* I thought. "Why don't I go and ask Nicholas?" I said. "Perhaps he knows where your mother is."

I'd been trying to be diplomatic in my phrasing, but Poppy's eyes told me she knew all about the nature of her mother's relationship with Nicholas, and she had no intention of letting me leave her alone on the landing. "I'm coming, too."

Nicholas's room was round the corner from the ladies' wing, strategically placed, Den had told me, so that he shared an outdoor balcony with Madeleine, and thus had easy access to her room without it being obvious. Knowing of Galeazzo D'Ascanio's legendary sexual appetite, I assumed he'd had the rooms designed that way so he could visit chosen female guests at night without his Celia catching on. Rather brazen of him, really, considering that her rooms were next door, but then a man who'd kept his wife down in the Villa delle Tempeste while living with his mistress mustn't have worried too much about protocol.

Nicholas wasn't answering his door, either.

I knocked again, feeling at a loss for what to do but wanting to look competent for Poppy's sake. I sympathized entirely with how she felt—my own tossings and turnings and uneasy imaginings had left me as on edge as if I'd had a nightmare myself, and this was not a reassuring house to be in after dark. The narrow corridor pressed closely and the musty smell of the oriental carpets underfoot when combined with the uncertain light of the wall sconces made the atmosphere darkly Victorian, morbid, decaying, like the stage set for some creepy Gothic melodrama.

I could have simply invited Poppy into my own rooms, and made her a temporary bed on the sofa so she wouldn't

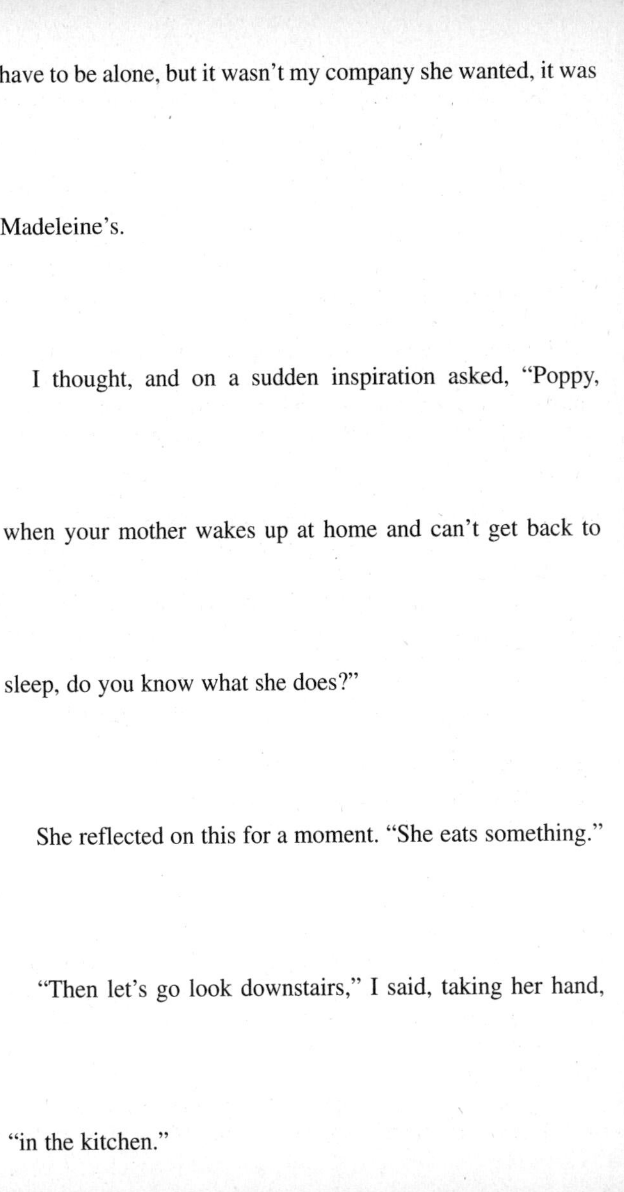

have to be alone, but it wasn't my company she wanted, it was Madeleine's.

I thought, and on a sudden inspiration asked, "Poppy, when your mother wakes up at home and can't get back to sleep, do you know what she does?"

She reflected on this for a moment. "She eats something."

"Then let's go look downstairs," I said, taking her hand, "in the kitchen."

X

THE door to the kitchen, tucked away around a corner at the bottom of the stairway that we came down from the ladies' wing, was an old-fashioned swinging door, covered in green baize that deadened all noise from outside as effectively as any soundproofing system. And the look on Poppy's face when I pushed the door open told me I had just been elevated in her books to the level of a Sherlock Holmes.

"You were right," she said, in open awe. "She's here."

"Yes, well, I rather thought she might be."

Madeleine, sitting at the thick oak kitchen table, looked as though she hadn't been to bed at all—she still wore the pleated soft trousers and jumper she'd worn at dinner, cosmetics intact, her hair only slightly rumpled on one side as though she'd been resting her head on her hand for support.

She wasn't alone. Den, across from her, looked round with surprise as we came in. And then he grinned. "You see?" he said to Madeleine. "I told you we'd get busted." The bottle of wine on the table between them explained, I thought, both his good mood and his grin.

Madeleine's eyes went directly to Poppy. "Oh, Poppet," she said with great sympathy, rising, "what's wrong?"

"I saw the ghost—the woman in the photographs. I saw her standing right beside my bed."

"Oh, darling. Come here. This is my fault," she said, over Poppy's head, to Den and me. "I was talking to Nicholas, earlier . . . Poppet, you know I wasn't being serious at all when I said those things about the woman in the photographs."

"What woman?" asked Den.

"Celia Sands. The first one," she explained, with an apologetic look at me. "I have all these pictures of her in my room, you see, and Nicky was saying she seemed to be everywhere, and I said it was probably her who broke in on our séance. I was only joking." She hugged her daughter closer. "I didn't mean to give you a bad dream."

Poppy, no longer in the throes of immediate terror, submitted to her mother's hug with the typical stiffened response of a twelve-year-old who knows she's being watched and is determined not to look too much the baby. "It wasn't a dream," she said in that same stubborn tone she'd used yesterday with Nicholas. "She was there."

"Oh, Poppet," Madeleine said again, smoothing a strand of the girl's hair away from the childish cheek. "Here, come and sit down. Would you like anything? A glass of water? Cocoa?" Looking at Den, she asked, "*Is* there cocoa?"

"I don't know. Let me look." He stood and rummaged through the cupboards as though it were his kitchen, not Teresa's.

The kitchen was designed, I thought, for function more than comfort. It had one small window, curtained, on the far wall, and beneath it was a single sink and draining-board, scrupulously scrubbed and as white as they must have been the day they'd been installed, no doubt as part of Galeazzo's modern upgrades in the twenties. The tiled worktop ran along two walls and ended at a frighteningly archaic-looking cooker, all knobs and hobs and shelves, that looked as though it might explode if one pushed the wrong button. There were mod-cons as well—a microwave oven, a spidery gleaming espresso machine—but the overall look was traditional, competent, much like Teresa herself.

Den found a tin of cocoa in the cupboard and milk in the fridge, mixed them both into a mug and set the microwave to heat it while he fetched an extra wineglass for me. "Give this a try," he said, nudging the bottle towards me on the table. "There's lots more where this came from. I think we found Teresa's private stash."

The label, turned towards me, had a rich, exclusive look to it, as though it had been pasted on by hand. "Or else," I ventured, "this is one of those rare vintage things that the D'Ascanios have kept for an investment."

"Could be." He didn't sound overly concerned. The microwave beeped and he retrieved Poppy's cocoa. "Here you go, honey. Just the thing for curing nightmares."

Poppy took the mug, and in a small but firm voice said again she hadn't had a nightmare. "She was real. Our séance brought her back. No, Mummy, I *know,*" she said, when Madeleine would have interrupted, "I saw this thing on television last year and the same thing happened, these people accidentally raised a ghost and then it wouldn't leave, and it did all these horrible things, until an expert came to make it go away again." She seemed very sure of her facts, and I knew it would be useless for us to try to tell her otherwise. She was twelve, after all. At that age, one knew everything.

Madeleine smiled. "Well, in that case," she said, neatly working her way round the problem, "in that case, we'd better have Mrs. Farrow hold another séance, so she can lay this ghost of yours to rest. All right?"

That suited Poppy. "Can she do it soon?"

"I don't know. Perhaps Celia could ask her."

I lifted an eyebrow. "Why me?"

Madeleine told me, "I think she likes you best of any of us."

Den agreed, with a happy smile that told me just how much wine he'd consumed. "No one," he said, "could say no to that face."

"Well . . ." I hesitated. I had a feeling Alex wouldn't like it if we had another séance—he certainly hadn't thanked us for encouraging his grandmother the first time out. But on the other hand, there was Poppy to think of, and if this would help stop her nightmares . . .

She looked at me, large eyes imploring.

"I'll talk to Edwina tomorrow," I promised, "and see what she says."

xi

"NO."

I stared at her, taken aback. It was not at all the answer I'd expected her to give. "I'm sorry?"

"Well, my dear," she explained, with a smile to soften the words, "for one thing, I haven't the time. I am leaving tomorrow."

I didn't like to be reminded. In the two days that she'd been here I had grown rather fond of Alex's grandmother, and when I'd spotted her this morning from my window, strolling through the gardens as though on military inspection, I confess it hadn't been solely the thought of my mission for Madeleine that had hurried me into my clothes and downstairs through the still-sleeping house—I'd been eager for Edwina's company.

I'd never had a grandmother myself; at least, not one I'd been aware of. My natural father, whoever he was, might have parents still living, but Mother's had died long before I had made my appearance. And Rupert and Bryan, for all their love and nurturing, hadn't been able to help much in that area—Bryan's parents, like my mother's, were long gone, and though Rupert's mum had managed to hang on a little longer than the others, she'd been very ill, so ill that he had never taken me to see her, and she'd died when I was small.

I rather envied Alex all the schoolboy holidays he'd spent at his grandmother's 'draughty house in Norfolk' with the forest and the ducks. The séances she'd held might have put him to sleep, I thought, but I doubted Edwina herself would have been boring.

She paused on the path to bend over a cluster of flowering

shrubs that I couldn't identify. "Shameful," she said, with a click of her tongue. "Look how the weeds have got in there. Alex will have to have words with his gardeners."

I didn't let her off the hook so easily. "I know that you're leaving tomorrow, but surely . . . I mean, you said yourself you're all packed and ready. Why couldn't we do it tonight, at the villa?"

She straightened from the shrubs with a faint smile. "Daniela would have a fit. She'd be crossing herself and complaining—she takes a dim view of the spirit world."

I couldn't picture Daniela crossing herself, personally. It implied a certain level of humility and piety that didn't fit my image of the woman. Aloud I said only, "I shouldn't have thought that you'd worry about her approval."

"Oh, just look at the state of this border," Edwina said, stooping again. She poked at the greenery, shaking her head.

"And anyway, Daniela doesn't *need* to know. It was only a thought, you know, using the villa—we felt it might be more convenient for you, that's all. But we can always do it at the main house, if you'd rather."

She didn't answer me directly. Wandering a few steps further on along the path, hands clasped behind her back, she appeared, in fact, not to have heard me. Above us the morning sun broke through the clouds with a tentative air, as though testing the waters. Reassured by the chattering song of the birds, it gained confidence, pushing its way clear to cast a weak shadow at Edwina's feet.

"It's criminal," she told me, "what has happened to these gardens. When my daughter was alive, you know, the grounds were kept immaculate. She used to love to hold enormous parties then, and dances at the Peacock Pool, just as there'd been in Galeazzo's day. A shame her husband let things fall to ruin."

Realizing that I wasn't making any headway in my efforts to persuade her, I gave in for the moment and went with the flow. "What's the Peacock Pool?"

"Haven't you seen it? Well, come then, it isn't far. See for yourself."

A short distance on, the path forked, running off in one direction to the trees that ringed the hollow where the theatre lay, but we chose the other turning, winding uphill between fragrant pines and mossy-trunked magnolias till we came upon an avenue of cypresses. These opened out in turn into a setting that brought to mind pictures I'd seen of the Taj Mahal—a long, narrow pool flanked by broad marble paving bleached white by the weather and sun, with a miniature temple affair at the far end that might once have sheltered musicians or elegant ladies who liked to sip tea in the shade. The effect was exquisite.

Even in neglect, with vines winding round the pillars of the temple and the water of the pool turned black and clogged with vegetation, the place retained its aura of formality, of grandeur. I could easily imagine couples dancing here, under strings of paper lanterns with the moonlight making shadows on the wide white marble paving. I looked for the source of the pool's name and found at last, half-hidden in the weeds that choked the water, six stone peacocks in a perfect line that marked the very centre of the pool, beginning close by where we stood and running clear down to the temple end. The birds were tailless, which puzzled me until Edwina explained the design.

"There were fountains, you see, for each statue. Lovely fountains that came up as high as me, higher, and fell in a fan, and those made the birds' tails. In the evening, with coloured lights shining on the water, it was beautiful." She sighed, as though remembering, and I tried to cheer her.

"But surely Alex will restore this, too, in time."

"He may. One never knows. He's rather bound, in some ways, by what Daniela wants to do, and she takes more of an interest, I think, in the buildings. She wasn't very keen, from what he told me, on doing the theatre, either. He had to push to get that project started. And once the estate has been signed over to the Trust . . ." She raised her shoulders in a shrug of resignation. " 'To every thing there is a season,' and these gardens had their day."

Looking down, I nudged a bit of fallen tree bark with my toe. "Edwina . . ."

"Yes, dear?"

"Are Alex and Daniela . . . that is, have they been together long?"

"Since last autumn, I believe."

I didn't know what had made me ask so personal a question. I could feel Edwina watching me, although I didn't lift my head to look. To cover my embarrassment I said, "They make a striking couple."

"Yes." She didn't sound approving. "And I don't doubt that Alex sees her as an asset to this great campaign of his to be accepted as a bona fide Italian."

"Well, he *is* half Italian."

"He is. But the other half's English."

I did raise my head then, and found her studying me with speculative eyes. "It will be interesting to see," she said, "which side wins out."

Beneath her gaze I felt slow colour rising in my cheeks, and I felt tempted to tell her that I wasn't in the competition for her grandson, but she'd already changed the subject. "Your rehearsal starts at ten? We'd best head back, then; you don't want to miss your breakfast."

As she turned to lead me back the way we'd come, I tried again to plead my case for the second séance. "It would be such a great help to Poppy. You know how great the power of persuasion is—you'd only have to pretend you were holding a séance, that you were telling this ghost of hers to go back where it came from, and Poppy would believe you and sleep easier."

Edwina turned her head and fixed me with a kind and patient gaze. "But the spirits, my dear, wouldn't know it was a 'pretend' séance, as you put it. And what if the spirit that spoke with us yesterday comes back again and says more? You do know," she said gently, "whose spirit it was?"

I didn't know exactly how to answer that without appearing to disrespect her beliefs. "Well, I—"

"I'm afraid I couldn't risk a second séance. There are consequences, Celia, for each action that we take—isn't that in fact the message of your play? It's called *Il Prezzo,* isn't it? In English, that's 'the price.' Your characters pay a great price for their choices," she said thoughtfully. She looked away, and for a long moment said nothing. She seemed to be focussing hard on the overgrown temple that rose at the end of the Peacock Pool, darkly reflected in what little water remained. "When dealing with the spirit world, one needs to choose sometimes between the living and the dead. One can put wounded souls to rest, but at what cost?" She brought her gaze back round to mine as overhead the morning breeze wept damply through the pines. "Sometimes it's better, Celia dear, to let the past be past," she told me. "Let the past be past."

The day the workmen finished with the fountains in the Peacock Pool he threw the largest party he had held for many years. The night was fair and warm, the stars were out, and everywhere his servants had strung coloured Chinese lanterns so the pool became a fairyland of light and music, clinking glass and wafting cigarette smoke and the lilting sound of laughter.

At the centre of it all was Celia, dressed in silver, luminous herself, so young and lovely that it set his heart to racing just to look at her. With drink in hand he stood and watched her, proudly.

He was aware of nothing else until Francesca, at his elbow, said, "She must be very good, that girl, to hold your interest for so long. The other women you brought home were lucky to be here a month."

"She is not like the others."

"No." A thoughtful tone. "I think perhaps you love her."

"Does that make you jealous?"

"Caro, to be jealous one must care, and I stopped caring years ago." She raised her glass and toasted him. "Do hurry up and write your play, I simply long to read it." And she laughed and walked away from him, along the bright reflecting pool that caught the dazzling spray of each stone peacock's tail beneath the Chinese lanterns.

ACT IV

Noise and Tumult within.

Such welcome and unwelcome things at once
'Tis hard to reconcile.

Shakespeare: *Macbeth,* Act IV, Scene III

i

THE house seemed a quieter place with Edwina gone.

Not that she'd been in the main house that much to begin with, but I missed her at mealtimes. Her quick mind and quicker tongue had, more than once, thrown Daniela Forlani off balance and caused the younger woman to withdraw into a self-defensive silence. I'd enjoyed that. But without Edwina there, Daniela soon reclaimed her former place as centre of attention.

Poppy didn't like her, I could tell. A few times I'd caught the girl giving Daniela the same look she often gave Nicholas, open contempt mixed with something more private, as though she were wishing they'd just disappear.

I couldn't really blame her in Daniela's case—I frequently found myself wishing the very same thing. Not only because of the way she behaved around Alex, in the same manipulative, doe-eyed way my mother acted with her men. And not because of Alex's predictable response, though I admit that might have been a tiny part of it—for every smile he showed her, my dislike of her increased, for all I told myself it wasn't any of my concern. But what I really took objection to was how Daniela spoke to Poppy.

In fact, the Saturday after Edwina's leaving I nearly forgot my resolve to keep my mouth shut when Daniela at dinner retorted to something that Poppy had said about spirits and séances, "Only fools believe such things."

I wanted to reply, but Den took up the fight instead. Deliberately misunderstanding her target, he answered her calmly. "Oh, I don't know. Alex's grandmother didn't strike me as being much of a fool."

And I had the satisfaction of seeing Daniela's poise waver, of watching her own words come back to trap her as she quickly looked at Alex. "Well, of course I did not mean—"

"I know what you meant," was Alex's rather dismissive reply, and unsmiling he turned to resume his discussion with Rupert. They were talking about books. "But of course if it's plays that you want, I don't know that we have any, other than my grandfather's, that is. If there are any others, they'd most likely be in the Veranda della Diana, the room I now use as my office. My grandfather wrote there, and the bookcases haven't really been touched since his day. You're welcome to have a look through them, if you like, though I'm afraid most of the books won't be much use to you unless you know German or Latin."

"Latin, yes," Rupert said. "German, no."

I joined the conversation out of curiosity. "Did the German books come from the Casetta Fiorita, then?" I asked, remembering what Edwina had told me about Galeazzo clearing out the Austrian's belongings from the house in Venice.

Alex sent me a look down the length of the table, impressed. "Yes, but how did you know about that?"

"Your grandmother told me. When I was down at the villa I happened to see a cup . . . a chalice, your grandmother called it . . . in the cabinet, and I mentioned that it looked like one I'd seen in the basilica in Venice, so she told me the story."

Rupert was looking a question. "What story is that?"

Edwina, I thought, knew it better, but I did my best to tell Rupert what she'd said about Galeazzo D'Ascanio and the Casetta Fiorita—how the house had once belonged to the descendants of a knight of the Fourth Crusade, and how it had come down at last through marriage to the Austrian who'd lost it, temporarily at least, in World War I, and how the poet Galeazzo had, on hearing he would have to leave the house that he'd been renting, helped himself to all the treasures he could find.

Rupert's interest increased. "Are there many things here that came out of Constantinople?"

"There is a small collection," Alex said. "Some silver, the chalice, a few bowls, a sword. Those are down at the villa.

And then there are the tapestries in the Stanza d'Arazzo, those came from Venice also, and they're Byzantine. And these heads"—he motioned to the marble heads of a man and a woman set behind him in the wall niches—"my father always called them Jason and Medea, though I don't know if that's really who they were."

I'd always assumed, myself, that they were meant to be Galeazzo and Celia the First, though I hadn't been able to see the resemblance, and now I knew why. They weren't portrait pieces commissioned by the poet, but rather trophy heads broken from statues as part of the plunder of the Fourth Crusade. I looked at them more closely, the brave but faithless Jason and his bitter wife Medea . . . still appropriate for this house, though they made a better fit with Galeazzo and his wife, Francesca. She would, I imagined, have been bitter, too.

Daniela had developed a suspicious look, as though she expected us all to run down to the villa and invade her private space. "These things you speak of at the Villa delle Tempeste, they are in boxes mostly, not for viewing."

Alex admitted that many things had been packed away for safety while the restoration work was going on. "But I could show you a few of the items sometime, if you like. They're quite lovely."

Den raised an eyebrow. "And valuable, I guess."

"Yes, we have them separately insured."

Nicholas, predictably, showed interest at the mention of money. "You're never giving those things to the Trust, as well? They'd be worth a bloody fortune. I should think you'd want to hang on to them, for an investment."

Alex shrugged. "I have other investments. And besides, things so beautiful shouldn't be hidden away, they are meant to be shared."

Daniela smiled. "Yes, you are right, *caro*. This is a wonderful thing that you do, and this Constantinople collection, it will be well cared for in the years to come, admired by many visitors." And then, as the maid came in to clear our plates, she changed the subject. "You have had news, Alessandro, of that girl who ran away? Pietro said so."

I wasn't sure, initially, why Pietro would have any special

knowledge of the matter, until I remembered that he had supposedly been going around with the first maid, and that it had possibly been an argument between the two of them that had made her run off to begin with.

Alex was nodding. "Yes, her family had a letter from her yesterday, to say she had found work in Milan. It's been a great relief to them. Her mother called to let me know."

Madeleine looked relieved, too. "Well, that's good news, then. I confess I've been worrying myself, about the girl—so many things can happen, these days." Her gaze brushed her daughter, protectively; passed on to Den, who agreed.

"*My* mother," he said, "would have killed me herself if I'd pulled a stunt like that, just not showing up for work one day and taking off."

"I wonder why she left?" mused Rupert.

Alex answered. "That I don't know. It's difficult to tell what goes on in the minds of young women."

Den grinned. "It's not just the young ones. Women of any age are a mystery," he said, with a quick wink at Madeleine that made me wonder if something might not be developing there. I would certainly have been far more approving of Den as a partner for Madeleine than I was of Nicholas, who never had given a good explanation to my mind of what he'd been doing Monday night when Poppy and I had knocked at his door. He'd claimed to have been sleeping, but I doubted that anyone slept quite that soundly. And then there was the matter of his lighter being left down at the Villa delle Tempeste on Sunday.

He had it back in hand, now, and was using it to light a cigarette while we waited for coffee. "So that just leaves you one, now, unaccounted for," he said to Alex. "I don't suppose Giancarlo's in Milan, as well?"

Ignoring the innuendo, Alex shrugged. "I really don't know. He'll turn up when he's ready, he always does."

Daniela shook her head, uncomprehending. "I do not know why you are permitting such behaviour from a servant. When he returns you should tell him to pack his bags, go. But you will not, I know. You have too forgiving a heart."

"This is Giancarlo's home as much as mine," said Alex

quietly, explaining to the rest of us, "his father worked for my father."

I wondered whether it was loyalty that made him keep Giancarlo on, or simply a desire to maintain some kind of connection to his own past. With both his parents gone, and Edwina living so far away, perhaps he needed someone like Giancarlo, who remembered.

The maid returned with the coffee, but Alex declined. "You'll excuse me, I have an appointment. But please," he said, speaking to Rupert, "do feel free to have a look at the books, as I said, in the Veranda della Diana."

"Never mind, it can wait till you have the time. I wouldn't feel right, poking round your office with you not there."

"Nonsense." Standing, he said rather casually, "Celia can show you the way, she should know it by now."

And with a nod to all of us he took his leave, and left me sitting, coffee cup half-raised, to face the roomful of enquiring eyes that turned in my direction.

He crumpled the paper with both hands and tossed it the length of the sunlit veranda. It was hopeless, he told himself, hopeless.

He should have died young. A talent like his was intended to flare up in youth and burn brightly . . . by old age it sputtered and choked on its ashes. He'd known this—he'd seen it himself, in his writing. But the fires of his youth had been so brilliant that most people were still dazzled, still prepared to call him genius, and for years now it had been enough to simply hint from time to time that he was hard at work on some great masterpiece.

Francesca, he suspected, knew the truth. That was why she'd suggested he write a new play, for his Celia; why she kept going on and on about it now, and always with a smile, as though she knew she had tied him a Gordian knot and was finding his struggle amusing.

And yet, he thought, why should *Celia not have a play? He had written plays for several of the others, for Francesca . . . and Celia was above them all, as like to them as wine would be to water. Had he met her in his younger days her beauty might have moved his pen to write a work so perfect it would live for an eternity.*

Pausing, his pen inked and poised on the paper, he lifted his gaze to the bookcases, searching the spines of the leather-bound volumes. A work that would live an eternity . . . Surely his Celia deserved nothing less.

After all, he thought, smiling, the best way to deal with a Gordian knot was to cut it.

ii

"SO," said Rupert, looking around at the comfortable masculine warmth of the Veranda della Diana, "you've been here a few times, then, have you?"

I sighed. "It wasn't like it sounded. I came to send Bryan an e-mail, I told you."

"Yes, I know that's what you told the others, and a very good story it was, too . . ."

"Oh, Roo."

He relented with a smile. "I'm only teasing. Mind you, I like Alex," he said, crossing to switch on a floor lamp beside the long glass-fronted bookcases. "And the fact that he likes you just proves to me he's got good taste."

"He doesn't like me," I corrected him. "Not that way."

"My dear, I have eyes. There's a definite interest."

I glanced up, a little too quickly. "There can't be. I mean . . . he's already in a relationship."

"Ah," said Rupert.

"And anyway," I said, ignoring his quietly knowing expression, "Alex is too old for me. He's thirty-two, Den said."

Rupert pointed out that a ten-year gap meant different things at different times. "There's nearly ten years between me and Bryan, and trust me, when you get to our age, no one really notices." He paused in thought a moment, backing up a mental pace. "When were you talking to Den about Alex?"

"A few days ago, I don't remember. And we weren't talking about Alex, not specifically . . . we were only talking." Then, because Rupert was starting to get that fatherly-protective look again, I said, "I think Den fancies Madeleine."

"It's possible," said Rupert. "Dennis fancies a lot of women." His tone shut the door on that topic, and turning, he carefully opened the glass door of the nearest bookcase. "Now then, let's see what we've got here."

Moving up beside him, I joined in his perusal of the rows of books, inhaling the pleasantly musty smells of old paper and leather. The books in this case nearly all had identical bindings, and as Alex had warned, nearly all of the titles were German. I assumed Rupert was still looking for the elusive play he thought existed somewhere here at Il Piacere, the play Galeazzo had supposedly plagiarized into *Il Prezzo*.

"That's right," he said, when I sought to confirm this. "Although I have a hunch it won't be here—that what I'm really after is a book much larger than these ones, and very much older."

"And what makes you think that?"

"The tale you told at dinner. I didn't know, you see, that the Casetta Fiorita had been built by a Crusader."

"Well, Edwina said it might have been the *son* of a Crusader . . ."

"Either way. If the Crusader, whoever he was, managed to carry chalices and tapestries and silver out of Constantinople, then he might have brought home something else . . . something that would really have appealed to Galeazzo."

Frowning, I followed along with his train of thought. "Books, you mean?"

"It's possible. Remember I told you that the library at Constantinople was one of the finest in the world, before it burned in 1204. It held the complete works of Euripides, Sophocles . . ."

"Oh, Roo." I smiled a little at the far-fetchedness of the theory. "You don't honestly think that Galeazzo stole a play from Euripides?"

Entirely serious, he said, "I'd be inclined to think Sophocles, actually. There are some intriguing points of similarity—the cadence of the dialogue; the single hero, or in this case heroine, who marches blindly on to self-destruction, in spite of other people's warnings—these are very Sophoclean. And

Sophocles, of course, was the first to introduce the third actor, to complicate things. Before him, there'd only been two." Shutting the door of the first bookcase, he moved on to the next.

"So you're saying there might be an unknown play by Sophocles floating around undiscovered?"

"Well, think about it. He wrote over a hundred plays in his lifetime, my dear, and we only have seven today. And we know from the fragments, the bits that survived on scraps of papyrus, or as scattered quotes in other people's letters—'I saw this marvellous new play last night, and in it the characters said such-and-such,' that sort of thing—we know from these that Sophocles wrote a play called *Shepherds,* about Protesilaus and the landing of the Greeks at Troy. You remember Protesilaus?"

To prove I'd been paying attention when he'd told me the myth in Venice, I parroted back, "Protesilaus, the chap who sacrificed himself at Troy so the Greeks would win the war, like the oracle promised."

"Precisely."

"But our play's not about Troy."

"The Greeks," Rupert said, "liked their trilogies. It's possible that Sophocles followed his *Shepherds* with the story of how Protesilaus's wife, Laodamia, had him called back from the underworld."

"Ah."

"It's a rather remote possibility, I admit . . ."

"*Very* remote, I should say." I thought it highly unlikely that a book so ancient and important would go undiscovered so long, but when I said as much to Rupert he merely shrugged.

"It has been known to happen. Lost manuscripts do surface from time to time, and unknown Rembrandts turn up in people's lofts."

"But even so . . ."

"I'm only looking. There's no harm in doing that, is there?"

"No."

"Well, then." Reaching out he drew a volume from the

shelves and smiled. “It looks like Galeazzo had an interest in the spirit world, as well.” Holding the book up, he turned the cover so I could read the title: *Ghosts and Hauntings: A Study of Spirits.*

“May I see that?” Taking the book, I leafed through the front pages and read down the table of contents. “It looks kind of interesting, actually.”

“Not the best bedtime reading for you, though. You’ll have nightmares.”

Head bent, I ignored him. “I wonder if Alex would mind if I borrowed it?”

“If the way he was watching you at dinner is anything to go by, I don’t think he’d mind if you borrowed the whole library.”

I looked up, frowning faintly. He was only teasing me, I knew, and yet . . . “He wasn’t really, was he? Watching me, I mean. Because I haven’t done anything to encourage him.”

“Perhaps you should.”

I stared at him as if he’d grown an extra head. “You’re giving me *advice*?”

“Oh, no, only commenting. You do what you like. Just remember it’s not every day that one finds oneself being pursued by a wealthy and handsome young man.”

“Yes, well, this wealthy and handsome young man has a girlfriend.”

“I see,” Rupert said, understanding. “And you’re not your mother, is that it?”

“Exactly. It’s like Bryan says—”

“Oh, Lord. Bryan.” Rupert cut me off in midstream, looking at his watch. “I was supposed to ring him at ten o’clock. Damn. Is there a phone in here, I wonder?”

“On the desk.” I pointed, then looked hopefully on as he dialled the number. “Can I talk to him, too?”

Rupert smiled at me indulgently. “I thought you liked your e-mail.”

“Well, it’s not the same as talking.”

I had missed the sound of Bryan’s voice. It came across the crackling line like soothing music. “Angel, what are you still doing up? You ought to be in bed.”

"I *am* an adult."

"Only just. You've been getting my e-mails?"

I assured him I had. "Only you mustn't send so many of them. They come in on Alex's business computer, you know, and he has to deliver them to me."

"Who's Alex?"

"D'Ascanio."

"Ah. Well, no worries," he told me. "It probably brightens your Alex's day, Angel, reading my jokes." He laughed. I had missed that, too. "Anyway, how has your week been?"

"Not bad. We did have some excitement on Monday." I gave him an edited version of Edwina's séance. "Kind of creepy, actually, and it frightened Madeleine's daughter half to death—she's still having nightmares about it, I think." She'd been sleeping in Madeleine's room since the night of the séance, and Madeleine, to ease Poppy's mind, had removed all the pictures of Celia the First that had hung on her wall. "We wanted Edwina to hold a follow-up séance, to convince Poppy that the spirit had gone away, but Edwina wouldn't do it. She took it very seriously—said that we ought to just let the past lie."

Bryan surprised me by asking, "And what do you think?"

"Oh, I don't think it's *real*—"

"No, I mean about letting the past lie," he specified. "Do you agree?"

I wasn't sure why he was asking me, but Bryan rarely asked without a reason, so I gave the matter thought. "I don't think I do, no. I think, if there really were something worth knowing, then I'd want to know it."

"I see." Then he changed course completely, and moved on to talking about something else. "So, what's Dennis O'Malley been up to?"

I could have told him heaps of anecdotes, but I was very aware of Rupert standing close behind my shoulder, and I knew how much it bothered him whenever I talked about Den. "Nothing much," I said. "Look, I really ought to let you talk to Roo, now. He's been waiting very patiently, and like you said, it's time I was in bed."

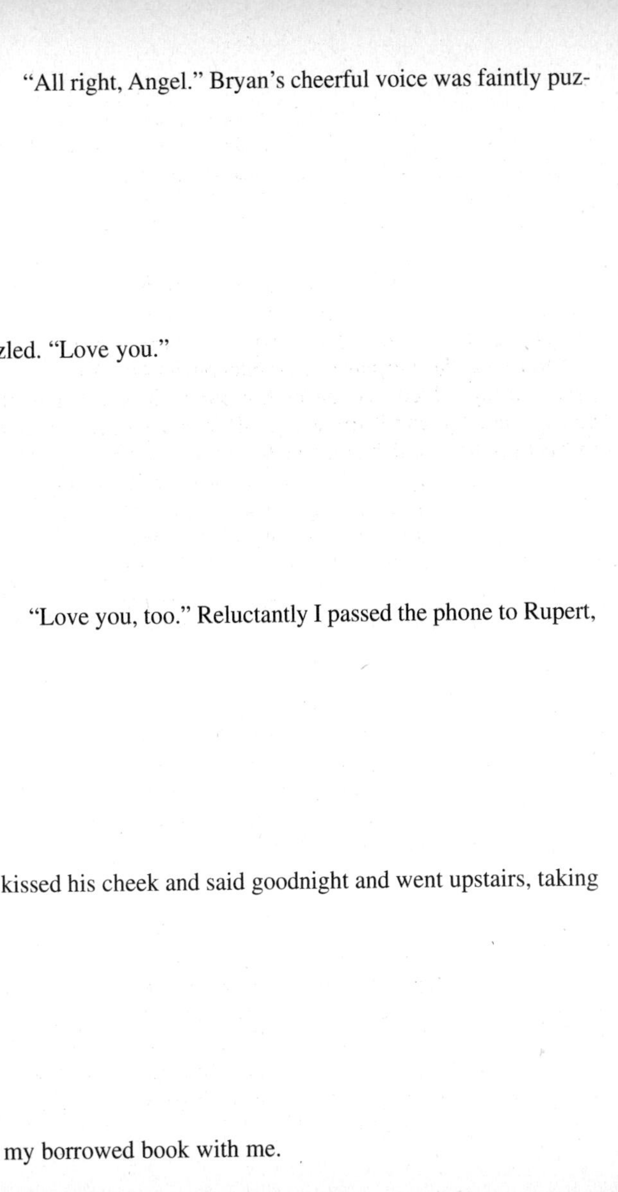

"All right, Angel." Bryan's cheerful voice was faintly puzzled. "Love you."

"Love you, too." Reluctantly I passed the phone to Rupert, kissed his cheek and said goodnight and went upstairs, taking my borrowed book with me.

iii

IN bed, I reached first for the book of Galeazzo's poems, to check a reference. Having seen the marble statuary heads in the dining room tonight, the 'Jason' and 'Medea' heads that had supposedly come out of Constantinople, it occurred to me that somewhere in *The Season of Storms* was a poem that mentioned Medea.

Yes, here it was, in his twenty-ninth poem 'To Celia,' where after telling Celia for the twenty-ninth time how matchless she was, he then compared her to an unnamed woman—probably his wife, I thought—who wandered through a putrefying garden,

> *. . . like Medea, with my children's blood upon her hands,*
> *an evil breath upon her lips,*
> *Her rival's flames around her head like some despoiled*
> *halo . . .*

"Ugh," I said, and closed the book. I could understand why others thought that Galeazzo's final play had been a plagiarism, though I didn't agree with them. Most of these poems had, after all, been written in the years that had followed his affair with Celia. He'd written the play while they'd been together, and love, I knew, had inspired many an artist through the ages to great heights of achievement. Petrarch had had his Laura, Dante his Beatrice, and Galeazzo, for a few years anyway, had had his Celia. So I thought it wholly possible that *Il Prezzo* had burst from some unfettered recess of his writer's mind, a final act of beauty like the singing of a swan about to die.

The poems, though, as Rupert said, had come from somewhere else.

I set them aside and instead took up *A Study of Spirits,* the book that I'd borrowed from Alex's study, deciding that reading about hauntings and ghosts would be less gloomy and depressing. I was two chapters in before I realized that I'd made a big mistake. Rupert had been right—this book was not the sort of thing that I should read before I went to sleep. Already my imagination was creating goblins underneath the bed, and unseen watchers in the shadows.

Even when I'd reluctantly set the book down I had trouble convincing myself I was really alone in the room. Every sound, every creak of a carpeted floorboard or knock of a pipe in the wall, took on a new sense of malevolence. As the curtains at my windows ruffled slightly in a draught I imagined that I saw Teresa's stern face looking at me through the glass, and heard her voice. *Is not a room for guests,* she said. *Things happen.*

Uncomfortably aware of the watching eyes of Celia the First's portrait above my head, I burrowed deep beneath my sheets and closed my eyes.

iv

I woke from fitful sleeping to the early morning sunshine and the twittering of birds, the combined light and noise making any thought of drifting off again impossible. So much for enjoying a lie-in on my Sunday off, I thought, rubbing the grit from my eyes as I came down the stairs.

No one was up yet, not even Teresa. The kitchen was quiet.

"Damn," I said. I was desperate for a cup of tea, but even if I'd known where Teresa kept the kettle I could not have braved that cooker. Just the look of it, a monster built of gleaming pipes and hobs and knobs, made me feel hopelessly incompetent. If I'd so much as touched it I'd have surely burnt the house down.

Pushing up the sleeves of my jumper, I took a look round and decided to go with the microwave. It wouldn't be *good* tea, I thought, but at this point I didn't care. I found a mug easily enough in the cupboard, near where I'd seen Den get the glasses the night we'd drunk wine. Filling it with water, I popped it into the microwave to boil and started searching for the teabags.

Head in the cupboards, I rummaged with growing frustration. "It shouldn't be this difficult to find a bloody teabag." I wasn't complaining to anyone in particular, and given the whine of the microwave oven I wouldn't have thought anyone would have heard me, but somebody did. From behind me a hand reached up, brushed past my shoulder, and took a tin box from the second shelf up, bringing it down till my own hands could grasp it.

I jumped. Spun around, banged my head on the cupboard

door, then dropped the tin with a whopping great crash, spilling teabags out over the hard tiled floor.

"Careful," said Alex, one hand outstretched in what might have been either an instinctive attempt to steady me or an equally involuntary effort to protect himself from my erratic movements. It apparently hadn't occurred to him that his coming up on me like that, so close behind me, without warning, might have scared me half to death.

I'd been holding my breath, and I let it out now in a long, controlled sigh. "I didn't know that you were there."

"I wasn't trying to be quiet," he excused himself. "I thought you would have heard me."

"Well, I didn't." That came out a bit more peevishly than I'd intended, but I couldn't help it. My heart, which I would have expected to slow in its pounding when I'd identified the person who'd surprised me, had instead speeded up at the sight of him, and to hide my consternation I was forced to bend and make a show of picking up the teabags, letting my hair fall forward to screen my reddening face.

Alex, unaware of my confusion, knelt to help me. He didn't have the dogs with him, which meant, I assumed, that he'd either been with Daniela or was on his way to see her. I tried to use that knowledge to restore my equilibrium. "I thought Teresa would be in here," I said, seeking to justify my presence in the kitchen even though he hadn't made an issue of it. "I only wanted a cup of tea."

"It's Easter Sunday. I've given Teresa the morning and afternoon off, to spend time with her family in Mira."

The microwave finished, its hum abruptly ending in a bell that sounded rather like the ones that mark the end of fighting rounds. Alex gathered up the last few teabags, took the tin in hand and straightened, looking round the kitchen. "She said that she'd make up some baskets of bread and preserves for me to set out in the dining room, so you could all just help yourselves to breakfast. I was going to make coffee," he said, bringing his gaze back to me. "I suppose I could boil a kettle, as well, for your tea."

"That's all right, I've got it taken care of."

Glancing at the microwave he said, "You can't drink that."

"It's not so bad."

"It's not real tea," he told me, very definite. "You need a teapot." Brushing past, he opened the door of a cupboard beside me and drew out a plain silver teapot, setting it down on the worktop with such determination that I couldn't help but smile, just a little.

"That's your English side showing," I said.

He looked up as though I'd surprised him, but his shrug was purposefully Latin. "Oh, I don't know. We Italians have a thing for food and drink—we like things properly prepared."

"I see." I watched him while he searched another cupboard for the kettle, found it, filled it at the sink. Head bent in concentration, he looked younger somehow, almost like a boy, and I found myself thinking of what Edwina had said about Alex not fitting in anywhere, not being wholly Italian nor wholly an Englishman, trapped in a kind of a cultural limbo.

Perhaps that was why he was trying so hard now, I thought, as Edwina had said, to be accepted as Italian—why he was willing to give away his home to gain approval, with Daniela's help . . .

Thinking of Daniela and their relationship centred my thoughts again. As I looked away, yawning, Alex asked, "Didn't you sleep well?"

"Not particularly, no." I didn't tell him about my foolish imaginings and the bumps in the night, but instead shrugged it off with the comment—not a lie—that I'd been having trouble sleeping for a few nights, now. "Den thinks it's because of the weather."

"Well, if Den says it, then it must be true." I thought I detected a hint of sarcasm in his voice, but I couldn't confirm it by looking at him since he'd bent his head again to watch the kettle. "He's up early, as well. I saw him on my way up. He was heading, I believe, towards the theatre."

I registered only four words: "On your way up?" From the villa, I expected. From Daniela.

Alex answered without turning. "Yes, from the boathouse.

We've been doing repairs on a few of the boats and I went down to see what was fueled up and ready to go. I need to make a run to Sirmione later on."

"Sirmione." The name rang a bell, but I couldn't recall . . .

"It's a town," he supplied, "at the southernmost end of the lake, on a peninsula. A very ancient town."

"Oh, right." I remembered, now. We'd talked about it on our first day here. "The place with the hot springs. The Romans built a spa there, Den was saying."

Glancing up he said, "The Grotto of Catullus, yes." The kettle boiled. He made the tea. The silence stretched between us.

"Well, you've got a lovely day for it," I said at last. "Your trip, I mean." I gestured towards the window, where the morning sun angled in shallowly, strongly, and clear sky showed blue through the lace of the curtains.

"Yes." He set the teapot by me on the worktop. "You will need a cup."

"I have one in the microwave, actually. No, I'll get it, that's all right. I only need some milk, if you—"

"Come with me," he said suddenly.

I turned from the microwave, mug in hand, staring. "I'm sorry?"

"To Sirmione. I promised before that I'd show you the sights when you had a day off, and there's a lot to see in Sirmione. We could have lunch there, and you could tour the grotto while I do my business."

"Oh. I—"

"It is your day off?"

"Yes."

"So come with me." His tone was persuasive, but . . .

"I'm sorry," I said. I'd be no better than my mother, I thought, if I went on what amounted to a date with this man, when he was already involved. That said, he was still my employer, and I couldn't just turn him down flat—I needed an excuse. "I mean, it's kind of you to offer, but I can't—I promised Rupert that I'd spend the day with him. In fact," I compounded the lie with a glance at my watch, "he asked me

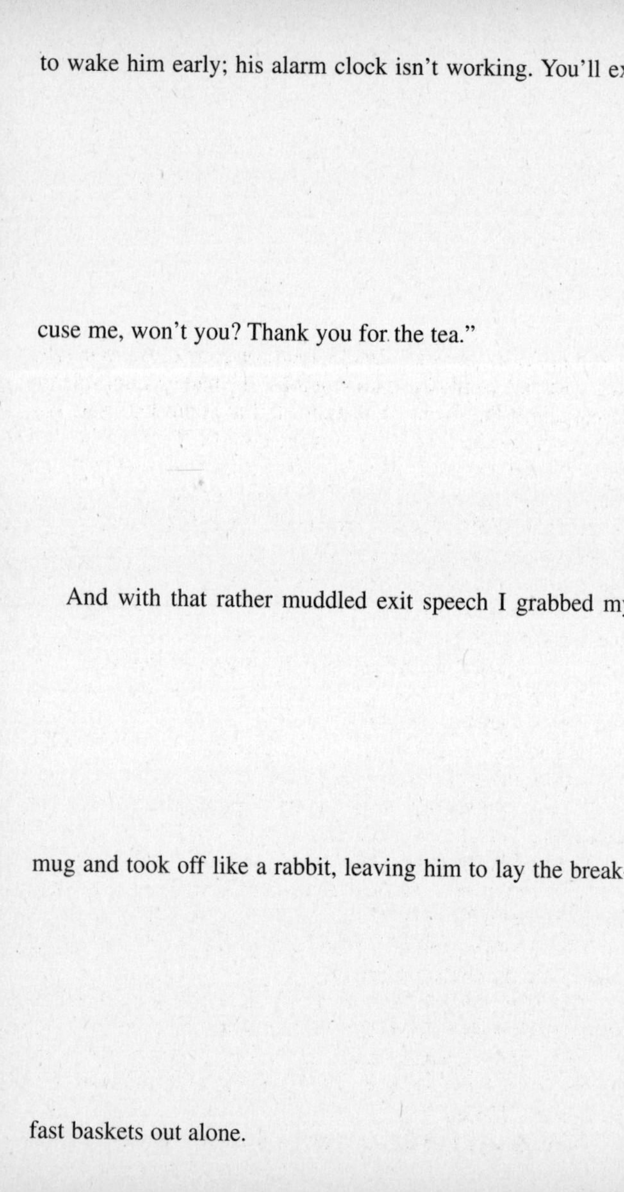

to wake him early; his alarm clock isn't working. You'll excuse me, won't you? Thank you for the tea."

And with that rather muddled exit speech I grabbed my mug and took off like a rabbit, leaving him to lay the breakfast baskets out alone.

V

I didn't really need to wake Rupert, of course. Anyone who knew Rupert would have known that—he had an infallible internal alarm that went off without fail at about half past six. When he answered my knock at the door of his room he was fully dressed, shaved, with his bed neatly made and a book laid open on the table near the chair beside his window.

He looked at the mug in my hand. "Is that for me?"

Following his gaze I noticed for the first time that in my haste to get out of the kitchen I'd forgotten the milk for my tea, and I couldn't drink tea without milk. Rupert, on the other hand, liked both his tea and coffee black. I thrust the mug toward him. "Yes. I thought you might like room service."

He smiled as he ushered me in. "And I thought you were fed up with serving people."

"Oh, well, I've got to keep in practice, haven't I? I'll likely be back waiting tables by Christmas."

"You never know," said Rupert. Moving to the table, he closed the book he'd been reading.

I peered at the cover. "Bulfinch's *Mythology*?"

"I found it on the shelves in Alex's study last night. I haven't read it in years."

"You've been busy," I said, noting that he'd marked his place near the end of the book.

"Yes, I'm into the legends of Charlemagne, now. Exciting reading. Though I still prefer the Greek myths overall."

"You and Galeazzo both. He keeps popping gods and heroes in on every third line of his poems—in the last one I read it was Medea."

"I've always had a soft spot for Medea," Rupert said. "A

much-maligned character. Madeleine played her, you know, years ago."

I hadn't known that. Madeleine had starred in so many productions, and I'd been lucky enough to see most of them, but I'd missed her Medea. To be honest, I'd probably missed it on purpose. There was something about the idea of watching her play a woman being cast off by her husband, being abandoned along with her children so that he could go and marry someone else, that hit a little close to home. I don't know that I *could* have watched it. Still, I knew if any actress could have made an audience feel sympathy for a character who killed her own children and poisoned her husband's new lover, it would have been Madeleine.

"You'd have been about two at the time," Rupert went on, "a little young for me to take you, but it was a great performance. Your mother, of course, didn't think so—she'd read for the part herself, you see, and thought she ought to have had it. That was what started it."

"Started what?" I felt myself frowning.

He glanced at me over the rim of the mug as he sipped his tea, and I saw him censor himself. "Nothing. Sorry, I spoke out of turn."

"Tell me."

"I'll owe Bryan a pound if I do," he said, referring to their gentlemen's agreement not to say anything negative about my mother in my presence.

"Yes, well, you could buy a small country for what Bryan owes you on that count, and besides, I won't tell him if you don't. So, what are you talking about? Started what?"

"The thing," Rupert said, "between your mother and Madeleine." And then, as I went on looking at him, uncomprehending, he asked, "You did know they were rivals?"

"Well, obviously, yes, because of Mother's affair with—"

"Oh, no," he corrected me, "it started years before that, years before. *That* was the end of it, not the beginning."

"It was?" I felt the way the first explorers must have felt when offered proof the world was round, unable to let go of their belief the earth was finite, flat, with monsters at its edges.

"Decidedly the end. A *coup de grâce.* Mind you," he said, "your mother may have won the final battle, but the war ran fairly even up to then, as I recall. You ought to ask Madeleine, sometime. I'm sure she could tell you some stories."

"I've no doubt she could." My voice sounded vague as I searched through my childhood memories for any remembrance of this war that he was speaking of, but I drew a total blank.

I was still trying to absorb this minor bombshell when Rupert asked, "Have you been down for breakfast, yet?"

"No, I . . ." I thought of Alex downstairs setting out the breakfast baskets on the sideboard, laying plates and making coffee, and the image made me remember why I'd come up here in the first place. "Actually, I came to ask a favour."

"Oh, yes?"

"Alex asked me if I'd like to go to Sirmione with him, and—"

"You see? Didn't I say that the boy had his eye on you?"

"Roo, I'm not going. I told him I'd already arranged to spend today with you, so I was rather hoping . . ."

". . . that I'd back you up in your lie?" He finished the thought for me, smiling.

"Only until Alex leaves. We don't have to do anything special, I'll just tag along, if that's OK."

He shrugged a noncommittal shrug and raised his mug of tea. "I was about to take my walk," he said. "You'd better get your coat on."

vi

I should have told Alex I'd made plans to spend the day with Madeleine, I thought, or Poppy—somebody more sedentary. I hadn't been out of doors for fifteen minutes before I was perspiring, legs burning from the strain of keeping up to Rupert's pace. Thankfully, here in the gardens the air was still cool, though the sunlight fell warm on my face, shining down from a sky that was robin's-egg blue, fading down to a paler white-blue at the peaks of the mountains. A few innocent-looking puffs of small white cloud hung overhead, barely moving, and lighter clouds wrapped round the top of Mount Baldo like gauze, so transparent I could make out the folds of the mountain beneath.

Last night's rain had left a litter of sodden leaves across the garden path, and a scattering of forsythia, and above us the leaves of the olive trees glistened like silver. The water droplets hung in the thick hedges and on the splayed palm fronds where, caught by the breeze and the sunlight, they glimmered like diamonds.

Songbirds flitted everywhere among the cypresses and weeping pines, and over their small joyful voices we heard, now and then, church bells pealing below in the town to remind us that today was Easter Sunday.

"A beautiful morning," said Rupert, with typical understatement. "You see what people miss when they sleep late?"

I didn't answer him straight off. I'd spotted a familiar-looking turning in the path ahead and was trying to gather enough breath to speak. When I finally did manage it, the words came out in a rush: "Have you been to the Peacock Pool, yet?"

"To the where?"

I slowed my pace purposely, drawing in air. "Oh, you have to see this, Roo. You'll love it," I promised. I led him up the winding path, more convinced with every step that I was headed in the right direction, although I wasn't really sure until I came upon the avenue of cypresses. "Edwina showed me just before she left. It's really something. There," I said, a few steps on.

The peacocks looked a little less forlorn this morning, standing in the sunlight that reflected where it could along the surface of the water, in between the choking reeds.

Rupert agreed with me that the Peacock Pool looked like a miniature Taj Mahal. "But the mausoleum here is very Western, very classical. It's not the least bit Indian."

"It's not a mausoleum," I corrected him as he wandered ahead of me, mounting the steps of the pale marble temple and peering round the columns. There were seated stone greyhounds that guarded the steps, carved no doubt by the same sculptor who'd created the peacocks. I touched the head of one as I passed. "Edwina said that there used to be dances here. I think it's more of a tea house. You know, for the dancers to rest in."

Standing with his back to me, hands clasped behind him in the manner of someone patrolling a portrait gallery, he said, "You haven't looked closely enough."

The open-fronted temple blocked the breeze but I still felt a chill when I joined him. Here in the half-light, deprived of the sun's warmth, the marble walls dripped with green stains, breathing damp. Fighting off a shiver, my nose wrinkling slightly at the sharp dank smell of stone, I moved up close to Rupert's shoulder, following his contemplative gaze towards the row of age-tarnished brass plaques set into the wall.

"'Brutus,'" I read the names, "'Jango. Napoleon.' What are those, dogs?"

"I would hope so. They'd be unfortunate names for children."

"They must be dogs," I said. "Besides, Galeazzo only had the one son, didn't he? Alex's father. And I don't see his name here, anywhere." Looking down the wall I started counting the plaques, but gave up when I'd reached thirty. "Do you suppose they're all actually buried here?"

Rupert thought it possible. "There must be a crypt of some sort, underneath, though I can't see how one gains access . . ."

The answer came from several feet behind us. As always, I hadn't heard Alex approach. He told Rupert, "My father had the crypt sealed off. He thought it much too dangerous, because I played here as a child."

Rupert, turning, smiled a welcome. "Good morning, Alex. Happy Easter."

"And to you."

"We're not trespassing somewhere we shouldn't be, are we? Not risking the wrath of Pietro?"

His mouth curved. "No, there's nowhere in the gardens that you may not go. And if Pietro gives you trouble you must tell me, I will talk to him." There was a rustling from the path behind him and the dogs came bounding out to join us, apparently enjoying a last run in the garden before Alex left for Sirmione. Max came straight to me, tail wagging, and as I petted his head I could feel Alex watching.

"We've been looking at the dogs," I said, diverting his attention to the row of tarnished plaques. "At least, we assumed that's what they are . . . or rather, were."

"Yes, my grandfather's greyhounds. He was a sentimental man." Alex didn't climb the steps to join us in the little mausoleum. He stayed down beside the pool itself, hands deep in the pockets of the dark jacket that he'd thrown on over shirt and jeans since last I'd seen him. "He wanted to be buried here himself; had his artisans build him a marble sarcophagus, a huge thing, it's down in the crypt, but it's empty—my father wouldn't hear of such a burial. He was very devout, my father. And a practical man, not the least bit romantic. He didn't bury any of his own dogs here."

I looked at Max and Nero, wondering what would happen to them when their time came, whether Alex would lay them to rest with the bones of their ancestors, down in the crypt with Galeazzo's empty sarcophagus.

Alex asked, "So, where are the two of you going today?"

I turned to Rupert, hoping he would answer that. He did,

though not exactly in the way that I'd intended. "Actually," he said, and smiled, "there's been a change of plan. I have some work I need to do with Den." He met the accusation in my eyes with innocence, and smiled.

Alex looked at me. "Then you are free to come to Sirmione."

"Well, I—"

"Go ahead, my dear," said Rupert, waving me on as though giving permission. "Enjoy yourself. We'll do our thing another time." And leaning close he brushed me with a Judas kiss.

"Another time," I promised, and gave him a glare, but he didn't look at all concerned. He looked, in fact, rather insufferably pleased with his cleverness.

Left with no polite option, I turned to face Alex. "Thank you, I'd love to come. When were you wanting to leave?"

vii

SEEN from the water, the hotels and houses of Mira del Garda formed a long, unbroken sweep of ochre walls and red tile roofs along the lakeshore, while behind that line a smaller scattering of rooftops climbed the darkly wooded hillside, growing sparser till they hardly showed at all amid the lush green trees and cypress spears. And higher still, I glimpsed the sprawling splendour of Il Piacere—here a patch of roof tile, there a flash of yellow wall, a slice of terraced garden, and the chimneys of the Villa delle Tempeste.

For the first time I could see the mountains looming up beyond our own steep hill, too far back for me to see them from the windows of my room, massive grey stone mountains etched with white and capped with snow, like the more imposing peak of Mount Baldo that now lay behind us.

My view of the opposite shore was less clear. A haze had settled over it, blending the speckle of towns and the rolling green hills into one smudge of colour, washed pale by the sun. And between that shore and me lay Lake Garda, deeply blue and roughed with tiny rippling waves that mirrored back a million fragments of the sunlight overhead and, dancing, slapped and rolled the boat whenever Alex slowed the motor.

I'd expected that his boat would be expensive. I was right. It had looked modest enough in the boathouse, surrounded by the larger craft, but here on its own on the lake it commanded attention, a twenty-foot-odd sleekly tapered motorboat, long-nosed and gleaming red, with leather seats and streamlined windscreen and a spoiler rising wing-like at the back that I presumed was meant to hold us on the water at high speed.

I'd expected to feel seasick, too, but I didn't—likely because we were moving so fast that my body hadn't time to feel the motion. I'd only ridden in boats a few times, and Alex hadn't helped my confidence any by handing me a life-jacket when I'd climbed on board, but now that we were underway, with the boat kicking up a cold three-cornered spray to our rear and the lake spread before us, both shorelines in sight, I'd begun to relax.

It helped that the noise of the motor made conversation difficult; impossible at times. If Alex felt the need to point a bit of scenery out to me he throttled back so I could hear him and then turned away again without requiring me to answer. Which was fine by me. The less I spoke the better, went my thinking. I'd been working at looking the part of a casual cosmopolitan to whom boat rides like this one were commonplace, and I didn't want to spoil it all by opening my mouth and coming out with something stupid.

So when Alex asked me, "Are you cold?" I simply shook my head and smiled and leaned back in the leather seat, adjusting my sunglasses, looking away. I wished I'd thought to change my clothes before we'd left, not so much for warmth's sake as for style, but I was stuck with the rather plain outfit I'd put on this morning. I wished, too, I'd taken the time to eat breakfast. My stomach was starting to rumble. But I knew I could hold out till lunchtime, I'd done it before.

To distract my mind from thoughts of food I watched the passing shoreline. We went by a few towns that were smaller imitations of Mira, each one strung along the water's edge with stately promenades and harbours, porticoed buildings and villas-turned-hotels that looked like elaborate stacked wedding-cakes, painted in holiday colours of yellow and deep pink and white. And round them rose the everpresent cypresses and lacy silver olive trees and palm trees, and the trailing mounds of flowered vines and shrubs that gave the whole western side of the lake the appearance of one giant tropical garden.

I wasn't sure which I liked better—my view from the bus on that first day, with the lake spread beneath me, or what I saw now from this lower perspective, encircled and made to feel small by the mountains and hills. Both vistas held beauty.

Alex, turning, throttled back and pointed ahead to a finger of land jutting out from the distant flat shore at the base of the lake. I couldn't see much detail, only a ridge of high cliff at the finger's tip, facing us, and greenery on top. "That's Sirmione," he informed me. "Not too far, now."

We swung wide on our approach, giving me a slightly better look at the peninsula. It snaked out very narrow from the mainland, growing wider at its tip, and all along the shore on our side narrow jetties marked the spas and hotels tucked among the trees. The main port, roughly halfway down the strip of land, called attention to itself with a row of tall flagpoles set into the low harbour wall, flying multicoloured flags of many nations as a welcome.

Alex steered our boat towards it, manoeuvering expertly through the narrow entrance and around the other vessels to an empty mooring place. Having taken off my life-jacket, I thought it best to wait and let him help me up onto the quayside. I was not a practised sailor and my feet weren't very steady on the slickly painted surface of the boat.

This was only the second time Alex and I had actually touched since the handshake we'd exchanged when I'd arrived at Il Piacere, and I was unprepared for the wash of awareness that swept through my system as his fingers closed around mine, firmly, warmly, without hesitation. For an instant when he let me go I felt that I might still be on the boat, the ground beneath my feet seemed less than stable, and I was grateful for the sunglasses that hid my reaction.

Alex said, "I'm afraid the crowds will be a bit thick—this is one of our busiest holiday weekends."

The quay, I thought, wasn't too crowded, but off to the one side a bustling car park appeared to be spouting out tourists in one steady stream. They passed beneath shade trees, paused by the vendors offering lemons and oranges from stalls beneath gaily striped awnings, then carried on over a little stone bridge, disappearing at last through a massive medieval stone gateway.

We pressed ourselves into the chattering, laughing procession and passed in our turn over the bridge, which spanned what looked to be a stone-walled canal or a moat running out of the harbour . . . moat, I decided, as having passed through the great gateway I found myself standing in a large and spacious square before a castle, squat and angular with crenellated towers. Detaching myself from the crowd, I crossed to have a closer look, leaning my elbows on the waist-high wall protecting the moat, that I now saw ran right round the castle.

"This is the Rocca Scagliera," Alex said, behind my shoulder. "In the thirteenth century, Lake Garda was under the rule of Verona and the della Scala family. They built fortresses, or *rocche,* all round the lake, to defend it."

"From whom?"

"I don't know. Anyone who wanted to invade, I suppose."

The only invaders that I could see now were a motley assortment of ducks paddling round in the moat, above the darker, darting forms of giant carp-like fish who rose now and then to the clear water's surface to battle the ducks for a breadcrumb tossed down by a tourist. Still, the castle could, I thought, have held its own against all comers. Baked a blinding yellow-white beneath the late morning sun, it loomed solid and sure overhead, dwarfing everything close to it, even the towering palms in the square.

Alex looked at his watch. "I'm afraid I don't have enough time before my meeting to take you through the Rocca Scagliera, but perhaps after lunch?"

I agreed, settling in the meantime for a quick stroll round the shops. Letting him lead me away from the castle, I followed the flow of people into the tight narrow streets of the town.

This part of Sirmione reminded me of Venice's commercial promenade—both seemed in some ways artificial, made for show. Oh, the setting might be real enough, the town's antiquity quite evident, but in spite of its castle and its cobbled streets and all the olde-world atmosphere, Sirmione was very much part of the present. It shouldn't have been, but it was. It was too slick, too fast-moving, too full of tourists; and well-heeled tourists at that, if the number of people emerging from shop doors with carrier bags was anything to go by.

The holiday weekend had brought out the foreigners, mostly Germans from what I could catch of their conversation, travelling in pairs, or pairs of pairs, cheerfully intent on enjoying themselves in spite of the still-cool weather. Laughing often and loudly, they passed us in a mix of ages—older couples, quartets in their thirties, and one couple who didn't look old enough to be out on their own, a true Romeo and Juliet, their wedding bands still shining new on their clasped hands. There were Italians, too, in family groupings, with babies in pushchairs and toddlers who pulled on their mothers' arms; and I heard French spoken now and then, but not English.

Only once, and that was by Americans—a middle-aged woman buying a cuddly toy dog the size of a real-life Alsatian for her daughter, a girl of about Poppy's age. Which made me think maybe I ought to buy Poppy a trinket or something, a small souvenir. She was ill, after all, and could do with some cheering up.

I chose a little necklace of delicate seashells, and Alex stood beside me while the shopkeeper wrapped up my parcel in bright coloured tissue-paper, tying it with ribbon.

"And this is for Poppy?" he asked, in a curious tone.

"Yes. It always makes you feel better, getting gifts when you're ill, don't you find?"

"I wouldn't know. No one ever gave me gifts when I was ill."

"Oh," I said. Rupert and Bryan had brought me things all the time—chocolates and story-books, puzzles and games. When I'd had the chicken-pox, Bryan had bought me a book every night on his way home from work, and we'd read it together at bed-time. "Well, take it from me, it does make you feel better. And anyway, it's not expensive jewellery, or anything. If she doesn't like it, she can always throw it in the bin." Picking up the parcel, I turned to face him. "I haven't made you late for your appointment, I hope?"

He cast a glance down at his watch. "No, I have a minute left. Come, let me show you the road to take to the Grotto of Catullus." Outside, he pointed me in the right direction. "You can't miss it, really. You just go up there, up the via Catullo. The gate to the grotto is right at the end."

I nodded. "If you'll give me a time and a place where you'd like me to meet you . . ."

"I'll find you," he assured me. He likely only meant he knew the grotto well, and so would have no problem finding someone in it, but the certainty with which he made the statement made me feel a little fluttery inside. I watched him walk off through the jostle of tourists. His fair head blended easily with those of the Germans, and yet I had no trouble at all in singling it out, as though it were already so familiar that my mind retained its imprint.

My stomach grumbled. It had actually been making noises for the past hour or so, but now the rumblings grew insistent, to the point where I was sure they would be audible above the chatterings of passersby. Temporarily postponing my visit to the ruined Roman grotto, I began a search for food, a search that led me to an open square that fronted on the lake, ringed round with restaurants and cafés and tables set out on the pavement.

I didn't even bother to compare the menus—I simply took a seat at the first outdoor table I found and waited for service. It was still a little early for a proper lunch, but a small sandwich and a cold drink filled the void. I would have enjoyed the food more if it hadn't been for the man sitting two tables over, a suave-looking man in a bright red shirt, who seemed always to be staring at me when I raised my head. His stare was rather more appraising than malevolent, and he might have been the sort of man who looked at all women that way, but I found it uncomfortable.

I purposely waited until he had gone before I paid my bill and headed out again in the direction that Alex had shown me.

Not that I really needed direction—I simply had to follow along in the wake of the crowd and I found myself swept from the narrow claustrophobic streets of the old town and into the via Catullo, surrounded by others making the same gradual ascent up the wider, tree-lined road, as though I'd somehow joined a pilgrimage in progress.

I'd got partway up before I missed my tissue-paper parcel.

"Damn." I had set it on the table at the restaurant, with my handbag, I remembered, but I didn't have it now. I must have forgotten it. Wheeling in my tracks, I started down again, cursing my lack of attention. I wasn't going to have much time to look around the grotto, I realized, not after all this. I had already spent all that time eating my sandwich and walking up here, and now here I was doubling back.

Luckily, the waiter hadn't got round to clearing my table. I picked up the tissue-wrapped necklace and tucked it safely away in my handbag.

In my absence, a large white passenger hydrofoil had docked at the lake end of the open square, discharging a new flood of daytrippers into the already congested streets. The man in the bright red shirt was back, standing now at the end of the dock, lounging against the rail like a wolf on the make, watching the women pass by. In my eagerness to slip away before he noticed me, I turned too fast, colliding with another man just passing by the restaurant.

"Oh, I'm sorry, excuse me," I said, and he nodded, preoccupied, stepping round me without stopping.

He had, I thought, one of those faces that I felt I ought to remember—sharp-featured, brooding, rather hawk-like . . . Then I *did* remember. He was the same man I'd seen going in to have a word with Alex in the Veranda della Diana on our first day of rehearsals. One of the workmen, I'd assumed, only seeing him here it seemed rather more likely that he was a business associate, or something. He might have even been the person Alex had come here to meet.

Only that would have meant that their meeting was over. Forgetting the hawk-faced man, I hurried back to join the pilgrims' procession up the via Catullo so I could at least reach the grotto before Alex came looking for me.

I had made it as far as the level gathering-place at the top of the road, with the iron grille of the entry gate in sight, when a pair of running children heading downhill knocked my arm by accident, throwing me slightly off balance and sending my handbag flying. Their mother murmured something that I took for an apology as she brushed past me in the children's wake, her eyes distracted, but she didn't stop to help. With a sigh, I turned and bent to gather up the rolling items that had tumbled from my handbag when it hit the pavement—scattered coins, both Italian and British, a couple of Biros, a lipstick, the little seashell necklace in its tissue-paper parcel . . .

"Let me help." A second pair of hands joined mine in the retrieval effort as Alex crouched down to my level. Stuffing a few things back into my handbag, he righted it on the pavement and looked round. "Is that everything?"

"Yes, I think so. Thanks."

He straightened with me, watched me brush my arm and readjust the strap against my shoulder. But when I raised my head he looked away, his gaze travelling uphill and back as he tucked his hands deep in his pockets. "So you're done with your tour of the grotto, I see," he said. "What did you think?"

I could have told him the truth, I suppose, and confessed that I hadn't yet been, that I'd wasted the past hour in eating and running about, but it seemed easier to simply reply, "It was lovely. But crowded," I hastened to add. "That's why I came out here." I waved a hand around me at the low stone walls surrounding the large open gathering-place near the entry gate, high on its cliff overlooking the lake. "I thought I'd have a seat on the wall, you know, enjoy the view and wait for you. Make it easier for you to find me."

He looked at me intently for a moment, saying nothing . . . so intently that I thought he maybe knew that I was lying. The blood rose pounding, guilty, in my ears, so loud I nearly didn't hear him.

"There are better views," he said. "Come, let me show you."

viii

I hadn't seen the signpost on my way up the via Catullo, nor the footpath leading off from it, and even if I had I doubted I would have been moved to investigate, because the word on the sign—*Lido*—was at least a word I knew, and I would have expected a bathing beach, even this early in the season, to be crawling with people.

It wasn't. There were tourists here, to be sure, but fewer of them and they seemed a different breed than those I'd been among before. These ones were quieter, more leisurely. They strolled.

The beach was a long strip of golden white sand, with a long wooden pier stretching into the water and a blue-roofed restaurant baking in the sunlight at the shore end of the pier. From the sand's edge a garden of olive trees rose in grass-covered terraces, sleepy and serene, its neatly trimmed pathways and benches sheltered by a stone retaining wall above which I could see the peaceful steeple of a little church.

We hadn't come too far from where we'd been—the tall pale cliffs on which the Grotto of Catullus ruins sat curved off immediately to the north, and to the south, beyond a stand of cypresses, I saw the tall stone tower of the Scagliera castle in the town. And yet it felt like we had gone a million miles from Sirmione.

I looked at Alex, keeping pace beside me as we passed the restaurant's umbrella-dotted patio and headed for the pier. He was being, I thought, quieter than usual, if such a thing were possible, as though he were still working over some detail of the business meeting in his mind. Whatever the reason, he was clearly preoccupied. I had visions of him stepping off the pier into the water without knowing it.

The water here, at least, was very shallow, perhaps only a metre or so deep, and a perfect pale peridot green, crystal clear to the slabs of flat rock growing algae at the bottom. Two ducks dozed alongside us, bobbing along to the motion of the water, and near them a lizard lay sunning himself on the pier. Further on, in imitation of the lizard, a young boy had stretched out flat on his stomach, absorbed in watching schools of tiny minnows darting in among the rocks. Stepping over the boy's legs, I continued on towards the long pier's end, enjoying the spring of the wood underfoot and the lapping of water below and the freshening bite of the breeze on my neck with the warming sun full on my back.

To be safe, though, I stopped several feet short of the end and, turning to Alex, said, "You're right, it is a lovely view."

That roused him, as I'd hoped it would, from his distracted mood. He stopped walking. Looked up, at the water around us, the sun on the cliffs, the deep violet blue of the opposite shore with the long ridge of snow-covered mountains behind. "Yes, I've always thought so. It's sort of a blend of the Swiss Alps and the Mediterranean."

I'd never seen either place, except in photographs, but to admit that would have spoiled the sophisticated image I was trying to present, so I only gave a knowing kind of nod and levelled my gaze on the jewel-like green water that deepened to blue farther out off the end of the pier.

"Over there," said Alex, pointing straight out where I was looking, "is the Fonte Boiola, the hot spring that has fed the thermal baths of Sirmione since the Romans came."

I couldn't actually *see* it, of course, but I nodded again. "Yes, Den said that there were spas here."

"Yes, well, Sirmione's waters are supposedly useful in the treating of arthritis, and complaints of age. That's likely why he knows about them."

I gave a laugh, half-turning. "I don't think Den's that ancient."

"No? I assumed he was roughly the same age as Rupert."

"A few years younger, I should say."

He glanced at me. "I gather Den's been married?"

Which struck me as rather an odd question for him to ask, but I couldn't see the harm in answering. "Yes, he's divorced."

"Ah. And he's only had the one wife, has he?"

Looking at him sideways, I replied that I had no idea. "Why do you ask?"

"I just wondered. He strikes me as the type of man who might have three or four wives in the cupboard."

"Den? A Bluebeard?" I smiled at the image. "Oh, I wouldn't think it likely. I'm sure he has hordes of old girlfriends, but wives? No, it isn't his style. Like he said himself, he isn't any good at being married."

"He told you that?"

"The first day we met him in Venice," I said with a nod. "In fact, I believe it was one of the first things he *did* say. Mind you, he might be softening his views a little, now."

I felt Alex turn to look down at me. "Might he?"

I bit my lip to stop myself from being indiscreet, and saying more about the way that Den was getting on with Madeleine. Not only would our play's producer not be overjoyed to learn that there might be a romantic triangle developing between his SM and two of his actors, but it was only speculation, after all. Bryan always said it only got one into trouble, spreading gossip.

Instead I deflected his question with one of my own, shielding my eyes with one hand as I looked at him. "That sun's awfully strong, isn't it?"

"We can sit in the shade, if you'd rather."

We had to leave the pier and climb the olive grove to find an empty bench among the trees. From up here the beach appeared even more lovely, more secluded, and the people on it even more remote and insignificant. Above our heads the olive leaves rustled ever so slightly as the breeze blew by, and by my feet a scattering of tiny white-and-yellow daisies nestled in the grass. I'd expected Alex to lapse back into silence, but he surprised me by asking, "So, how are the rehearsals going?"

"Very well. I really should thank you for giving me this

part—it's been a dream of mine, you know, to work with Madeleine. She's wonderful."

"And Nicholas? How is he to work with?"

"Pass."

"Pardon?"

I shook my head. "Bryan says that if you can't say something nice about a person, you should keep your mouth shut."

Alex smiled. "I see."

"Besides, I can think what I like, but the man is a tremendous talent, really, and successful, whereas I'm still doing walk-ons." I caught myself. "That is," I amended, aware that I'd just shot my sophisticated image all to pieces, "I *was* doing walk-ons . . ."

A moment passed. A tiny grey-brown lizard had come out to bask upon the tree trunk nearest me, and I focussed my attention on it, envying its stillness.

Alex said, "You didn't have a walk-on part in the play that I saw. You had lines."

My head came round so quickly that I startled the lizard—it shot down the tree trunk and into the grass like a bullet. Not that I paid the poor creature much notice. Staring at Alex, I asked him rather stupidly, "You saw me in a play?"

"Last autumn. Last October, actually. In *Happenstance*."

An awful farce. I'd had four lines. I'd been onstage so briefly that my own friends might have missed me. "You'll be one of the rare few who actually saw that play, then. It got horrid reviews. It only ran a week before it folded."

"Yes, I know. I must have caught you on your final night. I went back to see it again, but the theatre was closed." He fixed his gaze idly on the lake, watching the wake of a small boat, far out on the water. "I did manage to locate your agent, through Equity, but the same day I did that I also met Rupert for lunch—our first meeting—and he said he knew a young actress who'd be perfect for the widow's role, and that her name was Celia Sands, and wouldn't that be good for our publicity. And then he pulled out his wallet and showed me a photograph." He paused, and his gaze slid back to me. "And I told him yes, he was right. You were just what I wanted."

Time stopped, and my heart did a curious flip in my chest,

and I didn't know quite what to say. So I said nothing, and after a moment I felt his gaze leave me and swing out again to the water.

The lizard, encouraged by the silence, crept warily out of the grass again and up the gnarled tree trunk till it reached the spot where it had been before. I said, "But hang on . . . in the programme for *Happenstance*, I wouldn't have been billed as Celia Sands. I used my stage name: Celia Sullivan."

"Yes, I know."

"So you had no idea I was Celia Sands until you talked to Rupert?"

"That's right."

"But you made it a condition of your offer, that I use my real name."

He gave a small shrug. "Because Rupert was right, it was good for publicity. You can't buy a publicity angle like that; it would have been foolish to waste it."

It seemed an improbable chain of coincidences, really—that he'd seen me at all in that horrible play, and that the director he hired should turn out to have such close connections to me, and that I should turn out to be named for the actress who'd starred in the play he himself was reviving. But when I pointed this out to Alex, he only smiled.

"My grandmother would argue that there are no coincidences."

He turned the smile on me, then, and I suddenly felt like I'd stepped off the long pier myself into water well over my head.

"Shall we go find a place to have lunch?" Alex asked.

I didn't remember, afterwards, too many of the details of what followed: where we ate, or what, exactly . . . only that the restaurant was a small one, tucked discreetly down a narrow street, and that the waiter glided like a ghost, and that our table had a vase of fresh-cut daisies in its centre. We drank wine and ate and drank more wine and talked through the meal about nothing and everything—theatre and books and, of all things, astronomy, though I was never too sure how that subject came up. And later, full from the meal and languid from the wine, I walked with Alex through the back streets, trying to absorb the sights he showed me, though the only ones that truly made an impact were a quiet church with pillars and a marble porch of chequered red and white, a blue plaque mounted on an alley wall in memory of an English woman writer who had died at Sirmione, and a little unexpected garden fronting on the lake—a sort of gated courtyard with a small well at its centre, gay geraniums and, facing one another, carved stone statues of an older man and woman in medieval dress.

Alex told me who they were, but I'd forgotten by the time we reached the harbour and the boat, and then it hardly seemed to matter because all my attention was claimed by the sun in my eyes and the spray of the lake water cold on my face and the exhilarating feeling of speed.

It seemed a much quicker trip back, but that might have been partly the fault of the wine, and the fact I was lost in my thoughts half the time watching Alex's shoulders in front of me. By the time we arrived at the boathouse of Il Piacere I knew I was not only over my head but beyond hope of rescue. I'd fallen, and hard, for this man who was turning to help me up out of my seat.

I wasn't sure how it had happened, or when, but it had. I was stuck with it.

And now, I thought, I was no better than my mother. She, too, would have smiled at Alex as he handed her onto the dock, and looked at him with eyes that showed exactly how she felt, and let him kiss her on the cheek. A short kiss, friendly, just a glancing brush along my cheekbone, but it tingled through my system like a jolt of electricity.

I stepped back quickly, tucked a strand of hair behind my ear, and stammered something incoherent about needing to find Rupert. "Thank you for a lovely day," I told him, and with that I turned and made a coward's dash out of the boathouse and began the uphill climb along the path towards the house.

ix

I came up the terrace steps frowning, and was halfway across before I realized I was not alone.

Daniela, elegant in black and wearing sunglasses, uncurled herself like a cat from the chair she'd been lounging in, shifting to face me. "You're back," she said simply, and yet something in her tone made me feel for an instant like a teenager caught coming home past curfew. I halted in my tracks a little guiltily.

She smiled. "Did you have a good time?"

So she knew. "Yes, I did, thank you." I didn't know exactly how to handle this—whether I ought to explain, or apologize, or what. As I tried to decide, Daniela leaned back in her chair, assessing me, I thought, the way a careful politician might assess the opposition.

The sunglasses threw me off a bit—it was always harder to read someone's expression when you couldn't see their eyes. Her voice, when she finally spoke, was decidedly neutral. "When I was young," she said, "there was a neighbour's dog that liked to come onto our property, chasing our goats, so my mother put out poisoned meat. The dog died, and our neighbour he was angry, but he could do nothing. My mother had a right to do the thing she did, because the dog was trespassing." She paused, and lit a cigarette, holding it between her perfectly manicured fingers as she added pleasantly, "You understand what I am saying?"

I'd have had to be an idiot, I thought, to miss the threat, but as threats went it seemed so unlikely and over the top that I found myself quite at a loss for a reply. I'd probably have laughed if I wasn't so taken aback. I could feel my face starting to flush as it frequently did when I faced an unjust accusation. Carefully, I said, "I think you're telling me that Alex is a goat."

Her lips compressed, a tiny sign that I'd succeeded in annoying her. "You know he's taken."

I was getting annoyed, myself. Which explained why I forgot my guilty conscience long enough to snap, "You'd best tell *him* that, then." And deciding that would make as good an exit line as any, I turned and started walking off.

Daniela's voice followed me, cutting. "I've heard this is a habit for the women of your family, stealing men."

I stopped. My flush became a burn that spread not only up my face but through my veins as well, blurring my reason and leaving me frustratingly unable to defend myself with words. And in the midst of this I heard approaching footsteps, heard Daniela greeting Alex in Italian in a voice as smooth as honey, heard him say to her in English, "Yes, a good day." Then a pause, and I could feel his eyes on me. "Is everything all right?"

"Of course." I kept my back to him—I knew my cheeks would still be flaming, and I didn't want to let him see that, didn't want to give Daniela any cause to feel triumphant. "Of course it is," I said again. And straightening my shoulders I excused myself and left them with a calm, unhurried walk that plainly said I wasn't bothered.

But I was.

X

IT took some time, once I had reached my room, to recompose my thoughts. Splashing my face with cool water, I frowned at the mirror, replaying the scene in my mind—only this time I rewrote my lines so that for every one of Daniela's remarks I had the perfect comeback, not so rude as to sink to her level of bitchiness, but classily sharp, in control. The more I rehearsed it, the better the scene became, and the more satisfaction I felt, though I would have been happier had I been able to do it for real, when it counted.

Still, I thought, it didn't matter. *She* didn't matter. And as for Alex, she was welcome to him, with my blessing. I washed my hands of the pair of them.

As I went through to my sitting-room the faint sound of Daniela's laughter drifted upwards from the terrace and I pulled the window closed to shut it out. Almost immediately, a nearer, more appealing laughter echoed from the landing. Looking out, I saw Poppy and Den at the head of the stairs. Den was holding a flat cardboard box in his hands.

"Hey, you're back," he said, seeing me. "Great. Care to join us in a friendly game of Chutes and Ladders?"

"Snakes and Ladders," Poppy corrected him.

"Whatever," said Den. "We're just on our way down to the dining room—figured the table down there was the best one for game-playing. How was your trip?"

"Fine. Oh, hang on a minute, I've got something for you," I said, remembering as I looked at Poppy. Pushing my door all the way open in invitation, I turned back into my sitting-room to hunt for my handbag.

Den followed, intrigued. "What, you brought me a gift?"

"Not for you," I said. "For Poppy."

The child hovered in the doorway, her dark-eyed face a mix of curiosity and doubt. "For me?"

I'd found the handbag, and the little parcel that had caused me so much trouble today. "That's right." I passed it to her with a smile. "We went round a few of the shops in Sirmione, and I saw this and thought you might like it. It's nothing too fancy, but—"

"For me?" she repeated, as though she hadn't quite taken it in.

Den gave her a nudge. "Well, open it."

Her small hands tore the tissue-paper, easing off the ribbon, and the seashell necklace slithered out into her waiting palm. She stared. "It's beautiful." From the way she held it up and looked in wonder at the tiny tinkling shells you'd have thought that I'd given her diamonds. "Thank you so much."

Such genuine appreciation, I decided, made the trouble all worthwhile. "You're very welcome."

"Wait till I show Mother," she said, slipping the necklace over her head as Den, beside her, pushed his lower lip out in a pout.

"And there's nothing for me?" he asked. "Typical."

I smiled. "Maybe next time."

"I'll hold you to that. So you went all that way to go shopping?"

"And sightseeing."

"Well," he confided, his amused gaze meeting mine in conspiracy over Poppy's head, "you've put someone on the warpath, so I hope that it was worth it."

An hour ago I'd have told him straight out that I hadn't intended to go in the first place, that I'd been tricked into going by Rupert, and that Daniela had a right to be upset. But coming fresh from the encounter on the terrace I felt less sympathetic. I said, "He's not wearing a collar and lead that I know of."

Den grinned, as the mention of collar and lead pulled Poppy's attention away from her necklace. "Are you talking about the dogs? I got to play with them today. We saw the kennels, didn't we, Den?"

"We did indeed."

"I don't think Max and Nero like it in the kennels," she went on. "Not when they're used to the house."

Den explained that the kennels were nearly a part of the house, and that Alex likely only put the dogs there when he planned on being out all day. "And anyway, he's home now. They'll be able to come out."

Not so long as Daniela was out on the terrace, I thought—the greyhounds would have to stay somewhere else, out of her way. Which was probably, I conceded, not such a tragedy for the dogs after all. Better to stay somewhere else than to have to put up with the woman's presence.

"Where are the others?" I asked.

"They abandoned us, didn't they, Poppy? Took off into town to have tea at the Grand Hotel."

"And they didn't take you?"

"Well, Poppy was sleeping," said Den with a shrug and a look that told me he had volunteered to stay behind and babysit. "And I didn't feel like walking all that way."

"I see." I wouldn't have minded playing Snakes and Ladders with the two of them, but the dining room, where they intended to set up the game, was a little too close to the terrace for my liking. "When did everyone leave?"

"About an hour ago." Interpreting my tone of voice, he checked his watch. "They're probably still there, if you wanted to catch up with them. Of course, it would mean leaving *us* . . ."

"Would you mind?"

"Nah. We'll make our own fun, won't we, Poppy?"

She nodded, but her faintly disappointed look prodded me to promise, "I'll challenge you both to another game later, though. Say after dinner?"

"You're on," Den said, holding me to it. "But be warned, I'm damn good."

He was good at a few things, I thought, as I watched him

disappearing down the stairs with Poppy, noticing their natural and easy interaction and how quickly he restored her happy mood. I wondered whether Den had any children in New York. He might have been, as he proclaimed, a wash-up as a husband, but I fancied he would make an all right dad.

From where he sat he saw the boy at play, a lonely figure pushing toy cars round the garden path.

It shamed him, in that moment, that he had not been a better father. True, the boy had been Francesca's doing—her desire, her child to raise, but still, the fact that he could look now at his son and feel no love disturbed him greatly. He felt the way he felt whenever someone that he knew returned from visiting a land he'd not yet seen—a nagging sense that he'd missed out on something.

It would be different, he decided, with his second child. His melancholic mood was washed away by this new flood of expectation as he closed his eyes, recalling how she'd told him late last night, in bed, and how he'd placed his hand upon her belly, still so flat, so soft, and felt a wave of wonderment roll over him, as overwhelming as the sea at rising tide. And then had come the fears: he was too old, he was too selfish, he would fail her . . .

But she'd only smiled and held his hand against her and, still smiling, slept, and he had watched her till the dawn had slowly filled the room with light—a new day, ripe with promise.

Yes, he thought now, opening his eyes to look once more upon his son at play below him in the gardens—yes, it would be different, this time. He had learned from his mistakes.

xi

ACROSS the courtyard, Max and Nero peered at me hopefully through the wire of their runs. They looked rather lost in the long stretch of kennels that must, at one time, have been home to thirty or more dogs. Max woofed and wagged his whip-like tail so hard I felt compelled to cross and speak with him.

"It's all right, sweetie," I said as he poked his long nose through the wire in search of my hand. "Just hang in there, it won't be much longer. I'm sure he'll come let you out soon."

If I'd known how to unlock the gates, I might have let them out myself, if only for the momentary satisfaction I'd have gained from knowing they'd frighten Daniela. But the best I could do was give Max's smooth snout an affectionate scratch before I turned and took the steps down to the drive.

It seemed a much shorter walk out to the main road, I thought, when one wasn't lugging suitcases. At least I had a fair idea this time what direction I should go in. The Grand Hotel in town—that's where Den said the others had gone for their tea, and I'd seen the Grand Hotel from the water this morning. Alex had pointed it out as we'd passed, and its distinctive tall tower ought to make it easy enough to find once I got down to Mira.

The road itself was practically deserted. I heard the mosquito-like whine of a Vespa that had just passed by, heading uphill, but that was all. Still, I kept prudently to the edge of the road, facing whatever traffic might approach me on the left-hand side. The verge was bright with buttercups and daisies, set off further back by a handful of plum-coloured blossoming trees that had come into bloom since I'd last passed this way.

I was so absorbed in looking at the trees, I nearly didn't hear the car.

Then, too, it came on quickly. So quickly, in fact, it had all but gone by me before I reacted by sidestepping into the verge. I nearly lost my balance, but the bright red Mercedes whizzed past in a spray of dust and gravel, unconcerned.

"Moron!" I called after it, steadying my stance as I brushed the blown hair from my eyes. More indignant than injured, I cautiously edged to the side of the road again, soldiering on downhill, round the next bend.

I didn't recognize the thing for what it was, at first. In fact, I think my first thought was that someone must have thrown their rubbish from a passing car, a heap of clothes . . . and then I took another step, and I could see the clothes weren't empty.

They contained a man—a man who lay facedown, half-buried in the verge, one arm outstretched as though he'd tried to break his fall. He was still breathing when I reached him.

"Oh, God." I crouched to see how badly he'd been hurt. One leg looked definitely broken, twisted round below the knee so that his foot jutted out at an unnatural angle. And the red stain in the grass beside his ribs was spreading steadily. His face was turned away from me. I touched his hair, I don't know why—from instinct, I suppose. The human need to give an injured person comfort. "It's all right," I said. "You'll be all right. I'll go get help . . ."

Which was meant, of course, to soothe him, but my words came out so panicked and so urgently I can't imagine that they did him any good. Besides, he likely didn't understand, as I was speaking English.

But he heard me. As I made to stand, he moved his head and tried to move the outstretched arm that I now saw was broken, too, and bleeding. It must have caused him unbelievable pain, but he moved it anyway, and then with a supreme effort brought his head all the way round as though compelled to look at me.

I knew him, then. The hawk-faced man.

I caught my breath, and felt my eyes grow wide with recognition and surprise, while his glazed over. I had never seen death before, not like this—never watched somebody's face while the life left their body, nor heard the rattling breath that stopped midway, unfinished. I suppose I'd always thought that death would either be violent or peaceful, but this one was neither. It shook me rather more than I'd have wanted to admit.

I don't know how long I stayed kneeling there, staring in shock. It might have been a minute or an hour. I only know the sound I heard next, and what snapped me from my stupor, was the sound of Rupert's voice. Not the words, not distinctly, but only the voice, the calm familiar timbre of it just as I remembered it when, waking as a child, I'd heard him talking in the sitting-room with Bryan.

I did stand, then, and looked towards the sound. There was blood on my hand from where I'd touched the dead man's hair, and I held it out stiffly away from my body as though I had touched something dirty. I wasn't aware at that moment of crying, but something felt warm on my face and I must have looked a fright because when Rupert finally did come into view, with Nicholas and Madeleine behind him, he took one startled look and immediately quickened his pace, reaching my side out of breath and concerned. I went into his arms as if I were still seven years old.

"There now," he stroked my hair. "Hush, it's all right."

And then Madeleine and Nicholas were there, and I was telling all of them, in a strangely flat voice that sounded nothing like my own, exactly what had happened, and then Madeleine stepped away a little and said, "Oh, my God," or something like that, and Nicholas asked, "What?" and she replied, "Well, darling, look who it is," and he moved to look, too, and he swore.

Turning my head against Rupert's shoulder, I frowned in their direction, trying hard to keep my gaze from drifting

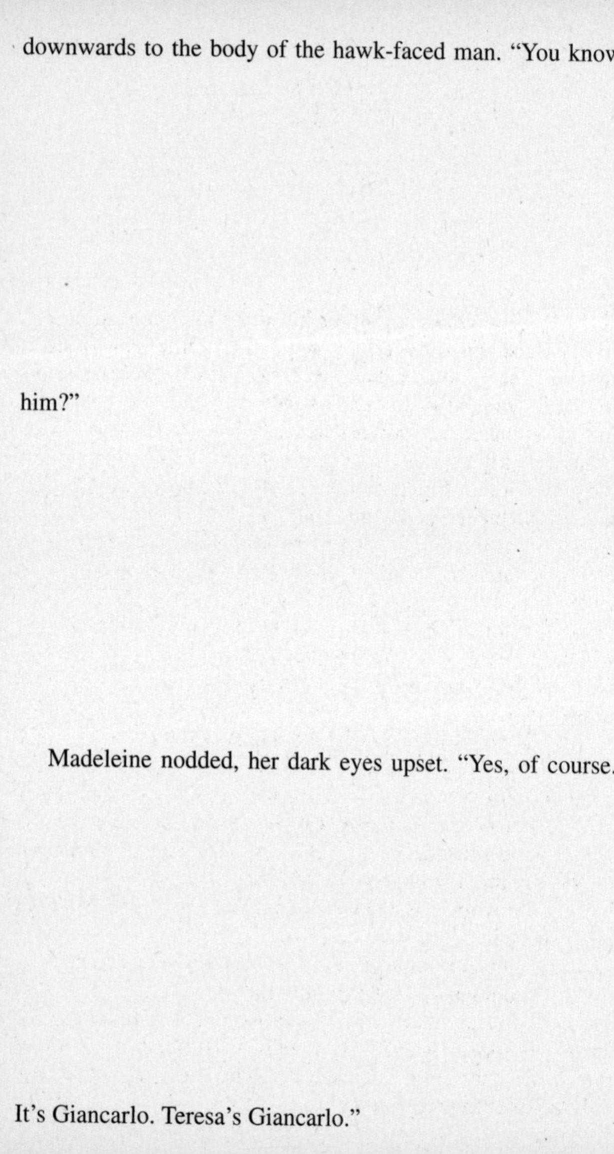

downwards to the body of the hawk-faced man. "You know him?"

Madeleine nodded, her dark eyes upset. "Yes, of course. It's Giancarlo. Teresa's Giancarlo."

xii

THE breeze had grown teeth. I drew my knees up tighter to my chest and wrapped my arms around them, blocking as much of the wind as I could with my back. I could have put my jacket on, but it was underneath me at the moment, serving as a makeshift groundsheet, keeping out the damp and protecting my trousers from grass stains. Feet braced against the angle of the sloping hill, I sat looking down on the theatre below me, tucked peacefully into its hollow.

I wasn't entirely sure what instinct had driven me here—I had only intended to take a short walk in the gardens, to get away from everyone and clear my head, but my feet had developed a direction of their own and I'd found myself here, with the circle of sheltering pines at my back and the soft blowing grass and the wooden roofed stage sitting silent beneath me.

In less than three weeks I'd be down on that stage, I thought, trying to persuade the people watching me that I was someone else, to make them set their knowledge of reality aside and trust illusion—to convince them there were walls where none existed, that a ghost could walk and talk among the living, that my character's emotions were as genuine and worthy of involvement as their own. The actor's art was, after all, a study in deception.

I'd grown comfortable with this, and with the fact that, in the theatre, things were never what they seemed. A door that appeared to lead out to a street really only opened onto a tiny curtained corner of backstage; sunrise was simply a trick of the lighting; the chilled gin and tonic the butler delivered was only room-temperature water.

But that was the theatre. I didn't like being deceived off the stage. And I didn't like knowing that Alex had lied.

I was thinking this, resting my chin on my knees, when the cold bluntness nudged at the back of my neck.

I didn't jump. I froze. And then the cold thing gave a questing sort of snuffle and I twisted round to face the dog that owned the nose. I might have expected that it would be Max, the flirtatious one, his long brindled snout only inches from my face, his mouth half-open in a doggy grin of self-congratulation, looking pleased that he had found me.

Nero, never so bold, had stayed further back. Beside the man who stood against the circle of the trees.

As Alex came forwards I turned my back to him again, sparing a scratch on the ears for the dog who had come round to sit by my side. His master either didn't recognize the snub for what it was, or didn't care. A pair of long denim-clad legs stepped within my peripheral vision.

"I thought I'd find you here," said Alex.

There seemed little point in responding, so I didn't.

He sat, half-turned towards me with one arm slung across his up-drawn knee, as Nero collapsed with a grunt on the long grass beside him. "You didn't come to dinner."

"Yes, well, I figured that dinner was off," I said, not looking up. Which was truthful enough. Teresa had, understandably, not been in any condition to make anything, and the house had been in chaos when I'd left.

"We managed with cold ham and pasta," he told me. "Rupert helped. He's quite a good cook."

"Yes, I know."

He paused, in reaction I think to the shortness of my answer. Then he said, "We did leave some for you."

"I'm not all that hungry, thanks." Pulling a few blades of grass from the ground I chose the longest one to toy with, sliding its smoothness through my fingers and wrapping it with precision round my thumb. Alex watched me a moment, then shifted to look down where I was looking, at the stage.

"It must have been a shock," he said, "to find Giancarlo's body."

"Yes, it was."

"Unpleasant."

"Yes." I took a breath. "Of course, I didn't know it was Giancarlo."

Alex shrugged. "You couldn't have. You'd never met him."

I stayed silent, but my silence spoke. I felt his gaze return; heard the frown in his voice as he prompted me, "What?"

The blade of grass snapped in my fingers. I threw it away. "I didn't know it was Giancarlo," I repeated, "but I recognized the man."

"How did you—" he began, then stopped as though a thought had just occurred to him.

I turned my head then; met his eyes. "I'd seen him three times, actually, although the first time I couldn't see him clearly, it was dark. You were with him on the terrace," I said, watching him remember. "And the second time, you met him in your study. And today in Sirmione."

"Celia . . ." Alex said.

"You lied."

He looked away, and yanked up a handful of grass himself, sifting it absently into the wind while he thought.

Unable to leave it alone, I said, "You said you hadn't heard from him—you said so to Edwina. And you let Teresa worry . . ."

"No." He set me straight on that. "Teresa knew. Perhaps not right away, but she was told."

Thinking back, I did remember that the day I'd seen the hawk-faced man going into Alex's study, Teresa's mood had brightened and she'd lost her air of melancholy, lost the furrowed lines between her eyebrows. "But why tell the lie at all?"

"Because I promised." I couldn't tell from his voice whether his impatience was directed at me or at the situation. "Giancarlo asked, and I promised."

It seemed an odd sort of request for an employee to make, and an odder one still for an employer to grant, but then I didn't know how long the two men had known each other, or on what terms. I didn't know much about Alex at all, really. Certainly I'd never seen his face take on this particular expression, the skin at the sides of his mouth and his eyes etched with weary lines that told me that Giancarlo's death had hit him on a level that was personal.

I didn't press the issue. I simply sat there, head down, stroking Max's head, and felt the distance spread between us.

Alex took a breath as though he meant to make a statement, and then let it go again without a word. He flicked a sideways glance at me, too quickly for me to read any emotion in it, but I felt his hesitation. He was measuring the risk, I thought, of telling me a secret.

At length he drew another breath and said, "It's rather a long story." But his tone of voice implied he was prepared to tell it to me, so I waited. He stretched himself out on the hill, leaning back on his elbows. "The night Giancarlo first came home, the night you saw us talking on the terrace, he was explaining to me where he'd been all day. I was angry with him, you understand, for not having done what I'd asked him to do; for leaving the three of you stranded at Desenzano. I assumed he'd been drinking—something he hadn't done for a long time, or else I never would have sent him down to fetch you in the first place—but he swore that this wasn't the case. He'd been playing detective. You have to understand," he said, "Giancarlo is a very loyal man." And then he caught himself and paused, rephrasing in a quiet voice: "He *was* a very loyal man. Loyal to me, and to Il Piacere. He was born here, he'd lived his whole life here, he hadn't ever gone away like I had, so I imagine he felt more connected to Il Piacere than I ever did—more protective of the house and what was in it. He wasn't overly pleased with my decision to give the estate to the Forlani Trust. Seeing Il Piacere pass out of my family was not a thing that he looked forward to, but on the other hand he was happy to see the place finally restored, and to know that the furniture and artworks would be kept intact and cared for by the Trust. He was not an educated man, Giancarlo, but he had a connoisseur's soul. He was born with it, born with a passion for beautiful things."

He paused again, but because I sensed that he was leading up to something I said nothing, only nodded once to show that I was following.

He said, "A while ago, about a week before you came, Giancarlo got it into his head somehow that things were being taken from the house. He said a few objects had been moved or were missing, and that he wasn't the only one who had noticed. I took a look myself, but I saw nothing out of place. Giancarlo, of course, blamed the Trust, but I tried to make him see how unlikely that was. The Forlani Trust is a highly respected organization—I couldn't see that they'd risk their reputation stealing items that would, in a few months, belong to them anyway. Still, just to set my mind at rest, and on the theory that you can't ever be too careful, I phoned my friend—the one who put me on to the Trust in the beginning—and I asked him if anything had gone missing during the work on his villa, and he said no, he hadn't had a problem. And of course, none of our own staff would have done a thing like that."

I arched a speculative eyebrow. "Not even the maid that took off for no reason, and went to Milan?"

"Especially not her. She was *very* religious, that one—never said anything bad about anyone, never told lies. And she'd never have stolen. Her conscience would not have permitted it."

My eyebrow, of its own accord, moved higher. "And she was going around with *Pietro*?"

"Yes, well, I was just coming to Pietro, actually. He was the reason you didn't get met at the station. Giancarlo was on his way to the car, ready to leave for Desenzano, when he saw Pietro going into the garage—'skulking,' in Giancarlo's words—looking as though he didn't want to be seen, and carrying a bag, a kind of rucksack. Giancarlo," Alex told me, "didn't like Pietro."

I didn't blame him, and said so. "Pietro isn't exactly a likeable man."

"They'd had words before, on more than one occasion. Over what, I don't know, but Giancarlo didn't like him. So when Giancarlo saw Pietro with the bag, it made him instantly suspicious. He was sure he'd found his thief. And instead of driving down to Desenzano to meet your train, he took the car and followed Pietro. They ended up in Sirmione."

Where we'd been today. I found that I was curious myself about Pietro and his rucksack. "And what happened?"

Alex shrugged. "Giancarlo wasn't sure. He saw Pietro go into a shop, a jeweller's shop, and come out again, still with the bag, but Giancarlo said he thought the bag looked different somehow, emptier. He couldn't prove anything, though. That's what he wanted to talk to me about, that night. He wanted me to let him have some time to investigate, to look for evidence. I've known Giancarlo for a long time, and I knew he wouldn't let this go until he'd done it, so I said all right. It seemed harmless enough, for a few days, to let him pretend to be off on a binge while he played at being a detective."

Interpreting his tone, I said, "But you didn't expect him to find any evidence, really?"

Again the shrug. "There's nothing missing from the house that I can see. And this thing between Pietro and Giancarlo, it was personal, so no, I didn't take his accusations very seriously. I figured he'd be back in a week or so, when he didn't find any proof." Beside him Nero shifted, and laid his head along his master's thigh, his dark eyes rolling to regard me with a studied lack of interest. Alex went on, "But he didn't come back. Only that one time, the day that you saw him coming to the Veranda della Diana, and that was only to ask me for money so he could rent a room in Sirmione."

They must have had a very close relationship indeed, for an employer and employee, I decided, for Alex to humour Giancarlo to such an extreme. "So it was Giancarlo you were meeting today, then—it was him you went to see in Sirmione."

"I meant to. He'd phoned me yesterday; he wanted me to come and see the jeweller's shop, the one he'd seen Pietro going into. He said it was important. I went . . . the shop was closed for Easter Sunday, and Giancarlo never showed. I waited outside in the street for an hour, and then I gave up and came looking for you at the grotto. No point wasting the day."

I was frowning. "But he was there."

"Who was?"

"Giancarlo. He was there in Sirmione. I saw him myself. I

bumped into him, actually." And I told him about the outdoor restaurant in the open square, and how I'd collided with Giancarlo as he'd passed.

Alex frowned in his turn. "And which way was he heading?"

"Towards the dock, I think, but I'm not really sure . . . there were so many people coming off the hydrofoil, the square was pretty full. He might have turned off down one of the alleys."

"Either way, that would put him going in the opposite direction from the jeweller's shop. I wonder why?"

The only person who knew the answer to that, I thought, was Giancarlo, and he was beyond telling anyone. I'd been trying not to think about that body in the dust, but I thought of it now. It was hard for me to picture someone running down a man along the road like that without the driver knowing . . .

Shattering the silence, I asked, "Alex, what sort of car does Pietro drive?"

"A Fiat Panda. Why?"

"I just wondered. A red Mercedes passed me on the road a minute or so before I . . . well, before I found Giancarlo. It was going awfully fast. I wondered if it might have been the car that knocked him down."

"You told the police this?"

"I mentioned it, yes." They had noted it down before leaving. They hadn't stayed long at the scene.

"It wouldn't have been Pietro," he said, very sure. "A tourist, maybe. Lots of people come down here for the Easter weekend—you can tell them by the Audis and Mercedeses and the Porsche 911s." His mouth quirked. "If Pietro started driving a Mercedes, on his salary, even I might be convinced that he was up to something."

When I didn't respond to that, he changed the subject, looking out across the rise of land opposite, towards the distant mountains. "We're losing the light," he said.

The evening was settling down into dusk with a creeping inevitability, stealing the colour from all that it touched as it spread out its mantle of flat bluish-grey. Another half-hour would bring darkness.

The breeze blew past me, stronger, colder. At my side Max raised his head and sniffed.

"I suppose that we ought to head back," Alex said, sitting upright.

"Yes, I—"

Max interrupted by springing alert to all fours with an ear-splitting bark. Nero, taking the cue, rose as well, pointed nose to the wind as though testing a scent. His low growl was much more unsettling to me than Max's barking.

Both dogs, as one unit, erupted into motion, bounding uphill at a breakneck pace that blurred them into shadows. Alex called out a command that stopped them just shy of the pines.

They waited, whining and impatient, till we joined them.

There was nothing there, no danger in the pines that would seem to have warranted such a great show of alarm. But looking down at my own feet I saw that someone had dropped a cigarette end—it had rolled to the edge of the path, still smouldering, the filter stained bright red with lipstick.

Seeing it and knowing that Daniela had been spying on us made my temper surge. She could watch all she wanted, and think what she liked, but I hadn't done anything wrong. I'd come down to the theatre alone, for some privacy—Alex had come after *me*. And as for thinking she could threaten me with tales of poisoned dogs . . .

Max and Nero whined again, and, "False alarm," said Alex.

I didn't tell him differently. It wasn't up to me to tell him what sort of woman Daniela was—I was not at all involved in their relationship.

He smiled a faint apology. "It must have been an animal."

"A cat, perhaps," I said, and ground the cigarette end underneath my heel as we walked on.

xiii

POPPY met us as we came in from the terrace. From the way she knelt to greet the dogs, I gathered she'd been waiting more for their return than ours. The girl was mad about the greyhounds. And they, in the face of so much adoration and affection, consented in an almost lordly manner to be petted, standing patiently with long tails moving slowly side to side, the greyhound version, I suspected, of the royal wave.

"They like you," Alex told her with a smile.

"I used to have a dog," said Poppy, rather wistfully. "I'd like to have another one, but Mummy says we can't while I'm at school, because there wouldn't be anyone home to take care of him."

Alex agreed that dogs needed a lot of attention, companionship. "These two are angry with me now, because I've been away all day."

Caressing Nero's neck, Poppy said, "They don't like being left in the kennels."

"No, you're right, they don't," said Alex. He tilted his head as though thinking. "Perhaps next time I need to go out for so long, I'll let you look after the dogs, keep them company. How would that be?"

"Would you really?" Her eyes glowed. "Oh, that would be brilliant, I'd love to. D'you hear that, boy?"

Nero's response was subdued—just a tolerant twitch of one ear—but it seemed enough for Poppy. She gave him a passionate hug. And then, with the ease of a twelve-year-old, changed from a child to an adult in one breath. Straightening, she looked at me. "We saved you some dinner. Shall I heat it up for you? Rupert showed me how to work the microwave," she said.

She looked so keen to please that I found myself nodding in spite of the fact that I still had no appetite. "I'd like that. Thank you."

"And afterwards, maybe," she said, "we could play Snakes and Ladders? You said that you might, after dinner. Unless there's another game you'd rather play . . ."

"Snakes and Ladders," I assured her, "will be fine." And even preferable, I thought, to sitting round with all the others going over the details of Giancarlo's death. Having witnessed the event, I had no great desire to speak of it. I wanted to forget.

I had the feeling Alex understood. He said, "I'm not much good at games," and with a quiet nod to both of us excused himself and walked off down the corridor, with Max and Nero padding at his heels.

Poppy's obvious pleasure at having me all to herself was quite touching. Seating me rather decorously in the dining room, she went off to reheat my meal in the kitchen and returned bearing my plate before her with such proper form one might think she was serving the Queen. I was careful not to smile because I still remembered how, at Poppy's age, I'd been in awe of my headmistress; how I'd longed for her to see me as an equal, not a little girl. Remembered, too, the day I'd served her tea, and just how desperately I'd tried to play the perfect hostess. Everything that could have gone wrong did—the tea was far too strong, the biscuits stale—but my headmistress hadn't once let on. She'd endured the whole thing graciously, and in so doing had made my twelve-year-old self feel wonderfully special.

She was very much in my thoughts now as I swallowed a mouthful of chewy cold pasta and assured Poppy that it was lovely, just right. My reward was a shy smile that made me at last understand why my headmistress had not only suffered through my awful tea, but had asked for a second cup.

She brought me wine, as well, that she had poured into a pitcher, and a buttered roll. And then, at my insistence, took the seat across from mine.

From her look of concentration I guessed she was trying to think of something suitably grown-up to say to start a conversation. "It's terrible what happened to Teresa's husband, isn't it?" When I agreed it was, she carried on, encouraged. "Alex said she'd better stay with relatives the next few days—you know, until after the funeral. He said he'd find somebody else to cook till then. That's really nice of him, I think, don't you?"

"I do, yes."

"Very rich people aren't always so thoughtful with their servants, are they?" she said, in a tone that had travelled the world and met hundreds of very rich people. "But Alex is. And he's like that with everyone, too. Even us."

"He's a very considerate man," I said, spearing another forkful of pasta.

"He was really worried about you."

"Oh, yes?" I glanced up, keeping my expression casual, and Poppy nodded.

"Yes, at dinner, when you didn't come. Rupert tried to tell him that you sometimes liked to be alone when something had upset you, but Alex said finding a body was more than upsetting and that someone ought to look for you to see you were all right."

She had, I thought, a parrot's ear for dialogue. I made a mental note to watch what I said in her presence in future.

"Mummy said she'd go and look, but Alex told her no, he'd go himself." And then she added, as an afterthought, "Daniela didn't like that."

Reaching for my wine to wash down a largish lump of noodles, I said, "No, I don't imagine that she did."

Poppy studied my face for a moment with eyes that were very adult. And then, in the tones of an ally, she told me, "I don't like Daniela. I don't like the way she talks to Mummy. And she's nicer to men than to women. Some women are like that, I know, but I think that it's stupid." She frowned. "Men don't notice it, though, do they? Nicholas doesn't." She stopped there; caught herself as though afraid she'd said too much. I couldn't help but wonder what the girl had seen, how much she knew about whatever had been going on between

Daniela and Nicholas. She was clever for her age. I had the feeling that she didn't miss much. Sitting up straighter, she tossed back her hair. "Nicholas," she said, "is such a jerk. I don't know what my mother sees in him."

I shrugged, careful not to offer any opinion that might find its way back to Madeleine. "They've been together a long time," was all I said.

"Not really. Only since last summer. And only because Nicholas was being thrown out of his flat for not paying the rent. He didn't pay too much attention to Mummy till then," she said. Her exhaled breath was cynical beyond her years. "He's just like all the others. He doesn't want Mummy at all, only what she can give him."

Astute as well as cynical, I thought. I was trying to think of what comforting bit of advice I could offer when she carried on without me.

"Den's not, though. He's rather different, don't you think?"

I nodded. "Quite different from Nicholas, yes."

"I like Den."

I could have told her that I thought her mother liked him, too, but I kept my observations to myself. No point in getting the child's hopes up, I thought. Besides, given Poppy's own powers of observation I had a feeling she'd start noticing things herself, before long, if she hadn't already.

Forcing my last bite of food down with wine, I pushed my plate away. "That was very good, Poppy. It did hit the spot."

"It's really only the first course, you know. There's ham still, and vegetables . . ."

Holding my stomach with a protective hand, I shook my head and smiled. "No, honestly, I'm full."

"I'll just make the tea, then," she said, jumping up to clear my plate, "and we can start our game."

Her tea, to my relief, was infinitely better than the stuff I'd served my poor headmistress all those years ago. I took a long sip while she set up the game board between us. It was an older board, well-creased and scuffed with use.

"There's a whole cupboard full of games, under the stairs," Poppy said, when I asked her where she'd found it. "Teresa showed Den, after lunch. She said she didn't think that Alex would mind if we played them. This one's a baby's game, I know," she put in, a bit self-consciously, "but all the others were Italian, and I didn't know the rules."

"That's all right. I quite like Snakes and Ladders." I touched the board and tried to picture Alex as a small boy, playing this—an English game . . . a present, perhaps, from the mother he couldn't remember.

"Den isn't very good at this," said Poppy. "He kept landing on the snakes this afternoon."

Which was appropriate, I thought, considering that the snakes were all associated with human vices, things I fancied Den O'Malley had his share of.

Poppy said, "He lost most of the games. But he said if we'd been playing the *American* version he'd have beaten me every time." She didn't appear to have taken him seriously. "He comes from New York, in America. Have you ever been to New York?"

"No, I haven't." I rolled the die, advancing my game piece a measly two squares.

"Too bad. One more and you'd have had a ladder." Rolling six, she slid up a ladder herself and went on, "Mummy's been to New York, with a play. She says it's nice there. Not as scary as they make it look on television. Mummy travels a lot with her acting." She glanced at me, tentative. "I'm going to be an actress, too," she said, watching carefully for my reaction. When I didn't laugh or make a patronizing comment she relaxed. "Den thinks I'll make a good actress—he says I have the memory for it, and with luck I'll have the genes."

"Well, Den's been in the business a long time," I told her, encouragingly, as I slid up a ladder for doing good deeds. "He knows what he's talking about."

She looked pleased. "What did he mean, about me having the genes?"

"He probably meant that you'll have inherited some of your mother's talent."

"And my father's," she reminded me. "He's an actor too, you know."

I knew. I'd have preferred to forget, but . . .

"I don't take after him much, though," she said. "I'm glad of that. He broke my mother's heart." Her words were solemn, with the ring of something she had heard repeated fairly often through her childhood. "He left her for another woman, when I was a baby."

"Oh," I said lamely. She didn't know, then. Didn't know I was the 'other woman's' daughter. Not feeling able to look at her, suddenly, I bent my head and shook the die as though my life depended on it.

"*She* was an actress, too. She still is," Poppy said, and named my mother with distaste. "But she didn't stay with Father. She went off to live with someone else. Doesn't matter, though, she's still a bitch," she said, revelling in her use of the grown-up word, "and I hate her."

I let go the die. It skidded off the game board and went halfway down the table. Poppy leaned over to read it. "Five," she announced. "Oh, bad luck. That's a snake."

For my vices, I thought, as I slid my game piece down the laughing serpent. *For my vices.*

xiv

WE came off book the next day at rehearsal.

This was always the most terrifying time for me, the time when I felt certain I was the worst actress ever; when I felt certain even Rupert, having witnessed my ineptness, would politely send me home, recast my part. Even though we'd been rehearsing the play for two weeks now, my memory, as usual, seemed to have failed me completely. Deprived of the script in my hands, I was hopeless—remembering one speech, forgetting the next, and then faltering on, stopping every few minutes to ask for a prompt.

I felt the panic starting now within my chest as I wheeled to face Madeleine, whose character was poised to have mine ushered from the 'room.' "No, please, you mustn't, I—" Oh, damn, I thought. I'd lost it. "Line," I said.

Den supplied it. "You are my final hope . . ."

Oh, right. "You are my final hope, the only person who can bring me peace." How on earth, I wondered, could I have forgotten something so simple?

She fixed her lovely eyes on me and said, "I cannot change the past. If he is dead, he will remain so."

"But I have heard that you can give the dead a voice."

Considering, she crossed a step in front of me, confusing me a little as I tried to remember whether I was meant to move in response.

"The price will not be small," she warned. "Are you prepared to pay it?"

My thoughts still on the blocking, I looked at her blankly. "Line."

Den, in his clear level voice, said: "I have money."

"I have money."

Rupert stopped us there, whether from pity or because he couldn't stand it any longer I didn't know. "All right," he spoke up from his corner, "that's fine, let's leave it there and take ten minutes, then pick up again with—"

Den leaned over, interrupting him with a low comment, and Rupert glanced down at his watch in surprise. "So it is. Right, change of plan then, everybody. Celia and Maddy, your first wardrobe fitting is scheduled for three o'clock, and since it's nearly that now we'll take a full hour and start back at four o'clock with scene . . ."—he flipped a page back in his script to check—"scene three. All right?"

Freed from my torture, I was about to apologize to Madeleine for making such a mess of our rehearsal when she met my eyes conspiratorially, raising one hand with a sigh to massage her neck. "God, I do hate this," she said. "I feel like such an idiot without my book—I never can remember my lines properly. And age only makes things worse."

"But you were perfect," I protested.

"Hardly. Den," she asked him, turning, "how many times did I ask for a line?"

Strolling over to join us, he grinned. "I lost count. You were both keeping me pretty busy."

Madeleine sent me an 'I told you so' look. "You see?"

Den raised an eyebrow. "Why? What's going on?"

"Celia thinks that I'm perfect."

Den winked at me. "Don't worry, honey, no one's ever perfect when we take their scripts away. There are some stories I could tell you . . ."

"Darling," Madeleine broke in, using the endearment rather naturally, I thought, "I don't suppose you'd be a prince and bring us both a cup of tea? We won't have time to fetch our own before the fitting."

"Tea it is. Where are they doing the fitting, in here?"

"Yes, I think so. I haven't heard otherwise."

"Okay," he said. "I'll be back in a minute."

He'd forgotten, I think, that Teresa was no longer in the house, and her replacement—a dour-faced woman on loan from a hotel in Mira del Garda—was neither as efficient nor accommodating. It wouldn't have surprised me if he'd had to make the tea himself. At any rate, it was nearly twenty minutes later by the time he reappeared, by which time the wardrobe mistress had arrived with a bright-eyed assistant in tow who had cheerfully pinned us both into our half-finished costumes and was fitting a wig on my head to assess the effect.

I didn't like the wig, myself. The style was all right—a close-fitting sweep of tight waves with small curls on my forehead—and the colour was necessary. Galeazzo had written *Il Prezzo* for Celia the First, after all, and there were any number of references in the script to the blondeness of the widow's hair. The problem was that the hair in this wig had turned out to be spot on the same shade as Mother's. It didn't matter that her colour came from a bottle, or that our facial features weren't at all alike—when I looked in the mirror I saw Mother's hair, and it bothered me.

If Madeleine saw the resemblance as well, she was too gracious to say so. She looked lovely herself, in the close-fitting costume of lavender silk that moved lightly each time that she shifted position, her arms held out gracefully, like a dancer's, to allow the wardrobe mistress to achieve a proper fitting of the sleeves. Madeleine looked, in fact, so very lovely that I didn't think Den would be able, or inclined, to take his eyes from her. So it came as a surprise when I looked up to find him staring straight at me.

Madeleine noticed him, too. "Oh, our tea. Dennis, thank you so much. You can put the cups there, on the table, if you don't mind."

He looked at the cups in his hands, as though surprised to find that he was holding them, then set them on the table as requested before lifting his gaze once again to my face, rather strangely, as if he were looking right through me at somebody else.

"Do we look all right?" Madeleine asked.

"What? Oh, yes, you look gorgeous, the pair of you."

The wardrobe mistress straightened like a warden; shooed him off. "No men," she said firmly, in accented English. "You go now and close the door."

"But surely—"

“*No* men.”

Defeated, he turned, pausing once at the door to look back. In my blonde wig, I decided, I must have looked more like my mother than even I had thought. Den—who had worked with her once, he’d said—seemed to be seeing a ghost. I half-expected him to comment on it, but then his faint frown disappeared, and “Blonde hair suits you, Celia” was the only thing he said before he passed into the corridor and shut the door behind him.

He steepled his fingers and watched while his publisher read the last page. The veranda had become so quiet he could hear plainly not only the to-and-fro beat of the pendulum in the long-case clock behind him, but the even subtler ticking of the minute hand as it marked out the hour. It clicked again now as his publisher set down the page and reordered the manuscript.

"Extraordinary," was the publisher's pronouncement. "You've outdone yourself, my friend."

"I was . . . inspired." Turning his gaze to the window he looked at the two figures seated outside in the gardens, on the bench beneath the walnut tree—the still-slender woman like sunshine herself in a pale yellow organdie dress, and the young man beside her . . .

"That's quite a moustache," said the publisher, looking out also. "I take it that's the boy who'll play the soldier?"

"Yes. He was a friend of Celia's once, in London. She suggested him." He tried to say that lightly, letting none of his misgivings show. After all, had not Celia assured him the boy meant nothing to her, that there could be no one else? "You'll come to the performance?"

"Wouldn't miss it. May I take this script with me?"

"Of course. And the poems, as well."

"Ah, the poems." The publisher picked up the second typescript with less enthusiasm, but politely. "Do you have a title for this new collection?"

"I call it The Season of Storms, *from a quote I have found in the book of the Crusades by Charles Lamb, the Englishman—a speech the*

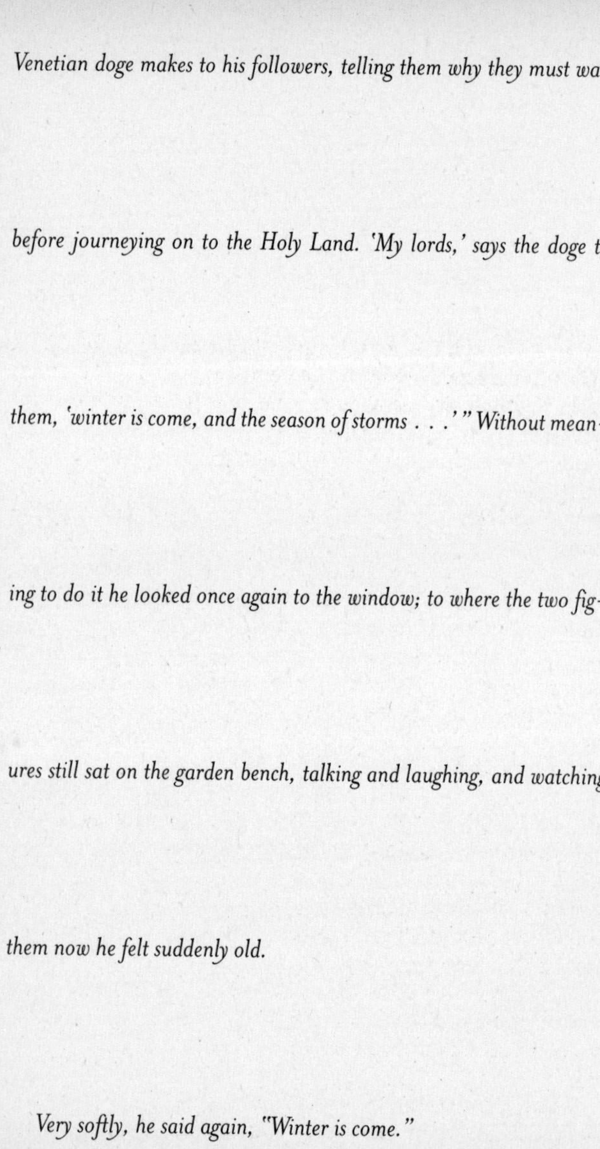

Venetian doge makes to his followers, telling them why they must wait before journeying on to the Holy Land. 'My lords,' says the doge to them, 'winter is come, and the season of storms . . .'" Without meaning to do it he looked once again to the window; to where the two figures still sat on the garden bench, talking and laughing, and watching them now he felt suddenly old.

Very softly, he said again, "Winter is come."

XV

I was seeing ghosts myself, or rather, hearing them. That night after dinner, alone in my bedroom, I heard the floor creak rhythmically as though someone were walking towards me. The creaks stopped, then a few minutes later approached from the opposite side of the bed. It didn't help that I was sitting up reading *A Study of Spirits,* the book about hauntings and ghosts that I'd borrowed from Alex's study.

I liked to have something to read in the evenings. The others had taken to gathering down in the Stanza d'Arazzo for drinks and a rehash of what had gone wrong or—less frequently—right, at rehearsal. I sometimes sat in, but more often now I simply went upstairs and read, to unwind. Even in London, I'd never been part of the set that went down to the pub every night to talk shop. I found the work itself so hard and tiring that the last thing I wanted was to let it carry on into my social hours. And working far from home like this, with such a small group of people, made the experience that much more intense, and left me more in need of balance.

But *A Study of Spirits* simply wasn't doing the trick tonight, and I'd already been twice through *The Season of Storms.* Remembering that Rupert had a bookcase in his room, I went to see what he could offer me, happy to have an excuse for a few moments' break from my creaking floor and the ever-watchful eyes of Celia the First's portrait over my bed.

Rupert's door was locked, and he didn't answer when I knocked, which more than likely meant he wasn't in his room.

Thinking to find him downstairs with the others, I stopped by the Stanza d'Arazzo but Nicholas was the only one in there, sitting with brandy in hand, and a cigarette.

I paused in the doorway. "You haven't seen Rupert, by any chance?"

"He was here a minute ago. Went to look at books, or something, in D'Ascanio's study."

"Thanks." Looking round the room, I asked, "Where's everyone else, tonight?"

"I really couldn't say." He took a lengthy sip of brandy. "No one tells me anything."

"Ah." I left him there, not wanting to get too closely involved in the romantic entanglements of my fellow actors. Instead I turned my steps towards the Veranda della Diana. Rupert, I thought, must have overcome his reluctance to poke round the study with Alex not there. Alex, I knew, was out—he'd left the dogs in Poppy's care just after lunch with the warning he might not be back till quite late. She'd been thrilled. Daniela, finding Alex not at dinner, had been less pleased. "Such fuss for a funeral," she'd said. "It is the family who should arrange these things, not Alessandro."

Madeleine had replied that perhaps Alex felt that Giancarlo *was* family. "The two of them must have been children together."

Daniela had shaken her head. "No, Giancarlo was older by ten years."

But I'd understood Madeleine's point, and agreed with it. Alex had told me himself that Giancarlo had lived his whole life here; that he'd had an intimate connection to Il Piacere . . . and indeed the house itself seemed to be mourning him. The rooms I was passing through now appeared deeper in shadow than usual, everything round me respectfully hushed.

I didn't like to disturb the silence by knocking at the study door, and at any rate Rupert had left the door slightly ajar, so I just nudged it open and put my head round.

"Ah, Celia," Rupert greeted me, and waved me in. "Come look at this."

He was standing with Alex, a few feet away, bending over some large book that they'd spread open on a side table. Alex turned as well, when Rupert spoke, and as I came into the room he stepped aside to make a space for me between them.

"What did I tell you?" asked Rupert, and for a moment, from the delighted look on his face, I thought he might actually have found his longed-for lost play by Sophocles—a large book, he'd said it would be, and an old one, and this was decidedly both. But when I looked down at the open pages I could see that it wasn't a play. It looked more like an illuminated manuscript, with brightly painted pictures of religious scenes.

"I told you the Crusaders carried books out of Constantinople," said Rupert. "Have a look at this prayer-book—have you ever seen anything so marvellous? Alex brought it down to show me."

Alex raised a shoulder. "Yes, well, you were asking me about the Fourth Crusade, and I know how interested you are in books. This was one of my father's favourite private treasures. It's never been properly authenticated, mind you—I don't think it left my father's room while he was living, and he certainly wouldn't have permitted anyone to have taken it away to be studied, or properly dated. I suppose I ought to have it done, myself, sometime. Send it off to an expert."

"You might never get it back," said Rupert. He was looking rather covetous himself, I thought. He loved old books, and this one was positively ancient—leather-bound with parchment leaves that showed the wear of centuries, their edges rough and browned and stained in places with the evidence of damp.

I couldn't read the writing, which was Greek, but Rupert could. Gingerly turning the pages, he read aloud in rough translation various prayers and rites of the Greek Orthodox Church.

I wasn't really listening. I was too aware of Alex standing next to me to concentrate. From time to time I fancied I felt him glancing down at me, and once I shot a quick look up myself and our eyes met, just briefly—mine hesitant, his tinged with something that looked like impatience. I broke the contact, looking down.

"Here's one for your grandmother, Alex," said Rupert, reading aloud: " 'A Prayer for the Laying of Ghosts.' "

The illustration for that prayer was unexpectedly lovely, a radiant sunburst against a cloudy sky, as though the heavens had opened to admit a wandering spirit that had just been laid to rest.

Rupert started to read the words to us, but the telephone rang on the desk, interrupting.

Alex stepped away to pick up the receiver, speaking curtly. "*Pronto.*" Then his voice changed, and although I couldn't understand the language I could tell that he was talking to a woman. He said something calmly, soothingly, and nodded, ringing off. "I'm afraid I must go out," he said.

Rupert closed the prayer-book with reluctance. "I should let you have this back, then."

"Oh, no, keep it for a few days, if you like. It's just gathering dust on its shelf; it deserves to be read and enjoyed, and I know I can trust you to take care of it."

You would have thought he'd handed Rupert the Crown Jewels. "Are you absolutely certain?"

"Yes, of course. Take it back to your room."

"I'll come with you," I offered. I'd meant that for Rupert, of course, but Alex, who had turned towards the door himself, misunderstood.

"All right," he said.

"Oh," I said, caught off my guard. "Sorry . . . I mean, I was talking to Roo . . ."

Rupert, of course, hadn't heard me. He wasn't even listening to me now. Head down, he was happily lost in his prayer-book.

"Ah," said Alex. He looked, I thought, almost disappointed.

Trying to make light of the mistake, I smiled. "I shouldn't think you'd want me tagging along, anyway."

"On the contrary." Alex slanted a look down at me. "I'd very much like you to come."

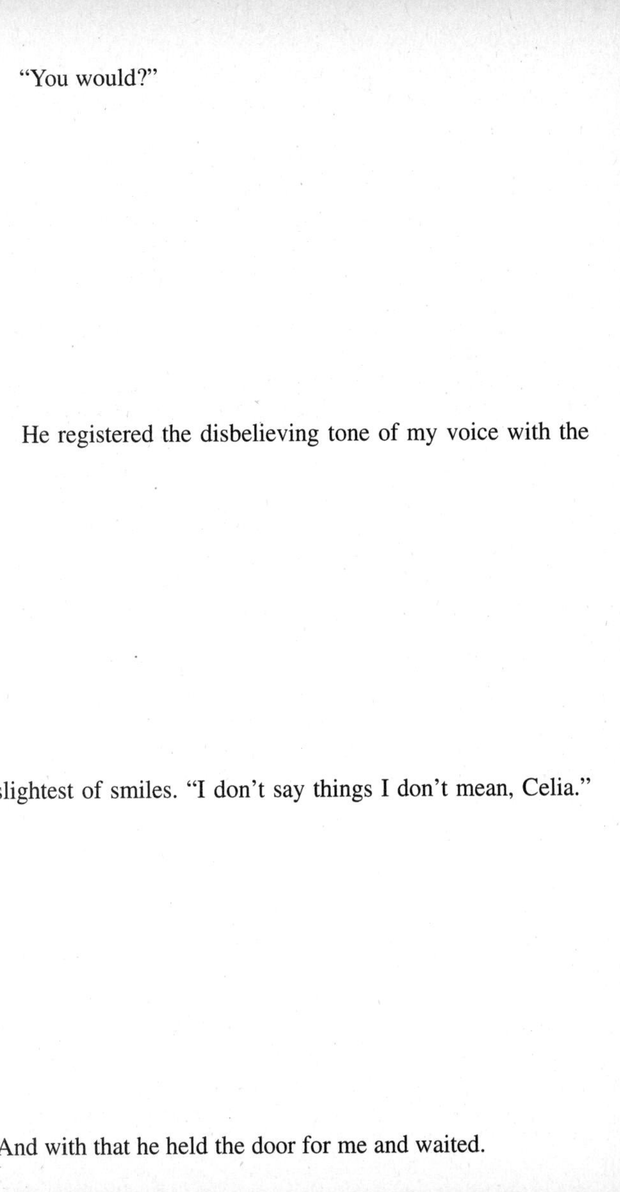

"You would?"

He registered the disbelieving tone of my voice with the slightest of smiles. "I don't say things I don't mean, Celia."

And with that he held the door for me and waited.

xvi

HE didn't say anything else on the drive down to Mira del Garda. Not that the drive was a long one, it probably took less than five minutes, but his silence and the close confines of the car made that brief time seem like an hour.

I still didn't know exactly why I'd come. After all, this wasn't like our trip to Sirmione—I'd been cornered into that one by Rupert, I hadn't had much of a choice in the matter. But this time I could have declined, without giving offence. The fact that I hadn't declined had, I think, something to do with the way Daniela had reacted to our Sirmione trip, with her threats and condescension. After that, I suppose, it was difficult for me to see her as a wronged party, or to worry what she'd think if I spent time with Alex. I knew full well she'd think the worst, no matter what I did.

And anyway, Alex had asked me to come.

I didn't notice which way he turned at the base of the hill, only that the houses where we stopped were small and warmly lit from within, and that the air around them had a kitchen-cooking smell that wrapped around me, welcoming, as I got out and stood.

"This way," said Alex, waiting till I'd joined him before walking round to the back door of one of the houses. He knocked. The old woman who came to the door clearly knew who he was. As she ushered us in, she called over her shoulder: "Teresa!"

So that was who we'd come to see, I thought, relaxing a little. That was the woman who'd phoned him.

Poor Teresa didn't look to me as though she had been sleeping. Dressed in widow's black, she looked paler, slightly older, but her walk still had the same firmness of purpose. Her surprise at seeing me was plainly evident, but Alex said something that took the distrust from her eyes. Speaking low and quickly in Italian, she motioned towards an adjoining room and Alex nodded.

He turned to me. "Teresa's brother, Mauro, wants a word with me in private. Will you be all right out here?"

I looked from Teresa's dour face to the sharply curious eyes of the old woman, who'd resumed her seat now at the kitchen table and was slicing mushrooms with a small but wicked-looking knife. I showed a brave smile to Alex. "Of course."

When he'd gone, though, my confidence wavered a little until the old woman made a gesture with her knife and said something. I didn't understand the words, but she had a kind voice.

Teresa said, "My mother asks please will you sit."

As I sat at the table, a little more upright than usual beneath the scrutiny of the two women, Teresa's mother asked another question.

Teresa said, "Do you like wine, Signorina Sands?" She was moving to the cupboard as she spoke.

"Yes, but please," I said, to stop her—she'd just lost her husband, after all, and it wasn't right that she should have to serve me—"I don't want to be a bother."

"Is no bother." Returning with glasses and an open bottle, she poured for the three of us, taking a seat by her mother.

"Grazie," I told her, and then turned to thank her mother, also. *"Grazie."*

The sharp eyes softened, crinkling at the corners. This time she rose herself, and fetched a plate. There were trays on the worktop, of small breads and savouries that had probably been specially baked for the funeral, but she filled the plate with some of them and brought them back to set between us on the table. *"Mangi,"* she instructed me, and pointed with her knife.

Obedient, I ate a pastry. Embarrassed by the hospitality, I looked at Teresa, wanting to express how sorry I was about her husband's death. The words came out rather more clumsily than I'd intended, but she didn't take offence.

"Signor D'Ascanio says you were there, with Giancarlo," she said, "on the road."

"Yes, I was."

She studied me a moment, then she told me, "Is a good thing. I am glad he did not die alone."

Her mother interjected, and Teresa said, "My mother asks how old are you?"

"I'm twenty-two."

Teresa's mother took this information in translation, smiled, and said something back in a tone of amusement. I caught the words 'Signora Forlani,' but Teresa didn't pass the comment on. She merely made a statement in her turn, and whatever she said made her mother look up at me, surprised. "No!"

Teresa nodded; turned to me. "I tell my mother that you stay in the ladies' wing, in the rooms of the English actress. She knows many stories of Il Piacere, of those rooms."

She was telling me a few of them now, apparently. Her face had grown animated, and the hand with the knife gestured widely for emphasis. When she'd finished, I turned to Teresa, but once again she didn't bother with translation, only shrugged and said, "Is like I said—things happen in those rooms."

Her mother, clearly dissatisfied with the interpretation service, tried to talk to me herself, aiming the point of the knife at my necklace and stabbing the air. "*Angelo* . . . good, good." She smiled at me. "*Dio* protect."

She was saying, I gathered, that God and his angels would guard me from harm. I touched the little gold-and-diamond angel that I wore and smiled to show I understood.

She would have told me something else, I think, but the door to the other room opened again at that moment, and Alex stepped out. He carried a parcel the size of a shoebox, wrapped up in brown paper. Exchanging a few words with Teresa and her mother, he looked at me. "Ready to go?"

I stood and thanked the women, leaving behind my unfinished wine as I followed Alex to the door. Teresa's mother, sit-

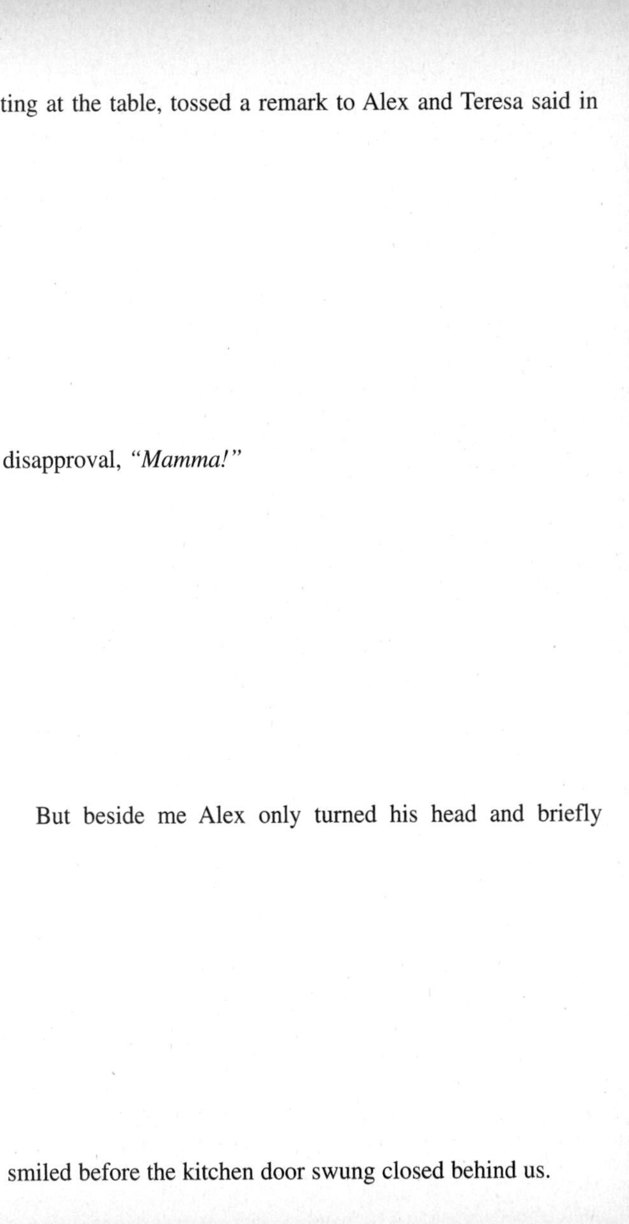

ting at the table, tossed a remark to Alex and Teresa said in disapproval, *"Mamma!"*

But beside me Alex only turned his head and briefly smiled before the kitchen door swung closed behind us.

xvii

WHEN we came into the house I would have said goodnight and headed to my room, but Alex stopped me. He'd been quiet on the drive up, so preoccupied that I'd assumed he'd want to be alone with his thoughts and the brown paper parcel that he'd carried so carefully up from the garage, but now here he was with his hand on my arm, saying, "Don't go just yet. Please. I could do with the company. Someone to talk to."

It surprised me at first that he'd asked, that he'd consider a virtual stranger like me 'someone to talk to,' until I reminded myself that Alex wasn't a man who had friends falling out of the rafters, and Daniela didn't seem the type to have a sympathetic ear.

He was Hamlet indeed, I thought, musing alone in this big empty house where the ghosts of his father and grandfather walked, in a figurative sense. But while Hamlet had at least had his Horatio, Alex had no one. Alex's Horatio, I suspected, had died Sunday night at the side of the road. Which left him with only the greyhounds as confidantes, and at the moment he didn't even have *them* . . . they were still up with Poppy.

So of course I said yes, I'd be happy to sit up a little while longer and talk.

The Veranda della Diana was empty when we got there—Rupert had long since departed, going back to his own room, no doubt, with the prayer-book, to study its pages in private.

Alex switched on a floor lamp that spilled a warm pool of light over the arm of a cracked leather chair and onto the wine-red oriental carpet. The striped draperies, closed round the room on three sides, lent the study a certain cosiness, a comfortably intimate feel that was helped by the low coffered ceiling and smell of old books. Behind the desk the bronze statue of Diana with her hunting dog and arrows gazed serenely past Alex's shoulder as he turned a second light on.

He set the shoebox-sized parcel with care on the desk, and stared at it so long that I was half-convinced he'd forgotten about me. I took a seat anyway, choosing a cushioned cane armchair across from the leather one, and waited. At length Alex raised his head, surfacing; turned. "I don't suppose you drink Scotch?" was the first thing he asked. "No? You don't mind if I do?" Assured that I didn't, he opened a drawer in his desk and removed a tall bottle and glass, bringing both with him as he crossed to the big leather armchair.

He sat. The light from the lamp at his side angled over his shoulder and caught the clear pale amber of his drink as he poured it. His face, though, was not in the light. He was frowning.

It was obvious that something had disturbed him, something connected, most likely, to the talk he'd just had with Teresa's brother, and the parcel sitting now on his desk. But I didn't like to ask, and since he was the one who had wanted my company, wanted to talk, I let him take the lead in conversation.

"I'm sorry I left you alone like that, down at Teresa's. I didn't know what Mauro wanted to speak with me about, you see, and so . . ." He frowned again. "I hope you didn't mind."

"Not at all. I was well taken care of. Teresa and her mother gave me wine and fed me and—"

"Mauro was friends with Giancarlo," he said, interrupting me not from rudeness so much as from the fact his mind appeared to be following a single track. "What he told me tonight . . ." He broke off for a moment and took a long drink, then looked over at me for the first time. "You already know half the story of what Giancarlo was up to—you might as well know the rest."

It crossed my mind to protest that he didn't have to tell me; that this was after all a private matter, and not really any of my business . . . but Alex was already leaning back, settling in for a lengthy discussion.

"Mauro didn't hear about Giancarlo's death until tonight. He drives a lorry, Mauro—he's been on the road since yesterday afternoon, and in all the confusion, I gather the family didn't bother trying to contact him. They knew he'd be back today, sometime. Anyhow, according to Teresa, when he found out what had happened he went mad, and kept saying he needed to talk to me. That's why Teresa phoned; why I went down." He paused, took a quick sip of Scotch, and went on, "It turns out you were right—Giancarlo was in Sirmione yesterday. He stopped in to see Mauro on his way back. He didn't have the car with him, Mauro said . . . he just turned up on the doorstep, walking. Said he'd caught the hydrofoil, which wasn't quite his style. Giancarlo never liked the water." I saw a brief shadow of memory and loss cross his face, but he steeled his expression against it. "Mauro was on his way out, with the lorry, but he thought it could wait a few minutes, while he had a drink with Giancarlo. He wanted to hear what was happening with Giancarlo's little investigation; whether he'd found any proof that Pietro was stealing. Mauro doesn't like Pietro, either," Alex said, as an aside. He drank again, and swirled the Scotch around his glass. "Giancarlo said yes, he had proof. He told Mauro he'd made friends with an assistant at the jeweller's shop, the shop he'd seen Pietro going into with the bag. Giancarlo said that this assistant—after several days and, one assumes, a fair amount of wine—had agreed to give him proof, and it was this Giancarlo wanted me to see, in Sirmione."

It was my turn now to frown. "So why didn't he keep his meeting with you?"

"Apparently he tried. He told Mauro that this friend of his, the jeweller's assistant, was sure they were both being watched. The assistant refused to hand over the evidence as they had planned; he insisted on finding another location, somewhere safe. In the end he chose the hydrofoil. Very cloak and dagger," Alex said. "Giancarlo told Mauro they had to jump on at the last minute, to be sure that this person—whoever he was—who had spooked the assistant, wouldn't be able to follow."

"But Giancarlo was able to get what he was after?"

"Yes. That box, there." Alex nodded at the desk. "Giancarlo asked Mauro to keep it safe there, at the house—said he didn't fancy carrying it around any more than he had to, he didn't want it breaking. He said I could come down and see it there as easily as anywhere. And then he left. Mauro offered him a ride up in the lorry, but Giancarlo said he'd rather walk. The first sunny day, he said, after so much rain—it was good to be walking." Again the shadow swiftly crossed his face. He raised his glass.

I said. "I am so very sorry. You were close to him, weren't you?"

"Like brothers." The words brought an ironic twist to his lips. "They say that every family has its curse. The curse of mine is infidelity. My grandfather's affairs are public knowledge, and my father . . . well, he was his father's son. Giancarlo's mother was a very lovely woman."

It took a moment for me to absorb what he was telling me, and then I simply said, "Oh," because I couldn't think of anything else *to* say.

"I don't have any proof of it. My father never acknowledged any children but myself, but I had my suspicions. Giancarlo did too, I'd imagine. He was more a D'Ascanio than I was, in some ways—he had the curse as well." Again his mouth curved, fleetingly. "But underneath it all he was a good man, and a good friend. Yes, we were close." He looked away at that, and his gaze found the box on the desk. "I did him an injustice, though. I thought that he was wrong about this business with Pietro."

"So Pietro *did* steal something, then?"

For an answer, Alex rose and fetched the box itself, returning to place it with care on the small round table by my chair. He and Mauro had already had the brown paper off once—when Alex broke the single piece of tape that held it on, the paper fell away in stiff folds, and the box lid lifted off. From its nest of polystyrene beads, Alex gently extracted the 'proof' that Giancarlo had managed to get from the jeweller's

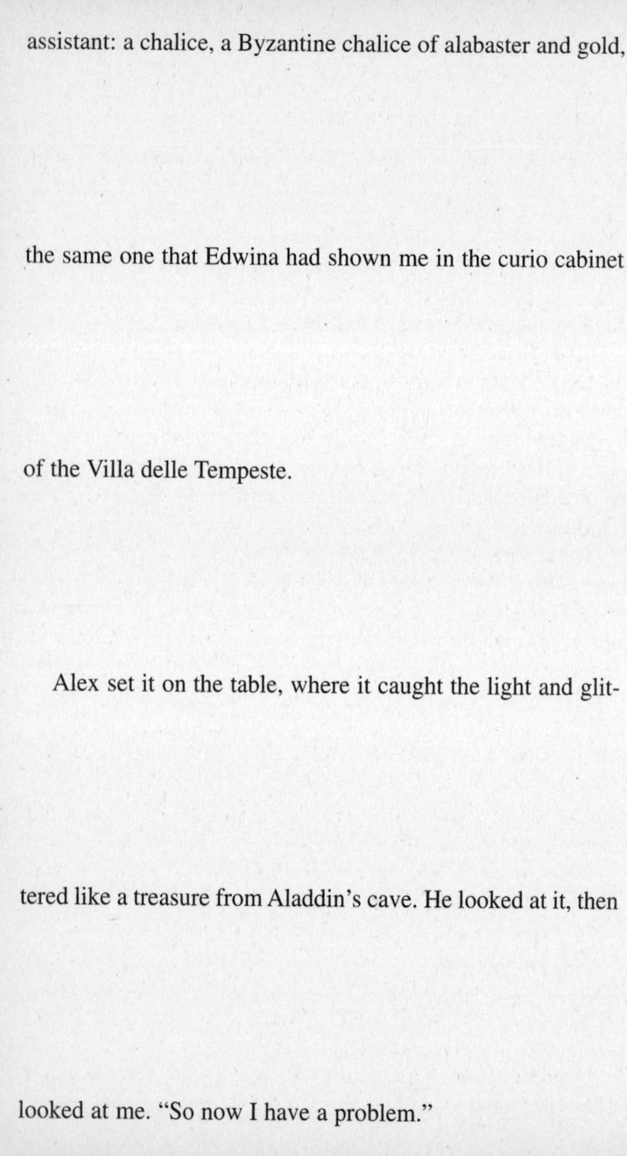

assistant: a chalice, a Byzantine chalice of alabaster and gold, the same one that Edwina had shown me in the curio cabinet of the Villa delle Tempeste.

Alex set it on the table, where it caught the light and glittered like a treasure from Aladdin's cave. He looked at it, then looked at me. "So now I have a problem."

xviii

DANIELA came to my room the next morning.

I was finishing up with my voice exercises when I heard the door to my sitting-room open and close. I turned in surprise at the sound, because everyone knocked, and I'd just begun thinking it must be the new cook and housemaid, Teresa's replacement, who might be excused for not knowing the unwritten rules, when Daniela appeared in the door leading through from my bathroom.

She looked rather different than she had at breakfast, an hour earlier. At breakfast she'd had the eyes of an ingénue. "And I, of course, had no idea," she'd told Nicholas across the table. "When Alessandro came to me last night"—the slightest pause, a glance at me to make sure I had taken in that point—"I was very upset, that Pietro should do this. I feel a fool that he could steal these things from the villa without my noticing, but I am not always looking in the cabinet, you understand, to see what is there and what is not. Fortunately, it appears he only took the chalice and a small bowl, and the chalice is recovered, thanks to God."

Unimpressed, I'd gone on spreading jam on my croissant, watching Daniela the same way I might have watched Mother perform on the stage. There'd been four of us there—Den, myself, and Daniela and Nicholas. Madeleine and Poppy had been down for breakfast earlier; their plates hadn't yet been cleared away . . . Rupert had still been on his walk, and Alex had been . . . well, somewhere.

Deprived of a full audience, Daniela had nonetheless given it her all. One would have thought Pietro had tried to murder her in her sleep, instead of simply stealing. "Never has such a thing happened at one of our properties. He is a beast, Pietro."

"But he's gone?" Den had asked.

"This morning, yes, before we could confront him. Alessandro thinks perhaps this jeweller in Sirmione, he has noticed the chalice not there at his shop any longer, and has telephoned to Pietro, to warn him. And the jeweller is gone, too. The shop, it is closed."

I'd found myself wondering what had become of the assistant, the one who had passed the chalice on to Giancarlo. I had hoped he wasn't lying in a ditch somewhere, himself . . . but I'd kept my thoughts silent, not knowing how much of the story Daniela had known. She hadn't once mentioned Giancarlo, after all, and Alex might only have told her the barest details of the theft. I hadn't wanted to repeat what he'd told me in confidence.

Den had remarked that it shouldn't take the police long to find a man as ugly as Pietro, and then Nicholas had said, "I'll bet he's hiding out in Milan with his girlfriend, that maid who did a runner. She's likely in league with him."

I'd joined the conversation for the first time. "I shouldn't think it likely. Alex says she's a very religious girl."

Nicholas had shrugged. "Most people put their principles aside," he'd said, "for money." And then, because I'd mentioned Alex's name and Nicholas loved stirring things up, he'd added, "You seem to be spending a lot of time with our Mr. D'Ascanio, Celia. You weren't the reason he got back so late last night, now, were you? Poppy had the blasted dogs till nearly midnight."

Den had come unexpectedly—and rather gallantly, I'd thought—to my rescue, commandeering the conversation with a tale about Poppy and the greyhounds, giving me time to finish my coffee and excuse myself to go and do my warm-ups.

But apparently he'd only bought me a temporary reprieve, for here was Daniela now, walking right into my rooms without knocking.

Momentarily knocked sideways by her arrogant invasion of my privacy, I could only stand and stare as she took up her position in the doorway, hands on hips, as belligerently posed as if *I* were the one intruding.

"You were with Alessandro last night," she accused me.

My first instinct was to make a rude reply and throw her out, but even as my blood pressure rose, I tried to hold my temper. Wiping my face clear of any emotion, I said in my coolest voice, "I don't recall hearing you knock, or inviting you in."

"You were with him."

"Did he say I was?" Turning my back to her, I gathered my rehearsal clothes with careful hands, keeping my movements deliberately slow, unconcerned.

She didn't like that. "If you play a game with me, you will be sorry. I am asking you a question, and—"

"And I suggest that you ask Alex." I faced her squarely, holding my rehearsal clothes against my chest. "Now, if you'll excuse me, I have to get ready."

For a long moment I didn't think she would give way, but at last she shrugged and moved aside. I went with her to the door and held it open, to make certain that she left. She turned on the threshold and paused. "Does he make love to you," she asked, "my Alessandro?"

Certain questions, Bryan always told me, oughtn't to be dignified with answers, so I gave it none.

Daniela smiled a viper's smile. "No," she said, "I do not think he does. For that he needs a woman, not a little girl." Her tone grew arch. "Be careful when you try to fight with someone who is stronger. You will find that it is dangerous."

"I'm not afraid," I said.

"You are a fool, then." And with that she turned and glided off, her footsteps on the stairs a grim reminder that again, as on the terrace, she had scored the final point.

Damn, I thought. Why was it I could never think of what to say when it most mattered? I'd find the perfect comeback line eventually, I knew—tonight in bed, perhaps, or in the bath, having replayed the whole conversation a hundred times over, perfecting my lines till the last stabbing comment was mine, not Daniela's. But that would be too late.

I sighed. And then, aware suddenly of a feeling of being watched, I looked up and over the landing.

Madeleine smiled. She was hugging her half-open door as though trying to keep out of sight, not from nosiness, I thought, but for discretion's sake. "I heard Daniela's voice," she said. "I thought you might need rescuing."

"I'm fine, thanks." My words did not convince her. I suspect I neither looked nor sounded fine, because her eyes grew rather thoughtful.

"Have you finished with your warm-up? Yes? Then why don't you come in and keep me company while I get ready?"

Holding up my folded rehearsal clothes, I said, "I need to change."

"You can do that in here," she invited me, pushing the door wider. "Plenty of room."

I could hardly say no.

xix

I'D never been inside Madeleine's room before. It had the look of her, somehow—a quiet, gracious beauty that exuded class from every corner. Thick carpets cushioned the floor; and the walls, wrapped in rose brocade, softened the light coming in at the lace-draped French windows. She'd made up the chaise lounge against the far wall for Poppy to sleep on—Poppy hadn't slept in her own room since the séance had given her nightmares—and a studding of nails in the rose brocade walls showed where the photographs of Celia the First had hung before Madeleine had taken them down, so as not to further feed her daughter's imagination.

"I'm just finishing putting my face on," said Madeleine, heading for the door of what I guessed would be her bathroom. "Won't be long."

I was dressed in my rehearsal skirt and blouse when she came out. Because I hadn't known where to sit, I'd stayed standing, moving round the room admiring furniture and objects with my hands clasped firmly behind my back, as though I were touring a museum exhibit. I didn't notice much of what I saw, though, to be honest. My mind was busy running through my conversation with Daniela, and though I thought I'd schooled my face sufficiently when I looked round at Madeleine, she must have seen it anyway.

She said, "My dear, you really mustn't let her bother you."

"I'm sorry?"

"Daniela Forlani. She's only trying to get your goat, as my grandfather would say."

"Yes, well, she's doing an awfully good job," I confessed.

"The thing with a woman like that," Madeleine said, "is that she thrives on power; likes to feel superior. You have to turn the tables on her—let her know you think that she's beneath you."

"No chance." I smiled. "I'm not clever enough, I can't think what to say."

"Darling, none of us can. I'm absolutely hopeless if the lines aren't written down for me. But it's not what you say, it's the way that you say it. It's acting."

"I'm not sure I follow."

Crossing to her dressing table, she chose a pair of earrings from her jewellery box and stood before the mirror to put them in. "You simply pretend that you're . . . oh, I don't know, a queen, for instance. Think of how a queen would move, the way she'd hold her hands, the way she'd speak. And then pretend the other person is the lowliest of servants in your palace. It's all in your demeanour," she advised me. "You could stand there and say nothing, and you'd still achieve the right effect."

"I'll give it a try, if you think it will work."

"I'm certain of it." Smiling, she turned from the mirror. "I've had plenty of run-ins with difficult women myself, in my life."

She meant Mother, of course. I flushed with shame and glanced down to hide it, focussing instead on a small framed photograph of Poppy, unsmiling in her school uniform. Touching the frame with an absent finger, I said, "You haven't told Poppy whose daughter I am."

"I haven't, no. I didn't see the point. Poppy's rather too young, yet, I'm afraid, to understand the intricacies of adult relationships. Her world is black and white—she loves and hates, there's nothing in between."

"She hates my mother," I observed.

"I know she does. That's why I didn't want her judging you with prejudice. I wanted her to like you. And she does."

I kept my head down; touched the frame again. "And I like her."

"Well, there you are then," said Madeleine. "One day Poppy will be old enough to understand you're not to blame for what your mother did, any more than Poppy herself could be held responsible for something that I—"

"But I am." I hadn't meant to say that, but the weight of my guilt suddenly seemed much more than I could bear and the words came out all in a rush with the air of a formal confession. Swallowing hard, I glanced sideways at Madeleine. "I *am* to blame."

"Oh, my dear, you can't possibly think that."

"It's true. I provoked her, you see. I told her that she couldn't act for toffee, next to you."

"My dear." Her voice was very gentle.

"I shouldn't have said it. I knew from the look in her eyes that I shouldn't have said it, but I—"

"Celia," she broke in, still gently, "it wasn't your fault. They'd been lovers before, you know. Long before I came along. And anyway, if it hadn't been your mother, it would have been somebody else. There were many, many others. He was not a faithful man."

I struggled to take in what she had just told me. My mother and Madeleine's husband . . . Surely Rupert would have mentioned that they'd known each other earlier, before their great affair. But then, I reasoned, why would Rupert tell me that? He'd never talked to me about the men that Mother slept with, just as I had never talked to him about that night, the argument, the awful thing I thought I'd done.

"You haven't thought this, all these years?" Madeleine came closer, her large eyes spilling sympathy. She shook her head and said something that I took for a quote from a play or a poem—I'd never heard it before. "'Oh, how the debts of the fathers are paid by the child,'" was what she said. And then, as if I were no older than Poppy, she folded me into her arms with my head on her shoulder, her hand on my hair. "Darling Celia, it wasn't your fault."

I'd never been religious, not in any standard sense. But as I stood there in her quiet room, held safe within her motherly embrace, I couldn't help but feel I was receiving absolution.

ACT V

A Storm, with Thunder and Lightning.

Sleep . . .
Secure from human chance, long ages out,
While all the storms of fate fly o'er your tomb;

Dryden: *All for Love*

i

MY dreams, in vivid colour, came that night in a relentless stream. I woke, and turned, and fell once more to dreaming—unconnected dreams that grew more wild and twisted as the night wore on.

In one of the more pleasant ones I was walking with Poppy, who'd grown up to be nearly my age, a lovely young woman. We were walking in a park, along a well-kept path with chestnut trees along it, and then suddenly the path became a flat and golden ladder, and the park a giant game board, and we slid up the ladder together, arms linked. Poppy looked at me, laughing. "I've always wanted a sister," she said.

But where there were ladders, there also were snakes. In the next dream, my mother was dragging me through the same park by the hand. I was small—maybe four or five, trying my best to keep up. I stumbled, and Mother let go of my hand and hurried on without me, not looking back, and I sat in the path and cried and cried until footsteps approached. Looking up, I saw Edwina standing over me, uncompromising. "Let the past be past," she told me. "Let the past be past."

And then in that strange, wholly natural way that things happen in dreams, Celia the First happened by in a soft yellow summery dress, and she scooped me up, laughing, and carried me off, setting me down all grown up again back in my bedroom at Il Piacere. I'd never heard her speak, of course, but in my dream her voice was soft and lyrical. It sang the words. "You will tell him I didn't run off?" She smiled as though reminding me of something I had promised. "I couldn't bear to have him thinking that, it's such an awful lie, and I do love him. Tell him I was murdered, won't you? Tell him I'm still here."

Still here . . . The words were echoing through the dark room when I woke. At my bedside the glowing numbers of my alarm clock read 3:22. Exhausted as a distance runner midway through a marathon, I reached to put the light on, sitting up in bed and raking back a handful of my dampened hair.

And then I heard the voice. A woman's voice—little more than a murmuring, actually, as though someone were talking very softly on the telephone. It seemed to be coming from my sitting-room.

Mindful of Daniela's unauthorized entry earlier, I sat up in bed, listening. It didn't *sound* like Daniela, the voice was too gentle. It sounded, I thought, more like Madeleine. But then what would Madeleine be doing in my room at all, let alone at this hour of the night?

Fully awake now, I slipped my arms into the sleeves of my dressing-gown, shrugging it on as I crossed through the bathroom and opened the door.

There was nobody there.

The sitting-room was empty except for my shadow, made huge by the angle of light spilling out from behind me and stretching the length of the carpet. The murmuring had stopped, and all was silent.

Frowning, I shut the bathroom door again and leaned my weight against it. I heard a creak, just faintly, and then a pipe inside the wall began to make a thunking noise and I relaxed.

This was an old house, I reminded myself, and not only would an old house harbour lots of little noises of its own, but other sounds would travel queerly here. The voice that I'd heard was most likely an echo from Madeleine's room that had somehow spilled over the landing.

But that didn't stop me from turning the key in the bathroom door lock before making my way back to bed, nor from pulling the blankets up over my ears so I wouldn't hear anything else.

I was glad when the light finally came. By then the birds were drowning every other sound with their exuberant singing, flitting through the branches of the trees beyond the terrace with an energy and joyfulness that made me feel quite limpid by comparison.

Rising to open the window, I caught a glimpse of Rupert walking down towards the orchard through the gardens. He seemed to be walking more slowly than usual, head bent, hands clasped behind his back—a lonely-looking figure. For a moment, from this angle, he looked old.

My conscience pricked. I let the curtain fall and, dressing quickly, went outside myself to try to catch him up.

ii

RUPERT had vanished from view by the time I got out to the gardens, of course, but I knew which path he'd taken and I started out behind him at a quickish pace, confident that this time I wouldn't get lost.

The sky was full of shifting clouds and sunlight that had fooled me, from my window, into thinking it was warm, but I wished now that I'd worn something heavier. The air felt freshly sharp, and by the time I'd reached the orchard my hands had grown so cold that I could barely work my fingers. Flexing them, I hugged myself and tried to warm my hands against my body for a moment while I looked around for Rupert, trying to decide which of the pathways he'd taken from here.

He might have gone right, through one of the long walls of stone columns and arches that had been purposely built to resemble an old Roman ruin, sealing the orchard off from the rest of the garden and giving it a sort of timeless feeling and a sense of peace. Or he might have gone left, along the path that wound its way into the wood. Or else he might have gone straight on, one terrace down into the tidily ordered rose garden, Celia the First's 'bit of England.' The new bed that the gardeners had been preparing the last time that Rupert and I had been down here was planted over now with spiny bushes, and already hedged with lavender. Behind it I could see a path that led along the copper beeches, straight towards the Villa delle Tempeste.

Above the trees the villa's upper windows showed against the rose-washed walls, and though they still were tightly shuttered I couldn't help but feel that they were looking at me, watching, as I stood and tried to choose which path to take. In fact, I felt exposed on all sides, watched from every angle, as though someone might be standing there, behind that crumbling column, or that hedge . . . that ivied wall.

I knew it was only imagined—a bit of paranoia left over from finding that cigarette end by the path above the theatre Sunday evening—but that didn't make me any less uncomfortable.

So when I thought I heard a rustling from the woods, instead of turning towards it as I should have done, on the logical assumption it was Rupert walking on ahead, I headed in the opposite direction altogether, down the narrow path that drove its way between the ruined columns.

It brought me to a quiet place, a Japanese-style garden filled with twisted-looking trees and ringed with tall bamboo that smoothly grew in peaceful, silent groves. Most of the sections of D'Ascanio's gardens, I'd noticed, were arranged around a fountain, but there was no fountain here. At least, not in the traditional sense. In its place, a see saw bamboo trough had been set up to catch the water dripping from an overhanging stone—when the bamboo trough filled, it tipped over with a pleasant hollow ringing sound, as though it had been struck by a hammer, and, depositing its load of water down into a trickling stream beneath, it righted itself with another sharp clack and prepared to begin the whole process again, keeping time at a leisurely pace.

As I left the Japanese garden, passing underneath an arbour draped with some sort of vine trailing tiny white flowers, the sound of the bamboo trough followed me, as rhythmic as a metronome. So rhythmic and hypnotic that at first I thought the other noise was part of it, a periodic snapping noise that followed just as faithfully as I moved on, past fragrant clumps of glossy-leafed oleander and jasmine to the next small sheltered enclave where a statue of a weeping girl poured water in a small round pond beneath a drooping evergreen. The path here grew soft and a little bit slippery, having been protected from the drying wind and sun by an enclosing ring of cedars. From the absence of footprints I knew that not only had Rupert not come this way minutes before me, but nobody else had been on this path, either, for some few days. Only myself.

I had paused and was standing, considering this, when the snapping noise stopped. And that's when I noticed it.

Cocking my head to the silence, I listened.

Given that the snapping had stopped when I'd stopped walking, I reasoned, it might have been a noise that I'd been making myself, without realizing. Testing this theory, I slowly walked on. For a few steps I heard nothing, then the snapping started up again, a sound like dry twigs being trodden on heavily, and this time I could tell that it was coming from behind me.

I stopped a second time, and turned. "Hello?" I called. "Is someone there?"

Only the breeze and the birdsong replied. The path behind looked innocently empty and idyllic, but as before in the orchard, I could feel the eyes.

I lifted my chin in defiance. "You're wasting your time. I'm not frightened."

But when the sound started again I turned tail like a rabbit and ran, pushing my way through the branches that blocked me, and stumbling a step as the path changed from plain dirt to paving stones. Recovering my balance I charged onwards, head down, running as though Death himself were after me. And when I rounded a bend and collided with a man who reached to hold my arms, to steady me, my first thought was to struggle.

"Hey, hold on!" Den's voice. "What's happened? Where's the fire?" He set me back a step to look me over.

Breathing hard, I glanced back. There was nothing there now, and no sound of pursuit. I met Den's eyes, embarrassed by my cowardice. "It's nothing," I told him. "I thought I heard someone behind me back there, but—"

"Got spooked, did you?" Nodding understanding, he released my arms. "I know, I feel the same way sometimes, walking through this place. Here, come and sit a minute, catch your breath."

I let him guide me three steps to the side, to have a seat on the curve of a low stone wall running alongside this part of the path. The thickly clipped yew hedge at my back offered some sense of safety, of privacy, making me feel more secure.

Den sat next to me, looking me over again. "Want my jacket? It's cold out this morning."

"No, thanks."

He took it off anyway. "Here, put it on," he advised me. "You'll freeze."

"Den, honestly . . ."

"I can't afford to have you catch a cold. We don't have understudies, remember? Put it on."

I put the jacket on, losing my arms in the folds of its sleeves like a child playing dress-up. I *did* feel much warmer, though. Settling back, I asked, "What brings you out in the garden so early?"

He shrugged. "Oh, just looking for Rupert. I wanted to go over something with him, and I know he likes to come down here and walk before breakfast. He's not easy to find, though."

"I know." I confessed I'd been tracking him, too. "He was heading for the orchard when I saw him last, but where he went from there I haven't a clue." I smiled. "He's probably back at the house by now, wondering where *we* are."

"Probably." Den folded his arms across his chest as though feeling the cold himself without his jacket, but he didn't complain. Looking round, he asked, "How many gardeners, do you think, does it take to keep on top of all of this?"

I didn't know, and couldn't guess. "There aren't as many as there used to be, though. Edwina was complaining that the gardens had been rather let go."

"I can't see it, myself. But then I'm not a gardener. I didn't even mow the lawn, when I had one. I've lived most of my life in apartments—I'm back in one now. My ex-wife," he said, "kept the house with the lawn." For all he said that lightly I still sensed that underneath his joking attitude there lingered disappointment, that he hadn't really wanted the divorce. Perhaps he had longed for the house with the lawn, and a wife, and a family . . .

I looked at him, curious. "Do you have any children, Den?"

He turned his head, I thought, a little quickly, eyebrow raised. "What makes you ask me that?"

"Oh, I don't know. It's only that you seem so comfortable with Poppy, I just wondered . . ."

"Yeah, well, Poppy," he said, shrugging in an offhand way, "she's one great kid. She's easy to spend time with."

"The feeling appears to be mutual," I said. "She thinks that you're pretty great, too."

"Really? What did she say?"

Because he looked so genuinely pleased I tried to recall her exact words. "She said she liked you, that you weren't like all the others."

"All the other whats?" he wanted to know.

I realized my mistake too late to backtrack, so I had to tell him, "All the other men who like her mother."

There was a pause while he digested this. And then he smiled. "I see," he said, neither denying nor confirming it.

"She didn't put it *exactly* like that. She was talking about Nicholas, I think, and how different you were, how much nicer."

"Well that," said Den, "goes without saying." His smile grew cocksure. "Anyone with taste would like me better."

"Shall I tell that to Nicholas?"

Shrugging again, he remarked, "Wouldn't matter. His ego's so big that I doubt if he'd take you too seriously." And then, as if remembering that it wasn't very politic to talk about one member of the cast with another, he brought the conversation back around to, "Anyhow, I'm glad that Poppy likes me. I'd hate to think I'd let myself be humiliated at Chutes and Ladders for nothing."

My turn to smile. "Oh, so you lost the games on purpose, did you?"

"Naturally." Grinning, he slanted a look at me sideways, his gaze dropping down to my neck. "Hey, you're about to lose your necklace, there."

Putting a hand up I felt the open clasp of the diamond angel pendant and refastened it gratefully. "Thanks, I must have caught it on something when I was running. It's a good thing you noticed—I'd hate to have lost it. Bryan only just gave it to me, for my birthday. He bought it at Tiffany's."

"Well, twenty-first birthdays are special, though, aren't they?"

"I'm twenty-two."

He seemed surprised by this. "My file said twenty-one. And I could swear that Rupert told me . . ." Here he stopped, and paused.

I heard it, too—a cheerful whistling, coming up the path the way I'd come. I recognized the tune, and turned expectantly as Rupert strode with characteristic briskness into view. He slowed when he caught sight of us, the whistle dying on his lips. Even at a distance, I knew his expressions well enough to know he wasn't thrilled with what he saw—me sitting here alone with Den in this secluded corner of the gardens, and wearing Den's jacket at that, and so I tried my level best to make it clear he hadn't interrupted anything.

"Good morning," I said. "We've been trying to find you."

"Oh, yes?" Drawing level, he stopped; looked from Den's face to mine.

"Yes. You lost me at the orchard," I explained. "I wasn't sure which way you'd gone, so I came this way, and ran into Den."

"In the literal sense," Den put in, with a smile. To Rupert, he said, "Are you done with your walk, now? Because if you have a minute, I'd like to get your input on the scheduling of our next production meeting. I'm supposed to call the lighting guy this morning."

"Yes, I'm finished," said Rupert. He glanced at the time. "It's nearly eight, anyway—we ought to head back and have breakfast."

Den made a face as he stood. "Let's hope it's better than yesterday's breakfast."

I teased him, "Missing Teresa, are you?"

"In the worst way. This new woman fries rubber eggs."

Rupert smiled in spite of himself. "Chin up," was his advice. "I'm sure Teresa will be back before too long. Once she gets the funeral over with—"

I interrupted, frowning. "When is the funeral?"

Rupert thought it was today. "This afternoon, I believe. Why, were you thinking of going?"

"Heavens no, I hate funerals. I wondered, that's all." Alex would doubtless be going, I thought. And for all I knew Daniela would be going with him. She seemed to have reclaimed her territory in a deliberate way since Monday evening—I hadn't seen Alex at all yesterday except for at dinner, and then he'd been quiet as always, politely withdrawn.

"—rotten shame," said Rupert, clearly finishing a comment that I'd missed.

I glanced up, guilty at being caught daydreaming, but he hadn't been talking to me.

Den was nodding. "It just goes to show you, you never can tell what's around the next bend."

Pushing Alex to the back of my mind, I wrapped Den's jacket tighter around me to shut out the chill of the rising wind, and fell into step behind the two men.

iii

"WICKED bloody weather," Nicholas complained, crossing the stage to gaze blackly out over the dripping wet landscape through the cascades spilling down around the edges of the high roof overhead.

We'd had a solid week of this, cold days and bitter nights and rain that came and went and came again, relentless. Rupert, keen to move us out of the rehearsal room and onto the stage, had been hoping for a break, and when this morning had begun with sun and lightly scattered cloud and all the signs that it might be a nicer day, he'd wasted no time in transporting us down here, to Galeazzo's theatre-in-the-round.

But the thunder had come on suddenly around eleven, with heavy rain that fell straight down and bathed the green surrounding hills in thick rain-forest mist. It didn't stop us from rehearsing—the roofed area over the audience seats was more than wide enough to give sufficient shelter. But the thunder added unexpected drama to what was meant to be a quiet, poignant scene, and the chill wind that whipped round my skirts now and then made me lose concentration.

After nearly two weeks without my script in hand I'd managed to regain my earlier confidence, but this morning I'd found myself once again asking for lines. It wasn't entirely my fault. This morning we'd been doing scenes from Act Two, between Nicholas and me—the scenes in which we, having been reunited by the medium for one brief hour, discussed the details of his death, the nature of the afterlife, the morality of war . . . The dialogue, plagiarized from Sophocles or not, was beautifully written and rich with emotion, but

Nicholas had an unfortunate habit of editing his lines to suit himself, which not only confused me at times but occasionally had the effect of making *my* next line sound out of place, as though I weren't responding properly to what he'd said. And that confused me more.

Normally, when one of us got a line wrong, Den simply made a note of it for later and the rehearsal went on uninterrupted. Rupert only rarely stopped rehearsals to correct us in our speeches. But this morning for the first time I had seen him losing patience.

Like the weather, he'd gone on watching for a time in an increasingly brooding silence, and then as the first clap of thunder had rolled overhead he'd exploded as well. At least, to me, who'd only seen him lose his temper on a handful of occasions, it had seemed like an explosion. Den and Nicholas would probably have deemed it rather tame: a quick slamming down of his pen on the clipboard, the order to break, and the slamming again of his clipboard down onto the seat in the front row beside him as he'd risen to his feet. Striding firmly up the aisle he'd stopped beneath the overhanging roof to stand, hands clasped behind his back.

Knowing that meant he was cooling his temper, I had prudently stayed silent, taking the opportunity to stretch my tense shoulders while Nicholas had moved to where he now stood at the far edge of the stage, head bent to light a cigarette.

The tone of rehearsal, I thought, was always different without Madeleine. She hadn't needed to be called this morning, naturally, because she wasn't in the scenes that we were working on. Other times all three of us were needed; sometimes only Madeleine and me. The curse of my particular part was that I was onstage the whole time, from beginning to end of the play. While the other two actors got breaks from rehearsing, I didn't.

Mind you, I still had it better than Rupert and Den, who in addition to their long days at rehearsal had to make time for production meetings afterwards some nights, and deal with the technical people and everything else. They'd had a production meeting last night that had gone on till all hours, and the strain of that was showing a little on Den's face this morning.

He normally broke the silence of a break by whistling or telling jokes, but this time he stayed quiet like me, making notes as he lounged in his front row seat, feet propped casually on the rail that encircled the stage.

The stage looked much the same as it had on the first day I'd stood here, except that now the furniture was in place—the chairs and table underneath a gorgeous reproduction gas-lamp with a red glass shade, suspended like a rare jewel by a cable from the lighting bar above.

I was looking up, examining its structure, when I heard Rupert's footsteps returning down the aisle towards us.

"Nicholas," he said, "I'd like a word."

I knew that tone. Its measured calm spelled trouble. And though part of me wanted to stay and watch Rupert put Nicholas in his place, experience had taught me that the best thing to do was to duck out of range for a few minutes. Catching Den's attention, I said, "I'll just be . . . you know." I nodded at the gangway leading backstage. "Back in two ticks."

"Oh, sure, no problem." As I started off the stage he called after me, "Be careful using water in this thunderstorm—don't keep your hands under the taps for too long."

"I won't."

"And watch your step back there. The workmen aren't quite finished."

He was getting every bit as bad as Rupert, I thought, worrying about my health, though with our opening performance scheduled for Saturday week I supposed it was part of his job to be cautious. Losing any one of us to illness or to injury would mean, at best, delays, and lost tour revenue for Alex.

Accordingly, I watched my step going down the gangway.

The passage was dim, lit by what little natural light filtered in from the stage, and at its farther end by a single wall-mounted fixture that showed me a rough concrete floor whose downwards slope carried me several feet under the seats overhead. Here the gangway ended in a broad semicircular passage that followed the curve of the stage, its plain block walls painted an unlikely pink.

That had been the original colour, so Alex had said. Apparently pink had been a favourite of Celia the First, and Galeazzo had, after all, built his theatre to please her.

The washroom was pink, as well, beautifully restored with lacquered white stalls and gilt-rimmed mirrors over twin pedestal basins. I dawdled as long as I could at the basin, although remembering Den's warning about thunderstorms and water I only washed my hands one time, and quickly. I was watching my reflection in the mirror, testing various expressions, when something flickered at the corner of my vision.

I turned my head, but the impression vanished. Nobody was in the room but me. Still, when the thunder crashed above a second later and the lights went out and plunged the washroom into total darkness, I leaped for the door as if a whole army of ghosts was in pursuit.

The passageway was dark, as well, but at its end where the gangway came down from the stage there was light of a sort, filtered daylight, dim and mist-like, but enough to guide me out. At least, it would have been, if I hadn't been frozen in place by a sense of sheer terror; a feeling . . . no, more than that, really—a sudden *certainty* that I was not alone.

No imagined ghost, this time, but a living, breathing, solid human being. Close behind me. The stirring of the air, the hint of warmth, the faintly sweaty smell, these were no more imagined than the prickling rush that climbed my spine to settle like ice at the nape of my neck. But still I couldn't move.

Ahead, from the gangway, Den's voice called me. "Celia?"

I wanted to scream to him: "Here! I'm down here!" but my vocal chords weren't working, either.

"Celia?" He was in the passage, now. I saw his outline, grey and uncertain in the dimness, looking small and quite far off. He was holding a torch, beam pointed to the floor to help him find his way. "Are you all right?"

Again the air behind me warmed as though with someone's breath, and with a giant effort I wrenched myself free of the paralysed stance I'd been locked in and, aiming myself towards Den, I began to run.

For the second time in as many weeks, I nearly knocked him over. Only this time, instead of struggling to break free, I wrapped my arms around his neck and clung, face buried in his chest.

"Hey!" He stood in surprise for a moment. Some men, I suppose, might have misinterpreted the embrace, but not Den. When his own arms finally closed around me, slowly and uncertainly, they offered only comfort, nothing more. "It's all right, nothing to be scared of," he assured me. "The storm's just blown a power line down, somewhere. It's—"

"There's someone there," I whispered, panicked, into his shirt-front.

"What? Someone where?"

"Outside the washroom door. A man, I think. I felt him standing right behind me."

His hand moved at my back as he angled the torch to shine it down the passageway, sweeping the darkness from side to side. "Nothing there now."

Still clinging to him, cowardly, I turned to look, and as I did the lights flickered on again all down the long curving corridor, showing us nothing but empty pink walls and the bare concrete floor.

"See?" said Den. Raising his free hand he lifted my chin and dropped a quick kiss, reassuring, on top of my head. "No one's there. You were only imagining things."

A small cough interrupted us.

Standing halfway down the gangway, Rupert looked from Den to me, expressionless. There was absolutely nothing sexual in the way Den was holding me—I might have been a child as young as Poppy; younger, even—but from where Rupert stood I knew he wouldn't see it that way.

Aboveground the storm rumbled on and I could feel a corresponding swell of tension rise between the two men, trapping me between them. And then Rupert simply told us, "When you're ready."

And without another word he turned and walked back out onto the stage.

iv

"YES, I know, but—" A truck rumbled by and I set my back to the door of the call-box, trying to shut out the worst of the street noise behind me as I cradled the receiver to my shoulder and begged the international operator to try the line again. "Just once more, please. He's always home by now."

I could almost hear her sigh as she complied.

I was telling the truth, though. Bryan's routine could be timed by the clock: he always walked home from the office and came through the door of the flat at precisely ten minutes to seven; by ten minutes past he was sitting in his favourite chair with bottled beer in hand, deciding what to do for dinner. Even on the rare nights he decided to eat out, he never left the flat till eight. Which meant he should have been, at seven-thirty, sitting in his favourite chair and finishing his beer, beside the telephone.

The ringing, though, went on and on, unanswered, at the other end, until the operator told me I should give it up. She said it rather more politely than that, of course, but this time I could hear the firmness in her voice. I didn't argue.

"Right," I told her. "Thank you." Replacing the receiver, I pushed open the door of the call-box and stepped out, defeated.

I wasn't having any luck at all today, I thought. The afternoon's rehearsal, even with Madeleine there, hadn't gone any better than this morning's—while the weather had improved a little, Rupert's mood hadn't, and by the time we'd ended everyone had been a bit on edge. I'd longed all day to tell him that he'd misunderstood what he'd seen between Den and myself, but there was no point in trying to talk to Rupert when he got like this. He didn't listen, not to me. Only one person I knew had learned the knack of reasoning with Rupert in a mood, but that person was miles away in London and I couldn't get in touch with him.

My first thought had been to e-mail Bryan, asking if he'd please ring Rupert this evening and talk him round, only I hadn't been able to find Alex, or anyone who knew where he might have gone, and I couldn't very well use the computer without Alex there. Or the telephone.

So I'd come here, instead, to the call-box at the bottom of the hill, where the long road winding down from Il Piacere met the busier thoroughfare leading from town.

The walk down the hill wouldn't have been too bad, actually, if it hadn't started raining halfway down, and if I hadn't had to pass the spot where Giancarlo had died. The rain had eased and finally stopped while I was in the call-box, but now that I'd come out it started up again, colder now and hard enough to make me draw up the hood of my raincoat.

Across the street, a man and woman stood locked in a passionate embrace beneath the shelter of an awning-covered doorway. It was envy more than anything that made me notice them to begin with—envy because they were dry and quite clearly enjoying themselves, whereas I was sopping wet and feeling wretched. But my initial glance across at them was followed by another, longer look; a growing sense of recognition. Not that I could see either of them very clearly. The man's back was to me, and his body blocked a good part of the woman's. Still, he had a curiously heart-shaped bald patch on the crown of his dark head, one I fancied I had seen before. And when the woman moved and raised her head to look at him, I knew for certain.

So, I thought, Daniela's man from Venice was in Mira, now—the man I'd seen her with at the basilica, and later, at the restaurant. I'd thought her brazen to fool around with Nicholas under Alex's nose, but apparently she was even more of a risk-taker than I'd given her credit for. I was tempted to call over to them, wave hello, and let her know I'd seen her, but the rain was already beginning to soak through my shoes and in the end I decided it simply wasn't worth the effort.

Turning, I started my long uphill trudge, head tucked down, keeping close to the hedge to stay out of the way of the cars. I was passed only twice, but both times the spray of water from the speeding tires arced up and caught me squarely in the side. Dejected and drenched, I squelched up to the great iron gates of Il Piacere and pressed the buzzer for the intercom.

The temporary housekeeper answered. She started out suspicious, and she wasn't good with English, and the fact that my name meant nothing to her didn't help. "No, no," she said, and severed the connection.

"Oh, for heaven's sake." I buzzed a second time.

She came back on. "No, *no,*" she told me firmly, as though sending off a salesman, and again the line went dead. She wasn't going to let me in.

"I don't believe this." It was raining harder now, and when I moved my head the water from my hood sluiced down my neck. I buzzed again with a force that must have alarmed the poor woman, because there was a long pause before anybody answered; then a different voice said, "Celia? Is that you?"

Alex. I felt a small rush of relief. "Yes. Let me in."

"Where on earth have you been? We've been—"

"Alex," I told him, "it's *raining*. Please, just let me in."

The latch clicked as the gate began its inward swing. "Don't use the main steps, they'll be slippery," he warned me. "Come round by the terrace."

Apparently he didn't trust me to follow instructions—he met me at the bottom of the drive, with an umbrella. I must have looked a sight. I saw the concern in his eyes change to quiet amusement. "So, where have you been?" he repeated his question, holding the umbrella out to cover me as he walked with me round to the back of the house, past the garage.

"I went to use the call-box."

"The call-box?" He lifted an eyebrow. "But why? We have phones at the house."

"It's a long story. And anyway, I wouldn't have needed to

go at all if you'd been here, so instead of asking me where *I've* been you might tell me where—"

"Milan," he cut me off, remaining admirably calm in the face of my temper. "There was something that I needed to arrange." Starting up the terrace steps, he slanted me a quick look of apology. "I must have gone straight past you, in the car. I've only just got back myself."

At least his car hadn't been one of the ones that had splashed me—those had both been older cars, not like anything I'd seen in his garage. Relenting a little, I said, "Yes, well, I was probably in the call-box at the time, so you wouldn't have noticed me."

I sloshed across the terrace, pausing inside the door while he shook out the umbrella and reached to take my raincoat. "Here, I'll hang these up to dry," he said.

It was then I heard the laughter from the dining room. Laughter! And Rupert's voice mingling with all of the others. It didn't seem fair, I thought. Here I'd gone and risked pneumonia trying to find a way to pull Rupert out of his mood, and he'd managed to do it without me.

The laughter came again, more raucous this time, and I frowned and started walking past, preparing to go upstairs to change out of my wet clothes.

"Celia!" Rupert called me as I passed the open doorway of the dining room. "You're back, how lovely. Look who's here."

I looked.

The man beside him looked me up and down and grinned a welcome. "Angel, looks like you could use a hug," said Bryan, rising from his chair to give me one.

V

"I like your Alex." Bryan stepped out on my balcony to test the night-time view, his voice drifting back through the open French windows.

Fervently hoping there was no one on the terrace underneath him, I replied, "He's hardly mine."

"Well, whomever he belongs to, he's all right. Will you look at that lake? Bloody gorgeous," he pronounced it, as he turned and came back in again, shutting the windows behind him and drawing the curtains. "Bit cold, though. I wouldn't have expected this for Italy. You might have warned me."

"I didn't know you were coming, did I?"

"No, you didn't, to be fair. I didn't know it myself until yesterday," he admitted. "Not for certain, anyway. I had a job finding a flight."

"And Alex was in on this too, was he?"

"From the beginning." He sat on the end of my bed with a smile that told me how pleased he still was at the way his surprise arrival had gone off. "It was his idea, actually, my staying at the house here. I e-mailed him last week to ask if he could recommend a good hotel in Mira, but your Alex wouldn't hear of it. Like I said, he's a very nice bloke. I approve."

"Well, I'm glad," I said, with patience. "But he's already spoken for."

"We'll see."

"What is that supposed to mean?"

"It means I've got my eyesight, Angel," he said, sending me a dry look. "I was sitting between you at dinner, remember?"

"And?"

"And if you'd both been ten years younger, I'd have sent you to your rooms for misbehaving."

Drawing my legs up beneath me I leaned my back against the headboard. "Bryan, don't exaggerate."

He only shrugged and changed the subject. "So what's Roo been doing that's got you upset?"

I sighed and pulled my hair back with one hand, trying to explain. I told him what had happened earlier that morning, how I'd gone backstage and thought someone was with me in the dark, and how I'd run to Den for reassurance, and how Rupert had leapt to conclusions. "I mean, I know it wasn't only that. He hasn't been himself this week to start with, and then Nicholas was pushing all his buttons at rehearsal. Seeing me with Den was only one more thing. But . . ."

"But?"

I blinked the moisture from my eyes, glad to be sitting with someone who knew how upsetting Rupert's disapproval was for me. "He gave me that look. You know—the one he always gives when he's been disappointed. And he wouldn't even let me explain . . ."

"Oh, Angel." He moved to my side; put his arm round my shoulder and held me against him in sympathy. "Don't cry, it's all right."

I wasn't crying, not exactly. Sniffing, I said, "There is *nothing* between me and Den."

Bryan rested his chin on the top of my head. "I'll talk to him," he promised. "Don't you worry."

"Thanks." I sighed again, the small heaving sigh of a comforted child. "Bryan?"

"Yes?"

"I'm glad you're here."

I felt his jaw move and I knew that he was smiling. "Well, I was getting bloody lonely in that flat, I don't mind telling you. I can only eat meals out of tins for so long." Sitting back, he made a show of looking round my room, noticing the evidence of luxury. "I should have come a damned sight sooner."

I followed his gaze. "It *is* nice, isn't it?"

"Very posh." Nodding at the giant portrait hanging over my bed, he said, "That's the lady herself, is it?"

"Celia the First, yes." I twisted round, looking up. "Beautiful, wasn't she?"

"Sad-looking, I'd have said."

I studied the portrait more closely and saw it as well, the shadows in the large blue eyes, the almost wistful smile. "Edwina said she had an unfortunate aura."

"Edwina?"

"Alex's grandmother."

"Oh, right," he said, having been kept up to date by my e-mails. "The gypsy queen."

"Laugh all you want," I invited him, "but you wouldn't have laughed if you'd been here for the séance. I mean, I know it's all rot, but Edwina can be dead convincing. And I'm sure she isn't doing it for show—she truly does believe that spirits can speak through her. It was really rather creepy." The eyes of Celia's portrait held mine for a moment, compelling. "I wonder," I said, "if she really was murdered?"

"It certainly would explain why she never attempted a comeback."

"I'm being serious. What if she didn't run off with that actor chap? What if someone actually killed her and buried her here, in the gardens?" It would have been simple enough to do, I thought, recalling the freshly damp soil of the recently turned-over bed in the rose garden . . . even in this day and age someone could easily have popped a body in there and no one would have been the wiser.

"You think old Galeazzo bumped her off?" He looked at the portrait again, with a shake of his head. "I can't see it, myself."

I argued that it needn't have been Galeazzo. "It could have been one of his other women, someone who was jealous."

"Me, I'd put my money on the wife," said Bryan, joining me in speculation. "She can't have been too pleased to see Celia the First muscle in on her man."

I flushed a little, looking down, debating whether I should tell him anything about Daniela and her threats. In the end I decided against it. Bryan hadn't even met Daniela, yet—she hadn't been at dinner—and at any rate I was too old now to have him fight my battles for me every time I chanced to meet a bully.

He was talking. "Though on second thought, it can't have been the wife. Not on her own, at least."

"Why not?"

"Because, my little Miss Marple, crime novels aside, I don't think the average woman could dispose of a body without someone helping her."

"Oh." I hadn't thought of that.

"Anyhow, you don't want to be talking about all this just before bed," he told me. "You'll have nightmares."

"I have those anyway."

"I'm not surprised. It's how you always did react to stress."

As he started to stand I looked up at him, curious. "What makes you think that I'm stressed?"

"Angel." The word was a gentle admonition. "I've known you since you were a baby, I know your expressions and moods—they're just the same now as they ever were. Besides, it's common sense. You're in your first lead role, in a play with Maddy Hedrick, yet, and only a week or so left before opening night. That's plenty of pressure for anyone. And then on top of everything, you go and trip over a dying man. I shouldn't wonder that you're seeing ghosts and goblins in the dark," he said. "You'd have to be bloody superhuman *not* to be affected by all that."

"You're right, I suppose."

"I'm always right," he reminded me. "Now, be a good girl, get into bed and put the light out, get some sleep. It's nearly midnight."

"Are you going to tuck me in?"

He laughed. "How old are you?" But he did it anyway, tucking the blankets up round me and brushing my hair with a kiss as he'd done countless times through the years. "Sleep tight," he instructed me. "I'll see you in the morning."

I felt five years old again, and safe, and loved, and so I should have slept quite soundly. But the nightmares came.

I woke to hear the wind against my windows, then rolled and tossed and slept again to dream of being chased. It was dark in my dream, and dead silent except for the sounds of my breath and the footsteps that followed me, first through the labyrinthine corridors of the house itself, then out into the gardens where I ran in panic, searching for a place where I could hide. I found the Peacock Pool, and pressed myself behind a pillar of the mausoleum, in amongst the row of carved stone dogs; felt the coldness of the marble on my skin as from the shadows I watched the approach of my unknown pursuer. I couldn't see his face—I only glimpsed him from the back as he went past me, moving stealthily. I saw the heart-shaped bald patch on his head, and caught my breath, and at the sound he stopped and, as I watched in mounting horror, started turning . . .

I woke with a jolt, my heart racing. Blinking in the semi-darkness, I let my gaze flail wildly round the room, seeking reassurance from my surroundings. There was my window, my nightstand, the chair in the corner, the pale life-sized portrait of Celia the First, and the door to the bathroom . . .

My eyes fluttered closed.

It was only when I'd nearly drifted off to sleep again that it struck me—the image of Celia had been in the wrong place. It should have been over the headboard behind me; not standing alone, at the foot of my bed.

vi

"YOU don't look like you're sleeping well," said Madeleine.

"I'm fine." I showed her a smile as Poppy danced ahead of us along the garden path, momentarily distracting her mother's attention.

"Darling," Madeleine begged her, "slow down. You're too ill to be running like that."

"I don't feel ill."

"Perhaps not, but you know what happened yesterday—you wore yourself out early and then had to spend the rest of the day in bed."

Reminded of this, Poppy slowed to a more suitable pace, with only the occasional skip now and then. She did seem to be getting her colour back, along with these moments of energy, but her eyes were still shadowed and bleary, the eyes of a convalescent.

From the way Madeleine was looking at me now, I could only guess that my own eyes looked something like that, too. She frowned.

"You're not worrying about the play, are you? Because you shouldn't. You're doing brilliantly. You've really got the role in hand."

I couldn't help feeling a little puffed up by the praise. After all, I had never expected an actress like Madeleine Hedrick to say such kind things about *me*. It seemed faintly surreal. "Thanks," was all I could think of to say.

"I suppose I can't talk," she said, looking away with a smile of remembrance. "The first time I had to appear in the lead role, I don't believe I slept at all for at least a week beforehand. I still get nervous, even now."

"You do?"

"Oh heavens, yes. Rehearsals are one thing, but facing that opening night audience . . ." She left the thought unfinished, knowing I would understand. "Mind you, I wouldn't want it any other way. The day I don't get nervous I shall know that I've stopped caring, and it's time that I retired."

"I hope you're always nervous, then. No, really," I said as she sent me an indulgent glance. "I can't imagine the West End without you. And anyway, people like me who are still down the ladder need people like you at the top to inspire us."

"My dear girl," she said, "you are sweet."

"Mummy?" Poppy turned back on the path. "Do we have time to go and see the stone dogs?"

Madeleine glanced at her watch. "I suppose so. But only for a few minutes, mind—Celia and I have to get to rehearsal."

"Me, too," she said, importantly. "Den said that I could be his assistant this morning, and help with the prompting." She went on ahead of us, forging her way up the path to the Peacock Pool.

Madeleine shared her amusement with me. "She's certainly got the memory for it. I think she knows everyone's lines now by heart."

It was actually not a bad move on Den's part, I thought. He had so many things to keep track of in rehearsal that I didn't know how he had managed this far, on his own. He seemed to have six hands, two sets of eyes, and separate brains that could take note of every detail, every movement that we made. Even Rupert had said that Den was far and away the best SM with whom he'd ever worked, and given Rupert's background that was saying something.

Madeleine must have been reading my mind. "At least," she told me, "Rupert ought to be a little happier today, don't you think?"

"With Bryan here, you mean?" I nodded. "Yes, I hope so."

"They've been together quite a long time, haven't they?"

"Twenty-two years." I felt proud of the fact. My whole lifetime.

"It shows. Australian, isn't he? I thought so. I've seen him around through the years, you know, with Rupert at parties and such, but last night was the first time we actually spoke. He's quite charming," she said. "I can see the resemblance between you."

"You can?"

"Oh, yes. Not in a physical sense, but in your mannerisms. It's very marked," she told me.

"Really?" Pleased, I asked for specifics.

"You both stir your tea in the same way, and do this sort of sideways look whenever you're amused, and . . . well, I'd have to watch you both together, like I did last night, and tell you when it happens. I should think that it's all part and parcel of being an actress, having this gift of mimicry. Poppy does it as well, I've noticed, with people she admires." She smiled. "And I notice that both you and Poppy have picked up one of Den's habits."

"We have?" I lifted my eyebrows and Madeleine laughed.

"Yes, that's it," she said, nodding. "The one-eyebrow lift."

"Oh, I've always done that."

"Have you really?" That intrigued her. "Well then, maybe Poppy's imitating you, not Den. She thinks you're rather wonderful, you know." We'd reached the end of the avenue of cypresses, where the trees opened out to the Peacock Pool. Checking her watch again, Madeleine called ahead, "Poppy, love, ten minutes now, and we'll have to get going."

"All right." Poppy, unimpressed by the half-decayed beauty surrounding her, only seemed to want a few minutes alone with the stone greyhounds, anyway. Climbing the steps of the old mausoleum, she crouched by the pillars and patted the fixed, staring heads of the statues.

"Dog mad, that girl is," said Madeleine fondly. "I suppose I should be grateful it's not horses."

We were standing by the shallow pool and looking at the lily pads when Poppy called us. "Mummy, Celia, come and look! The cellar's open," she said, pointing down.

And indeed the large stone that had sealed off the crypt had been shifted to one side, exposing the smooth-edged square opening into the darkness below. There were no steps leading down, but I could see the upper rungs of a rusted iron ladder. A dank smell, damp and airless, drifted upwards.

"The workmen must have opened it," I said, noting the few scattered tools round the edge of the hole. "They must be doing restoration here, as well. Edwina will be pleased."

"What's down there?" Poppy leaned forwards, trying to peer through the blackness, and Madeleine grasped her firmly by the collar.

"It's nothing you need to be looking at, darling. Just a cellar. Come along now, we've had our ten minutes," she said, "and Den won't like it if his assistant comes late to rehearsal."

Which was more than enough to propel Poppy back down the path, on her way to the theatre, the stone greyhounds guarding the bones of their forebears forgotten. I spared them a glance as I passed, though, and something of the coldness of my dream of last night touched me, and I quickened my steps out of instinct to keep pace with Madeleine, suddenly not wanting to be in this place alone.

vii

BRYAN didn't come to rehearsal. He might have asked for—and received—permission to attend, as Poppy had, but Bryan respected the process too much to want to intrude. "You don't need the distraction," he'd told us at breakfast. "I'll wait till you start your dress rehearsals, when all the technical people are there. Then I'll hardly be noticed, I won't throw you off. In the meantime I'll find something to keep me out of mischief," he'd promised.

And he did.

When we returned at lunch, we found him on the terrace teaching Max and Nero how to balance biscuits on their noses. "Hang on a minute, we're having a breakthrough," he told us, without turning round. "My lurcher was brilliant at this. Alex, hand me one more biscuit, would you?"

Alex, sitting in a nearby chair and clearly amused by the whole undertaking, complied. "Max won't do it," he warned. "He's too greedy to ever—"

"Now, there you go. Good boy," said Bryan, grinning proudly as Max held his head perfectly still, the biscuit neatly balanced at the end of his long pointed nose. "All right then, you can have it. Go!" As the dog flipped the biscuit and caught it, Bryan turned to Alex. "See? He's bloody clever, this one. Never underestimate him."

Poppy, delighted, moved forwards. "Can I try?"

"Of course you can. Alex, biscuit? Thanks, mate. Now then, darling, you just put it there . . . right there, like that . . ."

Over the instruction, Alex met my eyes and smiled. "How is your rehearsal going?"

Momentarily dazzled by the smile, I had to wait until I'd

sat against the parapet to answer him. "Not bad." Rupert approached and I turned to include him. "I'm still having trouble with that final scene, though. I can't seem to get the knife stab right."

Bryan must have kept his word last night and talked to Rupert, because Rupert seemed a different man this morning—more his old self, mild and cheerful, his patience restored. "Yes, well, we can work on that this afternoon," he told me, "if you like."

Alex, frowning a little as he tried to remember the plot of the play, asked, "You stab someone?"

"Myself," I said. "At the very end, when I commit suicide so that I can follow my husband over to the other side. Only the action doesn't feel right, yet."

Nicholas, standing a few feet away, overheard me and added his expert opinion. "It's the weapon that's the problem. I mean, honestly, it's too archaic. Women in the Middle Ages might have stabbed themselves, but we're talking about, what? Nineteen eighteen? Surely you'd be able to lay your hands on a smart little pistol by then that would do the trick quickly."

Rupert remarked that the classical nature of my character's suicide was probably intentional. "Like in a Sophoclean tragedy."

"Rubbish," said Nicholas. "In a Sophoclean tragedy the widow would have stabbed herself offstage. The Greeks never did their violence in the open—they always went off and were killed or whatever and then someone came back on and told the audience all about it. And anyway," he added, "I don't see why we have to worry so much about keeping to the script exactly. Art should be open to interpretation."

Madeleine breezed past him, her expression almost motherly. "Nicky, darling, I believe you've lost that battle once."

He sulked at the reminder of his argument with Rupert. "Well, my lines *were* an improvement."

Rupert smiled, his restored good humour made all the more evident by his efforts to be tactful. "I never said they weren't. I merely pointed out that, in the interests of this particular production, we should opt for authenticity."

"All right, all right," said Nicholas. He raised both hands dismissively and looked at me. "But mark my words, it's the knife that's been giving you problems. No twentieth-century woman would use a knife to kill herself."

"I take your point," I said, "but I'm not sure I'd use a pistol, either."

Madeleine agreed. "Shooting yourself in the head in the middle of somebody's sitting-room, Nicky, is hardly a feminine thing. It's too messy. I simply couldn't die in peace," she told him, making light of it, "knowing that someone would have to clean up."

Den had been last to come up on the terrace and, coming late as he did to the conversation, changed its tone entirely, leaving me wondering how a simple question asked of me by Alex had evolved into a sort of parlour game. Looking at Madeleine, his grin an open challenge, Den asked, "So how would you do it, then?"

"Kill myself? Oh, sleeping pills, I suppose. But in my own house," she insisted, "reclining on the bedroom sofa, wearing something stylish. With Puccini on the stereo."

"You've got it all thought out, I see." Den's grin grew broader. "Me, I'd take a bottle of twelve-year-old Scotch and go sit in a blizzard."

"You'd freeze," she objected.

"That's the idea."

"What I mean is, it would be uncomfortable."

Den didn't think so. "No, only for the first few minutes. Then the cold would make you drowsy and the Scotch would make you happy and then bam!"—he snapped his fingers—"you'd be out."

"Brilliant," drawled Nicholas, exhaling smoke as he lit a cigarette. "And what happens if you don't find an obliging blizzard?"

"You drink the Scotch anyway," Den said, not missing a beat.

Madeleine laughed. "Go on, Nicky, it's your turn. How would you do it?"

"I wouldn't."

"Hypothetically," she urged him.

"No, I'm serious. I wouldn't. I think that it's morally wrong."

Bryan pulled his attention from Poppy and the greyhounds and looked round. "What is?"

"Suicide," said Nicholas.

"Ah." Bryan stretched his shoulders back, relaxing as he always did when starting a debate, but Rupert beat him to it, saying, "I suppose it depends on the circumstances, really. I remember you telling me that story, Bryan, about the farmer who lived near to you . . ."

"What, the one who got cancer?"

"That's right." To the rest of us, Rupert explained, "This man simply took his gun one morning and rode out to a place where he knew his wife and children wouldn't go—where he could be fairly certain it would be one of the station hands who found him—and he shot himself. Nice and quick, no fuss. To him, I suppose, that *was* the moral thing to do. No one likes to be a burden to his family."

Nicholas turned to Bryan, and his voice was condescending. "So is that the Australian way, then? That what you'd do?"

Bryan was still watching Rupert. He glanced up. "Who, me? Nah, I hate guns." Flashing another of his trademark grins he turned back to the dogs. "Me, I'd pour a beer and put the telly on and take a shot of insulin, enough to do the trick. The best part is it doesn't leave much trace, see, so they couldn't stop my insurance."

For everyone's benefit, Rupert explained that Bryan worked in pharmaceuticals. "He's rather an expert on medical poisons."

Nicholas blew smoke. "Is that a fact? I shall have to keep him away from my lunch, then."

"Speaking of which," Den cut in, with an appreciative sniff of the air, "something smells terrific in there. Smells like chicken."

Alex smiled. "Teresa's back."

"She is?" To see Den's face light up you would have thought he'd won the lottery. "That's great," he said. "I'd better go wash up."

His departure, coupled with the news that our lunch was being cooked by Teresa, seemed to be the signal for a mass exodus from the terrace. Madeleine went first, having pried Poppy away from her game with the dogs. Nicholas, a little unconvincing in his indolence, yawned and pitched the spent end of his cigarette over the parapet before strolling after them, his eyes fixed on Madeleine's back with a thoughtful expression that made me wonder if he hadn't begun noticing the way that she and Den were getting on.

Rupert was settling into a chair when Bryan, with a sharp glance at Alex and me, rose and stretched with purpose. "Come on, Roo, I need a wash as well. My hands are all covered in dog hair."

"Oh. Well, the washroom is just—"

"No," said Bryan, "you'll have to show me. I can't find my way round this house on my own."

With a sigh, Rupert rose as well and led Bryan into the house, leaving the terrace to Alex and me and the dogs.

I almost never saw Alex, these days. His business seemed to be keeping him unusually occupied.

His face was difficult to read, and so expressionless at times that I tended to project onto it what I wanted to see. Now, for example, I thought I saw warmth as he looked at me.

"I take it you're enjoying having Bryan here." He wasn't really asking me a question, but I nodded.

"Yes, I am," I told him. "Very much." And then, because I realized that I hadn't properly acknowledged what he'd done, I added, "It was really kind of you to invite him, and to fetch him from the airport, and everything. Thank you."

"It was no trouble."

"Well, of course it was. But anyway, it's meant the world to Rupert."

Alex fixed his gaze on me a moment, then he looked away and said, "It wasn't Rupert I was thinking of."

I answered, "Oh," because that was the only thing that came to mind, and then I looked away, too, watching the play of light over the lake, and in the brief silence that followed I could feel both greyhounds watching us with interest, as though they were the audience and we the actors, waiting for our lines.

I was, as it happened, trying to decide if he had meant what I had thought he'd meant, and if I ought to let his comment pass, or follow up on it, or . . .

"Actually," he told me, "it was curiosity on my part, mostly."

"Really? Why?"

"You're always saying 'Bryan told me this,' or 'Bryan says…' You use his name in conversation even more than you do Den's. It made me want to meet him."

I knew I quoted Bryan, but I hadn't been aware of using Den's name. I would have to pay attention, to avoid upsetting Rupert. "And so what is your opinion?"

"He seems very easygoing, very nice. I like him."

"Well, he likes you, too," I said. "He told me he approved—"

I stopped myself too late, and flushed, and looked away again as Alex asked, "Approved of what?"

"Oh, you know, just of you in general."

"Ah."

"That chicken does smell good," I said, trying to change the subject. "I suppose we ought to—"

"Celia," he said, calmly, "when do you have time off next? On Sunday?"

He ought to have known that, I thought, without asking. My schedule hadn't changed these past few weeks. But it appeared that he was only wanting confirmation, anyway, because without waiting for my answer he went on, "I was thinking we could take the boat out, maybe for the afternoon."

"'We' meaning . . . ?"

"You and me," he said. "The two of us."

I waited several seconds before answering. "Daniela wouldn't like that."

"Does that bother you?"

"I thought that it might bother *you.*"

"Daniela doesn't run my social life." He paused a moment, thinking, and then said, "Or has she tried to tell you differently?"

I felt the subtle shift of power; knew I could have told him, then—I could have told him everything I knew about Daniela, could have told him she was seeing someone else behind his back, and that she'd threatened me . . .

But even as the knowledge filled my mind, I bit my tongue. I didn't want to play Daniela's game, to sink to her level. Instead I said, "Of course she hasn't."

"Then you'll come with me on Sunday?"

"That depends on where we're going."

"Anywhere you like," he said. "I just want to go somewhere away from this house."

"Why?" I asked, but before he could answer me Rupert interrupted from behind us, poking his head round the door to announce: "Lunch, you two."

Alex looked at me and smiled a small and private smile. "I can't imagine."

viii

"CELIA, love, do please keep your mind on what you're doing. Thank you." Rupert settled back and began again. "Now, try crossing downstage left . . . there, just there . . . turn with the knife in your hand, so the audience sees it, and . . . that's it, you feel the point first, test it . . . both hands now, push it in. Good. That's much better."

I let my upper body arc around the imagined blade, and then crumpled and fell to the side as we'd practised. It did feel better that way, but, "I'm still not sure," I said. "It still feels rather awkward."

"Do you know," said Den, speaking up only when it became clear that the flow of the rehearsal had been broken, "much as I hate to agree with Nicholas, I think he might be right about the gun."

Nicholas pivoted in his position next to Madeleine, upstage. "Well, thank you *very* much."

Ignoring him, Den made his case to Rupert. "Not only would the action be easier for her, but it's easier to pull off in a theatre-in-the-round. Right now her body blocks the knife from half the audience, you see? Whereas a gun to the head would be visible to everyone. And then there'd be the sound of the gunshot, too, to let people know what had happened—they wouldn't just see her fall over for no apparent reason."

"But they've seen the knife," was Rupert's argument. "She takes it out and holds it while she makes her final speech, and turns, so everybody sees it. Besides, it's quite clear from her words what she's planning to do."

"I'm just saying the gun might work better, that's all."

Rupert passed the decision to me. "Celia, what do you think?"

I hesitated. Personally, I had to admit that the gun idea made more sense, but when I looked at Rupert sitting so belligerently in his chair, his eyes compelling me to answer, I couldn't help but feel whatever choice I made would somehow be, to him, a choice between the two of them, between himself and Den. A test of loyalty.

I cleared my throat. "I don't know that my character would use a gun. A knife seems more her style."

"Right then, let's try the blocking one more time," said Rupert, in a final tone that ended the debate.

We ran it through again, and then again, and I was plunging the imaginary knife into my breast for what seemed like the hundredth time when Poppy screamed.

I wheeled in unison with Madeleine, to face the chair where Poppy had been sitting, but she wasn't there. It took a second scream to tell me she had gone backstage.

"Oh, Lord." My memory of that presence in the dark down there, the terror of it, rose within my mind and I was down the gangway and into the corridor well before anyone else, running madly, in search of the girl.

"Poppy? Poppy, where are you?"

"In here!" a hysterical voice cried from one of the unfinished dressing-rooms down at the end of the passage.

I found her frozen to the dressing-room's blank wall, too frightened to move. "He was going to hurt me!"

I pried her from the wall and let her cling to me. "Who was, darling?"

"Him." Wild-eyed, she pointed to a heap of blankets spread untidily in one corner of the room, as though somebody had been sleeping there.

The others had reached us now. Out of breath, panting, they spilled from the corridor into the dressing-room. "What's happened?" Den asked.

Holding Poppy close I spoke above her head. "She says that some man tried to hurt her."

"He was over there," said Poppy, pointing again to the blankets, "lying down. I didn't see him when I first came in, but then I turned around and he was . . . he . . .” She broke off, burying her face against my shoulder. “He ran away when I screamed.”

Nicholas thought that convenient, and said so, a comment that earned him a fierce look from Madeleine.

“Darling.” She stroked her daughter’s hair in sympathy. “It’s all right, he’s gone now. It was probably one of the workmen, just taking a nap.”

“He was going to hurt me,” said Poppy, insistent.

I looked at the blankets, remembering again that awful feeling of a body close behind me in the darkness, breathing warm against my neck, of reaching hands . . . I shuddered, looked at Den, and knew he understood.

His face was grim. “I’d better go tell Alex.”

ix

DANIELA had been quick enough to offer up the culprit—one of the plasterers who, as Madeleine had suggested, had been catching forty winks instead of working. He hadn't meant to frighten Poppy, so he claimed. He'd only taken off running because he'd thought he'd be in trouble, having been discovered sleeping on the job. Daniela had apologized on his behalf, but when Alex had mentioned that it might be nice for the man to come up and tell Poppy himself he was sorry, Daniela had gone all protective, leaving me wondering, a little cynically, if perhaps the man might not have been a plasterer at all, but another of her boyfriends whom she'd stashed down at the theatre for convenience.

To be fair, though, she seemed to have quite enough men at the moment to keep herself occupied. I hadn't seen her balding chap recently—at least, I didn't think I had; I wouldn't have known him from the front, nor from the back if he were wearing a hat—but for all I knew he was still hanging around down in Mira del Garda, at one of the hotels, patiently waiting for scraps of Daniela's time after she'd finished with Alex and Nicholas.

And if I'd had any doubts at all about her being involved with Nicholas, they were laid to rest emphatically that evening.

It happened innocently enough. I didn't go out, at a quarter past ten, with the object of tracking down Nicholas. I was actually doing a favour for Poppy—she'd come to my room in a panic to say that the dogs had run off, that they'd somehow got out into the gardens and she'd called and called but couldn't make them come, and she was terrified that Alex would be angry with her, having left the greyhounds in her care, and could I please, *please* help her look for them?

Of course I'd gone, but I'd gone on my own, leaving Poppy behind at the house. The gardens in the dark of night were no place for a child. I wasn't all that keen on being out myself, but I didn't intend to go far. There was no point, really, in running after greyhounds—they could run like the wind, and you'd never catch up with them. Better to whistle, I thought, and rely on their hearing to bring them to *me*.

It was the one truly impressive talent I possessed, actually . . . whistling. I could whistle like a boy. I did it now, and called out, "Nero! Max!" and waited.

Thinking I heard a faint woof in reply, I moved off towards it. There was no rain tonight, and the broken-up clouds let through more than enough moonlight to see by. I didn't need to use my torch. Beneath my feet the path was soft, and my footsteps made almost no noise as I approached the little fountain with the dolphins.

Which was why the couple locked in an embrace beside the fountain failed to hear me.

I recognized Nicholas straight off, and at first I assumed that the woman, by simple association, was Madeleine. But then I noticed that this woman had longer hair; and the pair of them, when they finally drew apart to speak, were speaking in Italian.

There wasn't any kind of cover I could have made use of, if I'd been so inclined—I was standing right in the middle of the path, with the nearest shrubberies a good six feet off. But it didn't much matter. No one was looking my way.

Daniela raised herself on tiptoe for a final kiss and, turning, vanished down the path towards the villa. Nicholas, after a moment, turned, too. And stopped dead when he saw me.

In the stunned pause that followed I switched on my torch. "I don't suppose you've seen the dogs? No? Well, I expect you had other things to occupy you. Never mind."

He caught me up before I'd gone ten yards. The sprint had left him out of breath and his words didn't come with their usual suaveness.

"Look," he said, "hold on a minute, will you?"

I stopped walking, but only because he had grabbed me by the arm and swung me round to face him. "Look," he began again, letting go my arm to rake his hand through his hair in a gesture that was meant to be boyishly appealing, "I know what you must think of me, but honestly, it wasn't like that."

"Wasn't it?"

"No, we were just fooling around a bit, that's all. I'd never be truly unfaithful to Madeleine. Never."

"I see." I turned away again, preparing to continue on.

He stopped me for a second time, and this time didn't let go his hold. "You won't tell her, will you? Really, it was nothing, only Maddy has this thing about fidelity . . ."

I looked at him, incredulous. "I bloody wonder why."

The bushes crashed beside us and the greyhounds bounded out into the open, tails wagging at first at the fun of the chase; then, as Max noticed Nicholas holding my arm, his ears folded back and he growled.

"It's all right, boy," I told him, and pulled my arm free without looking at Nicholas.

"Celia . . ."

"Save it," I said, and whistling up the dogs I headed back towards the house, and left him standing there alone.

X

I didn't, as it happened, have to say a word to Madeleine.

It was obvious at breakfast the next morning that they'd had a falling out. Well, obvious to me, at any rate—a stranger entering the dining room might not have known that anything was wrong, so skilled was Madeleine at putting on a social face; but I had watched her long enough to know that she was acting. I saw the effort.

I think Poppy saw it, too. Children, in my experience, were like canaries in the coal mine when it came to adult arguments—they seemed to be able to detect the slightest whiff of tension in the air. It made them agitated. Poppy, no exception, had become a little chatterbox this morning, which was just as well, considering there were only the four of us down at the moment and three of us weren't speaking.

". . . and Den said he'd never seen anyone learn parts as quickly as I do," she said. "He thinks that acting's in my genes. I didn't know what he meant by that at first, but Celia told me that it meant he thought I might have inherited some of your talent, Mummy."

Nicholas, idly, said, "Celia should know."

Poppy looked at him. "Why?"

"Her mother's an actress as well," he said. "Didn't she tell you?"

Poppy's eyes were eager as they swung to mine. "Really? What's her name? Would I have heard of her?"

My own gaze flashed to Nicholas. I saw the smugness in his face before he could conceal it and I knew that he was doing this on purpose. I saw Madeleine realize it, too, but even as she turned to intervene he said my mother's name.

There was a silence, and then Poppy said, "It isn't true."

I looked at her. I didn't want to—didn't want to see the disappointment, the betrayal, but I gathered my courage and looked at her full in the face. It was worse than I'd imagined. "Poppy . . ."

"No." Her large eyes filled with tears. "It isn't true."

"I'm afraid that it is."

She shook her head; the tears spilled over. "No." And then she pushed her chair back violently and bolted from the room, fists clenched, arms stiff, as though she'd just been dealt a wounding blow.

Nicholas, still with that faint taunting curve to his lips, said to me, "Oh, sorry. Was that meant to be a secret?"

Madeleine turned in her chair to examine his profile, shaking her head. "Sometimes, Nicky," she said levelly, "you really are a bastard." She pushed her own chair back, and stopped me when I would have followed. "No, it's all right, Celia, I'll go have a talk with her. Don't worry."

Which left me facing Nicholas alone. "Why would you do a thing like that?" I asked him.

"Quid pro quo." He raised his juice glass in a mocking toast. "Since you so kindly saw it as your duty to tell Madeleine the sordid truth about myself and the fair Daniela, I thought the least I could do was to return the favour."

I might have used a term more strong than Madeleine's 'bastard' if I'd had the time to think of it, but my mind wasn't quick enough to come up with anything suitably cutting. I simply stood and stared him down and said, "I didn't tell her anything. I haven't said a word . . . not yet, that is. Perhaps I should."

His smugness faltered as I stood. "Now, wait a minute . . ."

"Quid pro quo," I told him, "as you said."

And then, because I liked that as an exit line, I made it one.

xi

THE day went rapidly downhill from there. Poppy stayed away from our rehearsal, which was probably just as well—all three of us were noticeably off. And that, in turn, made Rupert irritable, and set him snapping at Den, who in his turn grew short-tempered. It didn't surprise me at all when the skies clouded over in midafternoon, nor when the rumbling of thunder began to sound over the lake. Had I shared my former flatmate's superstitions I'd have been tempted to believe that the combined negative energy of our small group was having an effect upon the weather; that the storm was an extension of ourselves.

The only thing that got me through the day was knowing it was Saturday; that tomorrow would be a day off from the strain of rehearsing, a day to recover my balance. I clung to that thought all through the evening . . . through the long and awkward dinner from which Alex was, once again, inexplicably absent; through the long and silent hours that I spent reading in my room before I slept; and through the long and restless night in which my troubled dreams competed with the rain against my windows for attention.

But Sunday dawned as dismal as the day before.

The storms showed no sign of relenting, and when I went in search of Bryan, hoping he could cheer me up, I found him arguing with Rupert. The door to their room stood open a few inches, which was how I came to hear anything at all—I didn't make a habit of eavesdropping, and I certainly was in no mood to stand by and listen while they had a row. In fact, I would probably have turned back down the passage and left them alone if I hadn't heard the mention of my name.

"Celia has a right to know the truth," Bryan was saying, his voice not so much raised as insistent.

Rupert's reply was more forceful. "I'm not going to tell her. I'm not, and that's final."

"It's bloody well *not* final."

"Why, will you tell her yourself?"

"I might do."

I pushed the door all the way open. "Tell me what?" I was intruding in a private conversation, and I knew it, but with everything else going on at the moment I suddenly couldn't bear watching the two of them argue. As they turned in the surprised silence to look at me, I moved my gaze expectantly from Bryan's face to Rupert's, and repeated, "Tell me what?"

Rupert said nothing at all for a long minute. Then he coughed to clear his throat, and looked at Bryan, and I could sense the subtle shift as they allied themselves against me, like they'd always done whenever I'd confronted either one of them—forgetting their quarrel to form a united, unbreakable front. I'd had no hope against it as a teenager, and I doubted that the years had improved my chances.

"Angel," said Bryan, deliberately soothing, "it's nothing that can't wait till after the play's finished. This really isn't the time."

Which meant it was something they thought would upset me. Rupert and Bryan had always gone out of their way to avoid telling me anything upsetting at times they thought were special or important to me—they'd once kept the death of a friend of ours secret until I'd finished taking my exams. Recalling that, I looked at them suspiciously. "Has anyone died?"

Bryan shook his head. "No, it's nothing like that."

The second possibility that struck me was more horrible. "You're not . . . that is, the two of you aren't breaking up?"

"Of course not, Angel."

"Well, you wouldn't be having a row if it wasn't important, and you might as well just tell me what it is at this point, play or no, because what I'll be imagining will probably be a hundred times worse than the truth."

They shared another look, then Rupert stretched a hand towards me. "Celia, love, come and sit down."

I sat apprehensively, knowing the news would be bad. People, in my experience, didn't usually ask you to sit down otherwise. Perched on the edge of the bed, shoulders tensed, I tried to brace myself for whatever might be coming. Rupert closed the door, with care.

"Do you remember when my mother died?" he asked me.

I hadn't expected that. "Only vaguely."

Bryan, behind us, said, "Roo . . ." in a low, warning tone, but Rupert shushed him with a wave and kept his eyes on me. "Yes, well, you were very young, and she'd been ill for quite some time. She had HD," he told me. "Huntington's disease. They used to call it Huntington's chorea, in those days."

"Roo, for God's sake," Bryan said, almost pleading, but it was too late. Rupert had broken rank and was advancing on his own.

He went on, to me, "It's a nasty progressive disease of the brain—eventually one loses one's ability to walk, to talk, to reason. And there isn't any cure." Pausing, he frowned down at the carpet as though he were choosing his next words with care. "Most people, like my mother, don't show any signs of illness till they're middle-aged, and even then it can be only minor things . . . a stumble here and there, a change of temperament."

I stared at him, beginning to comprehend. "Oh, Roo . . ."

"It's an hereditary illness," he went on. "If your parent has HD then there's a fifty-fifty chance you'll get it, too. It's rather like carrying a time bomb inside you, and one with an uncertain fuse at that, because there's no way to know if you have the disease until you yourself reach middle-age. As I have."

"No." I shook my head, unwilling to accept what he was telling me.

"I've noticed the symptoms for some time," he said. "So has Bryan."

I glanced at Bryan for confirmation, and found it in his tight-lipped face, the sudden strain that showed behind his eyes. I looked away again. My insides felt as though a callous hand had crumpled them, and yet my voice, though hollow, sounded calm. "Are you very sure? About your symptoms, I mean. You're sure it's not just overwork?"

"I've had the diagnosis," he said gently. "I'd hoped I could spare you a little while longer—at least until we'd finished this production, but . . ." His shrug held regret. "Bryan said my behaviour was starting to worry you."

I wished now that I'd never mentioned it, never complained, as if my not knowing could somehow make everything better again.

Dry-eyed, I raised my head to look at him. "I don't want you to die."

"Darling." Sitting beside me, he drew me in close with an arm round my shoulder. "It's early days, yet. I could have another fifteen years, or twenty. It's a slow disease, HD."

I took no comfort in that, knowing I would have to watch him weaken, see him change. "It isn't fair."

"Life rarely is, my dear," he said, and pressed a sympathetic kiss against my hair. "Life rarely is."

We sat like that for some time. I was aware of Bryan sitting on my other side, his arm around me, too, and Rupert talking, going on about the play, about how fortunate we were to have this special time to spend with one another; but my mind had gone numb and his words didn't register fully. Only the comforting tone of his voice truly reached me. The rest of my brain was absorbed with the intricate whorls of the bed's woven coverlet, and how they pressed into my hand, reproducing the pattern. I would likely remember that coverlet forever, I thought. More than I'd remember Rupert's exact words, or how he had looked when he'd said them, or how I had felt. Memory worked like that, sometimes.

"All right?" Rupert was asking me. I didn't know whether he meant that generally or in relation to a specific question, but I nodded anyway, and he seemed satisfied. "Right, then," he said, "just let me finish shaving and we'll go and get some breakfast, have a cup of tea—you'll feel much better."

As he stood, his gaze locked with Bryan's reproachful one. Rupert couldn't hold the look. He gave a short, self-conscious

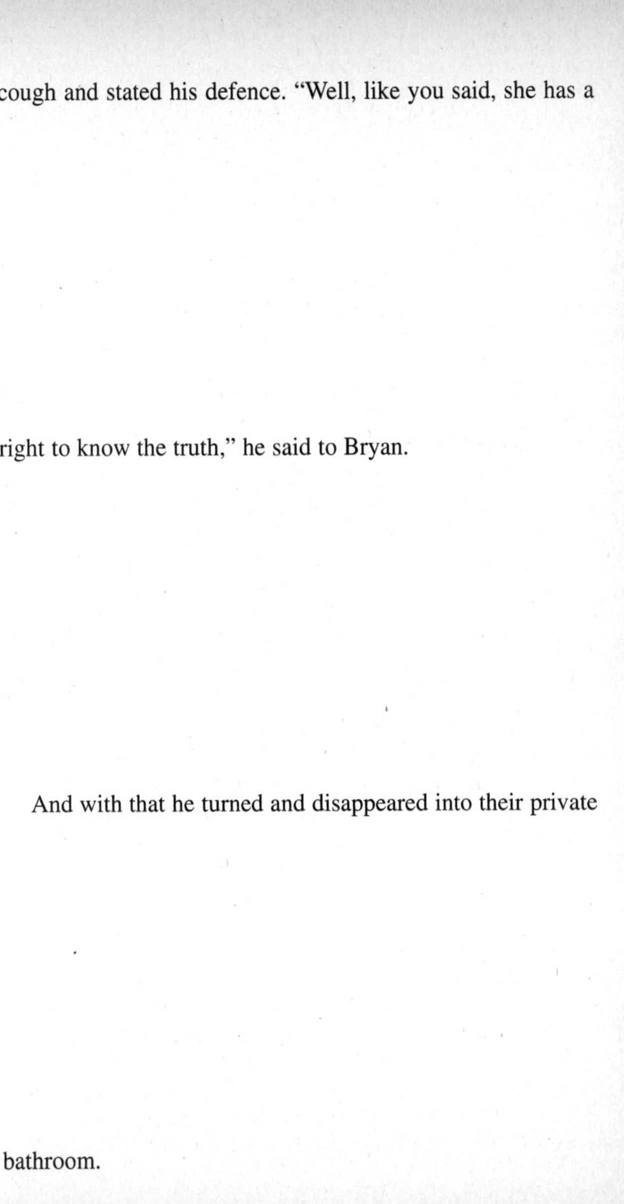

cough and stated his defence. “Well, like you said, she has a right to know the truth,” he said to Bryan.

And with that he turned and disappeared into their private bathroom.

xii

"TELL him I can't," I said to Teresa, who'd come to my room to deliver a message from Alex. "I'm sorry, but I don't feel well this morning."

Her dark suspicious eyes gave me a thorough going-over, as though she wanted to be absolutely sure herself before she carried the news back. "You are ill?"

I certainly felt like I was, and I didn't doubt I looked it, too. I'd spent most of the past hour crying in that slow and inconsolable way that always left my eyes red and swollen and dry and my sinuses blocked. "I don't feel well," was all that my conscience would let me admit.

Teresa didn't appear wholly satisfied by that, but having looked me up and down, sharp-eyed, a second time, she nodded briskly. "I will tell the signore."

Thanking her, I closed the door of my room and leaned against it, letting a wave of depression wash over me. The truth was, I would have loved to have spent the afternoon with Alex as he'd asked me, away from this house and its people and problems. But I simply couldn't. Not when I'd promised Rupert that I wouldn't spread the word about his illness. An actress I might be, but I didn't have the energy today to keep up the front for a full afternoon. Not with Alex.

At any rate, I didn't think I'd fool him. He was cleverer than that. So it seemed safer to avoid him till I'd had a chance to come to terms with things myself, and get my emotions in check.

A reasonable plan, I thought . . . only Alex himself spoiled it half an hour later when he turned up at my door in person.

His quiet eyes assessed me as Teresa's had. "May I come in?"

I started to refuse him. "Alex, honestly, I don't feel well enough to—"

"Yes, I know. Teresa said you told her you were ill." He came in anyway, and closed the door behind him with a certain unintended arrogance that might have been the product of his privileged upbringing or, more simply, of the fact that he was owner of this house. "She also said," he went on, turning in the middle of my sitting-room to face me, "that in her opinion you didn't look ill, but upset. She believed you'd been crying." Again his gaze levelled itself on my face. "Have you?"

I sidestepped the question, lowering my eyes as I lifted a hand to my temple. "I have a beastly headache, Alex." That was true enough—I didn't want to tell him lies if I could help it.

"And this is what has made you cry? I don't believe that."

"Don't you?"

"No." His voice sounded faintly impatient. "I know what has happened."

"You do?"

"Yes. I saw them together," he said, "in the gardens this morning. It was obvious even to me."

I looked up at him then, pressing my hand to my temple more forcefully as my headache intensified. "Was it?"

I sounded like an idiotic echo, and his impatience grew more pronounced. "Look, I can see that you're finding it painful, but if you'll permit me, I think it's a waste of your time. He's not worth it."

"He's not . . . ?"

"For one thing, he's too old—he's old enough to be your father. You might not think it's a problem now, but wait another twenty years and—"

"Alex . . ."

"Well, it's true. You throw your life away on such a man. It isn't natural."

"Alex," I said as he turned from me, raking a hand through his hair in frustration, "what *are* you talking about?" And then, because I had a good idea he wasn't talking about Rupert, I went on to ask, "Who exactly did you see this morning in the gardens?"

He glanced around, I think to judge whether I was being dense on purpose. "Den and Madeleine."

"And why would that affect me?"

"They seemed very . . . close."

"I know." Keeping my own voice deliberately clear so there would be no room for misinterpretation, I said, "I've known about the two of them for some time now. I think it's wonderful."

"You do." His turn to echo, and to frown. "So you and Den are not—"

"Of course not." Silently cursing whatever it was that made everyone so keen to bracket me with Den, I folded my arms in defiance. "Sorry to disappoint."

"Believe me," Alex said, "I'm not the least bit disappointed." And then, remarkably, he smiled, and when I saw that smile I knew beyond the shadow of a doubt that whatever there might once have been between him and Daniela, there was nothing now, no matter what she said.

That smile was mine, and mine alone.

I watched it coming closer as he crossed the room towards me, and when he stopped just in front of me, taking my face in his hands as he lowered his mouth towards mine, it was all I could see.

xiii

"I'M sorry if I've spoiled your afternoon," Edwina said, reaching to pluck a dead blossom from one of the low shrubs that lined this section of the garden path. "Teresa tells me you and Alex had an outing planned."

She'd arrived with her usual suddenness, a fairy godmother springing out of thin air, healthily tanned from her time in the Greek island sunshine.

The dogs, apparently overjoyed by Edwina's return, had come with us, and I had to stop walking for a moment to keep from tripping over Nero, who'd halted in the middle of the path to sniff at something. "You haven't spoiled anything. We'd talked about maybe going somewhere today, but then this morning I felt poorly, so . . ."

From her wordless sideways glance I had the impression that Edwina, like Alex and Teresa, was less than convinced by my illness excuse, but she at least was kind enough to keep it to herself. "All the more reason to be out in the fresh air," she said. "Staying indoors is no cure for a headache."

She believed in applying her medical theories with zeal, I'd noticed—she'd all but kidnapped me from my room, ordered me into a comfortable pair of shoes and a cardigan, and brought me out here. Still, I'd got off relatively easy, in comparison to Alex. The reason the dogs were with us in the first place was because their master had been dispatched to the Villa delle Tempeste, reluctantly, to break the news to Daniela that she was once again going to have to shift her things to make room for Edwina.

That alone improved my mood.

Edwina snapped another dying blossom off and clucked

her tongue. "What *do* the gardeners get paid for? That's what I'd like to know. There's one, now," she said, spotting a dungareed man who appeared to be pruning a flowering bush a short distance ahead. "I'll just go have a word."

It was, I thought, watching, an uneven match. Edwina, making up for the fact that she spoke very little Italian by speaking quite loudly and pointing a lot, was clearly overpowering the poor gardener, who seemed able to do little more than nod in the face of the onslaught.

"Hopeless," she dismissed him, as she came back shaking her head. "Doesn't know the first thing about pruning."

Over her shoulder I noticed the gardener had gathered his tools and was wasting no time in making his getaway down an adjoining path, looking a little bit shell-shocked. I smiled, and in the poor man's defence said, "Perhaps he's one of the new ones. Alex mentioned that he'd hired a couple of new men to help keep the grounds." Certainly the gardeners had been much more in evidence this past week. I always seemed to pass at least one of them whenever I was out. I told Edwina this, and added, "And Daniela's men are working at the Peacock Pool. I haven't been up there for a few days, but the last time I went, there was definitely something being done."

"You don't say? Let's go have a look then, shall we?"

Actually, it looked no different than it had the day I'd come with Madeleine and Poppy—a little more forlorn, maybe, under the overcast sky, but otherwise unchanged. There was still the long pool choked with stagnant-smelling lilies and the tailless row of peacocks wading through it and the carved stone greyhounds stoically ignoring the curious nudges and sniffs of their flesh-and-blood counterparts. Our footsteps today sounded very loud and lonely on the marble paving stones that ringed the pool.

"Max, get out of that!" Edwina called, as the dog began pawing at something in the shadowed corner of the mausoleum.

"That's where the men had been working," I pointed out. "They'd opened the crypt."

"How peculiar." She climbed the mausoleum steps to see

for herself. There were fewer tools lying about now, but the slab still stood off to one side and the square access hole still gaped blackly in the marble floor, with the old iron ladder descending into the darkness.

"They must have been making repairs to the foundation," Edwina said, peering down with interest. Max pressed past her with his nose in action, poking his head down the hole, and she pulled him away by his collar. "Back, you idiot. Yes, I'm sure you do smell all sorts of things down there, but there's nothing worth breaking your neck over, is there? Come on, get back. Off you go." And she waved him away with an imperious hand.

He went reluctantly, with a faint whine, and I wondered if perhaps he sensed the presence of his ancestors buried down there in the dark; if he'd somehow been drawn by their scent. I couldn't smell anything myself except the dust and mould and dampness of a stone vault that had never seen the daylight; but maybe Max, more sensitive, had caught the smell of death.

Edwina didn't share my fancies. "He's likely got wind of a rat" was her interpretation of the dog's behaviour. "I should think there'd be a few of them down there." She looked at me. "Speaking of rats, you must tell me, my dear, about this business with the workman that's run off . . . what's his name . . . ?"

"Pietro?"

"That's the one. I didn't like to ask Teresa for too many details—she's still quite broken up about Giancarlo's death, poor thing—but I gather, from what she said, that this Pietro had been stealing things, and that Giancarlo caught him at it. Is that right?"

I nodded, and told her the basics of the business, skirting round the few details that Alex had told me in confidence.

"A shame," she said, when I'd finished. "I was never very fond of Giancarlo—he had too much of his father in him—but for all his faults I know he was devoted to the family. His death will have come as a great blow to Alex, I'm sure." There was something indefinable in her expression that made me wonder whether she, too, believed that her son-in-law had been Giancarlo's father as well as Alex's. But she'd already changed course. She said, "You say Giancarlo managed to recover one of the pieces that was stolen, though? That was fortunate. So often these things disappear without a trace. A neighbour of mine had her house broken into last winter, and several of her good paintings were stolen. You'd think they'd be easy to hunt down, big items like paintings, but the police were telling her there's such a market internationally for stolen works of art, so many private collectors with more money than morals, that very often things just vanish. So it's lucky this Pietro person was stopped early on, before he could do too much damage. Lucky for Daniela, too," she added. "I'd imagine she could ill afford having her name connected in any way to a theft. From what I hear she's not too popular with the other trustees as it is—they only tolerate her because of her late husband's wishes. They wouldn't need much cause to get rid of her, and then where would she be? She couldn't live the lifestyle she's accustomed to, not without the Trust." She cast a thoughtful look towards the roofline of the house, behind us. "I wonder . . . has anyone else who's had dealings with the Trust had things go missing?"

"Alex already looked into that," I assured her, "and no, it doesn't seem so."

"Ah. Well, I don't suppose they'd be able to get away with running a racket like that . . . not for long, anyway. Word would get about. And even if they were a bunch of crooks they'd hardly be bothered to steal things *before* they took over a property, would they? They'd wait until afterwards, when the owner wasn't there any longer to notice."

"But Alex will be here," I said.

"Do you think so?" She looked around the cypress-sheltered garden with a dubious expression. "I can't see him staying on, myself—it isn't Alex, this place. He's a simpler sort of person. Oh, he may come back from time to time to visit, but to live?" She shook her head. "No, I can't see it. It's not his house, you see. It's his grandfather's, and it will be as long as it's standing."

I thought I knew what she meant. Il Piacere had the stamp

of Galeazzo everywhere—his tastes, his style, his decadence had settled into every room like dust that, being swept, would only rise and swirl and settle back still more tenaciously. One could only be a visitor in a house like this. No matter how long Alex lived here, or how much of it he changed, it would never belong to him.

I frowned faintly. "But where would he go if he didn't live here?"

Her shrug was philosophical. "The world is a wide place. Better to find a corner of it where there aren't so many ghosts."

She meant that figuratively, I knew, but I couldn't keep my lips from curving.

"What?" she asked me.

"Nothing, really. It's only that these past few weeks I've been tempted to believe in ghosts myself," I said, and told her of the 'footsteps' I'd heard walking in my room, and of the woman's voice murmuring late in the night, and my half-dream of seeing Celia the First at the foot of my bed. Smiling at my foolishness, I said in jest, "Perhaps your séance turned her spirit loose."

Edwina didn't share the joke. Dead serious, she answered in a thoughtful tone, "Perhaps it did."

"Oh, no, I didn't really mean—"

"Perhaps she didn't realize that I'd left, and she's been searching for a medium to help her to communicate."

I tried once again to use levity. "Well, in that case she's picked the wrong person. I'm no use at all in that department."

"No. I should think it much more likely that she'd try the little girl."

"Poppy?"

Edwina nodded. "The spirits frequently attach themselves to children of that age, I don't know why. Something to do with the onset of puberty, I'd imagine. Children passing through that time of life seem to release some form of energy that draws the spirits to them." To illustrate her point, she said, "That dream that Poppy had, for instance, after our séance—that might have been our Celia's spirit, trying to make contact."

Or it might have been a little girl's imagination, I thought, but because I liked Edwina and respected her beliefs I kept my skepticism silent. Instead I said, "Well, if it was, she didn't have much luck, because she's left the girl alone since then and set her sights on *me*." I smiled. "You're certain, are you, that you wouldn't like to hold a second séance, and send her spirit back to where it came from?"

"Quite certain. I told you before I left, my dear, that if we repeated the séance there might be grave consequences. We are, after all, talking about murder." With a final look down at the gaping dark hole in the floor at our feet she turned and strolled between the pillars, slowly descending the steps to the level of the pool. "The spirit of Celia Sands claimed she'd been killed by a woman. And I very much fear that the woman she spoke of was Francesca Tutti."

I followed her, frowning. "Galeazzo's wife?"

"She wouldn't be the first woman in history to do away with a rival."

I thought of Medea again, in the myth, poisoning Jason's new wife and his children . . . thought of Galeazzo's poem, black and brooding, speaking of the woman "*like Medea, with my children's blood upon her hands . . . her rival's flames around her head . . .*" Had he been writing of Francesca Tutti then, I wondered?

"Anyway," Edwina said, "there weren't too many other women here the night that Celia disappeared." Pausing at the bottom of the steps, she clasped her hands behind her back and gazed along the murky Peacock Pool, her expression so serious that I had to remind myself we were talking hypothetically, about the accusation of a nonexistent ghost.

"Did you know her?" I asked.

"Francesca? Oh, no, we never met. No, she died long before my daughter came to live here."

"Well then, what would it matter if Francesca did the murdering? She's dead now—they all are. The truth coming out couldn't hurt her."

"Ah, yes, but the sins of the fathers—or mothers, in this

case—reflect on the sons. Or the grandsons." She turned her head then, her gaze levelled on mine to make certain that I understood. And then, when she could see the implications sinking in, she said, "It's never nice to learn that one's descended from a murderer."

"No, I don't suppose it would be."

"*That's* why I won't hold a second séance."

I could understand, now, why she'd been so firm about the matter. She'd been concerned about upsetting Alex by casting aspersions on his forebears. And her concern wasn't totally unjustified, I conceded, because it wouldn't really matter that the 'message' any spirit might deliver at the séance would be only a projection of Edwina's own subconscious mind, nor that Alex himself didn't believe in such things; the barest suggestion that his grandmother had murdered Celia the First would be enough to start the trouble. Speculation, once begun, turned into rumour, and a rumour that couldn't be proved or disproved could take hold like a virus, infecting a family's good name.

It was better, as Edwina had advised, to let the past be past.

As we walked along the pool she said, "You might try explaining that to Celia's spirit, if she visits you again."

She said that so naturally, as if everyone conversed with spirits, that I couldn't help but smile, remembering my former flatmate Sally and her quirky 'white-witch' rituals—the strange chants and the rune-stones and the tarot cards. Edwina and Sally shared a kind of faith, I thought, that I could never fathom. Though I supposed that if I stopped and really thought about it, the tarot card reading had so far been eerily close to the mark . . . the selfish, cruel woman who'd cause me some trouble . . . the quarrels and illness in my family—at least, *I* counted Rupert as my family—and the man with light-brown hair who was meant to be my foundation, the man who was calm on the outside but emotional inside, as I had discovered this morning . . .

Edwina noticed the blush. She was, I think, about to comment on it when the dogs, who'd been snuffling for scents on the old marble paving stones, startled us both with a sudden eruption of barking. Heads lifted, they turned now in

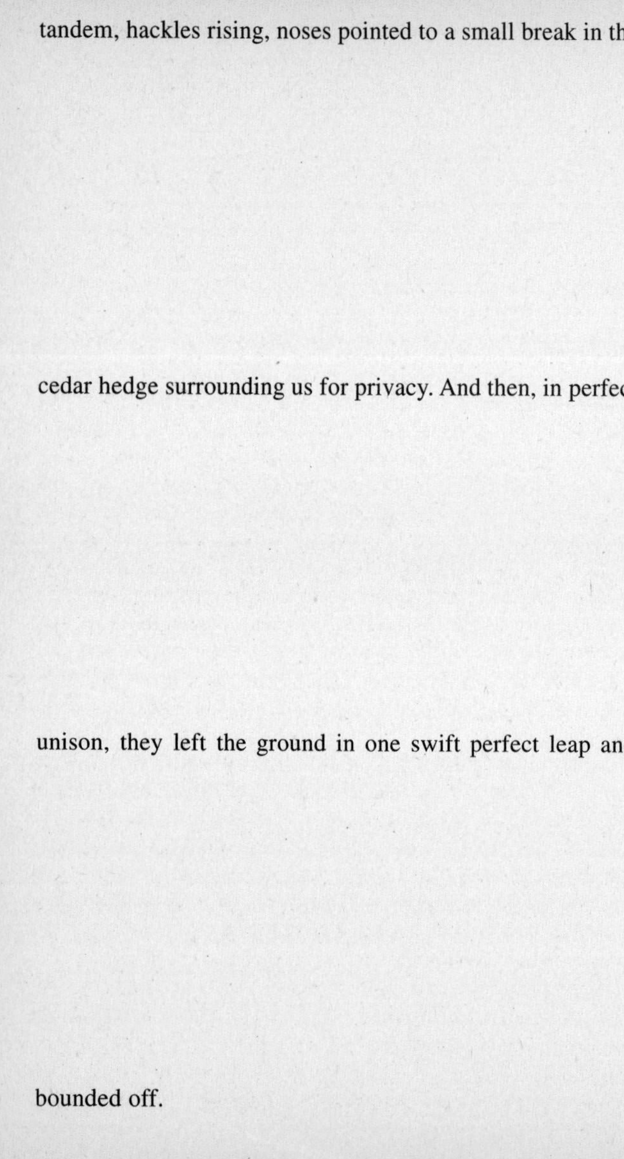

tandem, hackles rising, noses pointed to a small break in the cedar hedge surrounding us for privacy. And then, in perfect unison, they left the ground in one swift perfect leap and bounded off.

xiv

"AND did they catch anything?" Madeleine asked me the following morning, her eyes on my reflection in the mirror as I brushed my hair. We were sitting in what was to be my dressing-room backstage, having taken advantage of our tea break to get acquainted with the spaces we'd be occupying once we began our performances.

My dressing-room had been designed for Celia the First, and so was predictably pink, like the walls of the corridors, except in here the pink felt warmer somehow; cosy. The wall-mounted mirrors—one above the dressing-table, and another full-length one on the end wall—were framed in a pale wood that matched the dressing-table itself, and I had a small wash-basin of polished white marble. My chair, and the one in which Madeleine sat, were upholstered in soft pink brocade. It seemed altogether too pretty a room to be practical, but underneath the finery I fancied that the smell of grease-paint lingered, and there were a few cigarette burns on the top of the dressing-table that hadn't come out, a tiny but tangible link with the actress who'd sat in this chair over seventy years ago.

In the reflection of my mirror I could see her image watching me from the black-and-white photographs hung in an arrangement on the wall behind—the same photographs that had once hung in Madeleine's room, before she'd had them taken down for Poppy's sake. They were lovely photographs, showing the actress artistically posed at various places around the estate: Celia as Portia, in a long flowing gown like a Renaissance robe, standing sagely by the pillars in the orchard; Celia as *La Dame aux camélias,* half-reclining on a stone bench in the rose garden, all but buried by a scattering of flowers; Celia looking ghost-like, all in white, with one hand upraised dramatically beneath a gossamer veil through which one viewed upon her face a look of the most sublime terror . . . it had likely been that one, I thought, that had fueled Poppy's nightmare.

It was because of Poppy that I'd mentioned to Madeleine what the dogs had done yesterday at the Peacock Pool. "They didn't catch anything, no. And there may have been nothing there to begin with—I don't think a person could outrun a greyhound, those dogs move like lightning; but I just thought you should know, because with Poppy going down there all the time, if someone *has* been hanging round the Peacock Pool . . ."

"Oh, quite. I've already put it off-limits for her," Madeleine confessed. "I don't like that open crypt, it's far too dangerous, and besides, the place is rather isolated, and if the men are doing work there . . . well, one never knows, these days."

I knew exactly what she meant. I wouldn't have felt particularly safe on my own down here, after what I'd encountered backstage these past couple of weeks. Even though the workmen were now finished with these rooms and had cleared out, and though my reason told me that there was nothing and no one to fear here, I still felt wary walking through the passageways, and didn't want to be alone.

Even though Madeleine and I were the only people backstage now, I kept the door to my dressing-room closed, to make certain that nothing could intrude and spoil the perfect peaceful haven of this room.

"Mind you," said Madeleine, meeting my eyes in the mirror, "I don't know how much good it will do, my warning Poppy off the Peacock Pool. Twelve-year-olds, I'm finding, rarely listen to their mothers."

"Well, she certainly wouldn't listen to *me*." Self-pitying, I set my hairbrush down. "She acts as though I don't exist."

"Oh, darling, I am sorry. She will get over it, you know; she just needs time to think things through. She's like her father, that way. I've tried talking to her—so has Den—but, like I told you, twelve-year-olds don't listen."

"That's all right. She was bound to find out about Mother eventually."

Madeleine still thought the timing unfortunate. "It really was unforgivable, what Nicky did. He can be such a child. When he gets in a temper he fires in all directions; it was just hard luck you happened to be in his sights. Really, it was me that he was angry with—I'd quarrelled with him earlier, you see, about his visits to the Villa delle Tempeste. I'm not a fool," she told me, with a smile at my reaction, "and I'm certainly not blind. But he'd been getting rather obvious, and I thought he should try to be a little more discreet, for Poppy's sake."

I studied Madeleine's calm face with new respect. "May I ask you something?"

"Of course."

"Why do you stay with him?"

"With Nicky? Oh, convenience, I suppose," she said. "And vanity. A thousand women want him and I have him—at my age, that does wonders for the self-esteem. I'm not unlike your mother, that way. Both of us rely on our young men to keep us youthful."

I couldn't let that statement stand. I shook my head emphatically. "You're nothing like my mother."

"You are sweet. But really—"

A knock at the door interrupted.

"Come in," I said.

Den poked his head round. "Break's over. We're starting again."

Madeleine twisted to look at the wall clock above her head. "We have six minutes left."

"Yeah, I know, but Nicholas is chomping at the bit, and—"

"We'll be there," she said distinctly, "in six minutes."

Den grinned. "Fair enough." Retreating into the passage, he closed the door behind him as Madeleine reached into her handbag and leaned forward in her turn to use the mirror, touching up her lipstick.

"Sit down, Celia. Nicholas can wait," she told me.

"Chomping at the bit or not, he still can't make his entrance till we've finished with the séance scene, and I won't be done with *that* until I'm satisfied I've got it right. I've half a mind to bring Edwina in again for guidance." Fitting the top to her lipstick, she sent me a smile in the mirror. "She did tell you why she came back, didn't she? No? Oh, my dear, it's just too marvellous. I overheard her telling Alex yesterday, right after she arrived, because apparently she hadn't planned to come back here at all; she had a ticket booked to fly straight home from Athens, or wherever, so he asked her what had changed her mind, and she said she'd had word that she was needed. And when Alex asked her who had told her that, what do you think her answer was?"

I didn't have a clue. "A ghost," I guessed.

"You're not far off. Her *spirit guides*. Now, don't you think that's wonderful? She claims to have these spirit guides who act as her advisors, and they popped up out of the blue while she was on her tour in Greece and told her, so she says, that something momentous was going to happen at Il Piacere, quite soon I believe, and she ought to be here when it happened."

I could only imagine Alex's reaction to the news. "I don't suppose these spirit guides gave any clue as to what this momentous event might be?"

"Unfortunately not." Amused, she swivelled in her chair. "Perhaps they meant our opening night. That's soon."

"Don't remind me. I'm panicked enough as it is."

"I thought you might be." Meeting my enquiring look, she said, "You're not your usual smiling self today. I thought you might be thinking of how close we are to giving our first performance."

I hadn't been, actually. I'd been thinking of Rupert, watching his expressions and his movements with the urgency of someone who would soon be going blind, trying to construct a memory of him and carefully store it away so I wouldn't forget . . . But I couldn't tell Madeleine any of that, so I shrugged and said, "Well . . ."

"You'll be fine," she said, smiling.

I wasn't so sure.

XV

BY midweek our rehearsal hours, which until now had regularly been from ten to six o'clock, had shifted round to run from noon to midnight as we started into technical and dress rehearsals, a hectic and exhausting time when technical and backstage staff from all departments—lighting, sound, electrics, props, and make-up, wardrobe and the like—came on board at last to do their bit. The first day, Wednesday, was the longest and the worst, being our technical dress rehearsal or, as everyone I knew preferred to call it, our 'stagger-through.'

The purpose of this session was to fix each problem as it surfaced, and it seemed like every several lines we had to stop acting at Rupert's command while someone adjusted a light or complained about something.

Not that we were really acting, anyway. It would have been impossible for us to keep in character with all the interruptions, all the stopping and the standing round and waiting till the problem had been sorted out and people had stopped grumbling and Den had given us our cue to go ahead.

This was the week when the reins of control were passed subtly from Rupert to Den. It began in the stagger-through—Rupert told us when to stop, but only Den could tell us when and where to start again. By Thursday he was totally in charge, running the nonstopping dress rehearsal in the same way he would a performance, while Rupert sat quietly several seats back, taking notes.

The tension between the two men seemed to have eased off a little, and I mentioned this to Bryan as we sat out on the terrace Friday morning with our coffee in the unexpected sunshine.

"Your talking to Roo must have had some effect," I said.

"Yeah, well, I do have my uses." He stretched out his legs and leaned back with a smile, looking down across the pointed tops of the cypresses to the glimmering blue lake. "Mind you, it's probably the pace of work this week, as much as anything, that's mellowed him. He's been too busy lately to be rude."

"We all have."

"All of you except Nicholas. He seems to be able to be rude under any circumstances."

I smiled and said, "I meant we've all been *busy.*" All of us including Alex—I hadn't seen him at all since last Sunday, not even at mealtimes. Ordinarily, I might have let that worry me; I might have wondered whether what had passed between us last Sunday had meant more to me than to him. But as it stood, with this being our production week, I simply hadn't had the time to think.

"You know, I've never understood the logic," Bryan said, "behind the scheduling of these last few days before first night. You all come out bloody exhausted and borderline ill, which to me seems a hell of a way to begin your play's run." He turned his head to look me over. "I mean, have you seen yourself this morning?"

I confessed I'd been avoiding mirrors. "It's all right, though. Today's our last long day—our final dress rehearsal."

"Well, just see you don't collapse. More coffee?"

"Please."

He poured from the pot on the little round table between our two chairs and I watched him, thinking of all the times he'd done this for me; all the second cups of coffee we had shared while talking through my problems. "Bryan?"

"Mm?"

"Do you remember Rupert's mother dying?"

Setting down the coffee pot he handed me my cup with care. "Yeah, I do."

"Was it very horrible?"

"It wasn't pleasant." Bryan had never been one to sugar

the pill. "It's a nasty disease, but it's slow, Angel. Roo will have years, yet."

"But it's changing him already, isn't it? That's why he's retiring."

"Yeah." He topped up his own cup and sat back again. "He's starting to forget things, and the moods are getting worse. There are some physical things as well, movements he can't quite control. He's been good at hiding them so far—that's why he likes to keep his hands clasped—but they'll only increase. Eventually he won't even be able to walk."

"He'll hate that."

"He'll adjust. We all will." Levelling his eyes on mine he told me, very gently, "Look, I know it's hard, but try not to dwell on it, okay? You never know what lies ahead, what medical advances they'll come up with in the next few years. There's no point in worrying too much until we've got something to worry about."

"Yes, but—"

"Anyway, Roo wouldn't thank you for worrying," Bryan reminded me. "Not now, when you've got the play to be thinking about. I'm sure he's kicking himself for having told you at all."

I might have pointed out that Rupert likely wouldn't have said anything at all had Bryan not been urging him to tell me the truth, but at that moment the door to the house swung open behind us and Poppy came out onto the terrace. On seeing me she stopped and stood, a little hesitant at first, then turned her head in an exaggerated gesture as though wanting me to recognize the snub for what it was. "Good morning, Bryan," she said, in tones that quite clearly implied he was the only person present.

"Morning."

"I've finished my breakfast," she informed him, "if you want to play that game again."

"You're on. You go set it up, then—I'll be in just as soon as I'm done with this coffee."

As she turned and went inside again, I arched an enquiring eyebrow in his direction and he answered my unspoken question.

"I'm teaching her cribbage."

"You cheat at cribbage."

"Exactly. I got tired of being beaten at Snakes and Ladders." Raising his cup to drink, he added, "You really should talk to the girl, Angel."

Surprised by the advice, I said, "She doesn't want to talk to me. You saw her just now. She ignored me."

"That doesn't mean she wants you to ignore her in return. A twelve-year-old isn't a rational being. Believe me, I know." His expression was wry. "If I had a penny for every time you stopped talking to me back when you were that age, I'd be retired now and living off the interest."

"Was I really that bad?"

"You were deadly. The trick is, I never stopped talking to *you,*" he explained. "To a child, when a person stops trying, it means they don't care."

"I do care. I like Poppy."

"So talk to the girl."

"Well, I couldn't do it today," I hedged. "I've got that reception thing with the press before lunch, and then photos, and then final dress . . . I'll be lucky if it's over before midnight."

"I'm sure you'll find a minute somewhere."

I still thought it would be a waste of time, and told him so. "She isn't going to listen."

"Take a chance. She might surprise you."

XVI

POPPY did surprise me, later, by turning up to watch our dress rehearsal. She hadn't come out for a week, and it caught me off guard when, taking my place on the darkened stage for curtain-up, I noticed Poppy sitting halfway up the centre aisle. Bryan had settled himself, as was his habit, in the very last row, ostensibly so as not to distract me, though I'd always suspected he did it so I wouldn't be able to see his expression if the play was a bad one. At any rate, the only person whose presence *might* have distracted me wasn't in the house. Not only was Alex nowhere in sight, but Poppy appeared to have charge of the dogs for the evening—they sat calmly curled at her side, Nero half-sleeping while Max fixed his gaze on the stage with the well-mannered patience of a seasoned theatre-goer.

I didn't notice whether Edwina and Daniela were there, because by then the lights had come up and the play had begun and my concentration shifted of necessity to the performance, and stayed there till the lights came down again sharp at eleven.

For the first time we were greeted by applause, an unexpected sound that sent a surge of pleasure charging through my system and reminded me why I so loved doing this for a living. It was scattered applause to be sure, coming mostly from the technicians and Bryan, but coupled with the smile on Rupert's face it was reward enough.

"Excellent," said Rupert. "You should all be very proud of yourselves. Just do it like that again tomorrow, and you won't have any problems. Now, I only have one or two notes . . ."

As I'd predicted, it was getting on for midnight by the time

I'd changed out of my costume and wig into jumper and jeans, and Poppy had already left. No one remembered her leaving, but Den put Madeleine's worries to rest.

"She'll be perfectly all right. They've installed all those lights on the path to the house, now," he said, "so she can't lose her way. And she's got the dogs with her. I'm sure she's just gone back to go to bed. We must have bored her to death. Now, have a glass of wine, you've earned it." Filling the glass as he passed it to her, he looked at me and held the bottle up in invitation. "Celia?"

"Oh, no thanks, I'm totally done in. I'm going back to get some sleep, myself." To Madeleine, I offered, "I can look in on Poppy, if you like, and see that she's all right."

"Are you sure?"

"It's no bother." It might be a good time, I thought, to take Bryan's advice, and try to have a heart-to-heart with Poppy; try to smooth things over.

Refusing Bryan's offer of an escort home, I left the others drinking wine and celebrating while I walked slowly back on my own along the newly lighted path, working through, in the silence of my own thoughts, how best to attempt to make peace with the girl. It was not an easy exercise. I'd thought of and discarded four potential opening lines before I finally became aware of the sound of a dog barking, off to my right in the gardens, a short distance up the hill.

It was not a normal playful barking, but the high-pitched, continual bay of a hound in pursuit. And then all of a sudden the baying changed into a yelp that was cut off midway.

One of the greyhounds was hurt, or in trouble. And the last time I'd seen the dogs, they'd had Poppy with them. Without stopping to debate the wisdom of leaving the lighted pathway, I turned and ran towards the sound.

It was the actor who had telephoned up to the house. "You ought to come," he'd said, with urgency. "Your wife . . . you need to come."

"Something is wrong with Francesca?" It didn't seem possible. Scarcely an hour had passed since they'd finished with the dress rehearsal, and she had been well then, in fine spirits, so pleased that she had invited the three of them down for a drink at the villa. He hadn't gone himself, he had been tired . . .

"No, not Francesca," said the younger man. "It's Celia. She's . . . I think she's dead."

He had no memory of replacing the receiver, nor of running through the gardens. To his mind it seemed one moment he was standing in his bedroom and the next he was inside the villa, holding Celia's body in his arms, and rocking, willing her to wake.

Francesca watched him calmly from her corner, like a spider in her web. "You can do nothing for her, caro. *She is dead. I used the cyanide your gardeners use for killing wasps."*

"The drink," the actor said, and pointed to the spilled champagne glass that had fallen to the carpet next to Celia. "She poured us each a drink, you see. I didn't realize . . ."

"Why?" he asked Francesca, numb with grief. "Why would you do this? I've had other women, countless others, why—?"

"You said yourself she was not like the others," said Francesca. "She was carrying your child. She did not say as much, but I have eyes. And you already have a son. I will not have his future threatened."

"I'll ring the police," said the actor.

He raised his hand. "No." Even in his shocked condition one small detail penetrated. "Wait," he said, and setting Celia gently on the sofa he approached the actor privately. "I have a son, an innocent, who should not have to bear the shame of what my wife has done. I can at least spare him that."

The actor looked at him in disbelief. "You're asking me to lie?"

"To hold your silence. Will you do it?" He thought for a moment the man would say no. He had been Celia's friend, after all.

But then, "I'll do it," said the actor, rather coldly, "for a price."

xvii

I felt for a minute as if I were back in my dream, being chased, with the trees closing in blackly on all sides . . . only this time there were no footsteps behind me, and no shadows crossed the marble pavement underneath the moonlight as I burst into the long, secluded clearing of the Peacock Pool.

I paused to catch my breath, and look around. The tailless peacocks seemed asleep, the water lying still beneath its covering of lilies. The little mausoleum, too, appeared quite unaware of my intrusion, its row of stone sentinel dogs gazing blankly ahead in a slumbering silence.

And then, as I stood watching, one of the carved greyhounds slowly uncurled itself, coming to life, and detaching itself from the cold marble steps it came ghost-like towards me.

It wasn't a ghost. Nero's eyes held the light of the living. Giving the wide, high-pitched yawn of a dog under stress, he stopped several feet off and turned, urging me over his shoulder to follow. I looked round at the darkness, apprehensive. "Poppy?"

No answer came, and so I raised my voice and tried again.

"Here!" she cried. "I'm here!" Her voice echoed strangely and Nero gave a few sharp barks as though to make quite certain I had heard her. I approached the mausoleum with the greyhound at my side.

A beam of torchlight wavered from behind the pillars, deep within the shadowed corner harbouring the entrance to the crypt. "Down here," she called, and waved the torch again to draw me over to the square-cut hole. "I can't get out, I'm stuck. The ladder's broken."

I could hear the rising panic in her voice, although I couldn't see her. Dazzled by the light, I tried to calm her. "Don't be frightened, now, it's going to be all right. I'll get you out. Turn the torch to the side, would you? That's better." With the torch no longer shining directly into my eyes, I could see her some ten feet below me, standing underneath the iron ladder. She hadn't been crying, but her upturned face was pale and blotched and frightened. Frightened enough to not care who it was that had found her.

"How on earth did you get down there?" I asked. "Did you fall? Are you hurt?"

She shook her head no. "It was Max. He jumped, you see. And when I climbed down here and tried to help him out, the ladder broke."

For the first time I noticed the shining eyes beside her leg, and saw the darker figure of the dog, who wagged his tail in greeting. Ignoring him for the moment, I crouched for a better look down at the rusted iron rungs of the ladder. "Can you show me where it's broken? Shine the torch. Oh right, I see." It wasn't bad, I thought—a foot or so above her reaching hand. I could easily lift her that high, and then climb out myself. "That's no problem, then. I'll just come down there and give you a boost, all right?"

"What about Max?"

"Well, I'll try giving him a boost, too, but if that doesn't work we can go and get some of the others to help. Watch yourself, now. I'm coming down."

She took a step back from the ladder as I started my descent into the crypt. The ladder protested my weight a little, vibrating against the bolts that held it anchored to the stone, and I was glad to let it go and drop the final distance to the floor, landing with a thud that jarred my spine.

I'd only ever been in a crypt once before, and that had been on a school trip to Canterbury Cathedral, and this one smelled nothing like that one. This had a definite smell of decay and of death, and the walls breathed a bone-chilling damp. I was grateful for Max's exuberant welcome. Stroking his ears, I looked round, but I couldn't see much. The torch that Poppy held, still angled sideways, caught the corner of a wall niche that appeared to hold a smallish stone sarcophagus—one of Galeazzo's greyhounds, I presumed—but beyond that I saw nothing but the darkness.

Poor kid, I thought, turning back to Poppy. She must have been frightened half out of her wits, being down here alone. I reassured her with a smile. "Here, take the torch and I'll give you a leg up. Just put your foot there," I said, lacing my fingers to make a firm step for her. "That's right, like you're getting up onto a horse. Now hang on to my shoulder . . ." I hoisted her upwards as high as I could, until I could feel from the change in her weight that she'd managed to grab hold of the ladder. As her foot left my hands I warned, "Be careful going up," but it was rather a pointless warning as by then she'd already scrambled up and out and was kneeling on the marble beside Nero, who had kept a patient vigil by the opening above.

"Let's see if Max can do the same," I said. I had my doubts. The dog, although lighter to lift than Poppy, was somewhat more unwieldy and I couldn't make him understand exactly what I wanted him to do. In the end I had to crouch and persuade him to rest his front paws on my shoulders while I hugged his back end tightly to my chest, and then by straightening and shoving him straight up towards the ladder I managed to get him to shift his front paws to the rungs, more for balance than anything else; but he didn't like it. The unsteadiness, I think, made him nervous, and it took a few scrabbling tries before I finally got him heading upwards. Supporting his hindquarters with both my hands, I called to Poppy, "Lie down, if you can, and try to grab his collar; help him up." He didn't like that either, but it worked. With one great lunge his back legs and tail vanished over the rim of the hole.

Poppy pushed herself upright, excited. "I've got him."

"All right. Now if you'll just shine the torch down here on the ladder . . . thanks."

I had to stretch my full height up to grasp the lower rung and pull my body up after, a move I hadn't practised since my childhood days of playing on a climbing frame. My shoulders, unused to the strain, gave out after a few rungs and I had to drop and start again. This time, it was the ladder itself that gave out—with a crack of complaint the rusted metal snapped several inches above my hands, sending me once again plummeting down.

I landed hard and lost my balance, rolling to the side. The torch beam followed me. "I'm fine," I called, as I righted myself to a sitting position, massaging my knee. "I'm not hurt. But now *I'm* stuck, I'm afraid. I'll need another ladder, or a length of rope, or something, to get out. You'll have to fetch one of the others to help."

The torch held firm, unwavering, and pinned me in its glare.

"Poppy?" I shielded my eyes with one hand, looking up. "Darling, everyone's probably still at the theatre. Just go and get Rupert or Bryan, they'll know what to do."

In the silence that followed, with the torch still shining full upon my face, I knew a moment of uncertainty, and less than pleasant thoughts began to creep into my mind. I was, after all, in a rather vulnerable position, and Poppy was only a twelve-year-old girl who had already more than demonstrated her ability to hold a grudge. She hadn't spoken to me for a week, and likely would have gone on not speaking to me if she hadn't been in trouble, hadn't needed my assistance. Now that she was safe, I thought, what motive did she have to help me out? What if she chose to simply leave and take the dogs and leave me down here in the crypt all night, with nobody the wiser?

"Poppy?"

This time the light moved. "I'm going," she said. Not the most reassuring of answers, really, but before I could think to say anything else she had turned from the opening above and I could hear her footsteps cross the marble floor and fade into the night sounds of the gardens.

I felt colder in the dark. Hugging my arms I stepped forwards to stand in the paler square of moonlight slanting indirectly down into the crypt. Slowly, my eyes began to make the adjustment, and I could see the nearest wall, although the other three were shrouded thick in blackness, their location only guessed at from my memory of the mausoleum's size.

The wall I saw was smooth and finely faced with marble blocks that fit so perfectly they seemed to need no mortar. I expected Galeazzo must have put his finest artisans to work on this, his final gift to his beloved greyhounds, and the place where he himself had planned to seek eternal rest—his own sarcophagus, according to what Alex had told us, was somewhere down here, lying empty because of his son's refusal to have him buried in it. No doubt it had been beautifully made as well, and at any other time I might have been in a mood to appreciate the craftsmanship; but not tonight.

Not standing here and shivering alone, trying not to dwell on where I was and what surrounded me. I was trying especially hard not to think of what might have enticed Max to jump down here in the first place, trying not to remember Edwina's voice saying, "He's likely got wind of a rat."

Standing in my little square of moonlight I strained my ears to catch the sound of anyone approaching.

At first I heard only the wind in the trees and the watery murmur of the Peacock Pool. A leaf scuttled over the floor of the mausoleum overhead, startling in its unexpected loudness, and then skidded to a stop against a sheltered wall. Close by, some kind of night-bird called, a softly furtive cry; and then at last I heard the sound of mingled footsteps drawing nearer.

My breath rushed out in pure relief. She hadn't let me down, I thought. She'd actually gone and found someone to help—maybe more than one someone. It sounded as though there might be a few of them, walking with purpose. The lighter, more rapid steps, those would be Poppy's; the others were heavier. Men, I decided. I didn't hear the dogs, but . . .

One man made a sudden comment, in Italian, and was answered by a female voice—a woman's voice. Not Poppy's, but Daniela's.

I clamped my lips around the breath that I'd been drawing in to call to them, and started shrinking back into the shadows, moving cautiously, my hands behind my back to feel for anything that might stand in my way. Bumping the side wall, I used it as a guide, backing from niche to niche in search of a hiding-place.

The niches, more for ornament than anything, were too

shallow to shelter a person, and the sarcophagi that held the bones of Galeazzo's greyhounds were neither long enough nor tall enough to be much help. If I'd known where Galeazzo's own sarcophagus might be, I'd have made a beeline for it, but as it was I could do little more than to press myself into the very back corner and hope that the darkness would keep me from being discovered.

I couldn't explain, later, why I'd reacted the way that I had, like an animal going to earth at the first sign of danger; but an instant later I knew I'd made the right decision, when I heard Daniela call the second man by name—'Pietro'—and heard him answer in a rough, unpleasant voice.

They were much closer, now. Their footsteps climbed the mausoleum steps and crossed to stop at the edge of the opening. I heard a strange metallic scrape as something dragged across the marble. So much for my hoping they wouldn't be able to come down because of the break in the ladder, I realized—they'd brought their own, a sturdier aluminium model that settled on the crypt's floor with an ominous finality. A torch switched on, its bright light shafting downwards as a pair of boots—a man's boots—appeared on the topmost rung.

Standing unprotected in my corner, I again felt that sensation of being awake in a nightmare. My dream may not have gone like this exactly, but the setting was the same, as was the pulse-pounding fear that went hand in hand with hiding in the darkness, desperate not to be seen.

The man with the boots didn't keep to my side of the crypt. He crossed to a spot in the opposite wall, where his torchlight found a large, arching niche, elaborately carved with images of saints and angels, that held a man-sized sarcophagus cut from white marble and topped with a recumbent figure—Galeazzo, I presumed.

I couldn't tell who the man with the boots was, though. His back was to me now, and he showed only as a shadow in the light from his own torch, too short to be Pietro, with an unfamiliar walk.

The ladder creaked and clanged again, and two more shadows crossed the floor to join him—Pietro's first, his bulk unmistakable, followed a few paces back by the smaller, more delicate shape of Daniela. She'd brought a torch, too, and as she lifted it to sweep the wall ahead of her it caught the two men squarely from behind. I saw Pietro's bear-like shoulders, and the first man's head, bent forward to expose his heart-shaped bald spot . . .

Not that that really surprised me. I'd already suspected the stranger might be Daniela's mystery man, but having never seen him from the front I was surprised now, when he turned to make a comment to the others, that his face should bring a flash of recognition.

I *had* seen him before, I realized—in the little square in Sirmione where I'd sat and had a bite to eat. He'd been the man in the red shirt who'd made me so nervous. The man who'd been watching the crowd when I'd gone back to fetch Poppy's necklace.

My mind went racing back to that night in the Veranda della Diana, after Alex and I had come back from Teresa's house down in the town, and I heard again Alex explaining to me why Giancarlo had failed to keep their planned meeting in Sirmione . . . *The jeweller's assistant was sure they were both being watched.*

Was this the man who'd been watching them? I wondered. The man who had possibly followed Giancarlo to Mira, and left him for dead at the side of the road?

I narrowed my eyes on his face as he smiled and extended his hand to Daniela, expectant. Because she stood behind the light I hadn't noticed that she was carrying anything besides her torch, but now I saw her swinging something forwards. It looked like a suitcase, one that might have served well as a prop for a play set in the sixties—sleek and hard-sided and covered in powder-blue leathery stuff that appeared to have suffered a few knocks and scrapes. Hardly the sort of case that I'd have associated with a woman like Daniela, yet she handled it with care and passed it over with reluctance.

Pietro stepped between them, intercepting the transfer. For a moment I thought that the man with the bald spot might protest the action; he frowned and drew breath as though meaning to speak, but in the end he let it pass, even raising one hand in a gesture of invitation as Pietro set the suitcase down on top of the sarcophagus and undid the clasps.

Both torches angled downwards to illuminate the contents of the case. At first I saw only some kind of a puffy white packing material. Pietro moved to pull it back but Daniela's more careful hand intervened, pushing the white stuff aside to uncover a series of objects that glittered and shone in the strong beams of light. She made a comment to Pietro, then, and if I'd had to translate from her tone alone I'd have guessed it meant something like: "You see? What did I tell you?" but still he reached forwards and picked up an item before she could stop him.

Immediately, both Daniela and the other man spoke out in urgent voices. It was easy to see why. Pietro's huge hand held a yellowish vase that appeared to be fashioned from jewel-studded glass, and looked fragile enough to shatter at the slightest pressure. Shrugging, he replaced it in the packing fluff and let Daniela fasten down the suitcase with a click.

So she *was* involved in stealing things, I thought, for all Edwina had imagined that Daniela wouldn't want to jeopardize her status with the Trust. From what I'd seen of Daniela I rather suspected it might have been that very element of risk that had appealed to her—she did like playing games. And of course, there was always the lure of the money. The vase that I'd just seen was very similar in style to the Byzantine chalice that Giancarlo had recovered from the jeweller in Sirmione, and must also have come from Galeazzo's Fourth Crusade collection—objects that would doubtless bring a high price on the clandestine market.

I was thinking this when something—some insect, probably—scuttled down the wall where I was standing, and I jerked away, not thinking, setting loose a tiny fall of damp stone flakes that would probably have gone unnoticed if the others had been speaking at that moment . . . but they weren't. I saw their heads come up and turn; I saw the torchlight start to swing my way.

There wasn't anywhere I could have hidden. And I didn't want the light to find me cowered in my corner as though *I* were the one doing something that I oughtn't to be doing.

Straightening away from the wall, I stepped forwards and was standing rather calmly by the time the torches reached me. The light dazzled, stabbing my eyes, but I kept my head high and my gaze fixed in front of me, remembering Madeleine's advice on how to handle sticky confrontations—pretend you're a queen, she had told me, and the others are servants.

Trying for the proper tone, I told them all, "Good evening."

I heard murmurs from the dark behind the lights. The sensation was not unlike standing alone on a stage with the brilliance of footlights obscuring the audience. The men's voices mingled at first, then Daniela overrode them both, in English. "What are *you* doing here?"

Determined not to give her any ground in spite of my own nervousness, I countered her hostile demand with the arch of an eyebrow. "Actually," I told her, "I was just about to ask you the same thing. I rather think your explanation might be more interesting than mine."

Again the men's voices murmured and again Daniela silenced them with some short phrase that sounded like an order being given, an impression that was strengthened when Pietro's shadow stepped between the torch and me and came across the floor. His grasp hurt my arm as he hauled me back over to where the other two were standing—I could feel the bruises forming underneath his massive fingers—but I concentrated on not wincing or reacting to the pain. I had a feeling my advantage lay, at the moment, in not showing fear.

The man with the bald spot asked a question in Italian of Daniela, and she turned it into English for my benefit. "How did you know that we were coming here tonight?"

This close, the light from his torch no longer dazzled me, and I had no trouble seeing his face. There was something in the way he watched me, waiting for my answer, that convinced me to tread carefully. I shrugged. "A lucky guess." In an attempt to deflect further questions I went on the offensive, nodding at the suitcase. "You can't honestly think Alex won't notice those things missing?"

To my surprise, Daniela seemed to find that amusing; so much so that she passed it to the others in translation so that they could share the joke. Pietro, standing close behind me, gave a short, unpleasant laugh. The other man simply smiled, turning to shine his torch down on a smallish wooden crate that had been wedged inside the niche, between the wall and the empty sarcophagus. Bending, he levered off the crate's lid and carefully pushed back the packing to show me what lay inside. His torchlight caught the glitter of the square-cut jewels that rimmed a fragile vase of yellow glass. Glancing up, the man gave some instruction to Daniela and she opened the suitcase a second time, displaying the vase's identical twin—the one that Pietro had handled a moment before.

Below that vase I saw the edge of what appeared to be a chalice . . . and as I started to grasp the significance of what I was seeing Daniela asked, "Which is the real one, and which is the copy? You know this? Of course not. And neither will he. As far as he will know, there will be nothing missing."

So this was what Giancarlo had uncovered, then—not simple theft, but theft by substitution. Having tracked Pietro to the jeweller's shop in Sirmione, he must have then learned, through the jeweller's assistant, that the shop was participating in the creation of fakes.

Thinking of Giancarlo sobered me, because although he might have managed to uncover what was going on, he'd been silenced before he could disclose the information, and it suddenly occurred to me that, in all the crime novels I'd ever read, it was never a good sign when the criminals, having cornered the heroine off on her own, began to tell her every detail of their operation. It meant they'd already decided that she was expendable.

My only hope was that Poppy had done as I'd asked her, and that at any moment now she'd be returning with the others—and the dogs—to give me help.

"Is good quality, no?" Daniela touched the glass vase in the crate, proud of her accomplishment. "It has taken many skilled artists to make these. The glass, it was specially blown in Venice . . ."

"Is that what the two of you were doing there, then? I did wonder." And calmly, as Daniela turned with a frown, I went on, "I assumed you were only fooling around behind Alex's back, but now I can see it was business."

She didn't look pleased. "You have seen us in Venice?"

"Oh yes, a couple of times. And I saw you together in Mira, the day Bryan arrived."

I could see her memory searching backwards, warily. "And you have mentioned this to Alessandro?"

Because it seemed to matter so much to her, I chose the answer I thought she'd like the least. "Of course. I thought he had a right to know."

The two men had been watching our interchange in silence, but now Pietro asked a question and Daniela answered shortly in a sentence beginning with 'Signor D'Ascanio.' Perhaps, I thought, I was weaving myself a bit of a safety net by letting them think someone else besides myself knew what they had been up to. I said, "Alex knows everything, anyway—more than me. Giancarlo told him."

The man with the bald spot glanced over and I knew he understood me because his gaze narrowed slightly, became more appraising. Dropping the pretence of using Daniela as his interpreter, he said to me, "I do not think so. No, I think you tell a lie. Because Giancarlo, I am watching him a long time, since our man in Sirmione says he thinks they may have trouble. I would know if Giancarlo is telling D'Ascanio something."

"He came to the house."

"Yes, but that is a long time ago, and Giancarlo, he knows nothing then himself. He is still asking questions." Without moving, he seemed to have shortened the distance between us, his body language confident.

Trying not to let him see how much he frightened me, I studied him. "I suppose you were watching Giancarlo that Sunday in the square in Sirmione?"

"You remember me?" He smiled. "I am flattered."

"And I suppose it was you who followed him back here, and ran him down in your car?"

Modestly, he shook his head. "No, no, that job I give to Pietro. He is already here—it is easy for him to be stealing a car and to wait for Giancarlo. Me, I take care of the traitor who has betrayed us." The jeweller's assistant, I gathered . . . the one who had given Giancarlo the chalice. The man's smile grew shark-like and satisfied. "He will say nothing to anyone either, I think."

That smile chilled me to the bone, and I found myself reversing my earlier wishes, and hoping that Poppy *had* simply gone off and abandoned me; that she wouldn't return, unsuspecting, with someone in tow. A man who could smile like that, without any emotion, was dangerous, and with Pietro at his side I didn't know what he'd be capable of doing.

Daniela looked a question at him. "What do we do now?"

"We change the plan."

And before I could guess his intention his gaze shifted sideways and he nodded past my shoulder at Pietro, and I felt a sudden impact, saw a thousand lights exploding in my brain, and nothing more.

The crypt was silent, peaceful, still, and suited to his purpose. Here at least he knew she would not be disturbed. With tears upon his face he leaned against the lid of the sarcophagus until it shifted, inch by painful inch. He was not young. It took him time.

At length he'd moved it far enough that he had room to lay her in, with care. He hadn't thought to bring a pillow for her head . . . tomorrow, maybe, he would bring her one. And roses. Yes, she must have roses all around her, she'd so loved their scent.

He pressed a kiss against her forehead, smoothed the soft pale hair. Here she could sleep, he thought. Here in this place where he kept what he'd loved the most, where he himself, in the fullness of time, would come also, to lie in her arms and find peace.

"Please, God," he prayed aloud, "let it be soon."

And then he knelt, and turned his face against her body where their child had been, and wept, for all that might have been, and all that he had lost.

xviii

I opened my eyes to a pale orange mist. I was floating . . . I wanted to sleep, but the flicker of light held me mesmerized. I had no idea where I was—in a dream, probably. Certainly things had that unreal, distorted appearance of dreams. And the woman who sat on the edge of my bed wasn't real, either. The dress she was wearing, a soft yellow summery thing, was decades out of date, and she herself had a faint luminescence about her that marked her as something not human. I met her eyes briefly and smiled before looking away, unable to focus in my strange, suspended state.

Finding nothing in the room that I could recognize, I drifted a moment, then brought my gaze round again with an effort. She was still there, at the end of the bed. But that was all wrong, I thought confusedly. She should be in the portrait.

"Darling, wake up now," said Celia the First, in the voice I had dreamed before, lyrical. "Everyone's waiting."

I tried to absorb the words. "Waiting for what?"

"Just wake up and come with me, there's a good girl." Standing, she held out a hand in encouragement. "Hurry."

It took me a few tries to stand—I seemed to have no control over my legs at first, they kept collapsing underneath me till I'd learned the knack of keeping them straight—and the first steps I took felt as wobbly as if I were walking on waves, but I did my best to follow.

The orange mist grew thicker, brighter, swallowing her figure as she led me down a staircase. At the bottom she was there again, and smiling. "This way."

I trailed behind, but slowly, feeling very far away, my head a light balloon that floated high above my shoulders. I was vaguely aware we were passing through rooms, unfamiliar. Somewhere ahead I could hear a dog barking.

I was losing Celia the First in the mist again, but I saw her half-turn to look back at me. "You will tell him, won't you, I didn't run off? You will tell him I love him?"

And then she was fading, and the mist grew choking, rising up to burn my throat and sting my eyes, and when it shifted again there was Rupert's face in front of me, his expression relieved. "Thank God," he said, and turned me in the shelter of his arm. "Let's get you out of here."

And then all at once I came properly to my senses. I heard the crackling sound and realized that the mist wasn't mist after all—it was smoke, and the shifting orange light I saw was fire. For a moment I was paralysed by panic, not knowing where I was or how I'd come to be there, and then I realized we were in the Villa delle Tempeste, a few steps from the entrance hall. Behind us I could just make out the remnants of the sitting-room, flaming fabric peeling from the windows by the fireplace.

As Rupert turned me I nearly tripped over something that I took to be a table till it moved. I felt its warmth; a wagging tail; a pointed nose that nudged my thigh. The dog—I wasn't sure which one—pressed forwards with a nervous whine as something fell on fire from the ceiling, landing near us with a splintered crash.

"Go on, now." Rupert aimed me at the front door. "Go with Max, he'll lead you out."

"But Roo . . ."

"I'll be right behind you. I'm just going to have a quick look for Edwina."

I hadn't thought about anyone else being in here, but now that my reason was returning the idea left me horrified. I turned. "Edwina . . ."

"Go," he told me, taking my shoulders in a firmer grip and pointing me back to the door. Another piece of ceiling fell and Max whined more urgently. Taking hold of his collar I crouched to get under the worst of the smoke, and did as I was told, letting the dog all but drag me through the jumble of debris until at last I found myself outside and standing on the doorstep.

I heard running footsteps before warm hands grabbed me, lifted me, and held me close against a rough-knit sweatered chest that smelled like Alex. Beneath my cheek his heart beat strong and fast and when he lowered his head his voice, close to my ear, sounded oddly unsteady. I didn't understand what he was saying, but the sound of his voice alone soothed me. Leaning against him, I was only vaguely aware of the other people round us; other voices, and a frenzy of activity.

At length, he raised his head and stroked my hair back from my face. "Are you all right?"

"I'm fine. But Edwina . . ."

"Don't worry." He guided me down the steps onto the lawn, to a safe distance where my view of the villa was framed by the towering palms. From here I could see the full extent of the fire, the flames that had swallowed the upper floor windows and were hungrily stretching now up to the steep tiled roof; and the silhouettes of people, small dark forms that called to one another as they moved before the brilliance with an orchestrated purpose. One of the figures, detaching itself from the others, came over the lawn towards us carrying what looked to be a blanket.

I turned my face to the roughness of Alex's sweater as another spasm of coughing seized me, and I felt the blanket wrap around my shoulders.

"For God's sake, Alex, give her air." Edwina's voice, close by. "The poor girl can't breathe with you crushing her like that."

He loosed his hold, obedient, but kept an arm around me as though loathe to let me go. The coughing passed. I raised my head.

Edwina looked, I thought, remarkably unscathed for someone who, like me, had just been rescued. "Thank heavens he found you," I said. "Where is he?"

"Who, darling?"

"Rupert." Her uncomprehending look worried me. "He told me he was going back to find you. He . . ."

She glanced from me to Alex as my voice trailed off. I

think that something of the truth began to penetrate at that point, as I realized that Edwina looked *too* unscathed, too clean, that she most likely hadn't been inside the burning house at all. My logic blurred, then, in a rush of pure emotion. I believe I called out Rupert's name and tried to run towards the villa, but Alex was quicker. His arms caught me once again, holding me tight. "Celia."

"No!" I remember I fought him, beating at his chest with both hands as I struggled to get free, but even if he'd let me go there wasn't anything I could have done. Far off I could hear sirens drawing closer but the silhouettes were scattering and shouting, moving back, and as I raised my head the villa's roof caved inwards in a splintering of beams, and the bright flames surged skywards in triumph against the black night.

xix

I often felt, looking back later, that it was the longest morning of my life, and yet I had no clear and certain memory of it. I didn't, for instance, remember walking back to the house with the others, and yet I must have done, because when the first rays of daylight crept over the rim of the mountains and the birds began to sing in every tree I was sitting upstairs in my room, and the doctor, on Alex's orders, was looking me over. I didn't remember, either, exactly how the doctor had come to be there, but being in no state of mind to analyse things I accepted his presence without question, though I did put up an argument—I can't imagine why—when he suggested that I have some tests in hospital. He didn't press the point. Having found no evidence of lasting damage, he'd left Alex with a list of things to watch for and instructions I should not be left alone and he'd gone off again, and then after a while Alex was gone, too, and Madeleine was sitting in the chair across from mine, and we were drinking tea.

"She feels just awful," she was saying, and somehow it penetrated that she was talking about Poppy. "She didn't tell us straight off where you were, you see, and by the time we got there you had gone, and we all figured you had somehow climbed out on your own, and gone back to the house. Den headed back there to look for you, and we'd have gone, too," she confessed, "if it hadn't been for Max."

I failed to see where the greyhound fit into things. "Max?"

"He went absolutely mad—I've never seen a dog behave like that. Leaping and barking . . . he practically dragged us all down to the villa, and Poppy felt sure he was tracking your scent. And then, of course, we saw the fire." She looked away at that, as though not wanting to remember. "Anyway, my daughter's not a very happy little girl, right now. She wanted to come and apologize to you, but I told her to wait until later . . ."

And then it seemed that even as I looked at her she vanished and the room spun and Edwina took her place, without the tea. Her eyes met mine kindly. "Nothing to apologize for," she said. "It's natural for you to cry. You've had a dreadful shock, and lost a loved one. Though in time you'll come to realize that you haven't really lost him—he's only passed over, that's all. He's still with you in spirit."

I felt the tears warm on my face as I looked round, half-expecting to see Rupert's ghost standing at my shoulder. With Edwina in the room, I thought, anything was possible. I didn't share her faith . . . well, not entirely . . . but something made me ask her, "Can they hear us when we're talking to them, spirits?"

"Yes, I suppose so, if they're listening."

I found a certain comfort in that. Sitting back, I brushed a hand across my cheek and hesitated, wondering whether I ought to say something about seeing Celia the First in the villa last night. Edwina, I knew, wouldn't question the sighting, but it was precisely that fact that kept me from telling her, because I really didn't want to have it validated; didn't want to have to think it truly might have happened. It was easier to write the whole episode off as a by-product of concussion.

My mind was decidedly not working properly, but whether that was the fault of concussion or grief I couldn't say. Time passed in patches, with great gaps between. Edwina vanished, too, and in her place Bryan appeared, having brought along the old parchment prayer-book to read while he sat with me.

The sight of that book made me think of Rupert, and how excited he'd been when he'd found it, and how he'd tried to share that excitement with me, but I hadn't been interested. Dull-eyed, I looked at Bryan sitting silent by the window, leafing slowly through the pages.

"He wouldn't have done it on purpose, would he?" I asked. "I mean, that day on the terrace, when we were all talking about suicide and Roo told us that story about your neighbour in Australia who had cancer. You remember—the one who shot himself because he didn't want to be a burden to his family. You don't think that Roo thought that he'd be a burden to us, do you?"

"No, I do not."

"But he must have known Edwina wasn't in the villa."

Bryan raised his head. "How would he have known that? She'd been out with Alex, hadn't she? They'd only just got back."

I did have some memory, vague, of Alex saying something similar, of him explaining how he had returned to find the villa up in flames, and how he'd felt when he'd been told that Max had tracked me, frantic, from the Peacock Pool . . . that I might be inside. I heard his voice now, telling me, 'I would have died . . .'

I thought again of Rupert and, my vision blurring, looked away, towards the sunlit window, through which I could see the snow-capped distant mountains standing clear against the morning sky, with all the callousness of nature, as if one man's death had altered nothing. But it had, I thought. It had.

I said, "He'll never get to see our play."

"He'll see," said Bryan, very gently. "And anyway, it wasn't the performance he was keen about so much as the rehearsals—just to work with you, direct you in your first lead role, that's all he really wanted. And he got that."

He was right, of course. As director, Rupert had finished the bulk of his work this past week, and was already passing the torch to his SM—from now on, the play was Den's baby.

I thought about this. It helped to think that Rupert hadn't died without achieving what he'd hoped for; that we'd had our 'special time' together, just the way he'd planned.

Bryan watched me. "I just wish he hadn't told you he was ill. That kind of spoiled things. It could have kept another year."

"Another *year*?" My forehead creased. "So what was all that arguing about then, when you told him that you'd tell me if he didn't? When you said that I deserved to know the truth?"

"Ah." He looked down again, distracted by the parchment

page spread open to his idly searching fingers. “Well, it wasn't about him being ill.”

“What was it, then?”

“I'm sorry?”

If I hadn't known him better I'd have thought that he was being deliberately evasive, as though he almost hoped I'd let the matter drop. I asked him, very patiently, “What was it that you wanted him to tell me?”

Head down, he went on reading. “Angel, I don't think that this is the time . . .”

“Bryan, nothing you say could possibly upset me any more than I already am.”

He turned another page in thoughtful silence, and then sighed and closed the prayer-book altogether.

And he told me.

XX

THE round stage, empty in the quiet of the afternoon, felt as though it were holding its breath almost, waiting. Beneath my feet the boards creaked lightly where I walked, then silence washed over again like a wave as I stopped downstage centre and gazed out at the thirteen rows of seats, expensively restored and ready for an audience. I couldn't help but travel back a moment to the time when I'd first stood here, full of wonder, on a day not unlike this one, with the sun beating down on the hills sloping up on all sides to the trees, and the breeze blowing airily under the high pointed roof overhead. I closed my eyes to trap the memory, breathing in the fragrance of the pines.

And now, as then, the words of that soliloquy from Sophocles came clearly and unbidden to my mind, the speech I'd recited for Den and for Rupert—Electra's opening lament, made more appropriate by all that had since happened. Electra weeping over Agamemnon's death: *"But, like some brood-bereavèd nightingale, With far-heard wail, Here at my father's door my voice shall sound . . ."*

My father's door . . .

The boards behind me creaked.

I didn't turn; not straight away. Den's voice said, "Sorry, I didn't realize anyone was here."

I let my eyes drift open, no longer Electra but only plain Celia again. "I was just . . ." But there was no real way to explain what I'd been doing, so I looked round instead and said simply, "I had to get out of the house."

Standing by the entrance to the gangway with a coffee mug in hand, he flashed a brief, self-conscious smile. "Yeah,

I know what you mean. I never was too good at grieving in groups." He held up his mug. "Want some coffee? I've just put a pot on backstage."

"No, thanks." I walked the few steps over to my opening mark and turned again to face the empty seats that in a few hours would be filled with people.

Den watched me. "Look," he said, "are you all right with this? It's not too late, you know, to cancel the performance. In fact—"

"No." I'd already had this discussion earlier, with Madeleine, and I was as emphatic now as I'd been then. "Roo would have hated for us to cancel on his account. This was meant to be a triumph for him, staging the unstageable play. If we didn't go on, we'd be taking that from him."

His eyes, though understanding, held concern. "It's just that, so soon after . . . well, it's bound to be a strain."

"I'll be all right."

"How's the head?" he asked, crossing to feel for the lump at the base of my skull. "That bastard really gave you a whack, didn't he? You're sure the doctor says that it's OK for you to be up and walking around like this?"

I assured him the doctor had said I'd be fine. "There's no permanent damage."

"Yeah, well . . ." He didn't look very convinced, but in the end he dropped his hand and asked, "Is Alex back yet, do you know?"

"I haven't seen him." Not since dawn, at any rate. I had a vague remembrance of him leaving in the wake of the police, and though I knew he'd told me where he was going I couldn't for the life of me recall his words right now.

Den obviously did, because he nodded and remarked that it was bound to take some time, Alex's errand. "I just hope he makes it back before curtain. I thought I'd ask him to read the announcement, before we go on. About Rupert. I don't think any of us would be able to do it without making fools of ourselves."

He had a point. I knew that I, for one, wasn't a skilled enough actress to make an announcement like that without getting choked up, giving vent to my grief. But I wouldn't have expected Den to have had the same problem. With new eyes, I studied him. "You and Roo knew each other a long time, didn't you?"

"Yeah." The single syllable came stiffly, as he bent his head to take a swig of coffee.

"It's so bizarre, in all those years, that I never met you," I said, as he moved off a few feet to stand at the edge of the stage, with his back propped against the curved railing.

"Yeah, well, I didn't come to England very much."

"You used to live there, Bryan said."

"Only briefly. Before you were born."

"Is that when you worked with my mother?"

He nodded. "I doubt she'd remember me."

Linking my fingers, I twisted them, searching for words. "Did you love her?"

His hand paused midway to his mouth with the coffee mug. Lowering it carefully, he looked at me hard a long moment. "Yes," he said at last, "I did." And then he tipped his head and I could see a question forming in his eyes. "What else has Bryan told you?"

Looking down, I told him, "Everything."

"Oh, Christ." He hadn't been anticipating that. He set the coffee mug down quickly, near the row of seats behind him; passed a hand across his face. "This isn't how I wanted you to . . . damn, I asked him not to."

I might have taken that the wrong way, might have even felt rejected, if Bryan hadn't also told me how emotional Den had been last Sunday morning, when they'd talked together over an early breakfast. So I knew just how much it was costing Den now, to hold all of that in as he faced me, with eyes that asked forgiveness.

"I didn't know, you understand. I wasn't told."

I'd always had a fantasy about how I'd manage this meeting, when and if it ever happened. I'd be poised and in control of my emotions. I would cross the room sedately—for some reason, I'd always envisaged it happening at a party, with plenty of people about—and I would face him as an adult, and extend my hand . . .

But fantasies, as Bryan was so fond of pointing out, were

unreliable. And in the end I wasn't in the least sedate. I went to Den on impulse, like a child, and wrapped my arms around his neck, and held him tightly.

And he held me back, as though he'd never let me go, his breath a sigh that stirred my hair. "I was afraid that you'd be disappointed."

"Hardly." I moved my head against his shoulder. "All this time I've been thinking what a great dad you'd make, how good you were with Poppy, and I never guessed . . ."

"Yeah, well, I didn't, either, till that day you and Maddy had your costume fitting, there in the rehearsal room. I mean, there had been little things before, but seeing you done up like that, in the blonde wig and everything, that really hit me."

I felt my forehead creasing, remembering the incident, the way that he had stared at me. "Did I really look so much like my mother?"

He shook his head. "You looked like mine. She died when I was just a kid," he said, "but I have pictures of her, how she looked when she was young. You have her smile, her eyes . . . I didn't see it, though, until you put the wig on. She was blonde, you see."

"So that's what made you realize . . . ?"

"Well, it made me suspect. I didn't know for certain till I'd spoken with your mother."

I drew back at that, to look at him. "You talked to Mother?"

"Yeah, I phoned her up. She didn't want to admit it, at first—I think she'd rather have people imagine your father was somebody famous, and I don't quite qualify—but when I pulled out the big guns and threatened her with DNA tests, she finally gave in."

"And when was this?"

"Oh, a couple of weeks ago."

"You might have told me."

"It's not the sort of thing you just blurt out at dinner. Not after twenty years."

"Twenty-two."

"Well, that was another thing," he told me. "Rupert saying you were twenty-one . . ."

"He might honestly have forgotten. His memory . . . that is, he'd been forgetting a lot of things, lately." But I knew the excuse was a weak one. I didn't believe it myself. The truth was that Rupert, whether he'd been jealous or afraid that he might lose me, or because he'd simply wanted this to be a special summer for us, him and me alone with no one else intruding—the truth was that he hadn't wanted Den to know about me. He'd even gone so far as to tell me he was ill, a thing he hadn't planned to do, rather than give in to Bryan's urging that he tell me who Den was.

But then, in all fairness, Bryan hadn't told me, either, and he'd known the truth at least as long as Rupert. "Your mother told us once, when she was drunk," he'd confessed, "and after that we both saw the resemblance, but Dennis wasn't . . . well, he liked to have his fun; he wasn't what you would have called responsible, and besides," he'd added, gently, "you were *our* girl."

And I'd understood him then, and could forgive them keeping secrets. I wondered whether Den could do the same.

"Anyway," he said, "however many years it was, you'd got on well without me. You were happy. What right did I have to ruin that?" He asked the question lightly, but his guard had dropped enough for me to see the hopeful light within his eyes, damped down as though he didn't want to advertise his vulnerability.

I rested my head on his shoulder again. "You haven't ruined anything. I'm happy now."

He stroked my hair in silence for a minute, then paused as his hand felt the lump on my head again. "You're *sure* the doctor said that—"

"Yes."

"Well, maybe I should call him . . ."

"Den."

"Hey," he said, in self-defence, "I've never been a dad before. I've got twenty-two years of worrying to catch up on. Which reminds me"—he drew back in his turn—"exactly what's going on, now, between you and D'Ascanio?"

xxi

ALEX came to see me in my dressing-room, an hour before curtain up.

I wasn't in costume yet, and had only just begun to do my make-up. I turned from the mirror to greet him, then looked round. "Where are the dogs?"

"In the kennels. They're nervous of crowds."

"I see. So the audience is starting to arrive?"

"A couple of the coaches are here, yes. It's going to be a full house."

At least, I thought, the weather had held fair and warm for those who would be sitting on the grass. Perhaps the rain, the storms, had finished for the season. "Come in and have a seat."

"No, that's all right. I'm sure you're very busy—I don't want to get in your way." But that said, he didn't move from the doorway. He only seemed to plant himself more firmly there, his gaze focussed rather intently on a point just past my shoulder. Having watched him all these weeks now I recognized this posture as the one that he assumed when he was wanting to communicate but didn't have the words to hand.

Turning, I went back to putting on my make-up, glancing at Alex in the mirror's reflection. "Did Den manage to find you? He wants you to make the announcement before we go on, about Rupert . . ."

"Yes," he said, shortly. And then, in a more normal voice, "I'd be honoured to do it." The thought seemed to trigger another. The brief look he sent me was quietly cautious, as though he were probing a wound and wasn't sure at what point he might cause me pain. "About the cremation . . . they said they could do it tomorrow, at ten. Would that suit you?"

"Yes. I'll have to check with Bryan, but I'm sure it will be fine. Thanks."

"Are you sure that you don't want some kind of memorial service? We do have a chapel right here at the house, and—"

I shook my head, cutting him off. "Roo hated things like that. He always said that when he died he didn't want to have a funeral, only to be cremated and have his ashes scattered round the garden. Bryan will probably ask a few of their friends round to the flat for an informal wake, when he goes home."

"He's leaving soon, I take it?"

"Wednesday, I think he said."

"But you're staying here?"

My head came up. I met his eyes, perplexed. "Of course."

"It's only that you said you weren't quite sure, last night."

"Oh. Well, I was rather out of it last night. I don't remember half of what I said."

"I see."

It was his tone of voice as much as anything that caught me. "Is something wrong?"

It occurred to me that his behaviour went beyond his usual reserve, beyond his trying to be sensitive to Rupert's death, not wanting to upset me. He had actually withdrawn again; grown distant.

I could see it in his eyes as they found mine in the reflection. "No, of course not. I realize you were under quite a bit of stress last night—I'm sure you said some things you didn't mean, and I won't hold you to them. I should hope I'm gentleman enough to stand aside."

I shook my head as though the act might clear it. "Stand aside for whom?"

"For Den, of course."

I sighed. "But I've told you . . ."

"Yes, I know. You've told me several times, but I'm afraid it's just not on. I came back earlier today than I'd expected, you see, and Teresa told me Den had been wanting to speak with me, so I came here looking for him . . ."

"Oh, Alex."

"It's all right, really. Only don't try to tell me there's nothing between you, because I saw the way that you were holding him, and it wasn't exactly a friendly embrace. I'm not a fool."

"You are, you know," I told him, rather fondly.

"What?"

"You're right about one thing—we are more than friends, Den and I." And I told him the whole of it, gathering confidence as I went, watching his face change as his stoicism gave way first to amazement and then, rather wonderfully I thought, to something that bordered on open relief.

"Your father . . ." He half-smiled, and studied my face in the mirror. "There is a resemblance, you know, once you look for it."

I nodded. "Your grandmother saw it."

"That doesn't surprise me." Still looking a little off balance, he drew a chair up to the side of my dressing-table and sat. The distance had vanished from his eyes and he was back to being Alex now, the man who'd held me close last night, who'd kissed my face and whispered . . .

"How's your head?" He reached his hand as Den had done and felt the lump, to check it.

"Getting better."

"If it helps, I've been told the police had to bash Pietro around a bit when they arrested him. He didn't exactly cooperate."

I didn't envy the police the task of taking down a man that large. "He's still the only one they've caught, I take it?"

"Not to worry. Once he realized that the others had left him on his own he started talking to the authorities. It's only a matter of time before they find Daniela and her husband."

My head turned so sharply my neck hurt. "Her *husband*?"

"Oh, yes." He said that so dispassionately that I had to look more closely to be sure he wasn't simply covering his emotions, but he really did seem to be neither surprised nor concerned about Daniela's marital status. He went on, "Celetti, I think his name is—the police knew him by a few others, apparently. Pietro said it was Celetti's idea that

Daniela marry Forlani—an elderly man with millions, he must have seemed a sure investment. Only then of course he went and made that will leaving everything to the Trust, which wasn't quite what they'd expected, so they had to find a different way."

"Stealing from the houses that the Trust acquired." I didn't need to see him nod agreement. I already knew from my time in the crypt last night how the scam had been worked, with the forgeries taking the place of the genuine articles, which in their turn had been passed on to private collectors who weren't too particular where their collectibles came from. Curious, I asked him, "Did you know what they were up to?"

"I suspected. It was the chalice, you see, that Giancarlo brought back from Sirmione. Poor Giancarlo," he said, breaking off for a minute with a slight frown. "If he hadn't loved drama so much he might still be alive. He must have known everything when he phoned me, the day before you and I went to Sirmione, but he wouldn't just *tell* me, not that way . . . he wanted the big scene—the jeweller's assistant as witness, the chalice as prop, himself as the clever detective revealing the plot." He sighed. "All I could get out of him that day on the phone was that he no longer thought we were dealing with a simple case of theft. I knew that myself, when I looked at that chalice."

"But how?"

"I'd been down to the villa myself the day after Giancarlo died . . ."

"Lighting Daniela's fires?" I asked him, innocent.

"Putting them out, actually. And I'd seen the chalice sitting in the cabinet, same as always, where it ought to be. So when Teresa's brother handed me a second chalice, I knew one of them was wrong. And when Daniela took the chalice back next morning without comment, then I knew she was involved, somehow."

It must, I thought, have caused Daniela a bad moment or two when she'd learned—as I assumed she would have learned—that the chalice had vanished from the jeweller's shop in Sirmione. She'd likely breathed a huge sigh of relief when Alex had handed the chalice back to her, with the story that Pietro had stolen it, a story she'd played into when she'd sent Pietro into hiding.

Alex was talking. "I wasn't entirely sure what to do with my suspicions, though. I wanted to be very certain before I called in the police, so I got in touch with a friend of mine—the same one I'd phoned when Giancarlo had first raised suspicions of theft, the friend who'd first put me in touch with the Trust . . . he'd given them his summer home on Sardinia. I asked him if he'd check again, to see if anything like this had happened there. He'd donated quite a few paintings along with the house, and some very fine glassware. I called him on the Tuesday, I think, and on the Wednesday he went back to tour his former summer home with an appraiser."

I admired the man's initiative. "And?"

"None of the paintings they looked at was genuine. All of them had been replaced by forgeries. *Good* forgeries," he said. "World class. Daniela and her husband didn't mess about. They had a whole network of artisans doing the stuff for them; they knew what they were doing. My friend said he would never have questioned the paintings himself. He was angry about it, really angry. Not because the original paintings were gone, you understand—he'd never liked them all that much, or he wouldn't have donated them in the first place—but because he couldn't prove the theft, and so anyone might accuse him of pulling a fast one himself, hanging on to the original paintings and putting in forgeries just before leaving the house. I gather," said Alex, "that someone from the Trust politely raised that possibility, when the appraiser got in touch."

I'd never thought of it, myself, but I supposed Alex's reputation might have suffered quite a blow, too, if it had later been discovered that he'd given over to the Trust a bunch of worthless copies of the treasures from the Fourth Crusade. "So didn't they believe your friend, then, the people from the Trust?"

"Oh, he managed to convince them." Alex smiled. "He can be very convincing, at full volume. The trustees themselves were the ones who called in the police."

"The police were involved?"

"Yes, I'm sorry about that. They had me bound to secrecy, on pain of death. Not that you wouldn't have kept the secret, too," he hastened to assure me, "but it was their game, and I gather they figured that the fewer the people who knew the details of what was going on, the less the chance of someone slipping up and maybe tipping off Daniela and her crew by accident." His eyes apologized. "I'm sorry, I'd have told you if I could have."

"Never mind," I told him. "You can tell me now."

I'd have missed his smile if I hadn't glanced over, it was that brief, but the amusement lingered in his eyes as he began with, "So I can. The idea was to arrange a sort of sting—someone from the police would pose as a buyer of Byzantine art, and make contact with Daniela, and then when it came time for the exchange . . . well, there they'd be, caught in the act. In the meantime there'd be officers watching the house and the grounds, to make sure nothing was taken off-site without our knowing."

"The gardeners!"

"That's right. They weren't too good at gardening—my grandmother noticed that—but they did a decent job of keeping an eye on things. I had one of them keeping an eye on you, as well," he admitted, "only he seemed to be making you even more nervous, so I called him off a few days ago. I shouldn't have, I suppose—if he'd been watching you last night . . ." He left the sentence hanging there unfinished; coughed to clear his throat. "Anyway, they knew about Pietro sleeping rough down here, and—"

I set down my make-up, feeling suddenly chilled. "So that was *Pietro* that Poppy surprised?" I could still feel the threatening presence behind me, in the darkness of the corridor, the day the storm had knocked the power out. Shrugging the shiver aside, I said, "It's a good thing that we were all here, then, to come to her rescue. The man's already done murder once, that we know of."

Alex corrected me. "Twice. I don't really believe that my maid ran away to Milan. She just wasn't the type to do something like that. It's more likely she caught on to what was going on—Giancarlo did say that he wasn't the only one who'd noticed things missing and moved—and she probably made the mistake of saying something to Pietro. They couldn't have turned her, she was too good a Christian to be dishonest. So . . ." He spread his hands in a gesture of finality. "The police did find some evidence of blood down here, but no body, not yet."

"Down *here*? In the dressing-rooms?"

"Not yours," he reassured me, as I looked around. "The one at the end of the passage. They're thinking that he might have kept her body here a day or so, until he could dispose of it."

Which might have been, I thought, why Pietro had come charging down the hill at us that first day, why he hadn't wanted anybody poking round the theatre. Something else stirred in my memory at the mention of a body being disposed of. "Oh, Lord," I said, "the rose garden. Alex, have your men checked the rose garden? Someone was digging a new bed there, right after . . ."

"They noticed that, too, yes. There's nothing there now. They've been thorough, I'll give them that," he said, of the police. "They've even recovered at least one of the fakes from what's left of the villa."

Forgetting the maid for a moment, I frowned. "How do they know that it isn't the genuine article? I couldn't tell."

"You would have been able to see the difference, if you'd had a chance to compare the items. Giancarlo threw a spanner in Daniela's works, you see. Not only did he take off with one of their best pieces, but he managed to leave us enough of a trail that the jeweller had to do a bunk to keep from getting caught. He hadn't finished with his work yet, but Daniela and her husband had already struck a deal with a buyer—not our undercover chap, but one we didn't know about—and that buyer didn't want to wait, and so the three of them had to find a way to switch the genuine Fourth Crusade things for the fakes, without anyone spotting the unfinished details. That's why they set fire to the villa," he said.

I frowned harder. "I thought they did that to get rid of me, make it look accidental."

"No, burning the villa was part of the plan. They set it very scientifically, to do as much damage as possible to the cabinets where we kept the Fourth Crusade collection, so there wouldn't be very much left to recover. As you said yourself, it's rather difficult, at first glance, to tell whether a melted lump of metal is a fake or the genuine article, and as far as they knew no one would have any cause to suspect that the items *weren't* genuine." He looked to see that I was following the logic. "All they had to do, Daniela and her husband and Pietro, was to take the real things from the villa and put in the replicas. That's what I'd imagine they were doing in the crypt, when you met up with them—they were making the switch."

I was still trying to absorb the fact that they hadn't set the fire because of me. I'd been carrying the guilt of that around with me all day, reasoning that if it hadn't been for me there wouldn't have been a fire, and if there hadn't been a fire then Rupert wouldn't have died. "I heard them say that they were going to change the plan . . ."

"Well, yes, they'd meant to set the fire tonight. This buyer of theirs had booked tickets, Pietro said, for tonight's performance and intended to come here by one of the holiday coaches, along with the rest of the audience, to collect his purchase."

Which explained why the stolen items had been packed in a suitcase. In all the confusion of the fire, no one would have noticed one more member of the audience returning with a suitcase to his tourist coach.

"At least, that was the plan," said Alex. "Only as Pietro said, things didn't quite work out the way they'd expected."

"Because of me."

"Because of you."

I didn't need that part explained—I knew that my showing up in the crypt had put Daniela and her husband and Pietro in a no-win situation. The three of them could hardly have let me go on my way unmolested, not after what I'd seen, because I would have blown the whistle on their thieving. But keeping me silent meant giving up their meeting with their buyer, because without me there could be no first-night performance, no chartered coaches, no audience.

No wonder they'd wanted to kill me, I thought. In one

move I'd ruined what must have taken them weeks to organize. Now, instead of a neat handover of the stolen artifacts, they were forced to improvise a getaway.

And so the villa had been set on fire a day ahead of schedule. The replicas at any rate still had to be destroyed, and since no one would ever have had cause to suspect that the genuine items had been removed from the villa, any works of art 'lost' in the fire would have been paid for by the insurance. And as an added bonus, I'd have been conveniently eliminated.

I frowned. "I don't understand, though, if they thought I'd be killed in the fire, why did Daniela run away? I mean, Pietro was under suspicion of stealing—all right, I can see that. And her husband presumably went to connect with their buyer. But Daniela could have stayed. With me dead there wouldn't be anyone here to accuse her of anything."

His eyebrows lifted. "What makes you think that I wouldn't have suspected her?"

It was, I thought, a difficult thing to explain to a man, how certain women always seemed to get away with murder. It had everything to do with beauty and sexuality, and how it was used. I'd have been willing to bet, for example, that Alex's friend with the summer home in Sardinia, no matter how intelligent a man he was ordinarily, had not believed that Daniela could be capable of pulling off a swindle. Even when he'd been confronted with the fake paintings, he'd almost certainly have made excuses for her, saying that she must have been a minor player in the game, that she couldn't possibly have known the full extent of what was going on . . . "Most men wouldn't," I said.

"I'm not most men." He left a little pause, as though he wanted that to register. "And anyway, she *did* stay, to begin with. She was standing outside the villa when we got down there, wrapped in a dressing-gown, doing her damsel in distress. Had they brought out your body I'm sure she would have been ready with a story to tell us about what you'd been doing there." His voice had gone harder than normal, and stealing a look at his face I decided—not without a certain flush of pleasure—that he really and truly hadn't been taken in by Daniela, and that he would have held her to account if anything had happened to me. "Only you came out alive," he said, "and sometime shortly after that, *because* of that, Daniela disappeared. No one noticed her leaving."

"She can't hide forever."

"Don't kid yourself. She and her husband will have met up with their buyer by now, and if he paid them even half what the Fourth Crusade objects are worth they'll be able to hide in style for quite some time."

"Oh, Alex, I am sorry."

"What, about my losing the collection? I don't mind," he brushed it off. "My own claim to ownership was questionable at best. My grandfather stole them from a house built by a man who had stolen them eight centuries before, and how they came to Constantinople in the first place is anyone's guess. No one owns things like that," he informed me. "They're passing through time, and we're only custodians, really."

"But you'd like to have them back, surely."

"If you're asking would I like to see Daniela and her husband caught, then yes, I would, but because I want justice for Giancarlo, and for Rupert, not because I want my things back. Losing you," he told me, "would have been the greater loss."

He was leaning in to kiss me when a knock at my dressing-room door interrupted.

I smiled. "That'll be Den, come to call the half-hour. He's developing fatherly timing already."

But it wasn't Den. It was Poppy. She responded to my invitation to come in a little timidly, her gaze moving instantly to Alex.

"Oh," she said. "I didn't . . . I mean, I thought you were alone. I'm sorry."

"That's all right," I said, but my attempt to ease her nervousness was clearly unsuccessful.

Shifting from one foot to the other, she said, "Den sent me to tell you it's half an hour to curtain up."

I could hear Den himself, down the hall, knocking at Nicholas's door—we didn't have a public address system backstage, like most theatres had, so Den had to do things the old-fashioned way, playing callboy.

I didn't know whether Poppy was helping him to pass the word to anyone but me, but having delivered her message she certainly didn't seem in a hurry to go anywhere. She hovered in the doorway, looking faintly unhappy, and I remembered what Madeleine had told me this morning about how awful Poppy felt about leaving me down in the crypt, and how badly she'd wanted to come and apologize. Even though the half-hour before curtain up was usually a time I liked to spend alone, preparing to go on, I simply couldn't leave her standing there like that, not when I knew from experience how rotten it felt to feel guilty. And I didn't want Poppy to carry her guilt for as long as I'd carried my own.

"Come and sit down," I invited her.

"Oh, no, I couldn't, I . . ."

Alex rose, pushing his chair back. "Here, she can have my chair. I have to go and get ready, myself, to make the announcement before you go on." He gave me the kiss, though, in spite of our audience. "I'll see you after."

When he'd gone, I looked towards the door again. "Poppy, it's all right, really. Do come in. I'm not upset with you or anything." I showed her my most reassuring smile. "Please."

Anyone watching us would have thought I'd called her on the carpet. Her feet dragged as she moved to take her seat, the very picture of reluctance. I took heart from the fact that she was wearing the necklace I'd bought her in Sirmione, the tiny shells clicking together as they brushed the red wool of her jumper.

"You ought to be," she said, in a miserable tone. "Upset with me, I mean. It's my fault you almost got killed."

"Oh, Poppy."

"If I'd gone and found somebody straight away, like you'd asked me, then—"

"Then you'd all have been walking right in on a very dangerous situation," I told her. "And you might have made things worse. A lot more people might have been hurt. No, your timing was perfect."

"It was?"

"And I'm told it was you who convinced the others to follow Max."

She glanced away, embarrassed. "Well, he was acting like dogs do in films, you know, running away and then coming back again, and barking, like he wanted us to come with him."

"So there you are. You actually helped *save* my life then, didn't you?"

Her small face brightened for a moment, then clouded again. "But Rupert had to help as well, and now he's dead, and—"

"Oh, darling," I cut her off, wanting to wipe the sad look from her eyes. "What happened to Rupert, that was an accident. Sometimes things . . . well, they just happen. They're not anybody's fault."

That only seemed to make things worse. Her eyes brimmed with moisture. "You're being so . . ." Breaking off, she blinked the tears away and went on steadily, "And I've been so horrible to you. Mummy told me so, and she was right. I've been childish, and I'm sorry."

Brave words for a girl of twelve. I held back my smile with care. "Well, you're not being childish now. It takes maturity," I told her, "to apologize in person. Lots of people twice your age—three times your age—can't do it."

She flushed with pleasure, and a glimpse of the old Poppy showed through her self-conscious features. "I was going to ask you . . ." she started, then paused, circling round for the right approach. "That is, I was wondering if you'd like to have lunch with me tomorrow, at the Grand Hotel in Mira. I'd pay, of course—I have money."

She was so painfully earnest that I was once again reminded of my own youthful crush on my headmistress; how I'd striven to impress her; how I'd longed to share her company. The thought occurred to me quite suddenly that if Den and Madeleine *did* get together then Poppy and I would be sisters of a sort, and it struck me that I'd like that. "Yes, I'd like that very much," I said.

"You would?"

"Very much," I repeated. "Now come on, help me get into my costume. I could use an extra pair of hands."

She left me when Den came round to give the fifteen-minute call and collect any valuables that might need locking away in his desk. "I hope you don't expect me to take *this,*" he said. "What the devil is it, anyway?"

Putting the finishing touches to my wig, I glanced over to see what he was talking about. "Oh. It's a prayer-book."

Bryan had left it in my room this morning, and knowing how fond Rupert had been of it I'd carried it down here for luck. It was my way, I suppose, of having a little bit of Rupert with me still, to see me through tonight's performance.

Leafing through the pages of the prayer-book, Den admired the illustrations. "Is it very old?"

"At least eight hundred years, I think." Quite possibly the only item from the Fourth Crusade collection to have survived the theft, I thought. I passed him my wristwatch and handbag for safekeeping. "Here you are."

"Thanks."

Left alone, I took the one valuable I hadn't given him—my little diamond angel pendant—and hung it with care on the edge of my mirror, where it could watch over me. I wasn't ordinarily superstitious about my performances, but the full weight of what I was about to do had begun to press in on me, the fact that in under ten minutes I'd be facing an audience in my first leading role, in a play that nobody, till now, had been able to bring to the stage. In under ten minutes I'd have to go out there and wait in the dark for the lights to come up, and in front of a full house I'd have to live up to my name, and hold my own with Nicholas and Madeleine, and give the sort of performance that would have made Rupert proud, and . . .

"Five minutes," Den called, from the passage.

In desperation I looked at the prayer-book, wishing that I could read Greek so I would have been able to call on some higher power for assistance. But I couldn't read Greek. I did, however, recognize the painted illustration on the page that Den had left the book turned open to—a radiant sunburst against a cloudy sky, as though the heavens had opened to admit a wandering spirit that had just been laid to rest. I remembered how Rupert had phrased the translation: 'A Prayer for the Laying of Ghosts.'

The eyes in the myriad pictures of Celia the First on my dressing-room wall seemed to watch me, as though she were waiting for something. I found myself searching the eyes of the images, seeking a connection across the long years that divided our lives. Of course I knew I hadn't really seen her in the burning room, or heard her in the night, and there were no such things as ghosts, but still . . .

"He knows," I told her, feeling only slightly foolish for talking to a photograph. "He knows you love him, and he knows you didn't run away." It occurred to me, gazing up at that famously beautiful face, that I was finishing what she'd begun—she'd never had the chance to play the role that Galeazzo had so lovingly crafted for her, never had the chance to speak the lines before an audience. Perhaps she'd cursed the play herself, I thought fancifully, not wanting anybody else to take her place.

She was smiling at me now, though, looking down with warm approval as if somehow she considered me a kindred spirit.

And suddenly my fears about the play and my performance disappeared, and were replaced with something calmer and more confident. The feeling held, through the moment when Den came to lead me out to take my place on the still-darkened stage, through the moment I spent standing there on my own, with the hum of the yet-unseen audience surrounding me . . . and then in one quick burst the lights came on, spearing the darkness with dazzling rays like the sunburst illustration in the prayer-book, and in that instant I knew everything was going to be all right.

I turned my face towards the light, and spoke the opening line.

He had forgotten how to pray. He turned the pages of the prayer-book slowly, hopefully, but no help came. These words were sterile, penned by monks—they could not speak the passions of his heart.

He felt that he was being watched, and turned to see his son within the doorway, standing solemn and unspeaking. The boy, he thought, was all that he had left now. All the family he could claim. "Come in," he said. "Come in, don't be afraid."

The boy came cautiously, his eyes upon the prayer-book. "What is that?"

"A palimpsest. You know what that is?"

"No."

"A twice-used book. There was a time when parchment was a rarity, and those who wished to make new books were forced to reuse old ones. This book was a play, a Greek play, when its life began, larger than this, but the monks who found it cut its pages into two and scraped the parchment clean so they could write their prayers and incantations. Only they could not remove the underlying words completely. Here," he said, "and here, you see them for yourself."

The boy stepped closer, looked, and frowned. "A pal . . . a palim . . ."

"Palimpsest." He liked the frown, the earnestness, the drive to understand. "It is a very special book, this. No one else has ever seen it, only you."

He saw that pleased the boy, and reaching out a hand he touched the shoulder of his son. "Perhaps one day you will learn all the secrets of this house," he said, and smiled a little wistfully. "Perhaps, one day."

EPILOGUE

But my fate ever in a frequent round
Turns . . . and changes character.

Sophocles: *The Lost Dramas,* Fragment 713

We don't go very often to Il Piacere, now.

The Trust has the charge of the house and the gardens, and although they detour the tourists round our private rooms while we're in residence, it still feels rather strange, as though we're part of the display. Teresa has several times turned people out of her kitchen, and once I came across a straggler who had stopped to use our bathroom. Still, the house works better as a showpiece than a home, I think, and I have no doubt Galeazzo's ghost is somewhere looking on delighted at the sight of people queuing for a glimpse inside his legendary bedroom, or the desk in the veranda where he wrote his final poems. As for the spirit of Celia the First, if she still haunts her rooms in the ladies' wing, she keeps a low profile. None of the Trust's workers, nor any of the tourists, have reported anything 'happening,' as Teresa would put it, in Celia's suite.

I myself am inclined to believe that what I saw and heard were mere imaginings, and yet . . . and yet, there is a part of me, I must admit, that wouldn't be surprised if someday someone chanced to stumble on the resting-place of Galeazzo's Celia, sheltered in the gardens of Il Piacere. Walking there, I almost feel her presence.

But so far only one body has been found at the estate, and that a more recent one—not in the gardens, but down on the small stretch of beach by the boathouse. As Alex had suspected, the little maid who'd vanished on the day I'd first arrived hadn't run off to Milan at all; she hadn't run to anywhere. I'm told that Lake Garda is known to not give up its dead, but it gave back the maid . . . gave her back very gently, and set her in plain view to bear a mute witness to murder.

Pietro, still in prison, claims it wasn't he who killed her, that Daniela's husband did it, and forged the letter to her family saying she was fine; but it's likely we shall never know the truth. The two of them—Daniela and her husband—have eluded the authorities for so long now it seems to me unlikely they will ever be found, let alone brought to justice. We actually had a postcard from Daniela, last Easter . . . at least, Alex did. It came addressed to him, at Il Piacere—a view of Buenos Aires, and on the back her signature, and nothing more. It had occurred to me that she must have truly had some feelings for him, to take such a risk, but when I'd said so to Alex he'd shaken his head and replied that women like that didn't care about anyone, really; that men, to them, were playthings. I could understand the argument—Daniela, after all, was a good deal like my mother, who had grown so accustomed to being the bright centre of the universe that, like the wicked queen in the fairy tale, she couldn't conceive of anyone being fairer than her—but I couldn't help but think that in Alex's case, Daniela had felt something more. I'd seen her eyes that day on the terrace, when she'd warned me off.

"And anyway," Alex had gone on, still holding the postcard, "she's not taking any risk, sending me this. They'll have moved on to somewhere else by now, take my word for it."

With the money they must have made selling the Fourth Crusade collection, they will doubtless be able to keep moving for quite some time. Where the stolen items went, we still don't know—they have, as Alex put it, merely continued their illicit journey from hand to hand, as they came down through the ages. The few fakes salvaged from the Villa delle Tempeste after the fire have been put on display by the Trust, and the story of the theft has found its own place in the tour guides' patter, one more curiosity to entertain the tourists.

But there is one piece yet surviving—the prayer-book, which Alex allowed me to bring with us when we left Italy. That, and the portrait of Celia the First that had hung in my bedroom, and which is hanging now above me as I write this, are the only things we've taken from the house, the only things we didn't want to leave behind. The rest is for the Trust, and they are welcome to it, Alex says.

He talks from time to time of putting on another of his grandfather's plays in the theatre, but I don't imagine anything will come of it. At any rate, it wouldn't be the same. We could never match the triumph of *Il Prezzo.*

It was *Il Prezzo* that first brought us to New York, by invitation, when our summer's run in Italy was over; and the play is running still, to good reviews, although the only original cast member remaining is Madeleine. Nicholas left two months after we'd moved to New York. He now lives in Los Angeles, where I understand he has been seen at several parties with the actress who last year received the Oscar for best work in a supporting role—which was, I thought, appropriate.

I'd have stayed on longer with *Il Prezzo* myself if it hadn't been for the fact that I was offered, unexpectedly, the lead role in a television miniseries, and when I wavered it was Madeleine herself who pushed me into it. I remember she and Den had been throwing one of their famous parties that weekend, at their house in New Jersey, and Madeleine and I had found a corner of peace on the covered back porch, and with our drinks in hand were watching Poppy throw a ball for her new cocker spaniel puppy, and Madeleine, making her case for the miniseries, had quoted from Shakespeare, from *Julius Caesar*: " 'There is a tide in the affairs of men which, taken at the flood, leads on to fortune . . .' "

And when she'd said that it had struck me that I'd had my tide already, and had taken it, and had indeed found fortune. Not only in a financial sense, though I'd be the first to admit that I've travelled a long way from that draughty fourth-floor flat in Covent Garden, but in those things that make one truly rich—in friends, and in my ever-growing family, and the joy of being able to perform.

I did the miniseries, though. I've learned it's always wise to take advice from Madeleine.

I took her advice about Alex, after all. She said I ought to marry him, and so I did, and that has worked out well enough—the evidence is sleeping here beside me in a Moses basket, guarded well by Max and Nero. Bryan and Edwina will be coming in a week's time for the christening. We had a small dispute about the name—Alex had felt that it ought to be Rupert, only I had argued that Rupert had never much liked his own name, and had several times said that he wouldn't have wished it on anyone else . . . and choosing between Den and Bryan would have been impossible for me, so in the end we had settled on Christopher.

"It's all his own name," I'd said, watching our son while he slept. "No one else's."

It had pleased me then, as it does now, to know he'll have no expectations to live up to on that count, and nothing that he'll have to prove. Mind you, it doesn't bother me so much these days to carry Celia's name. With the success of *Il Prezzo,* and the first episode of my miniseries scheduled to air on Sunday next, I feel more confident in my ability to make my mark.

According to Madeleine, I already have. Only this morning she came by to tell me how, at dinner last night, she and Den had chatted with an influential critic who'd been praising my performance in *Il Prezzo.* "And Den got to bragging, you know how he is, and he told the chap that, in his opinion, you had done a better job than the first Celia Sands could have done with the part." Whereupon the critic, so Madeleine says, looked up in some surprise and asked them, "*Was* there another Celia Sands?"

Perhaps they'll write that as my epitaph. I think that I should like that.

AUTHOR'S NOTE

The character of Galeazzo D'Ascanio and the estate of Il Piacere were inspired by the real-life poet Gabriele D'Annunzio and his grand home Il Vittoriale, built on the shores of Lake Garda above the beautiful resort town of Gardone Riviera. In paying homage to a fascinating man I did not, of course, mean to imply that any of the events described in this book actually took place—the story is entirely imagined, and my own.

For my research into D'Annunzio's life I am greatly indebted to the wonderfully colourful biography written by his friend and secretary, Tom Antongini, and published in English by William Heinemann Ltd. in 1938.

To all those others, both in Italy and here, who were kind enough to assist me in my research for this book, I give my heartfelt thanks; most particularly to the woman at Equity in London, whose name I never learned; to Humphrey Price; to Jane Bradish-Ellames of Curtis Brown; and last but by no means least, to the actress Cynthia Dale, who generously prompted from the wings.